SUMMON US

SUMMON US

A DARK ROMANCE NOVEL

MT ADDAMS

WET INK PUBLISHING HOUSE, LLC.

Additional Credit:

Editor: Chrisandra's Corrections

Cover Designer: DoElle Designs

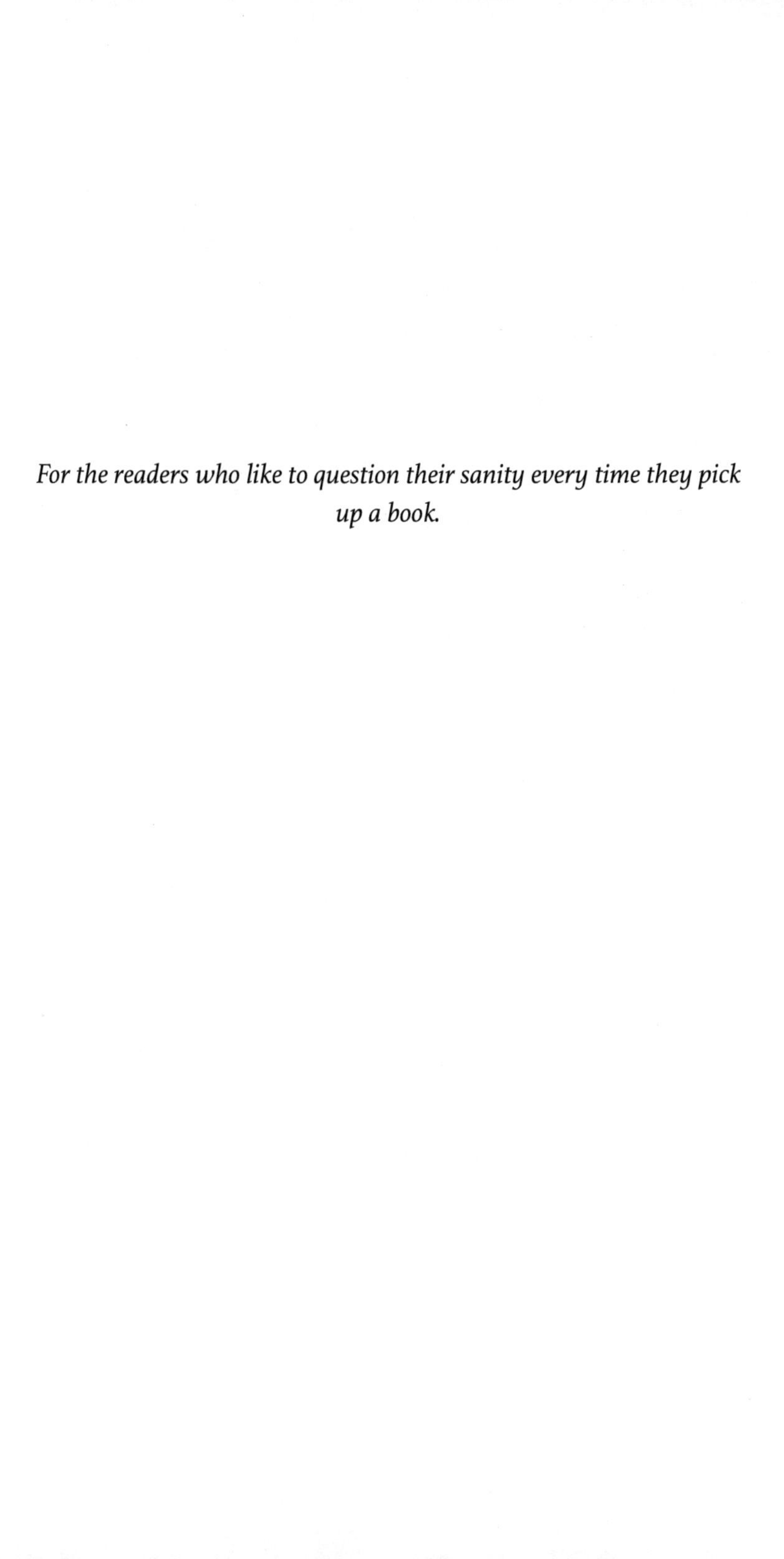

For the readers who like to question their sanity every time they pick up a book.

CONTENTS

CONTENT NOTES

Dear Readers-

This story contains certain themes that may distress some readers. **Reader discretion is advised.**

In order to adhere to the guidelines of the publication platform, I've moved and listed all of the dark content within these pages to my website. I *highly* encourage checking this list before reading this story.

Seriously, folks. I know some of you like to test the waters and go in blind—I suggest for this story that you don't.

For a full list please check my website at w w w DOT mtaddams DOT com.

1

Daisy

The sleepy town of Briar Glen is as boring as math class. Maybe even more so.

With a declining population that consists mostly of old people, shops that have been carrying the same items since the eighties, and a lack of any new or exciting restaurants, there's not a lot that happens around here.

At least most of the time.

Sitting on the grated metal catwalk with my arms folded and braced on the rusted railing of the old water tower, I can see the small town as clear as day. The streets are relatively busy this Thursday afternoon. The hustle and bustle seem out of sorts for the small town. With the Harvest Festival behind us and the county fair all but over, I can't seem to put my finger on what all this excitable energy is about.

Is someone retiring? Could there be someone important coming to town?

I mull over the questions briefly before letting them go. Who cares? It has nothing to do with me and I doubt it's as exciting as the adults below are making it seem. Anything even slightly new or different can cause the town to fall into a frenzy.

Pulling my gaze away from the place I've grown up in, I turn my attention toward the world outside of Briar Glen.

Surrounding the town are miles and miles of trees. Most of the terrain I'm pretty familiar with. The adventures I've gone on with my friends have, many times, led us through these woods. I'm pretty sure I know every nook and cranny of Briar Glen both inside the town and out.

My heavy sigh carries around me. Looking down, I watch as my feet dangle over the edge of the catwalk, swinging absent-mindedly.

Beside me, my friend clears his throat. I blink rapidly, clearing my drifting thoughts. Rather than straighten, I simply turn and rest my head on my arms to look over at Owen Woodlock. With brown skin darker than my own, thick hair that he lets grow out into a fun kinky afro, and glasses, Owen is utterly adorable. He's also the youngest of my friends by an entire year. While he just started eighth grade, the rest of us are in our freshmen year of high school. Despite his age, he's so much *smarter* than the rest of us. Nearly every time he opens his mouth, I learn something new and fascinating.

"We should get going," he says, shutting the book and letting it rest in his lap. "Oh, wait, let me try it this way."

His hands move, forming signs that I've taught him over the years, letting me know it's time to go. Ever since they learned that my aunt was deaf and I knew sign language, most of the guys have wanted to pick up communicating this way. It's turned into a game for them, to see if they can talk in our 'secret language.' Owen has picked up on it the fastest, but Drake's not far behind. Rather than answer him out loud, I sign back,

"The others should be here any second. Drake and Wyatt had to pick up Kingston."

"I thought Kingston was grounded?" Owen's brows furrow as he forgoes signing this time to speak his concern out loud.

I try not to mirror the expression despite the rock in my stomach. "I dropped off Mr. Winslow's favorite pastries this morning before school; that always wins him over. Kingston should be able to come out this afternoon, at least for a little bit."

Owen's face twists with skepticism. "You know that trick isn't going to work forever."

I do know that. Francis Winslow is a man with many faces. While he wears a friendly mask out in public, I've snuck over to Kingston's house before only to hear the real man beneath it. His cruel demeanor toward his wife and son is appalling. How Kingston keeps sane is beyond me. Maybe it's because King can be just as cruel as his father when pushed too far. He's the fearless one out of the five of us- that's for sure.

"I know, but it worked this time."

Owen chuckles. "That's because Daisy Murray can do no wrong. I swear all of our parents love you more than they love us."

I snort. "That's not true and you know it."

Thankfully, Mr. Winslow *does* seem to like me. His graciousness toward me occasionally rubs off on Kingston, giving him a break from time to time.

"In any case, I can't stay out too long. Mom and Dad say they have something super special for me tonight and they want me back right after we grab dinner at Ma's. Kingston won't be out long enough to get his dad any more upset with him than he already is." I look back over the town, wondering how far away our other friends are.

Owen opens his mouth to say something, but a sound drifts up from the trees below. We both straighten as the whistled tune of "A Spoonful of Sugar" drifts up to us. It's joined by a second whistle, then a third.

I'm on my feet before they finish the verse. "See! I told you they were coming."

Owen is slower getting to his feet. With a chuckle, he picks up his backpack and shoves the book he was reading inside.

"How you managed to get everyone to memorize that stupid song and use it as our calling card is ridiculous."

I laugh. "You're just annoyed you can't whistle."

"I can! It's just not that loud."

I move toward the ladder. "Come on, I'm starving."

I PUMP my legs up and down as fast as they will go. Sweat breaks out along my brow, even with the wind in my face. I don't have time to wipe at it. If I lose even a second of my concentration, my lead could be compromised. I lean over my handlebars, urging my legs to move faster. My lungs feel like they're going to explode as I raise up onto the pedals of my bicycle and lean into the curve.

It's the wrong move.

Kingston shoots by with a maniacal laugh. The silicon spikes lining his helmet jerk around madly as he speeds by. Gritting my teeth, I pedal faster. As we take another turn, my front wheel hits a rock and I lose control of my bike. Just before I topple over, I right myself. But it's time wasted. Wyatt, Owen, and Drake shoot by so quickly they're practically blurs.

"So long, *sucker*!" Wyatt shouts over his shoulder.

Growling, I chase after them. It's mid-October yet the heat is sweltering, the humidity making it even worse. My shirt clings to my body. It's uncomfortable. Gasping for air, I try with all my might to push through the discomfort. But my legs are done. They tremble as I lift and lower them, pushing my body weight up the last hill on Main Street. The guys have already crested it and disappeared on the other side, leaving me behind to suffer the immense task alone.

"Come on, Daze!"

I blink the sweat out of my eyes to see Wyatt reappearing and waving at me from the top of the hill where the traffic light is. With a grunt, I push until I'm right beside him.

I don't thank Wyatt for waiting for me, but I do shoot him a smile before sticking my tongue out. Speeding by him, I use the downhill to catch up with the others. Owen doesn't even see me coming and neither does Drake. They both have a tendency to slow down here, scared at the speed we pick up and the sharp turn at the bottom.

But it never scares me.

With tires shrieking, I make the turn and use the momentum to my advantage. Kingston is getting closer. From here I can see that his jet-black hair is plastered to his neck. The back of his shirt is drenched in sweat but rather than sticking to him, his shirt billows out behind him. I'm so close to reaching him, and our destination, I can almost taste success.

But it's out of reach.

Kingston crosses another street and just barely misses being clipped by a work truck that honks as it continues on its way. I'm forced to slow down so I don't slam into the back of it. By the time it's out of the way, Kingston's tires screech to a halt in the gravel parking lot in front of Ma's Diner.

Kings hoots as he pulls off his helmet and looks behind him at the rest of us.

"*Another* win!"

"You never won this much before," I glare at him as I come to a stop beside him and climb off my bike. He dismounts and reaches up to wipe the sweat from his face. My gaze drops to where his shirt has lifted enough for me to see the beginnings of muscle starting to form. Looks like soccer practice is really doing him some good. Embarrassed by my thoughts, I turn away.

"It's the new bike," Drake complains as he and Owen come up next. Both guys are sweating profusely as they glare at Kingston.

"How is it the bike? I'm just *that* good." Kingston protests then scoffs. "You're just jealous."

Wyatt comes up last, cruising, unbothered by the loss. He's always been more laid back than the rest of us. Even more than Owen, our bookworm.

"The bike is lighter, it gives you an advantage," Owen points out, wiping his brow. The rest of us walk our bicycles over to the bike rack.

As we lock them up, a few older high school students exit Ma's Diner, laughing with one another. The minute I see who they are, I brace myself for trouble. The juniors see us and rather than head toward their car, they saunter over. Chad's pompous grin stretches wide as his gaze lands on Drake, who has his back turned and doesn't see the threat. Chad's goonies, Mitchel and Borus, snicker behind him.

"Hey fatty, gonna wipe Mrs. Joanna's kitchen out this evening?" Chad asks. He moves to push Drake, but I step between them, forcing Chad to drop his hands.

Glaring up at the school's quarterback, I hiss, "Leave Drake alone."

His smile shifts as his eyes slide down my front. "Hey, pretty Daisy, ready to be plucked? I'll handle you with care if you—"

"If you finish that sentence, you'll walk away with a black eye, Chad," Kingston says, all playfulness gone as he steps up beside me.

"Hey, it's Kingston!" Mitchel steps forward, his sneer nearly identical to his leader's. "You coming out tonight?"

Letting Kingston take the reins from here, I grab the back of Drake's shirt and drag him away from the school's bullies.

"Probably," Kingston answers.

Wyatt and Owen look from Kingston to me as I head toward the door to the diner. I know their concerns. Since high school started two months ago, Kingston has managed to secure being one of the more popular kids in school. It's not surprising. Given that he's from one of the richest families in town, good looking, and carries himself with confidence, all the students seem to gravitate toward him. All of them, even Chad and his goonies. When he's not with us, he's with them, probably doing things he shouldn't be. Usually when Chad's involved, Kingston seems to get in even more trouble than normal with his parents. I've managed to help him escape some sketchy situations, but Kingston doesn't seem to want to learn from his mistakes.

"He's good," I assure everyone, pushing away my own doubts.

Drake moves forward, grabs the door for me and opens it. When I shoot him a smile, I note the red in his cheeks. My smile falters. Drake's incredibly self-conscious of his weight. Being just a few inches shorter than me but nearly triple the width of any of us, he definitely stands out. It doesn't help that his mom always gives him a bowl cut and embarrasses him by forcing him to wear shirts two sizes too small on purpose.

I hate the shame that flashes in his eyes as he looks down, away from me. As much as I want to assure him not to worry, I keep quiet. If there's anything he hates, it's attention or what he thinks is pity.

"Is he though?" Wyatt asks softly, coming up behind me, taking advantage of the open door.

"Of course he is, it's King," Owen states bitterly. "Why does he even bother to hang out with us when he clearly wants to be with them?"

It's a sentiment I share but don't speak out loud, hating the truth behind it. As much as we all hang out, it's clear from the incessant taunts that are borderline rude and the constant need to boast, Kingston clearly thinks he's better than us.

"It's 'cause of Daisy. You're the only one he really cares about," Drake mutters as we gather around the host stand.

"He loves us," I glare at all three of them. "Just because he can be an ass and hangs out with a bunch of assholes, doesn't mean he has any less love for us. By the way, I'm the first one through the door which technically means I won the race."

"Damn it, you're right!" Wyatt slaps my back as Mrs. Joanna, the middle-aged waitress wearing too much colorful makeup, nudges her head toward the booths.

"Go sit down in your usual spot and keep the ruckus down. I'll be with you in a sec!" she calls over to us from behind the counter.

Someone's hands land on my shoulders and guide me toward our favorite booth in the far corner. My heart does a funny flip at the contact. Wyatt is handsome in a wholesome way. His warm smiles, twinkling green eyes, and the unbothered way he holds himself make him easy to be around. He's also quite touchy-feely, and that touch? Well, lately it causes my heart to do a little cartwheel.

He's a friend. Remember, a friend!

Swallowing hard, I let Wyatt guide me through the diner. Owen brushes past me, eager to get a window seat. Drake's next, leaving me and Wyatt behind. Well, just me, because Wyatt lets go of my shoulders and gives chase.

"You guys aren't going to wait up for me?" Kingston's voice calls out from behind me.

I don't spare him a glance, but I do pick up the pace, knowing that he'll be quick to rush by me if I don't hurry. I'm right. He moves past me without even breaking into a jog. Laughter spills out past my lips as King tries to push Wyatt out of the way but fails. They grapple loudly, disturbing the patrons sitting at the table beside them. Owen takes advantage and slips in on one side. He slides across the worn leather seat to take the window on that side. Drake takes the other window seat before I can slip past Kingston and Wyatt.

"Gotta be faster than that," he teases as I slide in beside him.

"I *am* faster. That's why you guys owe me a milkshake today." I roll my eyes and grab for the large plastic menu on the table as if I'm not about to order the same exact thing I always order.

"It's someone else's turn to get a free milkshake," Wyatt whines, sliding in beside me. Both he and Kingston are a few inches shorter than me, so when I straighten, I can peer over Wyatt's head to look at the case of pastries on the counter.

"Hm, I don't think that's how it works," I tease him, eyeing the blueberry muffin. "*But,* if you split my burger with me so I can fit *that* into my stomach, I may let you guys just have my milkshake."

"I'll share with you!" Kingston offers, slamming his hand down on the table, startling the older folks behind us, and then shooting me a cocky grin. I hide my face behind the menu before he notices the way my cheeks heat up.

He's always had those dimples! Stop letting them get to you now!

"You know she always shares her shake anyway," Drake points out softly, staring down at his own menu.

Owen pushes his glasses up his nose and looks around at us. "We should just let Daisy have her milkshake. It's practically her birthday."

"It's *almost* her birthday," Kingston rolls his eyes. "It's not until tomorrow."

"Close enough!" I glare over the top of the menu at him.

"Not really." King spares me a bored look before yanking the menu out of my hand to look at it himself. "What are we doing for it anyway?"

I shrug, something he doesn't see. "I don't know. It's really not even a big deal. I'm kind of curious about what my parents have in store for me tonight though. They set something up for me, but they won't tell me what it is."

"Fifteen *is* a big deal. You'll be able to get your learner's permit this year!" Owen grins, excited. "Then you can drive us around."

"I'll be able to do that in a few months," Kingston glares at him. "It won't be a big deal when Daisy gets hers then."

Wyatt scoffs. "Yeah, like we'd trust *you* to drive us around."

"We'll die the first day," Drake agrees. "I don't trust you with my life, King."

"But you trust *Daisy?*"

At Kingston's skepticism, everyone responds unanimously, "*Yes.*"

I laugh, pleased by their confidence in me. Before Kingston can answer, Mrs. Joanna appears at our table.

"Alright you little heathens, what can I get you?" she teases, her smile warm and genuine. "Did you win the race today, Daisy?"

I beam up at her. "I did."

"So, a strawberry banana milkshake is in order, is that right?"

"Ah, c'mon, change it up!" Kingston moans.

I shoot him a glare. "You know what? No, I don't think I will." Turning back to Mrs. Joanna, I nod. "Yes please"

She chuckles. "Alrighty. One strawberry banana milkshake coming right up. The usual for the rest of you?"

Our table erupts with confirmation and laughter. Mrs. Joanna nods, scribbling it all down on her pad, and then winks at us.

"You guys are easy. I'll make sure your dinner comes out quickly."

When she's gone, my boys erupt into conversation. I sit back and smile, loving each and every one of them, even while they bicker and tease one another.

2

Kingston

"C'mon guys, I think it's just this way."

Drake sighs as he dawdles behind the rest of us. "Why are you whispering, King? There's no one out here."

I grind my teeth as I look around the woods. How many times have we crept around out here in the dark when we weren't supposed to? The woods are my home just as much as the water tower, railroad tracks, and Ma's Diner are. So why do they seem so ominous tonight?

Because you saw that knife and you heard them speak her name. My stomach churns.

Wrestling down my rising anxiety, I turn and make sure Drake notices my glare. "It's a party, of course people are going to be there. Now come on, we're nearly there."

"Why would *you* have to whisper if they know you're coming?" Wyatt asks, keeping close.

"*I* was invited. Not you guys. I'm going to need to sneak you three into this thing, so shut up and let's go. At this rate it's going to be over by the time we get there."

Keeping up this charade is exhausting. If I could just tell them why we're really out here, maybe they'd put some pep in their step.

Or maybe they would turn tail and run. I lick my dry lips and suck in a deep breath to keep from growing lightheaded. If I'm not ushering the others forward, I'm holding my breath, hoping that what I'd seen and overheard earlier had been just a wild form of miscommunication.

There is no way that the knife Dad was holding had anything to do with Daisy.

My plan tonight was to sneak out to meet Chad and drink some beers down by the railroad tracks. On my way out though, as I slipped past my father's office, I heard my name and stopped.

"—Kingston's going to be a good boy and keep his mouth shut and forget about her once the Murrays fulfill their end of the deal."

I had bristled at Dad's tone. Lately, he's been trying to dictate my life more than usual. What did he want me to do, or not do, *now*? I peered into the office just as he lifted the largest knife I have ever seen over his head. The tip was curved, and from where I stood, I could see the handle was made of gold.

"*This is the most important night of our lives, Georgia. Daisy Murray will be our salvation.*"

I shiver as I replay the moment. The zealous tone my father's voice had taken, the worried look I caught my mom wearing... All of it was too weird and alarming to ignore. After listening in to figure out where to go, I'd slipped out, and rather than head to the railroad tracks, I'd gathered the others.

So here I am, with my heart in my throat in the middle of the woods, hoping like hell that what I'd seen and overheard was wrong and that we won't find anything. Least of all, Daisy.

"—King?"

Owen's voice tugs me back into the moment.

"What?" I ask, my exasperation clear as I whirl around to face him. The scrawny kid pushes his glasses up his nose as he cringes away from me.

"I asked why you invited us if you're embarrassed by our presence."

Oh, this stupid party thing again. I sigh loudly.

"Because Daisy would want me to, ok?"

"You're only doing this 'cause you *love* her," Wyatt taunts, strolling by me in the direction of Solmer's Rock.

Heat rises in my cheeks. "No I don't."

"Yeah, *ok*. Don't think I haven't noticed you staring at her all the time."

"With that logic, I could accuse *you* of liking *me* since you're watching me. Besides, Daisy is always doing something ridiculous, of course I'm watching her."

That's a plausible excuse, right? Because admitting that I'm fucking *obsessed* with our friend isn't an option. She's too innocent and naive. Hell, she teeters on the verge of nerd and normal, jumping back and forth over that line every time she opens her mouth. What's worse, she *enjoys* hanging out with these guys. These *losers*. Maybe once I could tolerate them, when we were younger, but now? God they're annoying. The only thing holding me back from ditching them is the girl that may or may not be in trouble this evening.

My pace quickens. "Come on, you guys are so fucking slow."

"I hate the dark," Owen grumbles.

Tonight, I'm not a fan of it either. The full moon overhead is blocked by thick clouds, and the humidity is growing thicker. Is there a storm approaching? Shit, I hope not.

"After the party, we should climb down the cliff edge and swim in the river," Drake suggests.

"I don't think drinking and swimming go hand and hand. Especially not with how bad the current is. Dad tried to go fishing and said he nearly got swept away when he stepped into the water," Owen objects.

"How wasted are you going to get?" Drake replies.

God, they're so new to all this. At least Daisy started drinking this past summer. I'd stolen some of my dad's best whiskey after a tough night of him berating the shit out of me and snuck over to her house, knocked on her bedroom window, and she'd slipped out without a moment of hesitation. That night we talked for hours, just the two of us.

I'd never felt so seen. So heard. So loved.

But that's Daisy's gift. She can love anyone. It doesn't matter how flawed you are inside or out, she's there to accept you without judgment or hesitation. Maybe that's why I adore her so much. She's so easy to be around and has the brightest of smiles. When directed toward me, her smile can warm even the coldest parts of my soul. The rest of my life is shrouded in dark clouds. Resentment and bitterness are a stench I can't wash away. Lately, I've been worried that my growing cynicism will turn me into my father.

Could Daisy love me if I turned into him?

I push the thought away as Solmer's Rock comes into view. The massive boulder, the only one in the area, is tall and narrow. Faded graffiti covers the bottom of it. We're not too far now. It won't be long before we get to our destination. We're just here to take a peek, and if nothing is wrong, we'll leave. The guys will be disappointed that there's no party, but they'll get over it. They'll just call me an ass, like always, then they'll move on.

I circle the rock, trying to figure out which way is east. That's where my father said they'd be meeting, one mile east of Solmer's Rock. On my second time around it, my eyes catch something on the ground. As I move to pick it up, a hand shoots out and grabs the flimsy plastic ID before I can.

"What's this?" Wyatt asks, holding up the driver's license. He frowns. "Hold up, this is Mrs. Murray's."

For reasons I don't understand, bile climbs up my throat. I snatch the ID away from Wyatt whose brows slam together with concern.

"Since when does Daisy's mom come all the way out here?" he asks me. There must be something on my face because his brow's furrow even more. "Kingston, what's wrong? Why are we really here tonight?"

A scream, coming from somewhere in front of us, cuts off my lame response. It weaves through the trees, wraps around us, then shoots off in every direction. Rather than gradually fading off, it simply stops, leaving the woods silent once more.

The four of us stand there, rooted to the spot. Fear locks around my throat like a vice and cuts off my windpipes.

"W-what, what was that?" Drake asks, breaking the silence.

Owen shifts closer to my side. "A fox, obviously."

Wyatt stares at me. His long shaggy hair, parted in the middle, gives me enough of a glimpse of his face to see him piecing things together. He knows there's no party, but how much more has he surmised?

"Kingston, whose scream was that?" he asks, his voice quiet but firm.

Daisy. Her name in my head is the key to help shed the fear locking me in place. With no time to waste, I take off into the darker shadows of the woods.

"Come on, follow me!"

I don't need to know where east is. That scream told me exactly which direction to go. My feet fly over the ground. Even when the thick grass becomes less dense and the terrain turns rocky, I don't slow. The ground begins to climb. My breathing becomes ragged, but I don't slow down.

As I crest the top of a hill, my feet stumble over themselves as my eyes land on the sight below. Huddled together in a large semi-circle are at least a dozen people dressed in deep red robes. The color of the fabric catches in the large bonfire burning behind them, making it look like blood. In front of them is a large flat stone, and tiki torches are lined up along the other side of the group of people, creating a small barrier between the person laying bound by her wrists and ankles, and the surrounding trees.

Daisy.

Rather than the tee shirt and shorts that she'd been wearing earlier, she now dons a white robe that's parted, giving the chanters, and me, a look at her naked body. How many nights have I dreamed of seeing Daisy sprawled out before me, naked and wanting? Too many, that's for certain. I have the hard, crusty socks shoved under my mattress to prove it.

But this is a thing of nightmares.

A large bloody symbol is painted across her chest and stretches down to her pelvis. It doesn't look like anything I've ever seen before. What does it mean? And whose blood is that? Hers?

My legs give out beneath me. When my knees hit the hard earth, I barely notice. What the hell is this? What's going on? Blood is rushing in my ears, the roaring muffles the chanting going on below. My *parents* are down there. What about Daisy's? They wouldn't allow this, right?

But we just found Mrs. Murray's driver license...

The hooded figures chant softly, ignoring the struggles, pleas, and tears of my best friend. They're so absorbed in what they're doing that they don't hear the guys approaching behind me, huffing and puffing loudly.

"What the hell, King?" Wyatt drops down beside me, breathing hard. "You can't just—"

I turn and slap my hand over Wyatt's mouth. He fights me for a second before I press a finger of my free hand to my lips and jerk my head toward the scene below. Wyatt shoves me away and looks toward the bottom of the hill. His gasp of horror is followed by him shuffling back on his knees to get out of view.

"What the hell is that? Kingston, what is going on?!" he whisper-shouts.

I'm speechless. How the hell am I supposed to know what that is down there? Owen comes up the hill next, followed by Drake, whose gasping sounds like he may be having a heart attack.

"W-why. Are. We. He-he-here?" Owen gasps.

"Shut up and get down!" I demand sharply as the shock begins to wane. "Those people have Daisy.

"We have to do something. Find someone to help us or something!" Wyatt hisses.

Finally able to catch his breath, Owen looks between us. "Find someone to help with what?"

I scowl. "God, of course the bookworm can't grasp what's going on in reality. Look down there you idiot!"

Owen scowls and opens his mouth, but Wyatt shushes him and jerks his thumb down the hill. Muttering under his breath, Owen peers over the edge in front of us. I see the moment the panic hits him. I tackle Owen to the ground, holding my hand over his mouth. Behind my palm, Owen screams.

"What? I want to see!" Drake moves closer to us, drops to his knees, and looks. His gasp is muffled by his own hand, and tears well up in his eyes.

"Don't you dare cry," I snarl, keeping my hand pinned firmly against Owen's mouth. Emotional bastard. "Daisy doesn't have time for your freaking tears, Dre."

He sniffles and nods, dropping his hands away from his mouth. "What are we going to do?"

We? *We?* What *can* we do? I let go of Owen and sit up to look back over the hill. Jesus Christ....

"I have an idea!" Wyatt says suddenly. "Drake, do you have

your pocketknife on you?" At Drake's nod, Wyatt's mouth presses into a tight line before he sighs and says, "Here's what we're going to do."

A SINGULAR HOODED individual is shouting some nonsensical bullshit about a god. The others are paying close attention, swaying and chanting under their breath. On the stone altar, Daisy tries her best to fight her binds but she must be bound to something on the stone because she's unsuccessful. Her pleas have morphed into gut wrenching sobs.

Fear causes my hands to tremble, even as they fist at my side. Thankfully, a burning desire to save my girl, no matter the cost, keeps the fear from overwhelming me. And rage, so much rage, is gathering in my chest. This is my father's doing. Somehow, he's set this in motion. I'll fucking kill him after this.

As I move down the hill, just out of sight of the small crowd, I use the shadows as my cover. I don't bother trying to see if the others are trying to be discreet, I know they are. They're just as determined to get Daisy to safety as I am. And it's because of their determination that I feel confident that this plan will work.

As I get into position, I bend at the waist and pick up a handful of heavy rocks. When I straighten, I stare at my targets. The breath I'm holding lets out in a shaky whoosh. Resolve straightens my spine and my jaw clenches as I listen for the signal.

I don't have to wait long.

"A Spoonful of Sugar" breaks the silence of the woods, interrupting the cult's ceremony. My relief is a burst of cold delight in my chest before it locks down and fear returns. It's time. A second whistle pierces the air, coming from another direction. Then I join in, knowing that Owen can't whistle for shit, and so he probably wasn't even going to try. My lips purse and the sharp tune carries from the shadow.

Daisy stops her wiggling immediately and lifts her head.

That's right, we're coming, Daisy.

I wind my arm back and cast the first stone. It flies through the air, hitting the closest red-robed asshole. Their cry of alarm is mimicked by another as a second stone shoots through the dark from a different direction. I grab another rock and fling it forward, aiming directly at the hooded individual standing at Daisy's side, the one with a familiar knife in their hand. There's a cry of pain as they stumble back.

That's what you get asshole.

I reach down, grabbing two rocks at a time, and throw them as hard as I can at the crowd. The others do the same, keeping up the barrage of heavy fire. Every time a rock leaves my hand and hits someone, I laugh. It's a cold sound that doesn't travel far.

It's not long before the adults begin to back up. Even their leader, who swears loudly, is forced back. Rather than relent, I double my effort, sending as many rocks as I can in their direction. As I work, I catch sight of Drake running toward Daisy as fast as he can—which isn't all that fast. When we decided it would be Drake that saved Daisy, it was only because we knew his aim was the shittiest between the four of us. Rather than yell at him to hurry, I just focus on keeping the adults at bay. He knows our friend's life is at stake. He'll be running with all his might.

Wyatt and Owen must be working just as hard as I am because cries of pain become more frequent and panic begins to ensue. Some of the adults try to cover their hooded heads with their arms, others stumble backward and run. Most of those that run immediately trip over the uneven ground, going down hard. Two bolder individuals start to move toward the flying rocks. One is coming directly at me. My heart slams in my chest. Rather than stumble back and try to flee, my grip on the current rock in my hand tightens. I pulled it back behind my head and chuck it at the rushing individual. It hits them square in the face, taking them down.

"Run, run, run!"

Drake's voice startles me. I look past the person on the ground only a few feet away from me to see Drake and Daisy scrambling into the woods.

"No! Get her!" someone screams in rage.

As the two of them scramble toward the tree line, I focus on pelting more stones at anyone who tries to go after them. Wyatt and Owen must be focused on that too because rocks rain down hard and fast, sailing over Drake and Daisy as they dive into the shadows. The minute they're out of sight, the rock throwing stops on that side.

Shit. Time to go.

Keeping two rocks in my hand, I take off, racing through the woods after the others. As I move, adults start shouting. Someone's giving orders to go after Daisy. My heart leaps up in my throat. We didn't plan this far in advance. While I have a general idea which way they're running, we didn't talk about a meeting point. I lengthen my stride, hoping to catch up with them before the adults do. Rounding the clearing from within the shadows, I swing my arms hard and try to control my breathing.

Somehow, I manage to catch up to them.

I hear Daisy's half-sobs, half-gasps as she runs. Then I catch sight of the white robe. It disappears and reappears as she and the others weave through the trees.

"Hurry!" Daisy wails. "Wait, where's King?"

"He's coming!" Owen promises.

Before I can call out, a sound behind me catches me off guard. Something heavy slams into my back and takes me to the ground. The breath is knocked out of me as I roll, another body holding me tight.

"Got you, you fucking asshole," my father's voice snarls into my ear.

I gasp, trying to regain the breath I've lost. "Get off me!"

"I'll get her!" a robed individual shouts, running past us. I reach out to grab the hem of their robe, but they skirt around us and take off into the night. Three more sprint by us.

"No!" I wheeze, wrestling with the weight pinning me to the ground.

"You won't ruin this, *boy*! It is fate. It is her *destiny*!"

A fist slams into my face. My head hits the ground as stars blind my vision and pain radiates up my jaw.

My father growls before climbing to his feet. "I'll deal with you later."

With that, he takes off after my friends.

"*No!*"

With a groan, I roll onto my stomach and push myself to my feet. I stumble. Sucking in several deep breaths, the world stops spinning enough for me to move forward. I race after everyone. Further into the woods, there's a scream. It's followed by shouting. Someone swears loudly. As I close the distance between us, I hear the struggling. The shouts of pain and surprise litter the darkness. I push my legs harder than ever until I find my friends struggling with four hooded people. One has their foot against Drake's face as he lays on the ground. A knee meets Owen's stomach, taking him out, and Wyatt... Well he is fairing a little better. He twists out of the way of one and then body slams into the person holding Daisy. The motion jars Daisy free and takes her assailant to the ground.

"Run, Daisy!" Wyatt shouts.

"Get back here!" my father's voice bellows as he gives chase. His order follows him into the dark as he races after Daisy. I rush past everyone else, determined to beat him to her.

"Get her King!" Drake shouts weakly as I pass him.

I don't answer him, focusing on the glimpses of the red and white robes ahead of me. Daisy's broken sobs drift around the woods and stab at my heart. Whatever happens after this, I vow that she'll never cry again. That she'll never experience this type of fear. We'll run away if that's what it takes.

Her robe disappears as she and my father speed up.

"Daisy!" I call as the sound of rushing water reaches my eyes. "Daisy be careful! Go south!"

There's a screech. My heart jumps up into my throat, choking me. Daisy's sound of distress cuts off abruptly.

"Daisy?" I call out. "Daisy!"

"I'm here." Her weak voice doesn't travel far as I burst onto the scene.

There, standing on the edge of a sharp cliff, Daisy stands, shaking violently. Her arms wrap around her midriff, her wide eyes landing on me as I move toward her. In front of her is my father, his arms outstretched so she can't go anywhere. The sound of the river, far below, is alarming. How'd we get this far? And why is she standing so close to the edge? Her bottom lip trembles as she looks at me.

"Kingston..." Her hands drop from her waist and one lifts to point behind me, her eyes widening. "King!"

Something sharp and hard hits me in the back of the head. The next thing I know, my face is hitting the ground. My nose makes contact first. Pain explodes in my face, and I gasp for air. Even still, I push myself to my hands and knees.

"Oh no you don't," a stranger's voice hisses. A foot connects with my ribs and I spin, landing on my back. I stare up into the dark hood of the figure above me.

"Kingston!" Daisy's scream is of both fear and outrage. "Don't you touch him again!"

"Get over here and accept your destiny, Daisy," my father

orders. "You're not leaving these woods. Our Lord has chosen you and you will go—"

My father's cut off with a hard huff.

"Run, Daisy!" Owen yells.

I struggle getting to my feet. As I do, I see Owen standing there, breathing heavily, holding a large branch. He lifts it and brings it back down, hitting my father right dab in the face. Dad roars, grabbing the branch the next time Owen lifts it, yanking it from the scrawny kid's hands. Just as Owen is relieved of his weapon, Wyatt and two hooded figures burst out onto the scene. Wyatt elbows one immediately, causing that person to go down onto one knee. The second one makes it past him, toward Daisy.

They don't get to her. A rock goes sailing through the air and makes contact with their head.

"Take that!" Drake shouts as he appears, red faced and sweating.

There's blood on his face and shirt. His jeans are torn and he's missing a shoe, but the hard glitter of determination on his face says none of that matters. His assault takes the figure down.

"No!" Daisy shouts. "I won't do this!"

I turn around to watch my father reach for her. As Daisy twists out of reach, her foot also moves, taking a step backward. It doesn't find a perch behind her. Time slows down as my heart comes to an abrupt stop.

I reach out, as if I could stop what's to come. As if I wasn't on my knees, out of breath and in agony. As if I could save her. The frigid chill that courses through my veins and causes my stomach to twist is ignored. All I can see is Daisy. Our eyes meet before hers widen in terror. Her mouth opens as her arms shoot out to the side to help her find balance.

Her scream, so full of terror that I know I'll never get it out of my head, follows her as she tumbles backward, off the edge of the cliff and out of sight. I'm not the only one who screams out for her. Daisy's name peppers the air as time speeds up again. I scramble to my feet, ignoring the pain in my chest and face as I scream her name again.

Before I can get to the edge of the cliff, my father is there, staring down, swearing violently.

I come up beside him and look over. The drop has to be more than a hundred feet and the water below, high from the previous day's rain, is roaring.

There's no sign of Daisy.

No... no, no, no! My brain refuses to process what I'm seeing. Or who I'm *not* seeing.

"Daisy!" I scream as a fault line cracks and spreads in my chest. "*Daisy*!"

There's no response.

3

Daisy

(Five years later)

My Friend,

I'm alive but far from well. Thankfully, I am on the mend. I hope you're O.K. and living your best life. Maybe one day we'll see each other again.

Until then, take care.

Love,
D. M.

4

Daisy

(Five more years later)

My Friend,

In two weeks' time, Briar Glen will begin to burn as I exact my revenge. It will be ugly, there will be blood, and I'm hoping it will taste as sweet as Mrs. Joanna's strawberry banana milkshake.

If you're living your best life, watch out your window, wherever you are, and maybe you'll see the flames if I can get them to burn high enough.

But if you're interested in doing more than just watching, I have enclosed some special gifts made with love. You'll also find a time and place where I might just be.

Maybe you'll join me?

Whatever you decide to do, know that I love you with all my heart and wish you the best.

Love,

D.M.

5

Wyatt

Two weeks later

The plumes of dense, black smoke that cover the night sky send down ash that falls like snow. Even after two full days of endless work on the part of the Briar Glen Fire Department, the massive fire surrounding the town is still ravaging the woods with no end in sight.

Most of the houses now are covered in soot, as are any cars not parked in a garage, the roads, and all the street signs. Gray and black flecks of ash drift down onto my car's windshield, only to be batted away by my windshield wipers. With visibility being nearly zero, my trek through town to the police station is slow going and frustrating.

And unnecessary.

When Brett texted me that he needed to talk about something urgent, I nearly blew the guy off. He just doesn't get that we're not a 'thing' anymore. What that 'thing' was, I never did label it. But the brief interlude that we had together clearly meant a lot to Brett. He's been doing everything he can to get back with me. It's getting old *fast*.

"Damn it, Brett, this better be good," I grumble as I cross the empty street, or what I hope is an empty street, before turning into the station.

The smoke is thicker on this side of town for sure.

Hopefully, it won't be just the woods surrounding the town burning for much longer.

Briar Glen will begin to burn.

A smile splays across my face as I think about the note I received two weeks ago. I didn't know what it meant then, but now I do, and I can't be more thrilled.

Daisy's back and she's living up to her promise.

My heart races as my grip tightens on the steering wheel. I didn't know what to believe when I received the first letter. Seriously shaken, I almost threw the damn thing away.

Yet, for some reason, I kept it. I reread it over and over again until I could close my eyes and see that familiar handwriting behind my eyelids. It hadn't been long before hope started to melt away my wariness and seep into my psyche. It *could* be her. Heaven knew I wanted it to be so fucking badly.

Then Drake and Owen contacted me a few days later, out of the blue after years of nothing from either of them, wondering if I'd gotten a strange letter.

How would they have gotten a letter from Daisy?

After Daisy's death, the four of us were torn apart. It started with Owen's family moving him far away and cutting off communication with us. Then Drake was yanked out of school and practically disappeared for a few years before emerging just long enough to finish high school. He barely finished walking across the stage to get his diploma before dipping out of Briar Glen on the first ticket out of here. For a while, it was just me and King. Even that only lasted a year before Francis Winslow got tired of Kingston touting to anyone and everyone in town about his father's hand in Daisy's murder. He shut Kingston up in a way I could have never foreseen.

Did King ever get a letter? I doubt it given where he is. The letters *I* sent to him were always returned to sender.

For a while, I'd wondered if the letter was from someone in town, like Francis, messing with our heads. But why would he do that? Why would anyone? After her tumble over the cliff into the raging river below, the town had done everything in its power to erase her from its history. From her parents disappearing two days later and her childhood home being bulldozed shortly afterward, to any and all pictures of her around town, including the ones in our bedrooms, vanishing. Then there was the constant gaslighting we got from the adults around us when we tried to tell them what happened. All of it done to make sure it looked like Daisy was never here.

And they succeeded. It wasn't six months later before there was no sign of Daisy left.

So why would someone reach out to each of us, dredging up the past, after they worked so hard to erase it? My mind loved and hated the mystery of it. For five years I wondered if I could take the note seriously. I hoped... I even tried praying. When nothing else came in the mail, I'd nearly given up.

Then the second letter arrived. With it, a large package filled with ominous gifts. Since then, all my doubts have scattered to the wind. Daisy's coming home, and soon, I'll see her again.

This time around, I won't hold back my feelings for her. Growing up, I kept my adoration for our girl quiet. Now, I'll fucking shout it from the goddamn rooftops. The undeniable longing to just be in her presence causes my stomach to twist with nervous excitement.

Soon. I'll see her soon...

In the meantime, I have someone else I have to deal with.

Brett's cruiser is the only one in the parking lot in front of the small, red brick police station. Frowning, I park, lift the collar of my shirt so that it covers my mouth and nose, and push the door open. Quickly, I jog up the steps and yank open the glass doors before entering the police station.

"Wy!"

Dropping my shirt so that it falls back into place, I look across the small open area that Brett calls 'the pen' to find my ex-lover hurrying over to me. I have to admit, in uniform, Brett Runner is an attractive man. Tall, tan, and well-built, he would probably make a better model than a police officer.

"Thanks for coming. I know you said you needed some space but what I have to show you—" He shakes his head as he stops before me. A knowing grin stretches across his face. "Is something only you'd appreciate. This is *big*, Wyatt."

Is it though? Or is this a ploy just to capture my attention? Brett knows I'm a sucker when it comes to true crime shit.

Before I can ask what it is, Brett grabs my hand and leads me to the back. My teeth grind together and tension gathers in my shoulders. Maybe 'space' was the wrong word to use with Brett. 'Break up' should've been the phrase to use. Though we never actually *dated.*

I try to subtly pull myself free, but Brett keeps a firm hold.

"We don't have too long, but you'll have enough time to *admire* the crime scene," he says.

"Crime scene?" My frustration with my ex-lover vanishes as curiosity takes its place. "What are you talking about?"

Brett stops in front of a door and punches in a code on the keypad. There's a buzz before Brett pushes the door open and steps inside. He pulls me in with him and I let the door shut behind us.

What normally is a relatively empty room is now filled with

boxes of evidence, pictures posted on white boards, newspaper clippings, and long tables covered with stuff. I gape at the transformation of the otherwise sterile room.

"What in the world—"

"I told you this was big," Brett confirms, practically giddy. "Now, before I tell you what you've just walked into, you have to swear you'll never tell a soul. I shouldn't be jeopardizing my job like this. But I know you would love a good mystery and now Briar Glen has its very first one!"

It's most definitely *not* Briar Glen's only mystery. There's a well-hidden cult here that the townspeople pretend not to know about. Still, I'm interested in whatever this is. I tear my eyes away from everything to look back at Brett.

"You know I would never say anything."

Early on in our blossoming affair, Brett learned about my obsession with true crime and how my interest went far beyond the normal scope. I've got some twisted fantasies. They probably stem from my childhood trauma though I haven't looked too hard into the why of some of them. Luckily, someone in this small backwoods town is open to feeding into them. It's probably why I let what Brett and I had go on for as long as it did. No one else would be open to taking me to the coroner's office on a Saturday night so that I could have sex near someone recently deceased.

"I know, I just needed to say it again because this is—"

"—big, yeah, you've been saying that. Now spill. What is all this?" I wave my hands around the room.

Brett nudges his head and leads me over to the first table on our left. On it sits five evidence bags splayed out beside five full cardboard boxes. A bag containing a bloody butcher knife and another with a bloody mallet catch my attention first.

I look from them to Brett, unable to keep a smile from forming.

Brett chuckles. "I knew you'd like this. *Those* are potential murder weapons."

My stomach drops, who else was murdered in Briar Glen other than Daisy? "There's been a murder?"

The young cop nods. "Yup. Someone murdered a guy and left all the weapons behind."

Holy shit. "This would be Briar Glen's first murder in—"

"Over five decades," Brett supplies.

Wrongly of course. My jaw clenches tight. There's no point reminding him about Daisy Murray. He would've been too young to know about all that anyway. Besides, her existence has been deemed false. There isn't a single person in town willing to talk about the young girl whose smile could drag anyone out of their funk or whose heart was bigger than Solmer's Rock.

My attention returns to the items on the table. Judging by how dry the blood looks on the knife, this wasn't a recent attack.

I choke in surprise as my eyes land on the picture of a corpse. Whoever it was lost their head in a gruesome fashion. The skull is smashed to pieces, teeth and shards of bone litter the shag carpet beneath it. Sticking out of the skeleton's chest is the knife in the evidence bag beside the picture. A mallet rests in the middle of the skull fragments.

I grunt as my dick grows hard swiftly. My hand reaches out and grips the edge of the table to steady myself. The breath I draw in is shaky as blood warms my cheeks. Brett warned me to brace myself, yet here I am with my knees knocking together and my heart racing like a man in love.

"You like that?" Brett asks, stepping closer and his voice dropping an octave. With a hard swallow, I nod. "I knew you would."

"Who is that?"

"Does it matter?" he counters softly. It's followed by a

chuckle. "Who am I kidding? Of course it matters to you. That's part of the fun. You *enjoy* the details."

Hell yes I do.

"His name is, *was*, Oliver Grayman. We estimate his time of death was about five years ago. We'll know for sure in a few days."

I drag in a shaky breath. My free hand moves down to cup my erection through my pants. If I had known Brett wanted to show me *this*, I probably would have moved a little faster to get here.

"He'd be about seventy-two now if he hadn't been murdered," Brett continues. "He lived in the town over, in Chasm, but apparently, he owned about ten acres here in Briar Glen. At some point, Oliver built himself an off-the-grid cabin and has been vacationing there for decades. The fire that started two days ago out in the woods? It started on his property, but get this: the grass was soaking wet and there were two hoses still running when the firefighters stumbled upon his place. Whoever started the fire, purposely made sure the house remained intact."

There's so much to take in that I don't even know where to start. As I process the information, I squeeze my dick, trying to relieve a little pressure. I try to quell the rising wave of desire by wondering what Daisy would think of my reaction to shit like this, but even that doesn't cool the heat in my blood. A shiver runs down my spine.

"This is just the tip of the iceberg, Wy. Let me show you the pièce de résistance."

Brett waves me over to the next table where hundreds of pictures are strewn about. In them? Bodies. So many fucking bodies. My gasp of delight gets choked off however, when I study them further.

"WHAT THE HELL IS THIS, BRETT?"

Brett blinks in surprise, taking a step back while raising his hands in surrender. "What? You don't want to—"

"Those are young girls!" I snarl. "I'm not a pedophile."

Confusion brings Brett's brows together and he frowns. "I just figured—"

"What? That a dead body was just a dead body? Jesus Christ..."

I run a shaky hand through my mop of hair and glance back at the table. The disgust welling up in my chest softens my dick. Staring at dead bodies is one thing. Staring at torture scenes of young girls is a whole other ballgame. One I'm definitely not into.

"Who are those people anyway?"

"Oliver's victims," Brett grumbles. "There are thirty-seven girls here. It looks like a lot more because there are multiple pictures taken of the same girls."

As if thirty-seven wasn't already a lot of dead girls.

"Victims?" I repeat.

"Turns out that Oliver Grayman was a serial killer. Can you believe that? Right here in Briar Glen and no one knew." Brett laughs but it trails off as he shakes his head. "I'm not sure why I'm excited, especially given that I'm a cop and I should've noticed something was up."

Staring at the pictures, I notice the women and girls are *painted* in blood, not just covered with it. After a moment, I realize there's a pattern. I reach forward to start to shuffle the pictures together, but Brett stops me.

"Don't touch anything! Look, this is what you've probably discovered." He points to a picture on the other end of the table.

I move over to take a closer look. In this photograph, I can see that all these pictures laying out on the table before me were compiled into one large collage on the wall of some room. In this fashion, it's clear to see what Oliver Grayman painted on all the girls. Using the bodies and blood, he'd created a large symbol to display proudly. The V-shape with an arch and line crossing at the top doesn't look familiar but clearly, this was important to the sick bastard.

I stare at the sign, knowing that this isn't just some random symbol. My knowledge of crimes and cults is near frightening, given how much time and energy I've put into learning about them. And right now, my intuition is screaming this is important. A symbol like this, in a town with a cult? Not a coincidence.

"What does this mean?"

Brett hums thoughtfully. "We don't know yet, but we'll be running it through the database to see what comes up."

I don't know if I believe him. Ever since *that* night, I've learned I can't trust anyone. Not the other kids in school, who pretended not to know Daisy despite her popularity, which wasn't quite as impressive as King's, but was close. Not any adults, especially the ones we thought we adored, like Mrs. Joanna at Ma's Diner, or our parents and teachers who acted like they'd never heard Daisy's name before in their lives.

The symbol looks almost demonic. As I study it further, I realize there are three pictures missing from the collage. The missing images don't take away from the bloody work of the serial killer. But it's strange. Judging from their location, they would've been right smack dab in the middle of the symbol. An important piece. The *centerpiece* of this serial killer's obsession.

"What happened to these three pictures?"

Brett plods closer to stare at the pictures with me. "Who knows? The others think that whoever started the fire was one of his victims. One that might've escaped and never came forward to report him but wanted us to know what he'd done so they came back. Maybe they took them? God, if they were a victim, I can't imagine what they went through. If you'd seen what was in the room these pictures were in, you'd get it. It was a nightmare. I'm talking medical chairs, bloody tools, a dirty mattress, a drain full of—"

"Ok, ok! I get it!" My stomach rolls. I usually don't mind hearing, or even seeing, stuff like this. It must be because I'm not in the right headspace that the sight before me is making me uncomfortable.

Brett sighs. "Look, if we're not going to—"

"Officer Runner, what's your 10-20?"

I jump at the sound of dispatch coming through Brett's radio. Brett swears and immediately answers.

"I'm at the station, Pam, what's up?"

"All available units are needed on site at 236 Greenville Avenue. There's a 10-39 and a 10-12."

Brett swears loudly and rushes toward the door. "I'm on my way. Be there in ten."

He waves at me frantically to follow. I do, keeping close as we burst from the room to hurry down the hallway.

"What's a 10-39 and a 10-12?" I ask him.

We run through the station toward the exit. What's going on? Was there an accident? A thief? What could possibly have Brett so worked up—

"10-39 is a dead body and a 10-12 is vandalism. And that address?" Brett slows to a stop to open the front door for me. I slip out and he follows, locking up behind us. "That address just happens to be the mayor's house," Brett states grimly.

I KNOW I SHOULDN'T, but I follow Brett to Mayor Tobias's residence anyway.

The mayor lives in the nicer area of town. Here, the older homes are well taken care of, the lawns are nicely manicured, and the properties are at least double the size of the ones on my side of town. King used to live over here. Now it's only

Francis Winslow that lives in that large house a few blocks away.

While I've never been to the mayor's house before, it's easy to spot as I approach. If the flashing cop cars surrounding the building weren't enough of a clue, the sheer size of the house is. It is a well-known fact that Tobias likes to live extravagantly, so I'm not surprised he has the nicest, largest house on his block. I park a street away and scramble out of my car, covering my face with my shirt to avoid inhaling too much smoke.

My hands start to tremble as I approach the crime scene. I shove them into my pocket, embarrassed that they're my tell. Most people would probably assume that it's from fear or nerves, but they'd be wrong.

I fucking *love* the depraved and darker side of this world. I hate that I love it so much. Given where my fixation with death started, I shouldn't have this type of visceral reaction. One day I'll make it to therapy.

As I draw closer, I can hear cops yelling orders and clearing the premises. But I ignore them as I spot the 10-39.

"Holy shit."

With all the flashing lights hitting the brick building, I get an unobstructed view of Mayor Tobias's limp body as it hangs out a second floor window by its neck. The grizzly way his neck is bent has my stomach turning and my dick straining against my zipper. The long nightgown that he's dressed in is covered in blood, with a gaping hole in his chest.

I think it's safe to say this is definitely not a suicide.

With all the cops of Briar Glen fluttering about, desperate to secure the crime scene, I stop just across the street and stare in awe. Someone calls to someone else and then there's pointing. My attention drops to the driveway, where police are beginning to gather. I can't see what they're looking at.

As discreetly as I can, I cross the street and approach as close as possible without drawing too much attention.

There, in bold, bloody letters in the middle of Mayor Tobias's driveway, are the words: I'M BACK.

My gasp is cut off as an astonished bark of laughter tumbles past my lips. First the fire and now this? I cover my mouth to muffle the sound as my laughter grows louder and more hysterical.

She promised fire and blood and has already delivered.

Daisy Murray is back.

6

Kingston

Dry, cracked, lips press against my jawline as a wet pussy clenches around my dick. The nurse's breathless gasp in my ear as she cums around me is an echo of all the past ones I've been forced to listen to.

Judging by her desperation to get off, I'm assuming the honeymoon with her second husband didn't go well.

"*God*," Nurse Jenn chokes off as the fluttering of her filthy cunt subsides. At least one of us will leave truly satisfied this evening.

I hold back a grimace, even though her face is still buried in my neck. The only satisfaction I'm feeling right now is smug satisfaction. I haven't finished inside of her. *Again*. After being forced to become the fuckboy for all the female nurses, I've learned that not finishing pisses them off to no end. As desperately as my body *wants* some relief, I always fight it. It's the only way I can retaliate without catching time in isolation, or receiving the hard sedative that would knock me out for days at a time only for me to wake up feeling violated.

As it is, getting me hard is a chore for them. It's why they've gone to the extreme lengths of spiking my drinks and food with that damn blue pill to get me ready for their nightly escapades. Self-loathing and disgust stain my insides from years of this shit.

But no more. My stint in hell is coming to an end.

"Yeah, you like that, King?" Nurse Jenn asks, mistaking my grin for pleasure as she pushes up and straddles my waist. Her hand reaches forward so that she can skim her fingertips across the thick, gnarly scar across my throat.

Even if I wanted to tell her to fuck off, I physically can't. When dear old dad attempted to silence me after a year of my insistent pleading to the town to do something about the people involved in Daisy's death, he made sure I would never get to speak Daisy's name again. Not that this was his end goal. He'd wanted to kill me. When he realized his mistake, he had the judge throw me in here.

Thankfully, Daisy's daily sign language lessons stuck a little bit. They helped to get me by in the beginning while the administration scrambled to find someone who could communicate in the same manner here at Riverbend Asylum. Unfortunately, I can't use my hands to tell Nurse Jenn to fuck off right now either. With them currently above my head, I know that the moment I move them, Nurse Jenn will scream and bring security running in. *That* I learned the hard way long ago.

I stare up at the older woman, picturing my hands reaching down toward her neck. They'd wrap around her thick, saggy column of skin and squeeze until the life was snuffed out of those bland brown eyes. But other than wishful thinking, I don't acknowledge Nurse Jenn.

She doesn't expect me to.

The woman climbs off me and with a rough yank, pulls off the empty condom with an annoyed huff. She says nothing about my lack of release, however. She simply grabs the bottom of her scrubs off the linoleum floor and shimmies back into them. I don't watch. Instead my gaze finds the ceiling tiles and locks onto them. The soft sound of footsteps tells me I'm finally about to be left alone for the night. I wait for the familiar click as the door opens, but it doesn't come.

"You hear about Mayor Tobias's murder?" Nurse Jenn asks.

Murder? I blink in surprise before a sliver of glee winds its way through my limbs. Peeling my eyes off the ceiling, I look over to Nurse Jenn.

"Sheriff Ronney and your father are keeping it hush-hush while they continue to try and put out that fire in the woods, but I saw it on my way home last night. It was gruesome. It was something *you* would do."

Of course she believes that. *All* of Briar Glen believes I'm a psychopathic killer. My dad did a fine job setting me up to take the fall for him after he killed my mother. Now that bastard is free, while I rot away in an asylum.

I ignore her jab.

"Thought maybe you could jerk off to *that* information since you were a wonderful help this evening for me." The woman sneers. "Good night, patient three-oh-three."

With that, she makes quick work of leaving my room and locking me in. The door barely latches before my laughter slips past my lips. If I could produce any sound, my laugh would be booming, I'm sure of it. As it is, the wispy noise hardly fills the space around me.

Still laughing, I reach down between the mattress and the wall. I lift up the fitted sheet, dig two fingers into the small hole I'd made five years ago and dig out the small, rolled up slip of paper. My laughter dies down as I pull it free and unroll it.

One day, I'll come for you.
Watch for the flames.

Love,

- D.M.

My thumb slides over the handwriting. I've done it so many times, the ink has begun to fade. The simple note, slipped in by a security guard with a gaping wound, wild eyes, and radiating fear, has been the only reason I never succumbed to the insanity the town of Briar Glen believed I was so capable of.

The sign that I've been waiting for all these years, the flames that were promised, have been burning in the distance, having started three days ago.

But a murder?

How deliciously wicked. If it was Daisy that killed the mayor, it appears the flames were just the start of whatever she has planned.

I grin. *Come on Daisy. Let me help you paint this town red.*

7

Owen

"—With the unfortunate death of Mayor Tobias Bower comes a wonderful opportunity for the people of Briar Glen. Tobias was Mayor a long time, and well loved, but now someone else has the opportunity to step up and run Briar Glen how they see fit. We will be hosting an election this November." The man on the screen is clean shaven, sharply dressed, and smiles warmly into the camera. Those blue eyes are so painfully familiar to an old friend's' that I have to look away for a moment to catch my breath.

When I look back, my stomach rolls.

I fucking hate Francis Winslow. Kingston's dad tilts his head to give the town's local reporter his attention. The thoughtfulness of his expression seems so *real*. Maybe if I didn't have such an inside look at the true monster beneath the mask, I would believe the charade he's putting on for the town now.

Growing up, I believed he was a good man, despite how much Kingston complained about how strict he was.

"Do you believe this shit?" the man three seats down the counter mutters to the shorter guy beside him. "Ronney's telling everyone that Tobias died of a heart attack. If that's the case, why were they scrubbing his driveway so hard the night it happened?"

The shorter man grunts. "The better question is why they didn't tell us about his death until a few days *after* it happened. Man's been dead for five days now, and we're just hearing about it this morning? Weird, right? And why is Winslow doing the sheriff's job right now?"

"Ronney's a good man, but I swear he's getting lazier in his old age."

"Probably itching to retire."

On the screen Francis says, "Who? Me? No, I could never run for Mayor. Everyone knows how much I adore Briar Glen, but I'm much too busy to give the position the attention it deserves. I'm sure there are plenty of eager people gunning for it, though."

"He'd be a good mayor," the first man says. "He's the only one who really gives a shit about this place."

The second man doesn't answer right away. Instead, he finishes his drink and burps loudly. "I don't give a fuck who's mayor. As long as it doesn't affect me or my paychecks, I'll be good. Now let's get back to work."

With that, the two men get up, throw cash down next to their empty plates, and leave. With their departure, the lunch rush seems to be over. Now it's just me and a couple sitting in a booth.

The door to the kitchen swings open and I half expect Mrs. Joanna to appear. This is her diner after all. But it's not her. The young redheaded waitress that appears is all dolled up, chewing her gum loudly. Her uniform is a little too tight, but I'd bet anything that was on purpose.'

"Want anything other than water?" she asks me as she stops just on the other side of the counter.

"Naw, I'm good. Just waiting on a friend, then I'll be out of your hair." When I smile, she winks and returns it before sauntering off to help the couple sitting in the booth.

I twist from side to side on my barstool, not sure what else to do. Most people pull out their phones when they have a moment to themselves. Me? I don't trust them. It's why mine is in my car, despite having completely erased the firmware that it came with and setting up my own to protect my location, the sparse information I put into it, and lack of apps on it. So, I take the time to look around.

My attention lands on the pictures plastered around the window that looks into the kitchen.

Some have been here a long time. Those ones are faded and in black and white. Others are full color and clearly recently added. My eyes land on the picture right dab in the middle. There sits a picture of the four of us guys, sitting around our booth. There used to be five of us in that picture. That is, until someone photoshopped Daisy out of it.

Bitter resentment coats my tongue. I can't believe I'm back in Briar Glen.

Unlike the other's parents, my mother and father believed me when I told them what happened to Daisy. When the town tried to gaslight them into believing the Murray's never existed, my parents decided it was time to get the hell out of here. When we left six months after Daisy's death, I swore I'd never return. What happened to Daisy and then how easily this place erased her? It scared the ever-loving shit out of me. I wanted nothing more than to forget about this place. But forgetting was impossible.

So I did the next best thing: cut ties with everyone and anything that reminded me of Daisy. That meant no more contact with Wyatt, Drake, or Kingston. No more reading the books that Daisy and I used to love, and definitely not stopping in at diners or even in towns with a population of less than a thousand people. Who knows how many small towns are like Briar Glen, hiding in plain sight? I didn't want to know. I let fear keep me from a lot of things.

I thought I was ok with what I was missing out on.

But then I got the first letter.

With finding out Daisy was still alive, my whole philosophy changed. No more hiding or running away from the things that scared me. No more building walls between my future and my past. Five years ago, I opened up lines of communication with the others and it was the best decision of my life. Now Drake and Wyatt are a part of my life once more. We may not be *as* close as we once were, but slowly we have rebuilt a friendship that works for us.

Behind me the bell rings, indicating someone's just walked in. At the same time, the door to the kitchen opens and the waitress pokes her head out to flash the newcomer a smile.

"Hey, hon, sit wherever, I'll get to you in a second."

Behind me, heavy footsteps draw near. The seat beside me is taken by a hulking individual, whose shadow nearly engulfs me. I shoot the guy a quick glance but look away. Looks like Briar Glen has attracted some sketchy motherfuckers.

"Owen?"

My head snaps back around to the man beside me. He looks at me curiously, as if he doesn't trust what he's seeing.

"Owen Woodlock?" He uses my whole name this time, his voice gruff.

"Yeah...?" It's not until the word is out of my mouth that it registers who's sitting beside me.

Holy shit.

Gone is the chubby kid I once knew. Drake's grown about a hundred feet, lost the fat, and replaced it with heavy muscle. He sports a thick blond beard and has let his hair grow long enough to throw it into a messy bun. The tattoos up his arms disappear beneath his tight tee shirt then reappear, creeping up his neck. Around his wrist is one of those survival paracord bracelets, and there's a carabiner with a set of keys hanging off his belt.

"Jesus, Drake, I would've never recognized you! I was waiting for the old you to show up."

We may text here and there, but I haven't actually *seen* Drake since we were kids.

Drake grunts with a half nod. "Good, if you can't remember an old friend, maybe the people here won't recognize me either."

I slide halfway off the stool to throw my arm around his shoulders. "God, it's good to see you again."

"Yeah, it's been too long I suppose," he agrees as I slide back into my seat. "Is Wyatt meeting us here?"

I shake my head. "No, I didn't tell him any dates or times. I figured we could surprise him. Just so you know, anything we have to say, we say it in the safety of a debugged area." Drake's brow raises curiously. I nudge my head toward the old security camera in the corner of the diner. "Those aren't as old as the owners would like us to think they are and I'm *sure* they pick up more than we think they do."

"Why do you think that?"

"Just a feeling." *And the fact that I managed to scan the diner with the device in my backpack and found some high tech gizmos hidden within the walls.*

He shoots me a curious look.

"You know I own a small cyber security company. It's kind of my thing to know my way around technology and know when things aren't right." I grin sheepishly. "In any case, just be careful what you say in public or within *any* building here."

Drake nods.

"You want to order anything since we're here?" I ask him, glancing down at my watch, trying to judge how much time we have.

"Naw, I'm good." He slides off the stool. "Let's go."

8

Wyatt

I haven't been able to sleep since the night Mayor Tobias died.

Not because his death was gruesome. It's not even because I'm excited at the possibility that Daisy is nearby, though I'm sure that *is* part of it. No, my nights have been sleepless and rough because my mind, which is always searching for ways to connect the dots, has pieced together the worst case scenario about Daisy's whereabouts these past ten years.

Well, at least for the first five years of her disappearance.

And it's not good.

Five years ago was when I got the first letter from Daisy. In it, she'd mentioned not being ok. Being captured by a sadistic fuck would probably fall under the category of 'not ok', right? Given that Oliver has been dead now for almost five years, and the fire, *promised by Daisy*, was a way to bring attention to Oliver's cabin, it feels too weird to be a coincidence.

Could Daisy have been saved all those years ago, after falling from that cliff, by a psychopath?

The denial and logic didn't react well in my gut. The first night, when the pieces all came together, I threw up violently. Those pictures of the victims... Daisy could've been one of them. Once I finished turning my insides out, I grabbed my phone and pulled up the map feature. The only way Oliver could've saved Daisy was if he lived close enough to the river to either see her body floating in the water or if he found her along the shore.

Low and behold, his cabin is situated less than a hundred feet from the river's edge.

He had her. My friend. My girl... Oliver *found* Daisy and then he... God, the things he could've done to her.

It's *that* thought that keeps me up for the next five nights.

Drinking myself to near oblivion hasn't helped. It just ends up with me puking and dredging up memories I'd buried so deep I'd forgotten about them.

"Mr. Challahan?"

I blink and the world comes back into focus. Around me, students are rushing onto the buses to make it home on time and parents are sitting in their cars, waiting for me to release their kids from the line they'd all walked out of the building in. Looking down, I find Poppy staring up at me, waiting expectantly.

Fuck, did she say something? I clear my throat. "Sorry, what was that?"

"Can I go home now?"

Oh, that. "Yeah, sure. Go on," I wave my fourteen students away, releasing them from my responsibility.

I watch as they hurry toward their parents or the school bus. Some cross the green front lawn of the elementary school toward the sidewalks they'll take to walk home. Forcing myself to pay attention, I stand there and watch each student until all that's left standing in front of the school is me and a handful of other teachers.

I'm about to turn to head back inside to grab my belongings when my eyes land on two individuals leaning up against one of the tall pines on the school's property. I nearly pass them off as parents or older siblings, but something about them causes me to stare longer.

And as I stare, I realize I *know* them.

The scoff of disbelief that slips past my lips is followed up by a smile so big I swear it's about to split my face in two. I raise a hand and wave.

Both men push off the tree and head toward me. The moment they're out from the shade of the tree, I blink in surprise. Owen's grown taller. His smooth brown skin has lost all signs of acne, he's gotten rid of the glasses, and he's cut his fro off. The nerdy kid who wore bifocals and tee shirts that were too big for him, has morphed into a handsome guy.

My eyes jump from Owen to the guy next to him. Holy shit. Drake's definitely been hitting the gym. What happened to the fat kid? This brute looks ready to kickass and break bones.

I meet them halfway. Without hesitation, as Owen comes to a stop, I throw my arms around him and pull him into a hug. He chuckles as he returns it with an arm around my back.

"You guys came." Emotions cluster together to form a knot in my throat, making it hard to say more.

Owen flashes me an easy-going smile. "Of course we did. We wouldn't miss this for the world. Right, Drake?"

At the burly man's nod, I tear up a little.

We talked about this reunion for years in the hypothetical but neither mentioned that they would actually show up.

"Come on, let's head to my house. We'll catch up there, and then—" I drag in a deep breath. "I need to tell you what I've learned about Daisy's past."

9

Drake

As I drive my rental truck behind Owen, who drives behind Wyatt, trepidation keeps me tense. I hate it here. We drive through streets that once housed fond memories. Now those same memories are twisted with cancerous nightmares. Our lives were built on lies.

This town was never safe. The people who watched us grow up were also the ones willing to torture us.

We make a turn down one street, then another, until we're on a street so painfully familiar that I stop breathing. As we slow down to accommodate the legal speed limit of this residential neighborhood, I force myself not to look to the right. That structure with four exterior walls, a steep sloping roof, and an immaculate garden that never has a single weed or dead flower in it, is ignored.

My family was dead to me the moment I realized they were liars. They hid the truth, helped to erase the past, and tried to drive me to madness. The latter, they succeeded in. There's something wrong with me. Something fucked up in my head.

It's another few miles before we pull up to a small house, on a street filled with other small homes. Wyatt parks in the driveway while Owen and I park along the street. The cars will draw attention. I wouldn't be surprised if a neighbor didn't come knocking in the next twenty minutes to see who Wyatt had over for company.

People in small towns are nosy like that.

I grab my duffle bag and climb out, slamming the door shut behind me. Wyatt's house is probably the smallest on the street. The roof looks like it needs to be replaced soon, moss growing in patches here and there. His yard needs mowing too. It's not a jungle, not yet, but it will be. I'm surprised people haven't complained. There are some shaggy, overgrown bushes along the side and old trees growing over the house. One strong storm and a branch could take out half the building.

"Nice house," Owen mentions as we meet Wyatt by the front door.

I can practically feel the neighbors' gaze resting upon my back. Fighting the urge to roll my shoulders, I force myself to stand and wait patiently as Wyatt fumbles for his key.

When he finds the right one, he shoves it into the door and looks over his shoulder. "Yeah, once I moved back after college, I got that teaching gig at Sparkford Elementary. The salary was enough to get me something modest. It needs some updating, but I don't have the skill or cash for that just yet."

"I'm impressed," Owen mutters as Wyatt pushes open the door. "I still rent, and my apartment is the size of a tuna can."

I ask, "Where do you live now?"

We've been in communication since Daisy's first letter, but at Owen's urging, we've kept the responses and personal details to a minimum and infrequent. *Someone's* grown to be a bit paranoid.

"Greenwich, Connecticut," Owen responds as we all move into the house.

As I shut the door behind me, I'm hit and nearly overwhelmed by the stench of beer. I drop my bag next to the door as I grimace.

Owen whistles. "Jesus, Wy. You got a problem?"

I step around him into what must be the living room to find beer bottles everywhere. Bottles are on the floor, on the single side table, the coffee table, and they trail out of the room to the small kitchen that looks like it's from the mid-seventies.

"Ah, no, no problem." Immediately, Wyatt starts moving, fluttering around the room like a hummingbird, trying to clean up his mess. He manages to clear the couch, recliner, and the coffee table in nearly one fell swoop.

I shove my hands in my pockets and look around, noting the lack of pictures on the walls, or any sort of personal touch. There are a ton of books on the bookshelf, though they look old and worn. Are they his? Reading was more Owen's thing. I meander over, needing something to do. My eyes rake over the spines, barely processing what the words say. After a moment, I piece together that these books are medical ones. A lot of anatomy, some biology, and a few true crime stories.

Huh, weird mix.

Wyatt continues moving about as he picks up and throws away all the bottles. "I know it doesn't look like it, but I really don't drink all that often. It's just been, you know, this crazy week what with Dais—"

Owen clears his throat, drawing my attention back to him. He places a finger on his lips to indicate silence, then places his backpack on the ground. I watch as he pulls out a small, black device, and places it on Wyatt's end table. With a push of a button, a small red light flickers on, flashes a few times, then turns off.

"There, now your house is secure." Owen looks to Wy and adds, "You can never be too safe about who's listening in. Especially here, since your emails are being watched and tracked.

It's why I just wanted to text. I wouldn't be surprised if they had a bug in your house."

Wyatt's mouth opens and shuts in surprise. "Well, shit, that's good to know."

"In any case, we should keep her name out of our mouths outside these walls," I point out. "No need to alert the cult that we think she's alive and back."

The other two nod in agreement.

"Right, well, have a seat. I have a lot to tell you and it isn't good." Wyatt waves me over to the couch but I take the recliner instead.

It groans under my weight.

"You said it's about Daisy's past, right?" I try to get comfortable, but the recliner is old and well worn. I can feel the springs digging into my ass.

Wyatt collapses onto a couch cushion the same time Owen does. Despite the creeps this town gives me, I'm strangely at ease here with the two of them. It's weird not having the other two around.

I shiver as my mind drifts to thoughts of Kingston.

I wonder how he's doing now? Unable to receive visitors or letters, Kingston's been rotting away in the asylum sitting on the outskirts of town for nearly nine years, all on his own. Guilt twists my guts. There was nothing I could do for him then, and there's nothing I can do for him now. With how powerful his father is in this town, he's managed to secure a place for Kingston in hell all on his own.

I guess his cruelness is why he's the head of the cult here. Or, at least at one point he was. Is he still?

"Yeah... I think I know what happened to her and it all has to do with Oliver Grayman."

Owen frowns. "Who?"

Wyatt grimaces. His shoulders set as his expression clears and he looks around at us. "Briar Glen's serial killer."

"So Daisy was being held captive by Oliver, who drew runes across his victims, leading you to assume—"

"Not assume, *know*," Wyatt corrects Owen. "I *know* that means he's part of the cult. It's the same one we saw drawn on Daisy's body that night. It took me a while to remember where I'd seen it, but then it all came back to me. I'm not wrong."

I shake my head trying to connect the pieces. Wyatt's memory must be better than mine. I remember blood, but a rune? I can't remember if that had been painted on her body or not.

"Ok, let's assume that's true and this is where she's been," I tug at my beard thoughtfully. "You think she used the techniques Oliver used on his victims on Mayor Tobias? *Daisy*? The one that wouldn't hurt a fly?"

Wyatt snorts. It's dry and dark, and when he meets my gaze, that same darkness has leached into his eyes. "Judging by her letters, and our *gifts*, I have a feeling the Daisy we knew and the Daisy who's back for revenge are two very different people."

Yeah, I have no doubt about that. My gaze flickers to my duffle bag by the door. Her gifts sit inside, ready to be used.

"It's hard to believe, you know, that this is her," Owen whispers.

I glance over to him. He's staring down at the coffee table. Owen seems to be taking the news that Daisy's been with a serial killer poorly. I mean, we all are horrified, but Owen? His mouth hangs slightly ajar and his breathing looks shallow.

"You good over there?" I ask. *Should I grab a trash can...*

"Yeah, yeah... I, ah, am just... I'm just processing."

Wyatt and I trade skeptical looks. He gets up a second later and grabs a grocery bag from under the sink in his kitchen and brings it over to Owen.

"If you're going to puke, please do it in here." Owen takes

the bag without looking, his gaze still pinned to the table. "Now you understand all the booze."

As Wyatt takes a seat, Owen finally looks up at the both of us and says, "If it is her, you know she'll probably expect us to help her get revenge."

That's the same conclusion I came to two weeks ago. Ever since I received her letter and her gifts, I knew this wasn't going to be some lame-ass attempt to scare the town. And now that I know what she's been through, at least in part, I have no doubt this will be bloody.

"I've killed before," I admit, thinking of all the people that met their fate at the end of my scope during my time as a Marine. A grin stretches across my face that feels so cold it practically numbs my cheeks. "Truthfully? I hope that's exactly why she's calling us in."

Owen glances at me, his mouth twitching as if he wants to smile. Looks like he's not all that turned off by the idea himself. We both look at Wyatt, who leans back against the couch and throws an arm over the back cushion. The darkness in his eyes hasn't lessened. In fact, I'm almost positive it grows darker.

"I would've been pissed if she hadn't invited us to this revenge party." He glances at his watch. "We're supposed to meet her in a few hours. In the meantime, want me to order pizza?"

I chuckle. The sound lacks amusement. "We better fuel up. Sounds like we're going to need it."

10

Daisy

"You get home safe, ya hear? There's been trouble in the area, and I would hate to see a young woman like you get stuck in the cross hairs!"

Amusement tickles my insides, causing my mouth to curve upward in an unexpected smile. With my back turned, the man behind the counter doesn't see it. Knowing that it holds no warmth, I doubt he would feel so inclined to share the sentiment if he saw it.

Without a word, I push open the door, taking my bag of chips and new lighter with me. Outside, I shoot a glance upward at the stars. Tonight they twinkle brightly. The past few days they've been covered by smoke, but tonight, they're finally free.

They're not the only ones that'll be free tonight. The thought causes my smile to widen.

My old hand-painted black sedan sits by one of the only working pumps, looking as pathetically beaten and run down as I feel. Before reaching for the handle, I give the roof a gentle pat of appreciation and then slip into the driver's seat. I toss my bag of chips onto the floor on the passenger side. The seat is taken by a red container full of gasoline.

Turning on my car takes a few tries, but once it's going, I slowly pull out of the gas station and head back toward Briar Glen. The ride is silent, as are my thoughts. Knowing what needs to be done and having already done ninety percent of the work makes it easy to fall into autopilot. It's my favorite mode, and one that I go to often when I'm not plotting or sleeping. I'm especially grateful for the ease of which I can just turn everything off. Being back in Briar Glen has made sleeping nonexistent, and with the planning done, it's either turn my mind off or suffer the reemergence of old memories.

After a quiet car ride, I find myself pulling onto Main Street.

I wouldn't even be here again if I'd done the math right in the first place. Of course I was off only a single gallon. Math was never my strong suit. With a huff of annoyance aimed at myself, I pull my foot away from the gas pedal. Letting the car drift down the empty street, I reach over and pull the red plastic container onto my lap and undo the top. The driver's side window rolls down, and just as my car crosses the intersection of Main Street and Cedar Lane, I pour the contents out of the window and into the road.

The smell of gasoline burns my nose and makes me dizzy, but I force myself to take a deep breath of it in. I'm going to imprint this moment into my memories. Starting the fire in the woods wasn't supposed to be the start of my revenge, but the fact that no one had found Oliver after all these years? Or the evidence of his depravity? Well, that just wasn't going to fly with me.

But now my plan is back on track. *This* is how it was supposed to start, and now I'm fixing that.

Using my knee, I turn the car left to drive up First Street.

The gasoline continues to splatter along the street. When I get to the last intersection on this road, the gas runs out.

Perfect. *This* was where the gas was supposed to finish last time. I pull the car off to the side and park it. When I climb out, I toss the container onto the sidewalk and pull out the new lighter from my pocket. There's no one out and about to witness my crime, nor will there be anyone who will see me leave. Because they're all sound asleep in their beds without a care in the world. Mayor Tobias's gruesome death has been covered up, as I suspected Francis and the other Blessed Priests would do. No matter, they were the ones who needed to see it. How else would they know what to expect when I came for them?

In any case, they won't be able to cover *this* part of my plan up.

Another smile pulls at my mouth.

This sleepy town will never be able to sleep again once I'm through with it.

I toss the lighter onto the ground. Immediately, the gasoline reacts to the flickering flame. It catches and erupts. The line of fire shoots down the street the way I came and then turns down Main Street.

Wakey, wakey, Briar Glen.

11

Owen

"Are you sure that we can stay? I didn't want to presume anything, but I didn't make any other arrangements."

My mother beat enough manners into me that I do have a name and address of a motel in the next city over, in Chasm, but I figured, since tonight is when Daisy asked us to show up, that Wyatt would be ok with us crashing here.

"I'd be pissed off if you didn't stay." Wyatt opens a closet door in the hallway and pulls out an extra blanket. "I figured, if you were going to come, you'd at least show up on the date she gave us. So I made up the beds in the guest rooms in the hopes that we'd *all* stay here."

My heart squeezes painfully in my chest. Is it too much to hope that 'all' means Daisy too? When I was younger, I took our friendship for granted. When she'd taken me under her wing and let me hang out with her and the rest of the guys, I'd been so painfully shy that I could barely muster up more than a few words.

I think it's why I took a liking to reading so much. One,

because I wasn't *so* focused on the girl whose smile could stir up a fire in my gut and had a compassionate nature, making her easy to like. But two, because reading is what made us close. She never scoffed at the books I read, like nearly everyone else did. She'd sit with me wherever we were and read with me. We would share our thoughts on our current reads, how much a book sucked or was fantastic. What I didn't know until much later, when I was unpacking my books after my parents' move, was that Daisy had taken to writing little notes in the back of my books for me to find. It was always something sweet and encouraging.

Daisy was the only person who just seemed to understand me. Even now, I have a hard time relating to people. Will what I had with her still be there after all these years?

I hope so.

"I'd planned to camp out, but I'll gladly take a bed here." Drake's gruff voice floats down the hall from the living room.

Frowning, Wyatt and I head back to that room to find him standing and stretching.

"Camping?" I shake my head. "In September? It would get too cold at night."

He turns around to face me before shrugging. "The cold here is nothing to where I live now."

"Yeah, I bet. Anchorage, Alaska, gets cold as hell. Is that why you look like a bearded Fabio?" Wyatt asks.

The sound Drake makes is more of a bark than a laugh, but it's the most emotion I've seen from the guy since we met up this afternoon. He was never much of a talker, but then again, neither was I. But there's something different about Drake and it has nothing to do with the muscles he's added or the hair he's grown. He's rough around the edges now. I haven't missed how he's tracked our movements or how he moves silently despite his size. His silence isn't because he has nothing to say. He's listening, taking everything said and not said into consideration.

Drake clears his throat. "The beard helps keep me warm as I work on an oil rig. Though I don't hate that it makes me look dashing."

The laughter that spills out past my lips is loud.

"Got cocky after all these years, huh?" Wyatt chuckles.

Drake cracks a small smile before rolling his eyes. "Let's gear up."

"I'll grab my things and bring them inside." I move toward the door. "We're supposed to meet Daisy in a little over an hour and a half."

I open the door, ready to leave, but my foot pauses just over the threshold as the wail of fire trucks spill into Wyatt's house. Faded orange light floods the living room around me as I stare at the tall flames that have climbed high into the night sky.

"What the hell?" Wyatt hisses, pushing past me to rush outside.

Drake and I follow, gathering in his yard to stare up at the dark cloud of smoke wafting upward in the distance. The sound of fire alarms blare so loudly that soon the whole town will awaken, if it hasn't already.

"From the looks of those flames, the whole town is on fire!" I gape in wonder.

Drake jogs toward his truck.

"Let's go check it out. To the water tower!" he calls over his shoulder.

Wyatt and I exchange looks with each other before running after him. Drake's truck roars to life. Rather than reach for the passenger door, Wyatt and I jump into the bed. I whack the roof of the cab.

"Go, Drake!"

Carefully, Drake pulls away from the curb. He's careful to go just above the speed limit without being wild. It's a smart move.

People are poking their heads out of windows and doors, trying to figure out what's going on. A few glance in our direction but most eyes are glued to the sky.

The trip from Wyatt's to the old water tower is sickeningly familiar. How many times did we ride our bikes down these roads? We probably put more miles on those old bike tires than there are currently on my own vehicle. I'm nauseous by the time we get to the side of the road where the grassy hill starts. There is a thin line of trees halfway up the hill, blocking our view of the tower, but I know, once we get past them and climb up that old, rusted ladder to get to the top of the tower, we'll be able to see most of Briar Glen.

The moment that Drake kicks off the engine, Wyatt and I are jumping out of the bed of his truck and hurrying up the hill. To my surprise, Drake passes us.

"Since when do you run faster than me?" Wyatt shouts.

Drake doesn't answer, too far ahead now to even hear anything we say. It doesn't take as long as I remember to get to the top of the hill. Hadn't it felt like two, maybe even three, miles when we were younger? Drake is already halfway up the ladder by the time Wyatt and I get to the bottom of it.

"I haven't climbed up here in years." Wyatt peers up at the latter. "Were these bars always so rusty?"

I snort but don't reply as I start my ascent. By the time I get up to the grated catwalk, I'm out of breath and sweating. Moving out of the way for Wyatt, I turn and peer out over the town.

And gasp.

"No fucking way..." I stare at the pattern the flames have created down the streets of town.

"What? What is it?" Wyatt joins both me and Drake, leaning over the railing to take a look down at the town. "*Holy fucking shit.*"

Somehow, someone strategically lined specific streets with

something flammable, set them on fire, and the word 'LILITH' lights up the night.

What does that mean?

I can feel my bottom jaw dangling open, but I can't find it in myself to shut it at the moment.

Daisy really meant she was going to set fire to this town. I mean, I guess I expected *something*, but this? A literal interpretation? I'm not sure if I'm impressed or a little scared of the woman right now. Beside me, Drake grunts. When I look over at him, I *think* I see a smile. I'm not sure given how much hair there is around his mouth. Is he enjoying the sight before him? Is he not even a little nervous about what else Daisy is capable of? The Daisy we knew wouldn't...

No. I shake my head slowly, trying to dispel the notion of this Daisy and that one being one and the same. *That* Daisy, the one we all knew, is dead. Whoever took her place clearly has a penchant for destruction. And now, given what Wyatt told us about Oliver and his theory that Daisy had been with him, I can understand such a dramatic shift in her mindset.

But how far is she willing to go?

She's killed Mayor Tobias and set two fires, but what else does she have in store? I stand there, leaning on the rail and staring out at the burning town. The three of us are silent, each lost in our own thoughts. The smell of smoke finally reaches us after a few minutes, making it uncomfortable to breathe.

Wyatt breaks the silence first. "We need to get going. I need to grab my gifts from Daisy before we head out to Solmer's Rock."

I do too. We'd taken off without a second thought, but now we'll have to circle back to Wyatt's to grab what she put together for us.

Drake nods, and as one, we turn and head for the ladder.

12

Kingston

Daisy's near, I can feel her.

So near, in fact, that I can't sleep for fear that I'll miss whatever sign I'm supposed to be waiting for to come.

Lacking sleep is nothing new. All the thoughts in my head are always a jumbled mess. Dark memories and dangerous thoughts are all woven together with thick, heavy emotion, making it easy to never find peace.

But tonight, my thoughts are on my girl. She's here, lurking in the shadows of Briar Glen. A single secret among the others that the town hides. I suck in a deep breath. Though my lungs expand, I swear that ever since *that* night, I haven't been able to truly breathe. Part of me believes it is because guilt has taken up residence in my lungs. I failed Daisy all those years ago. I don't deserve to breathe easy. But while I may have failed her the first time, if she sets me free, I'll never fail her again.

C'mon Daisy. My eyelids slide shut of their own free will, my brain trying to abruptly shut down after so many sleepless nights.

What if tonight's the night?

With that thought, my eyelids pop back open.

The jostling of the security guard's keyring lets me know it must be nearly midnight now. It's the only noise besides the rattling of the failing air conditioning unit. Silence in the asylum is rare. Usually there is a patient or two somewhere wailing within these walls. Given how that's not the case tonight, I'm certain the overnight staff gave everyone a little extra help going to sleep.

Since I'm still awake, I guess my demons are stronger than whatever they gave us.

I wish my mind would quiet. Even if I can't sleep, it would be nice to have a reprieve from the memories of my father lunging at me with a blade. The same blade that he'd just used to gut my mother. Or the memory of Daisy as she topples over the edge of a cliff. In this memory, I can see the accusation in her eyes as our eyes lock. The condemnation. I let my family do this to her. If I had been faster… If I had just gotten to my feet, pushed my father out of the way, this all could've ended different—

Again, my eyelids try to close and once more, my brain jerks awake. This time, as my eyes open, I catch sight of movement on my ceiling. My gaze focuses on it and that's when I realize that there's a soft orange light coming in from the narrow window, casting an eerie glow and shadows into my room. How curious…

The silence within Riverbend is broken as the fire alarms begin to go off.

I don't flinch at the sound. But my attention is drawn to the flashing emergency light in my room. There's shouting and then the hard thundering of feet as security guards and nurses start to move. Doors open and shut, voices urging patients to move fill any remaining silence.

"Get up! Get up, quickly now. Get in line and follow

everyone else out to the back!" Someone orders. Urgh, it's Nurse Matthew. The guy walks around like he has a big cock. At least he leaves me alone, unlike his female counterparts.

My door unlocks and bursts open, the metal barrier hitting the hard walls.

"Patient three-zero-three, get up!" Nurse Matthew orders, stomping over to me. "There's a fire in the building and we need to get you up and out now."

A fire?

So this is how you're going to do it.

A grin stretches across my face, wider than ever, as I roll out of bed and march out into the hallway on bare feet. I follow the line of the other inmates—*patients*— here at Riverbend down the hall and stairwell to the first floor. The smell of smoke hits my nose as we're ushered down the hall to the back doors. It also registers that it's warmer on the first floor.

We're led out of the back of the building and escorted into the outdoor common space. Both in front of and behind me, patients are crying, wailing, whimpering, and shouting. The minute we're outside, a few of them try to make a run for it. It's a panicked run. Nothing planned or remotely thought through. Most of them can't even think about escape in that sense anyway. In any case, the nine foot high, chain link barbed-wire fence will keep them in.

"Trevor, I need your help here!" I think that's Nurse Kerri's voice floating back to us from the front of the line, but I can't be sure.

A security guard takes off after two patients that had run off in the same direction. Another security guard chases after the third going in the complete opposite direction.

"Single file lines everyone!" Nurse Kerri orders. "Careful, stick close. We don't want anyone getting hurt!"

We gather around on the cement slabs before we're called to a halt. Nurse Kerri quickly checks us over for any injuries before moving away to help locate any stragglers or elderly patients that are just now exiting the burning building. From back here, I can see that the left wing of the building is totally engulfed in flames. That would be the administration wing.

There go all our files.

Well shit. This is beautiful. Hell is on fire and it's so poetic I could cry. Instead, I laugh. The wheezing sound is lost in the madness. But what isn't lost is the signal I've been waiting for.

It comes in the form of a whistle.

The sharp, clear tune of "A Spoonful of Sugar" whips around like a bird flying overhead. It might as well be a shot of adrenaline and hope stabbed directly into my heart.

Pulling my gaze from the building, the fire and chaos already forgotten, I turn my attention to the darkness around the asylum. Just outside the fence is a few acres of rolling hills and then trees. My gaze slides across the chain link fence slowly, taking in every shadow and any movement. The whistling continues. It's not until the third full sweep that my eyes land on a person's silhouette just beside the white pine, on the other side of the fence. I just barely make out the nudge of the head before they step back behind the tree.

The whistling cuts off when they disappear.

My breath catches in my throat as something dark and hungry unravels in my chest. It twists with wicked delirium.

Daisy.

Looking over my shoulder, I watch as the staff of Riverbend run back and forth, trying to maintain some type of order. No one is watching me.

Without hesitation, I step back behind the line of patients, before making a mad dash toward the tree. My feet fly over the cement slab that houses picnic tables, hopscotch boards, and tetherball pole. When my bare feet hit the grass, my legs pump harder than ever. All those squats, push-ups, and crunches every night in my room have kept me strong. I knew there was a reason I needed to keep my mind sharp and remain physically in shape.

Under the deep shadows of the pine, I see her. Or rather, I see her silhouette. Beside her, a hole in the fence. My feet move faster but their speed is nothing to the way my heart is flying. There's nothing that can stop me now from reaching it. I'm almost to the hole in the fence when I hear someone shout,

"Patient three-zero-three! Get back here at once!"

The shrill shriek is grating to my eardrums.

Fuck you, Nurse Kerri.

"Matthew! He's making a run for it!"

I laugh again. They're expecting *Matthew* to reach me in time? That hulking mass of stupid couldn't catch me even if he tried. As I approach the hole in the fence, I realize that it's small. *Really* small. Is it big enough for me to pull myself through? I don't have the time to assess the merit of that thought. I can hear Matthew's booted feet behind me.

"Get back here!"

Taking three long strides, I close the distance between me and the fence, then dive through the hole. My scrubs snag, tearing in different places, and there's a flare of pain along my side as the sharp metal edges of the cut fence rake against me. Twisting, I land on my shoulder.

"Three-zero-three!" Matthew roars. "*Winslow*!"

I scramble to my feet, looking back as I do, to see Nurse Matthew make it to the fence. Our eyes meet and he lets out a snarl before bending at the waist and trying to climb through the hole.

A singular sharp whistle pierces the air. I turn to find the shadowed individual waiting down the grassy hill, by the edge of the road next to a small sedan.

Freedom. Daisy.

My feet are barely touching the ground as I move, running as if my life is on the line. Because it is. If I'm caught, my father will make sure I can never escape again. He'd find a way. Just like he found a way to silence me.

The individual who rescued me doesn't wait until I get there to climb into the vehicle. They open the driver's side door, and not a second later, the car sputters, grunts, and the engine turns over. I round it from behind and yank open the passenger door.

"Don't you get in there!" Nurse Matthew shouts.

I pause to look over the roof of the car to see him running toward me. I'm surprised to see that he even made it through the hole. With a muted laugh, I flip him the bird. I climb into the car and slam the door shut. The tires screech as we peel off. I'm thrown back into my seat, still laughing, as we veer down the two-lane road in the opposite direction of Briar Glen.

When my amusement dies down, I turn in my seat to take a good look at my savior, who is dressed in a black zip-up jacket, black ripped jeans, and wearing a strange mask. It has strange metal horns that curve upward and newspaper clippings adorning the smooth surfaces. It could be anyone beside me.

But it's not *anyone.*

I know Daisy even with everything covered. She's much smaller than I expected. Has she always been so short and thin? With the seat all the way up, her body is practically pressed against the steering wheel. Her nails are painted black, but they're chipped, and there are bruises on the backs of her hands.

My heart slams so hard in my chest that my ribs threaten to crack under the pressure. Any chance of breathing is left in the dust the car is kicking up behind us. I shake all over. God I want to throw my arms around her.

Then I want to throttle her. Doesn't she know how dangerous Briar Glen is for her? They tried killing her once. There's no doubt in my mind that if they know she's back, they'll try again.

"You're back," I say. It's not until I'm done that I realize she won't have a single idea of what I signed. The last time we were together, I could use my voice box.

Her head tilts in my direction. A second ticks by before her hand moves away from the steering wheel towards her face. Slowly, the mask slides upward to uncover her face.

I don't know what I expected after all these years when I looked into her face. Maybe the same fifteen-year-old Daisy Murray I'd thought of every minute of every hour of every goddamn day since we first became friends back in the fourth grade.

That's not who stares back at me now.

Instead, there's a woman with full lips, large brown eyes, and a small, pointed nose. The soft roundness of her face is gone, hardened by life. Her cheeks are hollowed, and dark circles hang under her eyes, as if she hadn't seen a good night sleep in too long. Long, dark, curly waves of hair spill over one shoulder. The other side of her head is shaved down. That missing hair, along with the jewelry lining both ears, gives her an edgy look.

For all these years, I thought Daisy Murray was beautiful. The memories I have of her have a halo over her head, shining a light upon the girl I loved.

I was fucking kidding myself. Despite the clear lack of sleep and one too many missed meals, the woman beside me is a succubus whose job is to steal my soul and heart. Well, she can have what's left of both, because they're all I have.

But I'll find a way to give her more.

"I'm here," she confirms. "It's good to see you again, Kingston."

She remembers sign language. My shoulders sag with relief.

As I gaze upon her face, I realize I have so much time to make up for. I have hundreds of questions, thousands of professions to utter, and a million apologies to confess. All the things that need to be said jumble in my head and cause me to freeze up. It takes a minute, but I decide to tackle one question at a time.

"Where have you been, Daisy?"

"Around." She swallows, her smile fading. "I would've come sooner if I could."

I shake my head quickly. "I would've waited for centuries. Just knowing you were alive inspired my will to live."

There's more to say, but staring at her dredges up so much emotion that my thoughts are a tangled mess. My hands curl in my lap as I lick my dry lips. My chest feels tight and my heart slams against my ribs.

We're together again.

Daisy fills the silence as the distance stretches between us and the asylum.

"There's so much I need to do in the coming days, King. A lot of it will be... unpleasant." Her lips curve upward again. Her smile lacks the warmth and amusement it had when we were kids. The one she wears now is cold, nearly a sneer. "In any case, I wasn't sure what you wanted to do once freed, so I have two options to lay out for you. The first is to get you to the truck I've stolen for you. The VIN number has been filed off, it's been repainted, and has legal plates. Inside is a bag of clothes, shoes, a driver's license I stole that you could pass off as and—"

"No." I lean forward so she doesn't have to take her eyes off the road for long and repeat myself so she understands how serious I am. "*No.*"

She eyes my expression. "Are you sure you don't want freedom? A chance at a normal life?"

Freedom? I spare a glance out the windshield. Can't she see I already have it?

"What's option number two?"

She hums thoughtfully, her eyes locking onto the road

ahead of us. The two lanes are dark, the trees around us are thick and seem to be closing in on either side of us.

"Option two is we kill your dad and all the Blessed Priests of the cult in Briar Glen. Then we make sure the town can never rebuild again."

My heart swells with demented glee. "Don't tempt me with a good time, Daisy."

"I'm being serious, King."

I reach out, my hand landing on her shoulder. She looks over at me curiously. Hating that I have to stop touching her to speak, I make what I say quick.

"As long as there is a 'we', I will kill until the streets are flooded with the blood of the guilty." I can't help myself from leaning over the center console and kissing her cheek. Daisy flinches in surprise before shooting me a confused look. I grin and settle back in my seat. "From now until death, I'm not leaving your side. Let's kill the people who tried to destroy us."

She tries to hide her smile, allowing her hair to fall in the way. But I see it and my grin grows wider.

"Alright then. We need to make a quick pit stop before the next part of my plan." She pauses before adding, "There's a backpack in the backseat. Grab the clothes and change into them, and we'll ditch your scrubs or burn them. And there's a little something extra in there as well... Put it on. You're going to need it."

13

Wyatt

The gifts Daisy sent each of us were a mask, a massive hunting knife sheathed in a fancy leather holster, and a black zip-up jacket that fits each of us perfectly.

The jacket and knife are nice, but it's the mask that really captures my attention.

It's remarkable and terrifying. When I opened the package, I nearly dropped it. The handmade, papier mâché mask has a humanoid face, but around the forehead are short horns, created with metal spikes that come out and curve upward. Where the eyes are is a thin, black plastic material that reminds me of a fencer's face mask. Clearly the intention is to be able to see through without showing any of one's face. The rest of the mask was created from old newspaper clippings. Most of them are missing person's reports. Others are obituaries. Taking the names from each story, I had plugged them into the internet's search bar and found that each woman had lived in or around Briar Glen.

Now, as I slip the mask on as the three of us walk through

the woods, I feel just as remarkable and as terrifying as the object covering my face. It's strange how much power I feel wearing it. I could be anybody, do anything, and the world would only see a terrifying mask. It's a heady feeling. Beside me, Drake and Owen don their own masks. They're identical to mine, except for the articles. Theirs have different people mentioned in the stories plastered across their faces.

None of us say a word as we walk through the dark woods.

My heart flutters and my stomach twists. I can't tell if I'm anxious, excited, or scared. What if none of this was from Daisy? What if it was the cult luring us somewhere? Since my return from college, I've investigated every possible angle about the cult. Who, other than Kingston's father, was a part of it? That night, I'd only seen his face but there were at least a dozen more people there. I was sure I'd be able to find out *something*.

Except I never did.

All I could surmise was that it must be people with deep pockets, in power, or both, running this thing. It's the only way they could keep their activity as quiet as it has been.

My heart picks up speed as, through the trees, I catch sight of our meeting place. Solmer's Rock looks just as I remembered it from *that* night: unsuspecting. But it's not the rock that we've come to see. My eyes search for signs of movement as we emerge from the woods into the small clearing.

Can the others hear the sound of my heart as it slams painfully against my ribcage? If they do, neither of them say a word.

We come to a stop and look around. There's no one about. The woods are relatively quiet, except for the sounds of cicadas and frogs. Overhead, the stars twinkle, though their luminous glow begins to dim as the smoke from the center of town drifts in this direction.

We're not standing there long when there's a shift. Gradually, the air seems to thicken. It's like time is beginning to slow down. Nature holds its breath, quieting the bugs and stilling the slight breeze moving through the leaves.

Breaking the stillness, someone steps from around Solmer's Rock. I start in surprise. Owen's soft gasp, muffled by his mask, is ignored as my eyes lock onto the individual.

Dressed in a black zip-up jacket and black ripped jeans, the person nearly blends in with the heavy shadow the boulder casts. But I can see the mask. It's just like mine. Just like *ours*. I'm pretty sure I stop breathing. My heart on the other hand, begins a full sprint. Is it...? Can it be...? My hands tremble at my sides and the woods around me begin to tilt.

We all just stand there for a moment, staring.

Then my legs are moving. I stumble but catch myself before breaking into a run. Crossing the short distance suddenly feels like an eternity. But then I make it to the newcomer. Before I can think it through, I throw my arms around them before lifting and spinning them around. There's a gasp, followed by a soft giggle.

A *feminine* giggle. I place them on their feet and then reach up to remove my mask.

"Daze? D-Daisy? Is it really you?"

There's another giggle before the person in front of me pushes their own mask up. All the air in the clearing evaporates as I stare down into the face of the beautiful woman before me. My knees knock together as blood gathers in my cheeks. She's back, she's here, she's alive and she's... she's *gorgeous*.

"Hey, Wy."

Her large eyes stare up at me as her cheeks swell from smiling so wide. I drown in their depths, unable to breathe properly under her gaze. I reach up, unable to stop myself, and touch her cheek. At first, it's just my fingertips that trail over her skin, but then I find myself cupping her cheek. She leans into my hand, never taking her eyes off me. I suck in a ragged breath as tears prickle in my eyes.

Before I can reply, Drake's there, knocking me out of the way and crushing Daisy's body into his wide chest. I catch Daisy's slight wince before she's laughing softly as she returns the hug.

"Drake, you've grown up a bit."

This time when the brute laughs, it's not a weird sound like back in my house. It's a booming laughter, twisted with the sound of relief, that drifts around us.

"Let her go, Drake! It's my turn."

Drake sighs but puts Daisy down. She's not free for a full second before Owen's arms come around her.

"God, Daisy, I can't believe it. It's really you." His words are muffled as he buries his face into her neck. It's not until I realize he's stooping that I register how short Daisy is.

Hasn't she always been taller than me?

"Believe it," she teases, briefly returning his hug.

When he lets her go, none of us really step back to give her room. We create a wall between her and the rest of the world. With her back nearly against Solmer's Rock, Daisy is practically caged in.

She looks around at us, her eyes wide, her smile even more so. While she looks happy at first glance, the more I stare, the more I'm beginning to notice there's something a bit *off* about Daisy. She looks different, yes. But it's not the piercings that line both ears or the deliberate shaving of one side of her head—giving her a tougher look—that is unsettling. I can't quite put my finger on it, and at the moment, I don't really care. She's here—that's all that matters.

"God, I can't believe we're all back together. I dreamed about this day for so long," she admits with a heavy sigh.

"Well," I hedge carefully. "Not all of us are here. Kingston's still locked up. Did you... Did you hear what happened to him?"

Her eye roll is so familiar that I have to fight back tears of relief.

"That he killed his mother in a rage and then went after Francis, who just *happened* to wrestle the knife away from him and managed to slit his son's throat to protect himself? Yeah, I heard."

Huh, I wonder how.

"But I don't believe it. Also, Kingston's here."

Her words don't register right away. I blink, trying to get them to process.

"Wait, what?" Owen sputters.

Before she can respond, a whistle pierces the night air. Drake, Owen, and I turn as one as Daisy's favorite musical number cuts through the air. As it ends, Kingston steps around Solmer's Rock and flashes us a grin.

Oh shit.

"King..." My voice trails off as he saunters over to us.

My god. Nine years has changed the guy I knew a lot. As he comes to a stop beside us, I'm reeling over his good looks. We used to be the same height back in the day. Now he probably has a few inches over me, making him taller than my six foot one. His skin has paled significantly. King practically glows under the moonlight now. He has a strong jawline, long nose, and he's lean. His dark hair, longer than I expected a psych patient would have, is a sharp contrast to his skin.

Owen, who's closest to King, throws his arms around him. "How the hell are you here, man? This is fucking awesome!"

I move next, feeling all sorts of off-kilter. When my arms come around his shoulders, I don't miss how there's still muscle beneath his shirt. Did they let him work out in Riverbend?

"I think I'm dreaming. How is this possible?" I ask as I step back and look between him and Daisy.

Daisy's smile turns smug. "While the town was busy trying to put out the flames downtown, I broke King out of Riverbend."

When I look back at Kingston, he's staring intensely at

Daisy. Is he still struggling to come to terms with her being here too? It's so surreal. Given the dark backdrop, and how we all came to be here this evening, this moment borders on dream-like. Afraid to blink and have everyone disappear, I reach out and take Daisy's hand. She looks down and watches as I weave my fingers through hers. I don't care how intimate the gesture may be, I need to touch her.

"Thank you for orchestrating this. I've missed you. I've missed all of you," I look around, meeting everyone's eyes before looking back down at Daisy. "It's been too long."

"Now that we're here, I'm assuming you have something for us to do?" Drake asks, drawing all the attention to him.

Daisy smiles at him. "I do. But only if you're sure."

"Sure about what? Revenge?" One of Drake's eyebrows raises. "Absolutely."

Daisy sighs. "I appreciate you all showing up. It means more than you could know. I wasn't sure if—" She shakes her head. "Anyway, I should warn you, what I want to do isn't legal. If we're caught—"

"Daisy," I step forward. "I watched you fall to your death after the people we trusted in this town tried to kill you. They washed you from its history like you were nothing more than chalk on the sidewalk. I've been waiting for a chance to strike back since then. I'm willing to risk my freedom and life to destroy this place. Just tell me what you want me to do. I'll do anything."

Owen clears his throat. "*We* will do anything."

Kingston and Drake nod. Daisy doesn't respond right away. I can't tell if she's judging how serious we are or if she's simply considering her next words. The darkness isn't ideal to scrutinize her expression.

"What if I asked for help with moving a body?"

This is a test. I watch as Daisy eyes first me, then the rest of the guys, warily.

Even if it wasn't Daisy asking, I have a sinking suspicion the word body would turn me on to any situation.

I grin as Drake answers her, "I'll kill for you, Daisy. All you have to do is say the word."

"I think we're all willing to do whatever you want us to do," Owen says softly, a little less intense than Drake, but still confident. "You asked if we wanted to do more than sit around, and here we are, ready to do whatever you need us to do. Briar Glen deserves whatever it is you're planning. They tore us apart."

Daisy nods. "They've done so much more than that."

"Whose body are we moving?" How is it that those words can tumble from my mouth so easily?

Daisy beams at us. I drag in a shaky breath. Daisy had been my childhood crush, but looking at her now, I know I'll always be head over heels for her. There's just something about her that draws me in. To know that she's alive, that I'll be able to look upon her everyday again? Shit, the things I *wouldn't* do for her are practically nonexistent. I would kill just to see her smile. I know it.

"It's not just one body," she starts, tilting her head as she eyes me. "It's multiple. And they're not really bodies. Not anymore."

I blink, confused.

"What?"

Kingston steps closer to Daisy, his eyes dropping to where I'm holding her hand then back to her face. He lifts his hands and they cut through the air deliberately. It takes me a second to realize that he's using sign language. Shit, I forgot about his inability to speak. It's been a while since I've used it or seen it being used. Blinking rapidly, I try to process the signs I do remember and piece the sentence together.

Something about looking forward to whatever we're doing tonight. Shit, I'm a crap friend. I make a mental note to start watching videos and refreshing my memory.

"Yeah, I bet you are down for anything at this point," Owen chuckles. "Being anywhere other than Riverbend is going to feel like a damn amusement park to you."

I gape at Owen. How is it that *he* remembers so well? Closing my mouth quickly, I simply nod.

Daisy flashes us another smile. "If you all are sure..."

I squeeze her hand. "Lead the way, Daisy. Wherever you go, we'll follow."

14

Drake

My fingers itch to touch Daisy.

Not just touch her, but to hold her. I want to wrap my fingers around the column of her neck, pull her against my chest and feel her pulse beneath me. I need proof of life. That this isn't some sort of hallucination.

Several times I catch myself as my arm raises and my hand reaches out to do just that. Thankfully, with Daisy in the lead and the others fanning out beside her, I'm left to watch her back, which gives me time to get myself under control.

It's hard.

The desire to hold her comes on the skirt tails of the emotions she's dredged up. It's like experiencing one's first love and the pain of first loss mixed together, strangling me. My breathing is shaky as we trudge along.

"—you been? Five years is a long time not to reach out, Daisy," Wyatt asks, bringing my attention back to the moment.

"It's been ten years, Wy."

"I know why you didn't reach out the first five years. I want to know what you've been up to these *last* five."

I watch as Daisy jerks her hand free from Wyatt's. Her steps falter. I adjust mine so I don't trip over her. Quickly, Daisy regains her composure and shoots Wyatt a look I can't see from here.

"How?"

"How what? How do I know what you've been through? Well, I don't know *exactly,* but I do know Oliver Grayman had you, and I saw what he was capable of," Wyatt says, reaching back out for her hand. I watch as she pulls away again. "I have a friend within the police force who showed me the evidence they collected at his house. It was insane. I saw the pictures, Daisy, and heard about that room of horror—"

"The pictures you saw weren't even the tip of the iceberg of what The Butcher of Briar Glen was capable of doing."

Her hiss is soft but so full of venom that it brings Wyatt to a complete standstill. She stops too, turning to face him, which brings us all to halt. The air around Daisy shifts. Tension gathers like a thunderstorm rolling in. The rest of us watch as she stares up at Wyatt.

"Yes, I was trapped with *him*. But I wasn't alone. The Butcher of Briar Glen had many victims during the time he had me. Grown women, young girls—he didn't particularly have a preference in who he scooped up, as long as they had no one to come looking for them. I knew their names, talked to them, consoled them... What do you want to know, Wyatt? I know how mysteries have always intrigued you."

I swear the air we're breathing is tainted with poison, which drips from each word that falls from Daisy's lips. Never have I heard someone speak with such deadly calm. My blood curdles.

"Look, Daisy, I didn't mean to pry," Wyatt sputters after regaining his composure. "I was just... I only wanted to know...." He gives up with a sigh, his shoulders dropping, and his head falls to his chest.

Daisy rolls her shoulders before letting out a heavy sigh. Around us, the tension lessens.

"You have questions, I understand." Her head bobs once. "My time with The Butcher is not a short, or pleasant, conversation. Maybe one day I'll tell you. But not tonight. Not now when we have places to be. In short, before I escaped his house, I made sure that The Butcher of Briar Glen was no more. As for afterward?" She shrugs. "The last five years consisted of me learning how to control and understand the monster he turned me into."

The hair on the back of my neck rises as my stomach twists. This woman isn't our Daisy. Whoever she is wears the skin of a killer. It should worry me. At least a little. Instead, the fucked up part of me is drawn to her even more than before. When she looks around at us, her gaze holds mine for just a bit longer than the rest. Can she see how our souls match more now than they ever did? Whatever monster she claims to be, I'll be her bigger and meaner one. I'm not the soft child from our past any more than she's the girl who was all rainbows and butterflies.

"Right, so let's go." She turns and continues to trek forward. Kingston follows right beside her, taking her right hand. I'm right on her heels.

Her empty hand reaches out as if to grab someone beside her. I move to take it, but Wyatt beats me there, shouldering me out of the way. His hand grabs hers and I catch the brief smile she sends his way.

"I won't push again." His vow is solemn. "You can tell us any and everything when you're good and ready. I'm sorry."

"Don't be."

Everyone is silent for the rest of the trek back to the road. We all steal furtive glances at her. If she's triggered by that conversation, what else will upset her? The Daisy I remember rarely got pissed. When we did manage to upset her, her anger was never long-lived. We walk along the road for only a few minutes before Daisy steps back toward the woods again only to stop and yank off camouflage netting from a waiting car.

"Where are we headed?" I have to ask, only because I need to know what trouble we're about to find ourselves in. I would rather not be taken by surprise.

She flashes me a grin as she pulls keys out of her pocket. I guess she's no longer mad. Some things just don't change I guess.

Or she's just gotten good at shoving things down like me. I push the thought away. Daisy isn't me.

"We, my friend, are off to the cemetery."

By the time we get to the cemetery, the others are rigid with tension. During the drive, Daisy refused to answer any questions about what the plan is, but she does share that it's not bodies we're here for but for a box of ashes.

"Whose ashes?" Wyatt asks. I can hear the hesitation in his question, clearly afraid to upset her again.

"All the victims of a friend of The Butcher of Briar Glen."

"Oliver Grayman had an accomplice?"

"No, not really. This man was his own breed of sick and twisted. He just worked in the safety of The Butcher's four walls to keep from getting caught."

Owen hums thoughtfully. "Who was it?"

"Who *is* it," Daisy corrects grimly. "He's still alive for now. You'll meet him soon enough. As a son of one of the town's leaders, this man knows he can bury the ashes of his victims here and they'll never be found. He told me once that he kept his girls in a box, separate from the Zarzuzian's sacrifices, so he could savor their deaths each time he came back to bury another."

Owen frowns. "Zarzuzian's?"

"Oh," Daisy shakes her head in amusement. "Zarzuz's followers: Briar Glen's cult."

Zarzuzians... It's a mouthful and ugly. A hard shiver rushes through me. "Were there many victims of the cult?"

"My guess? There were about a hundred and twenty." She parks the car down a side road not far from the entrance and cuts it off.

I grunt, choking on my own surprise. Owen gasps softly beside me and Wyatt visibly flinches. A hundred and twenty victims... Holy fuck.

We climb out quickly. I sigh with relief as I stretch. Sitting in the back seat of that small car, pressed against the door with Wyatt and Owen in the back with me, was stifling. Daisy moves toward the trunk and pops it. Out comes a shovel, several large heavy-duty trash bags, and an electric lantern. I move closer to her.

"Here, give me that."

"No, take the trash bags." She shakes her head and shoves the bags into my hand. "Don't touch anything where it may leave prints. I don't want Briar Glen to have anything on you."

"*You're* not wearing any gloves," Wyatt points out, frowning.

She gives him a rueful half smile. "I don't have fingerprints to leave."

"What?" My question comes out sharper than intended.

"They were burned off years ago."

Bile threatens to stream up my throat. Wyatt and Owen exchange horrified looks with each other. Kingston simply stares at Daisy's back, his face impassive. What does he think about all of this?

"Masks on and keep quiet. There is a caretaker that walks

around every now and then. Let's not get caught before I get that box."

We all do as we're told, slipping on our masks and falling silent. Kingston and I are the first to follow Daisy as she turns and leads the way, with Wyatt and Owen right on our heels.

Instead of breaking into the cemetery through the front gates, Daisy leads us around the stone wall that surrounds it until there's a worn down section, just wide enough for us to wiggle through. As we follow her through the grim and eerie place, I try hard to ignore the names on the tombstones. Most of them are faded anyhow. Beside me, Owen shivers. I don't know if it's from the cold or from hanging out with dead people. I hope it's not the latter. Given Daisy's recent actions, there's a lot of violence, and potentially death, on the horizon.

My mouth twitches into a smile behind my mask.

We walk until we're in the furthest part of the cemetery from the entrance, close to a tree that looks about as dead as the occupants who reside under the ground. There's nothing over here except for a small, unmarked tombstone. Wait... As we stop before it, I realize it *is* marked.

"I know that symbol. Ol—, I mean, *he* painted it on, um, ah, some people," Wyatt stutters.

Daisy places the electric lantern beside her then slams the shovel into the ground, where it gets lodged, standing straight up. She looks over at him, but with her mask on I have no idea what she's thinking.

"It's ok, Wy. It's not his name that's triggering. I just don't want to think about him right now. But yes, The Butcher of Briar Glen would paint the women he captured with this rune. It is the sign of Zarzuz, the god that the cult believes brings them prosperity and health." She looks at me. "Open the bags. The box shouldn't be that far down. You guys—" she glances around her at the others "—keep a look out for Marty."

"Will he even make it over to this part? It's deserted over here," Owen asks, already turning to look around.

"The higher members of the cult pay him to look the other way when they have someone they need to bury. They also use him to keep people from discovering this site. He'll definitely make sure this area is kept safe. Marty will show up eventually."

With that, she starts digging. I open up the trash bag with a sigh and watch. The others spread out, keeping close and to the shadows. I expect this will take time, so I brace myself for a long night.

But it's only a few minutes before her shovel hits something. A moment later, she unearths an urn. Kneeling down, she brings it to eye level and brushes the dirt off it.

When time stretches and still she doesn't move, I huff. "Daisy?"

She flinches. Her masks turns to look at me but swiftly turns back to the urn. She sets it to the side and continues shoveling. When she starts to breathe heavily and her pace slows, I offer to help again.

"No, I'm fine."

When she starts to tremble from fatigue, I nearly knock her away and take over myself. Just as I move forward to do it, her shovel hits something. With renewed effort, Daisy digs faster. A moment later, out comes a wooden box.

"Is that what you were looking for?" I ask, unable to tamper down my curiosity.

"Yes."

She heaves the box up out of the hole with a rough huff. I pick it up and shove it into the trash bag, realizing why she brought a few. As I start to double bag it, there's a short, sharp whistle from nearby. Both Daisy and I freeze.

"He's coming!" I think that's Wyatt's frantic whisper, but I can't be sure.

"Hello? Who's there?" A raspy voice drifts over to us.

Daisy straightens and looks at me. I place the bag down on the ground, ready to fight, but she nudges her head to the right. Following the direction, I catch sight of a wall. Does she want me to hide behind it? I snort. Loudly. Yeah, no. That's not going to happen.

"Hello?" The question is immediately followed by a sharp gasp. "W-what the hell? You're not supposed to be here!"

I turn halfway around to find a thin old man with fluffy white hair and an astonishingly cartoonish white mustache, wearing a gray jumpsuit. He carries a flashlight in his hand, which trembles, causing the beam of light to point almost everywhere *except* at me and Daisy.

It takes a second to realize we're not who he's looking at.

Around him, the others step forward and create a semi-circle, blocking his path of escape. Under the moon and starlight, the masks we wear give us a demonic appearance. The metal of our horns catches the light and reflect it, making them look as if they're glowing.

"Good evening, Marty." Daisy says, her voice slightly muffled through the mask. She drops the shovel and climbs out of the hole.

The man whirls around, pointing the flashlight in her face. "W-who are you?"

"Does it matter?"

"You're trespassing on private p-p-property. I'm going to call the cops!"

Daisy's answering chuckles lacks amusement. "They're a bit busy this evening. Besides, what will you say to them? That the grave you've been allowing the Zarzuzian's leaders to dump their finished sacrifices in is being desecrated?"

Marty sputters, searching for words. Shaking his head, he finally manages to say, "I-I don't know what you're talking about."

I frown as the man gasps repeatedly. His fear appears genuine enough. Does Daisy have it wrong?

"Oh, Marty, don't play dumb." Daisy slinks just a little closer. "I know all about that little retirement nest you keep under the floorboards beneath your bed. I also know that the Zarzuzians don't always burn their victims. Some of the lackeys for the upper members of the cult let you keep some of the corpses for a bit. I know how you used to *stuff* them and keep them in your basement until the bodies were too decomposed to hold up under your poor attempt at taxidermy."

The man's white brows shoot up as his jaw drops.

"How do you know about that?" he wheezes, his face contorting in pain as he continues to gasp. "How?!"

My hands curl at my side as shock and rage pool into my blood. He did *what*?

The caretaker reaches into his pocket and pulls out his phone. One of the guys, I think it's Kingston, steps forward and slaps it out of his hands. The phone hits the rocky gravel and the screen cracks.

Marty jumps away from him, his mouth opening and closing. I don't think any air comes in or out this time. His right hand comes up to cover his chest and suddenly he drops to his knees. Oh shit... His eyes widen as he looks back at Daisy.

"Please, don't hurt me. Call an ambulance..." He wheezes. "I'm not ready to die yet."

"Neither were the people in this grave," she hisses, closing the distance between them. I move with her, sticking close in case this somehow goes south.

Marty opens his mouth, but no words come out. His eyes roll up in the back of his head, and his upper half falls forward, his face landing by her feet. There's a short pause. Marty doesn't move and neither do we.

"Shit, is he dead?" Owen lifts his mask and moves closer.

Daisy crouches down and reaches forward to press her

fingers against his neck. After a few moments of tense silence, she nods.

"Yup. Dead." She frowns. "How disappointing."

Well, that was easy enough. I shove up my mask and stare down at the dead man.

Owen looks from Marty's body to her. "Disappointing?"

"I wanted it to be bloody. I'm here to revel in chaos and destruction, not watch old people die of natural causes."

My heart slams in my chest. Why does that response stir up desire in my veins like nothing else? Movement out of the corner of my eye grabs my attention. Wyatt's dragging the hem of his shirt downward, a failing attempt to hide evidence of his own stiff dick. I want to laugh. Not in amusement, but in disbelief. How it is that the two of us have become so fucked up?

Kingston pushes up his mask, waves to capture Daisy's attention and says, "There's always next time."

"You're right." She stands and comes around to stand by Marty's feet.

"What are you doing now?" Wyatt asks, stepping up beside her the same time I do.

Daisy grabs his ankles and starts to yank. "Dumping his body in the grave."

"Here let me—"

"You're not wearing gloves, Wy. You'll get DNA all over him."

Owen sighs. "Even if he did, I'll make sure to wipe any evidence of him, or us, out of any databases they throw it into." We all look over at him. Owen grins. "Hey, being a nerd comes in handy in a pinch like this, doesn't it?"

Wyatt squats, nudges Daisy with his shoulder to force her out of the way, then grabs Marty's ankles. I come up and hook my hands under his armpit. Together, we lift the caretaker and carry him to Daisy's hole. We aren't careful or considerate as we toss his body in.

Kingston grabs the shovel before Daisy can and begins to put the dirt back, covering Marty's corpse.

"Animals will dig him up," Owen points out.

Daisy's only response is to shrug.

Owen watches King from a distance as he asks Daisy, "What are we going to do with the box you unearthed?"

There's a short pause before Daisy answers. "I'm going to turn it into a bomb."

My shock at her response comes out as a bark of laughter. "No kidding?"

"You're going to make a *bomb*?" Owen shakes his head as if there's no way he heard our girl currently. "How? No, wait, *why*?"

I watch Daisy's body language closely, given that her face is still covered. She crosses her arms over her chest and her shoulders stiffen. Her feet shuffle apart ever so slightly, in a defensive position.

"How? Well, it's not like it's hard. I learned how to do it on the internet. This one will be low-key. Nothing too destructive. As for why? I want to use it to draw attention."

Wyatt guffaws. "Sounds like you've thought ahead *a lot*. Are you going to fill us in on anything else you're planning to do?"

Daisy looks over at him slowly. "Why? So you can decide if there's a line you won't cross?"

"So I know how to help, Daisy."

Her shoulders drop. I can't tell if it's in surprise or relief.

"Oh, well, why don't I just go over everything tomorrow? The sun will be up in the next few hours, and I still have things to do."

Wyatt nods. "That works. We can go get my car and then all crash at my place. I already have beds—"

"No." She shakes her head. "Kingston and I will hide out elsewhere."

Kingston leans against the shovel, staring at Daisy, while

the others sputter their outrage. I scoff at her audacity. "We're not splitting up."

"We have to." She looks from me to everyone else. "The police will most likely make an appearance at Wyatt's house to let him know that Kingston escaped. They'll probably keep an eye on your place for the day to see if that's where Kingston tries to go. So I need to keep him as far from your place as possible. At least for the next twenty-four hours."

As much as I hate the idea of splitting up, it's hard to deny the logic of it.

Wyatt opens his mouth to object, but I cut him off. "She's right. That's exactly what they would do, given our friendship with him. That being said, Owen and Wyatt can go back. I'm sticking with you."

"There's no doubt that word has gotten around that you and I are here visiting," Owen objects. "You have to stick with us, or it may look suspicious. We'll all play the part. We can pretend to be surprised and concerned about the fire downtown. If the police do come by, we can even offer to help them out anyway that we can." Owen tears his eyes away from me and looks at our girl. "We all go back, but Daisy... You aren't planning for you and Kingston to take off, right?"

Daisy pushes up her mask to look at him and smiles. "No, I won't leave you behind."

My hands curl up at my side. I don't want to do this. Daisy's my other half. Now that she's here, I'm whole for the first time in years. The thought of her slinking off into the night, without knowing where she is, has my whole being shying away from the idea. Daisy's not dead so there's no reason I should find myself without her. Ever.

Is that insanity speaking? Probably. But I don't have any fucks to give a damn at its presence.

"What if something happens to you between now and the

next time we try to meet up?" I demand. "I can't... I *won't* let you get hurt this time."

Daisy's smile is just as sweet as the one she gave Owen, but it's Kingston that responds.

"She'll be safe with me." I stare at Kingston, unable to be calmed by his promise. His mouth presses into a tight line, clearly reading my trepidation. "Death will have to come through me first before it can get to Daisy."

"You two are adorable, but I've gotten this far on my own just fine." Daisy's smile doesn't waver, if anything, it grows as she looks between the two of us. "I have a few hiding spots that I've been rotating between, each safe and secure. Kingston and I will lay low at one of them for a bit to get some rest before we head out to complete the next phase of my plan. We can all regroup at Zarzuz's altar tomorrow night at eleven."

I frown. "Where—"

"Is that where you were nearly sacrificed?" Wyatt asks, cutting me off. "That's what they call that place?"

At her nod, I grimace. "We should burn it down."

Daisy's smile twists until it's more of snarl. "We're going to do something so much better than burning it, Dre."

"Oh yeah?" I step closer, as if I'm being pulled into the darkness leaching out from that chilly expression on her face. "Like what?"

With a dark, beautiful giggle, Daisy responds, "You'll see."

15

Kingston

I got to sleep out under the stars.

Slowly, I wake to the sounds of birds chirping and the gentle caress of fog brushing up against my cheeks. As my eyelids flutter open, I find a squirrel staring down at me from a branch a few feet higher than the hunter's perch. It chatters down at me, clearly befuddled by my presence. I haven't seen a squirrel in so long. *Too* long. My heart squeezes painfully in my chest as I take a shuddering breath.

I'm free.

Tears start to well up, blurring my vision of the creature above me. But I can't help it. The relief I feel is overwhelming. Daisy did it. She came back for me. My heart untwists so that it can swell. She never forgot about me, just like I never forgot about her. Now that we're together again, from this day forward, it will be us against the world.

And anyone who stands in our way? We'll fucking kill them together.

I sigh, content.

My body still aches a little from the long trek here. After dropping the others off at their car, driving for another half hour, then pulling off on a dirt road, I helped Daisy cover her car with brush and camouflage netting. Then we made the long walk to this hunter's perch. I'd tried to talk to Daisy, but she fell into silence once we split up with the others. It was as if her mind had shut down. But even as zoned out as she was, Daisy worked hard to make sure we made it here safely. For the entire duration of the walk, she continuously kept covering our tracks, using deer spray from her backpack and leaves to hide our footprints in the softer mud. When I tried to help, she would just redo whatever I did. So, I dutifully carried the doubled-up trash bag with the box of ashes.

By the time we finally climbed up the rope ladder to our current place of hiding, we were spent. But her myriad of surprises didn't stop upon our arrival. Daisy had a thick sleeping bag, a second backpack full of extra clothes, a pair of work boots, and extra camping gear ready with me in mind.

She's planned for everything.

Better yet, Daisy had planned for me to stick with her. On some level, she must've known how much I adored her.

I grin through the tears and roll to the side. To my surprise, Daisy's awake. She sits with her back facing me, on the edge of the old, abandoned hunter's perch with one leg tucked beneath her while the other hangs over the edge. She has pulled off her jacket and tossed it to the side, but she remains dressed in a dirty white tee that clings to her too thin frame, a flannel shirt wrapped around her waist, jeans, and boots. As she hunches over, I can see the bones in her spine. Last night, I could tell she was thin, but I didn't realize how fragile she was. Frowning, I sit up.

Before I can do anything else, Daisy straightens, lifts something from her lap, and brings it up to her temple. I just barely catch the glint of metal from the barrel of the revolver. My heart comes to a grinding halt even while I reach out and scream. The muted sound is useless.

The click of the trigger might as well be the kiss of my own death.

I wait for the boom and blood splatter. It doesn't come. As the realization that she's not dead collides with my relief, my limbs unlock. I kick off the sleeping bag to scramble on my hands and knees across the short distance.

She must hear me because she starts to turn, but before she can finish the motion, I tackle her to the side. The gun clatters to the floor of the perch and skids away.

What are you doing? Why would you do that? What the fuck, Daisy? You would leave me? Now? Just when we've got back together?

I want to scream it all as Daisy starts to fight me. Her arms flail, her legs kick out, and she rocks hard from side to side.

"Stop, stop!" Her plea is wobbly as a hard sob wrecks her body. "Don't touch me, don't touch me, don't *touch me*!"

Rather than stop, I grab her hands that are trying to push me away, transfer them into one of mine, and then pin them to the wood floor above her head while I straddle her waist. Beneath me, I can feel her whole body trembling. It's a powerful vibration, and mixed with the sight of her tears, it causes my chest to tighten in despair. As does the utterly blank gaze behind those tears. She doesn't see me. Daisy doesn't know it's me holding her down. This fighting is a reaction to something else.

I've seen a few patients act like this when they were touched. But in their situation, it was from past trauma—It clicks swiftly, and bile climbs up my throat. *Fucking hell. Who touched my girl?*

Was it this Oliver, The Butcher guy? I'll have to ask one of the others who he was and what he could've done to our Daisy. In the meantime, I need to get her to see me.

Unable to call out to Daisy to drag her out of her panic, I reach forward and grab her jaw with my free hand. My grip is tight, borderline painful, forcing her to look straight up at me. Daisy fights a little harder for a few more seconds, but then she blinks. It's a slow one, her eyes coming back into focus.

But not fast enough for my liking.

Cautiously, I lower my head toward her face until I can rest my forehead on hers. With deliberate exaggeration, I take a long breath in through my nose before slowly letting it out through my mouth. I do this a few times. After a minute or so, Daisy starts to follow my lead.

One deep breath in. One long exhale out.

Together we breathe as one. Slowly, the tension in her body ebbs away. My grip on her jaw loosens and I let go of her wrists. Carefully, I turn my face so that my nose skims down Daisy's. When her eyes are crystal clear and she is breathing on her own, I sit up.

"King?" She squeezes her eyes shut, then opens them again. "Oh. Kingston. What—?"

I don't relax. Not yet. *She* may be calmer, but my heart is still racing, and cold dread keeps my limbs stiff.

"What the *fuck* were you thinking, Daisy!? You want to kill yourself? *Now*? Why? Why would you do that to me?"

"Kill myself?" Daisy's brows pinch together as she frowns.

I nudge my head toward the gun on the floor. She follows my gaze. "Oh, that. No, I wasn't... Yeah, it probably looked like it, but I wasn't. I promise, Kingston. I wasn't planning on offing myself." When she looks up at me, she gives me a soft smile. "The gun is empty."

"I don't believe you."

"Did I pull the trigger and is my head still on?"

I stare down at her, hating the sweet smile that's splaying across her lips.

"Do you think this is a joke?" I demand, baring my teeth in a snarl.

Her smile fades but her eyes twinkle with something wild and dark.

"I don't joke about death, King." She looks back at the gun. "I used to keep a bullet in there. Every morning, I'd get up, spin the cylinder, and pull the trigger. For a year I did that. After... After everything that happened, I wasn't sure what I wanted. Death, revenge, or a quiet life. So I let fate decide. I told myself if I wasn't dead in a year, I would take that option off the table." Daisy looks back up at me, her eyes hard. "Now I just do it to *feel* something. A short rush to wake me up when I'm still trapped in my nightmares. I just need to *wake up*."

A year of Russian roulette. She played with her life *every fucking day* for a year. A poisonous rage brews in my heart. How terribly I've failed her. I should've protected her that night I found her in the woods, and every night after that. Then she'd never play this game. I'll protect her now. I'll protect her from anyone and anything. Even from herself.

"From now until we're both buried and cold in the ground, *I'll* wake you from your nightmares." I stare down at her, willing her to see into my soul. "There is nothing I need more in this world than you, and I won't let anyone or anything take you away from me ever again. I have loved you since the moment I laid eyes on you back in the fourth grade. I don't know how I didn't see it then, but it wasn't until I watched you disappear off the edge of the cliff that I recognized the emotion for what it was."

Daisy's eyes go round. "Kingston—"

"No, wait. I need to say this. When I got your letter, I decided that if you did come, if I could see you again, I would tell you this because knowing that you never knew the extent of how much I cared for you ate me up inside. Whether or not you felt the same way, didn't matter. I need you to understand the lengths I will go to never feel so fucking lost again. This time around, you'll know how I feel and that I'll never fuck up and lose you again. I will fight to stay by your side until my dying breath, Daisy."

Before I'm even done talking, tears well up in her eyes again but they're followed by a small smile that tugs the edges of her mouth upward.

"I loved you too." Her small confession is followed by a frown. "And I still do. It's why I came back for you. But there's something wrong with me, King. I'm messed up here," she points to her heart and then to her temple. "And here."

I shake my head. "There's nothing wrong with you."

"Yes there is. It's why I want to do the horrible things I have planned and why I don't care who gets hurt in order to see it come to fruition." She scowls. "I've killed people, Kingston. I would've killed Marty if his stupid heart hadn't given out on him. You want to be a part of that?"

Murder the people who were ok with sacrificing a child to some bogus god? It's a no-brainer. My grin startles her. It's quickly followed by wariness as she realizes it's not from amusement.

"I've been craving revenge, nearly as much as I've been dying to see and hold you. Together, we'll flood the streets of Briar Glen with the blood of our enemies."

Her gaze shifts. The subtle drop to my lips doesn't go unnoticed. Oh fuck... A kiss. Daisy wants a *kiss*. A hard rush of desire pounds through me. Instantly, I grow hard. How I've craved tasting Daisy's lips. I can count on one hand the girls I'd kissed back in high school, wishing they were her. There's only a second of hesitation, a moment of mental recoiling. The last time someone's lips pressed against mine, it was repulsive. My stomach twists.

Don't let that ruin what could *be*, I tell myself.

When her gaze finds me, I take a steadying breath. "I want to kiss you."

A little color gathers in Daisy's cheeks. "You don't have to ask, King."

I cringe. "I do. I *really* fucking do. I wasn't given a choice in the matter these past few years. I don't want to put you in a position where you feel like you can't say no."

The color that rose in her cheeks drains away as her eyes widen in horror. No, no, no... Fuck, I hope I didn't screw the moment up.

"King—"

"No, I don't want to talk about it. I just want you; I've *always* wanted you, Daisy. Time hasn't lessened my hunger for you."

She stares up at me. As she does, the shock melts away. "Kiss me, Kingston. Please?"

A hard shudder rushes through me. There's no doubt that Daisy can feel it, but she doesn't say anything. I lean down slowly, holding her gaze and my breath. In my chest, my heart pounds loudly. When my lips press lightly against hers, time halts. The birds stop chirping, the fog stops moving, even the bugs scurrying around have paused, giving me this moment to imprint this kiss in my memory for all eternity. Daisy tilts her head slightly, deepening the kiss even more. The desire in my body causes me to grow warm. Too warm. I feel like my skin is on fire.

It's too much and not enough.

I pull away, shuddering once more. "I thought a kiss would suffice. Would help balm the obsessive need to have you, to *own* you. But I think I've just made it so much worse."

Daisy visibly swallows, her hips shifting against mine. I lean forward, pressing my erection into her stomach, willing her to feel how much I want her.

"What do you think will help you?" she asks, her voice no louder than a whisper.

As if she's afraid to break the spell around us.

"Nothing."

Her eyes widen as her lips curve at the corners. The smile is wicked and sultry, doing nothing to cool the fire burning beneath my skin.

"Maybe if we try again...?"

When I swoop down to kiss her again, this time there's no hesitation. Our lips crush against one another. Daisy opens her mouth, guiding me without a word. I take my cue and allow my tongue to snake in. Fucking hell. Did I really think a kiss was enough to satisfy my obsession? This is making it so much worse.

My dick strains against the zipper of my pants.

One of her hands takes my wrist and lifts it to her breast. While small, there is just enough for a handful. Through her shirt, her nipple beads. As my thumb teases the peak, Daisy gasps and wiggles beneath me. Good god, I'm ravenous for more of this. I cut the kiss short, but don't let go of her breast.

"Don't stop, please, King."

If I have a weakness, it's absolutely, unequivocally Daisy. I'll do whatever she wants, whenever she wants, and more. I lean down and go back for more, but she tilts her head away from me and says, "I want your hands on me. Is that ok, King? If not—"

My hand slides up from her breast to wrap around her throat. I don't miss how the action causes her pupils to blow wide or the soft gasp of delight. She likes this. I tuck the piece of information away for later.

"*You* can have whatever you want from me." It's a little harder to sign with one hand, but not impossible. "Just tell me what you want, Daisy. Be explicit. I need to know what you want me to do to your pretty little body and how you like it. What makes you squirm?"

She drags in a shaky breath. "Tell you what I want?"

"Down to the smallest detail."

"Your mouth... on my breasts, King. Please."

Gladly. I swoop down to kiss her lips one more time before skimming them down her neck. My free hand pushes up her shirt. I don't get far.

One of her hands flies to my hair while the other grabs my wrist. I freeze. Did I do something wrong? Fuck, I hope not. Daisy isn't holding my hair tight, her hand is practically just resting there, but I lift my head slowly, making sure this isn't her trying to hold me in place.

"I, ah, forgot about..." She can't hold my gaze. The back of her head gently hits the floor with a thud as she looks up at the trees. Her hands fall back to the floor. "The Butcher of Briar Glen marked me. Just... if it's too much to look at, you can stop. I'll understand."

I frown, waiting for more of an explanation. She doesn't say anything else though. Curious and wary, I continue what I've started, pushing up her shirt. As it lifts, I notice the scar. The more the shirt comes up, the more of the scar becomes noticeable. When her shirt is all the way up to her neck, I have a view of the entire grizzly marking upon her skin.

My eyes slide over the V first. Each point starting from either side of her collar bone and dragged in a perfect diagonal line down each breast, across her stomach, and meeting just above her belly button. When my eyes come back up, it's to trace over the gentle arch that cuts off the top of the V. Then finally they slide over the straight line, just under the arch, that sits below her collarbone.

I close my eyes to focus on choking back the futile roar of despair and fury. No wonder she didn't want me to touch her. These scars are not only deliberate, practically surgical, but they are so thick that I have no doubt she was cut open several times in the exact same place. It only confirms my earlier thoughts about why she freaked out when I tackled her.

When I open my eyes, I look up to find Daisy still staring up at the trees. Is she waiting for my rejection?

She'll be waiting forever for it then.

Letting go of her throat, I reach down to grab her breast, and I brace my other hand on the floorboards. When my mouth finds her other nipple, Daisy sucks in a sharp breath and arches into my mouth. Circling and sucking on the hard bud, I tease it, which, in turn, coaxes soft whimpers and moans from my girl.

"Tweak my other nipple, King."

God, my dick is so hard that it hurts. I do as requested though, pleased by the breathy sound she lets out.

"Yes!" Her body shivers as I play with her.

"Will you... Can we...?" She asks between pants, her hips raising up hard.

Fuck... How can I say no?

16

Daisy

Kisses. Heavy petting. Sex.

I've never really enjoyed any of it before. Getting off was just an itch that needed to be scratched every once in a blue moon. Sometimes that itch was harder to reach than others. Typically, doing it myself was better than anything any partner I've had could achieve. But even when the itch felt like a full blown rash, where I needed *some* human interaction, I never felt anything close to this.

But Kingston isn't just *some* interaction. This is one of the four boys I've crushed on from afar for longer than I can remember.

Kingston sucks on my nipple hard.

Fire barrels through my veins, on a mission to burn out the ice that's numbed me for far too long. My heart slams against my chest and my cheeks burn. King gives my nipple a softer suck before lifting his head.

Our eyes meet.

In the muted morning light, I can actually see Kingston in all his cold and dangerous glory.

There are remnants of the boy I knew, but there's so much change that I really have to look for him. No longer is he tanned from the summer sun, nor does he hold himself with the same cocky confidence. His mouth doesn't flash that familiar pretentious grin, nor does he continuously roll his eyes in exasperation. The man above me watches me with a predator's gaze and holds himself utterly still. The thick scar across his neck, almost as deep as my own, adds to the dangerous energy around him. Those icy blue eyes are striking against his pale skin and are even more pronounced as his dark bangs drape them.

"What do you want, Daisy? Tell me all your dirty desires." He waits expectantly as embarrassment and excitement tangle up in my chest. I've never been vocal about my desires. I just kind of did whatever my partner wanted. But here Kingston is, demanding I tell him everything.

As much as I want to be taken right here on the floor of the perch, after Kingston's confession, I don't feel comfortable asking him for that. But my body aches for him. What's more, King *wants* to do this. This boy—*man*—says he loves me. Reciprocating feelings I never thought he'd have for me. I'm going to take this moment and make the most out of it.

"Your fingers. I want your fingers inside of me."

His mouth curves. It's like watching stone being chiseled into a masterpiece the way his smile is slow in coming. Good god, he's stunning even with a darkness swirling in the depth of his eyes. Maybe even more so. Kingston shuffles back, off my hips, to sit alongside my thighs. His eyes drop to my pants, and his hands follow. I lift my hips as he pulls them down to my ankles.

With considerable care, he reaches down and cups my

mound. I bite my bottom lip as my pussy spasms, starving for touch. Kingston looks up and signs.

"I can now say I've held the world in the palm of my hand."

Before I can respond, his hand slides lower, and two fingers slip inside of me without any resistance. My loud groan carries through the woods as my body clenches around his digits. Kingston's smile grows incrementally as I repeat the noise when he pumps in and out of me.

"Deeper, Kingston, please."

He does as requested. His fingers dip deeper as he continues the slow and steady pumping in and out of me. When I think he's gone as far as he can go, he keeps going. Oh heaven and hell... *fuck*. I buck against his hand, gasping as the pleasure starts to mount.

"Kingston, King..." I gulp, not sure what I want as my eyes squeeze tight.

I'm not sure if it's a natural instinct or if he was taught, but his thumb comes down and lightly plays with my clit. My back comes off the floor with a start at the unexpected and pleasurable touch.

"Yes!"

My hiss is met with an airy breath of laughter. Kingston shifts his weight on top of me. I don't open my eyes, too wrapped up in the rising tension gathering between my legs. My body clamps down harder around his fingers, ready to fall into oblivion. Just as I'm about to reach the point of no return, Kingston withdraws his fingers.

I open my mouth and eyes to protest only to feel, and watch, as Kingston latches onto my clit with his mouth while he reinserts his fingers into me. All words die on the tip of my tongue and my thoughts scatter. His warm, wet mouth is heaven. Kingston's tongue twirls around my clit curiously, slowly growing more confident with each rotation and suck.

When I cum, it's with a force I've never felt before. I cover my mouth with the back of my hand, knowing we need to keep quiet, but it doesn't do much. My hips grind against his hand and face as my orgasm drowns me in pleasure.

When I'm finally spent, my body goes lax.

Kingston withdraws his face and sits up. His piercing gaze moves from my face to the hand he lifts up to eye level. It glistens with my arousal. He twists it left and right, studying the evidence of his success. When he's done, our gazes collide. Without breaking eye contact, King brings his fingers to his lips and opens his mouth. His middle and ring finger disappear inside, and he sucks them. Without any sort of rush, he cleans his fingers.

Oh. As I pull up my pants, I watch in fascination as he finishes up and that small smile returns. It's not *quite* smug, but there is a hint of the old Kingston is this one.

"Now that I've had breakfast, what's on today's agenda?"

I sit up, pull down my shirt, and reach out to take his hand. "Before we go over that, I want to reciprocate."

King's nostrils flare and his jaw clenches tight. He doesn't answer right away, and judging by the gathering tension in his body, I'm sure he's having some type of internal battle. How often did he endure such assault? I never once thought that, in all the places for that to happen, it would happen in Riverbend.

I suppose there are monsters everywhere.

"It doesn't have to be now. In fact, it doesn't have to be ever," I shift into a kneeling position before him. "I *know* what that type of touch can do to a mind and body, and how hard it is to overcome." If it's possible, his icy blue eyes harden into diamonds as understanding dawns on him. I don't elaborate or think too hard about those times in my life. Instead, I push through. "I'll kill those nurses one by one. It certainly helps the healing process."

He shakes his head once. "*I'll* kill them."

"Have you ever killed anyone before?"

Kingston might as well be made of stone with how still he holds himself. When he answers, it's sharp and dismissive. "I tried. It ended with me in a year of isolation."

A tall, heavy wave of anger and disgust rises in my chest, and when it crashes, it spills into every crevice of my body.

"I want their names, King."

Kingston looks away as he considers this. His pause is short though. When he looks back at me, he suggests, "We'll do it together. You'll have to teach me how to kill."

"Gladly." The rush that comes with a kill is addicting, I can't wait to share this particular drug with him.

And the others.

I start to get to my feet, but Kingston catches my wrist. Relaxing back into my kneeling position, I wait expectantly.

King lets go of me and studies my face. "I want to wash off the stench of that place, so it can't touch you. Then I'll bury myself so deep inside of you that there is no you without me. That's the *only* reason stopping me from doing it now."

Good lord, he's intense. I love it. Reaching up, I cup his cheek and lean forward. He meets me halfway, kissing me hungrily. When I break away, I'm breathless.

"As for *that*," he nudges his head to the gun on the floorboards. "*If* you decide to change your mind, we go together. That's nonnegotiable."

I blink in surprise before recoiling from the idea. Kingston *dead*? Bile climbs up my throat.

"It's the only way I'll allow you to even entertain such thoughts," he adds when I don't respond.

There are many ways this whole thing could end by the time I'm done with Briar Glen. A bullet to the skull of my own doing doesn't have to be one of them.

"Fine." King's mouth twitches like he might smile. "Come on, we should eat. I have granola bars packed in our backpacks."

Again, I start to climb to my feet, but as I do, the snap of a twig in the forest and the soft sound of voices causes me to pause. My head whips around in the direction of the conversation.

"—should be with the search party. Not all the way out here hunting deer, Ed. Besides, you know they don't hang out over here until later in the season."

Oh shit. I expected hunters, but not this far out. This area hasn't been touched in years.

"Quit your complainin'. There's a buck out here, and I'm gonna get it." This deep raspy voice must belong to Ed. Judging by the way he hocks a loogie, spits, and attempts to clear his throat, he might be a smoker.

"There's a lunatic on the loose, and you just want to wander about?" the first voice speaks up again.

Kingston and I exchange looks. One side of his mouth jerks upward in a harsh, half smile. I can't help but smile back.

There's a scoff. "Relax, Harry. If I were that boy, I'd be halfway across the country right about now."

"You think he's really gone?" Harry asks.

Ed responds without any hesitation. "Yup, and soon his old pals visiting the Challahan boy will be too. They'll grow bored of this place and dip out."

"Been hearin' rumors you know. A few people are saying that letting them leave is a bad idea. That they're here, up to no good, and should be stopped before they can carry whatever they learn back to wherever they came from."

"Eh, they're nobodies."

There's a pause. Beneath us is the loud rustling of feet. If these guys are looking for deer, they won't find any making all this noise.

"I'm with the others on this. I say we take care of them," Harry mutters after a moment. "It's suspicious they turn up as all this shit is happening in town."

I knew, with me coming back, that the town would turn its attention to the guys. It was a risk asking them to come home, knowing that town would notice their arrival right away. But it was also a risk contacting them in general. Who's to say they hadn't been brainwashed into participating in the cult's madness? Especially Wyatt, who has continued to live here *willingly*. Still, I took the risk. Now my guys might be in trouble.

Best to take the threat out before it becomes too great of a force to contend with, right? A cold grin spreads across my face.

Kingston notices. His pupils narrow on me as he starts to move but I hold up a hand to stop him. Despite the slight shift, the floorboards groan.

"Did you hear that?" Harry gasps in alarm.

"Look! Up there!"

Well, guess the cat is out of the bag. I get to all fours and shuffle toward the entrance to the perch and lean my head out.

"Hey, guys."

They see me at the same time, both jumping in alarm.

"Hey, you! Whatcha doing up there?" This must be Harry. His bushy, faded brown mustache twitches like a mouse's nose. The sweat on his shirt, which is too small for that massive gut of his, looks like he's gone swimming.

I flash a smile down at them. "Just wanted to camp out under the stars. Do either of you have the time? My phone died."

"Get down here! That thing is old as hell. It could fall straight outta that tree!" Harry demands, his brows coming together with concern, or maybe some suspicion. I can't tell.

Beside him, the younger man, rail thin and a bit starry eyed, simply stares. I don't know if he knows who I am or if I just startled him. Either way, I don't care.

"Alright, one second. I'll send down the ladder. Watch out," I move out of sight and turn to Kingston and signal to remain silent. He appears unperturbed by the situation and content to let me handle this. I grab the ladder and toss down one end. "I'm on my way down!"

"You're good!"

I make quick work of getting down, skipping the last two steps and landing in a crouch. As my booted feet touch the ground, Harry steps forward.

"You know it's not safe out here, camping all alone. There's a psycho on the loose."

Without a word, I yank the knife from my boot and move. Straightening, I twist around, bring the knife up, and attack. The way the blade slams into his chest causes blood to spurt upward, like a fountain. His eyes widen before he looks down where the blade has entered his body, right beside his sternum.

He tries to talk, but all that comes out is blood. I can feel the tension in the blade shift as his legs start to give out from beneath him. With a hard yank, I pull the blade free and let the guy drop. I don't give him another thought as I turn around.

A cold smile returns to my face as the other man, who must be Ed, stares down at his friend, his mouth gaping. His short orange hair is plastered to his forehead as sweat breaks out and he starts dragging in short, heavy pants. I take a step toward him. The man doesn't seem to notice.

"W-what have you done?" Ed squeaks in alarm. Has he forgotten he has a rifle to protect him? I guess so, because he doesn't raise it as I stalk closer.

Rather than reply, my blade cuts through the air, slicing across his chest. It's a shallow wound, but it's enough to get him moving. Ed cries out, staggering backward, away from me. It's then that he remembers his gun. As he takes another few uneven steps backward, he fumbles with the weapon, trying to bring it up while his hands shake. I juke forward with my blade, forcing him to focus on me rather than his weapon.

Behind him, something large and heavy falls from the perch. Kingston lands on his feet, behind Ed, and rises to his full height. Ed doesn't have a chance to react. Kingston wraps an arm around his neck and kicks out his feet, bringing the guy to his knees. Pathetically, the gun falls from his hands.

"No! Stop! *Please!*"

My knife is on the move again. The man chokes on a scream. Just before my blade makes contact with his cheek, Kingston jerks Ed out of the way. I freeze. My eyes jump up to King's.

"Show me how to do it," he manages to sign while struggling to keep the flailing man in his grasp.

Oh. He wants to have his first kill now. My heart swells with a twisted sense of pride.

"Ok." I nod, straightening. My eyes drop to Ed, who is beginning to turn red in the face as Kingston doesn't relent on the pressure around his neck. He kicks his legs out, trying to keep me away, while his fingers try to pry Kingston's arm from his neck.

"Get him on his stomach."

As I watch, Kingston wrestles the stranger to the ground with ease. The first flicker of doubt edges into the forefront of my mind. Am I really going to let Kingston kill this man? Killing has become so easy that I don't think about the consequences my own soul may face after my body perishes. Whatever happens next can't be worse than what I've already gone through. But Kingston? Now I'm playing with *his* soul.

King presses his knee in the middle of the man's back and looks up at me, expectantly. His expression is so unfazed that we might as well be having a nice morning picnic rather than a teaching lesson on how to kill properly.

It's his nonchalance that helps me shove the doubt away. If he didn't want any part of this, he probably wouldn't have helped bury Marty's body in a shallow grave and most certainly would've taken off after that. I flip the knife around and offer

King the handle. He reaches forward without hesitation and takes it.

"Please no!" Ed rasps, but his cries and fighting are futile. Kingston might be lean, but he's clearly strong. "Please, please, please, please... Why are you doing this?"

I watch tears stream down his face, unbothered by them. No one ever stopped because *I* cried. Why should I give him that grace this go around? Crouching down, I point to a place on Ed's back.

"To get to his heart, you'll need to be strong enough to make it through the ribs." I point elsewhere. "Same goes for the lungs. The spleen and kidneys would be easier. They're here. If you choose there, you're gonna need to stab those places a few times for good measure. Well actually..." I hesitate, looking back up at Kingston's face to make sure he understands where this is headed. "It doesn't need to be perfect. We'll be carving both men up. It's easier to hide pieces of a body rather than a full one."

Ed howls, his efforts to escape doubling.

Kingston nods and I roll back on my heels to give him space. He doesn't hesitate. King simply raises the blade high above his head and then brings it down. The sound of the knife tearing through flesh and hitting organs, and the sight of blood, have stopped bothering me. So as my knife tears through the man on the forest floor, I watch with fascination and pride as Kingston makes his first kill.

Ed wheezes. Because I'm facing him, I watch as his eyes bulge and his face turns a bright red as it lifts off the ground, his body flinching with pain. When his skull flops back onto the forest ground, the life in his eyes drops away too.

I rise to my feet at the same time Kingston does. He hands me back the blade and I take it, sheathing it before looking up to study to his face for any signs of distress. King grins. It's beautifully chilly and my heart flutters at the sight of it.

"One down, hundreds more to go," he declares with pride. "This was a great first date. Never would have thought of it myself."

This? A date? The laughter that bubbles up in my chest is an unexpected reaction to the relief and joy blossoming in my chest.

"Come on. Let me show you how to carve a man up properly." As I step away, Kingston moves to stand in front of me.

"Who taught you how to kill?" His eyes drop to my chest then back up to my face. "Was it this Butcher?"

All my amusement vanishes. Fuck, I do *not* want to talk about Oliver. Knowing that's exactly what I'll have to do sooner or later, I decide to hold off on the conversation until the others are with us.

"Yes." I swallow down the chill that seems to linger in my gut. "But that's not important now. We have to get moving. Once we're done with these two, we have to go to Chasm to pick up something for this evening."

I start to move around King, but he steps in front of me once more. Huffing in annoyance, I look back up at him. He dips his head down and steals a kiss. It's so swift that I don't have time to react before he's pulling away.

He grins. "Let's get started."

17

Owen

My teeth bare down on the screwdriver handle as I use my hands to adjust the camera angle.

"I still can't believe you brought all this stuff with you," Wyatt says from the doorway of the guest room. "But I appreciate you installing it. With our girl around, the more eyes and ears we have to keep a look out for trouble, the better."

My sentiments exactly.

"I don't leave home without extra gear," I manage to get out around the tool in my mouth. When I'm sure the camera is able to get the door and the window in its view, I pull the screwdriver out of my mouth and toss it onto the bed, then step down off the stool.

"Why?"

I grab my laptop and pull up the camera feed on my screen to double check that I've installed it correctly.

"I, ah, kind of have this paranoia that people are watching me. So to make sure no one is, I watch them. I bring cameras everywhere."

I glance at the five little windows on the top of my screen. They're so small they don't get in the way of what I'm doing, but big enough that I can see five women moving about their homes without issue. I can probably disable my access to their cameras now. After the last few years of watching Daisy look-alikes, I have the real thing.

I'll do it later, I make a mental note and push away that concern for the moment.

Wyatt's scoffs. "Don't tell me you became one of those tin foil hat conspiracy theorists."

Heat floods my cheeks, but my eyes remain glued to my screen.

"*No*! Owen, you're so much smarter than that!"

Swallowing down my embarrassment, I look up from my computer to glare at him. "An entire town wiped Daisy off the map. Once I had the ability, I looked up her social security number, birth records, *death* records, and everything in between to find *something* to prove she existed. There's not a single trace of evidence of her existence, Wy. *None*. How much do you want to bet everyone in that grave Daisy was digging around in last night has been erased as well? If a whole town can get away with this shit, what can a government with infinite resources do?"

Wyatt opens and closes his mouth before his eyebrows furrow as he considers this. While he ponders over my explanation, I pick up my laptop and stand.

"I'm starving. I think we have time to eat before you head off to work. Let's get breakfast at Ma's Diner. I think showing our faces and looking just as stunned as everyone else about the fire in town and at Riverbend might do us some good. Tonight, I'll go through everyone's phones and make them safe to keep around, then install the camera software in them so we all have access to it."

"Go through my phone, huh? I guess I should erase a few

pictures," he teases as he follows me down the hallway back toward the living room.

I snort. "Yeah, please do. I don't need to see any dick pictures you might've sent or whatever else you've saved—"

"NO!" Wyatt pushes past me, and races toward the kitchen.

I watch him in surprise as he approaches an opened door. When he disappears into the other room, I follow curiously. Just as I step out into the garage, Wyatt groans.

"Dre, what are you doing? How'd you get in here? The door was locked!"

My eyes land on Drake first, who's standing in the middle of the space with his arms crossed over his wide chest. In front of him are three massive whiteboards. On each are different newspaper clippings, headshots, candid photos of groups of people, dead bodies, and red string tying the pieces of information gathered together. The whiteboard in the middle of the three has considerably less than the other two.

Looking away from the whiteboards, my focus comes to a rest in the corner of the garage where a mannequin stands. Draped over it is a sickeningly familiar red cloak. My entire body stiffens at the sight of it. My heart skips a beat as I take a step back toward the door. My eyes finish their sweep by landing on the garage wall. There, I find a collage of pictures depicting dead bodies.

"Wyatt... what the *fuck* is this?" My voice is strained as I take another step back. My attention swings back to the red cloak.

Is he playing for the other side? No... No, that can't be. He saw what they did to Daisy. Why would he want to be a part of that? But the cloak! He *has* to be involved. The proof is right there. My mind shuns away that possibility. It's too hard to wrap my head around. There's no way Wy—

"It's not what it looks like, I swear!" Wyatt whirls around, his eyes wide and his face pale. "I'm not a member of the cult here.

That's not my cloak and those aren't, like, my victims, or anything!"

I want to believe him. His reaction seems genuine enough, but I can't seem to get past the red in the corner of the room. I start to shake my head, but Wyatt waves his hands frantically.

"I stayed in Briar Glen all these years to see if I could figure out who was involved that night." He glances back and forth between us anxiously. "I needed answers! Owen, you said you dug into Daisy's legal documentation for information, searching for clues. That was *your* way of investigating, and *this* is mine. It's the same thing!"

I shake my head immediately. "I think *this* is totally different."

Drake grunts. I'm not sure if it's in agreement or not, but Wyatt takes it that way.

"Look, you know how much I love a good mystery. That's all this is. Those boards? The two outer ones are centered around two different towns on either end of the country. They had a cult and eventually it was dismantled. I tried using those two places as a guide on how to figure out how Briar Glen's cult runs things so well. As you can see on the middle board, I've come up pretty much empty-handed."

I move a little closer to study what's on the whiteboard. But that cloak in the corner won't let me give anything else too much attention. "What about that?"

Wyatt swallows, his face paling further. "That's a replica I had made from memory while I was away in college. There was a chance that seeing it would jog my memory of that night. I know Francis Winslow was there, we all know that. But the others? I vaguely remember catching glimpses of faces, but everything about that night except Daisy's death has been a blur."

That whole night was like a nightmare where certain monsters and scenes stood out more than others. I don't remember seeing faces. But if Wyatt says he does, who am I to question how he tries to dredge up details of what he saw?

"Anyway, now that Daisy's back, maybe she can clue us in on all the missing details." Wyatt swallows. "I can show her what I have, and we can go from there. Look, I know this seems strange, but it's how I coped, alright?"

Drake finally looks away from the whiteboards. He glances at me, then at Wyatt, his expression unreadable. It's weird looking into the face of a stranger. There're no similarities, besides the blond hair, to show that this was one of my close friends growing up. The hard lines and even steelier gaze give no insight on what happened to the emotional kid I knew.

"Please, you guys have to believe me," Wyatt pleads softly, his shoulders falling as his brows pinch together. "I would *never* participate in a cult, let alone one that killed the girl I loved."

My whole body jerks as if electrocuted. Loved? He *loved* Daisy?

But *I* loved Daisy. I still do. It's why I'm here in Briar Glen ready to do only gods know what for her.

Does he feel the same way after seeing her last night? She's different, and I don't mean just physically, though there was no missing that she is now a woman versus the girl we knew. Her entire aura felt like a live wire, pulsing with energy and danger. When she laughed and smiled, both had an edge that wasn't there before. And the flippant disregard for Marty's life? The Daisy I knew would never have been able to stomach watching another suffer. This new Daisy is magnificently terrifying.

I never thought I could love anything more than the memory of the girl I knew, but I re-fell for Daisy last night harder than I ever thought possible.

Shaking my head, I point to the pictures on the wall. "What about the pictures? What do they have to do with the rest of this stuff?"

Color gathers in Wyatt's cheeks as his gaze slides away from me down to the floor.

"I, um, no. Those have nothing to do with anything else in here. They're just... pictures I found online."

I'm not sure I understand. "Then what are they up there? Jesus, there has to be over two dozen!"

"There's about fifty."

I gape at him. "For what purpose do you have pictures of fifty dead people hanging on your wall?"

Wyatt doesn't look up and doesn't answer right away. Using the toe of one foot, he pushes around the dust on the floor.

"Well, you see, I, um, have this, ah, thing—"

"*Kink,*" Drake interrupts.

I blink, not sure if I heard him correctly. Pulling my gaze off Wyatt, I watch as Drake nudges his head to the corner of the room. I follow the direction, where I find a large bottle of lotion and a few old socks laying in a pile.

It doesn't take a genius to deduce what's been happening out here. But it does, however, take me a moment to process what exactly he's been finding enjoyment in. My eyes look from the corner of masturbation material to the wall, then back again. Then I add Drake's word: kink.

When it dawns on me, I wish it hadn't.

"Oh, *oh*... Oh!" I think I might be sick.

Wyatt clears his throat. "We all have our things. No need to shame—"

"Makes sense why you were able to see all of Oliver's victims now," Drake muses out loud, cutting him off. "This cop friend of yours, does he know your dirty little secret?"

Though his expression doesn't change, I swear Drake's voice is a tad lighter, as if he finds all this rather amusing.

"Ah..." Wyatt's face turns beet red.

"Does he know it gets you off?" Drake pushes. Are the corners of his mouth twitching? They are! The bastard *is* enjoying Wyatt's embarrassment while he squirms. "He has to know, on some level, I suppose."

Before Wyatt can answer, the doorbell rings. We all freeze, exchanging wary looks with one another. It couldn't be Daisy. She wouldn't just flounce up to the front door in broad daylight. So who...?

"Expecting company?" Drake asks.

Wyatt shakes his head. "No."

Shit, could this be trouble? Determined to face it head on, I set my shoulders and head back into the main part of the house. I get to the front door just as the doorbell rings again. Yanking it open, I find a young cop waiting on the other side. Clean cut, with a baby face, the expression resting on the officer's face shifts from surprise to barely concealed suspicion.

"Can I help you?" I don't mean to sound rude but I'm not a fan of the way his eyes trailed over my chest.

I should've put a shirt on this morning. Once I got it in my head to protect this place and get it ready for Daisy's arrival, I'd simply rolled out of bed with just my pajama bottoms on.

"Who the hell are you?" the cop demands.

I blink in surprise. Well *that's* an interesting way to greet someone. I open my mouth to tell him to fuck off but then Wyatt appears at my side, his hand on my shoulder, laughing a bit breathlessly.

"Brett, what are you doing here?"

Oh, this must be the cop friend. The same one that showed Wyatt the evidence from the Oliver Grayman crime scene and that probably knows about Wyatt's special fetish for rotting flesh. I hold back a grimace.

Brett looks between us, his brows furrowing heavily and his frown deepening. Suddenly, Wyatt's hand is off my shoulder.

"Ah, Brett, this is, um, Owen Woodlock. Owen this—"

"I came by on official police business, Wyatt." Brett interrupts, his back straightening as his hands go to rest on his utility belt. "Did you hear about last night?"

Wyatt frowns, "I heard the neighbors talk about some fire downtown. We were going to drive to Ma's Diner for breakfast to check out the damage. Is everyone ok?"

The cop shakes his head. "Everyone is fine in town. I was talking about the fire at Riverbend."

I lean up against the door frame and cross my arms over my chest, schooling my face into interest.

"That's the insane asylum, right?"

My question is ignored as the cop stares intently at Wyatt.

"A fire at Riverbend? Last night?" Wyatt shakes his head slowly. "No, I didn't. Did everyone get out alright?"

"Yeah. Everyone is fine, but a patient escaped. We're going around to make sure everyone is aware to keep an eye out for him." Brett shoots me a wary glare before looking back at Wyatt. "The patient was Kingston Winslow. Rumor has it you guys were friends back in the day?"

Wyatt shrugs. "As kids, yeah. Why?"

"Well, he may search you out. You know, a friendly face and all that. He's dangerous though, so if he *does* make an appearance, call me immediately."

Huh, *me* not *us* as in the police force. Frowning, I stare between the two of them, noting the way Brett steps closer into Wyatt's personal space and the softening of his expression as he talks.

Wyatt scoffs. "Kingston wouldn't know where I lived now, and even if he did, I doubt he'd hang out in Briar Glen after what his dad did to him."

"What Mr. Winslow did was self-defense," Brett reminds him.

While my family and I weren't in Briar Glen when this all went down, I know King wouldn't have killed his mother.

However, Francis Winslow is more than capable of killing a person. I've seen that with my own eyes.

I scowl at the cop. "*Allegedly*. The only person there to point the finger at King was also the same person who slit his throat and locked him up in an asylum so he couldn't tell his side of the story."

"The court doesn't see it that way," Brett responds, still holding Wyatt's gaze. "And who knows what nine years in an asylum will do to a guy? I heard he was in solitary for a whole year after attacking a nurse coming around on her nightly visits. That sound like the guy you knew?"

Wyatt looks back at me, frowning. I mirror it.

If King got mad enough, he'd probably be capable of anything. But he has to have a reason and he's not rash. He also wouldn't go after someone who was innocent. King was a jerk at times, but he had boundaries.

"See? Dangerous," Brett says, taking our silence for worry.

I'm over this conversation. Nothing we say will change this guy's mind. Rolling my eyes, I push off the door frame and head inside. Drake is leaning against the counter in the kitchen, eating an apple. I move toward him, ready to find something to chow down on. Wyatt comes inside a moment later. I turn around as he shuts the door and leans against it with a sigh.

"Can this day get any worse?" he asks, more to himself than us.

"Why? What's wrong?" Drake chuckles darkly. "Upset we found out about what you're into? Or is your boyfriend jealous you have two dudes staying at your place?"

"He's not my boyfriend anymore!" Wyatt snaps quickly.

Both Drake and I still.

I blink. "Excuse me? *Anymore*?"

Wyatt runs his hand down his face. "Brett and I used to be, um, well, something. I broke it off though when he got too clingy."

"Oh." Huh, I didn't see this coming. Now I get why the cop didn't look so happy to see me. "So you're gay?"

Hadn't he just said he loved Daisy?

"*Bi*," Wyatt corrects without looking at either of us. Color gathers in his cheeks as he moves past the two of us, toward the garage. "I think I'll take down those pictures on the wall now. Then we can get ready to head out and be seen around town."

As he reaches for the door, I laugh. Hard. He stops to look at me, his face reddening even more.

"Well, that explains why the cop was shooting daggers with his eyes at me. Your ex was *jealous.* Did he think we hooked up last night? God, if looks could kill, I'd be on your front stoop in a puddle of my own blood! HA! I should've kissed you or something to really fuck with his head." For some reason this tickles me even more, and I laugh louder. "Better yet, Drake should've come out in just his boxers, *that* would have caused that dude's head to pop right off."

Drake chuckles and Wyatt's mouth twitches as if he wants to smile.

"You're not... you guys aren't weirded out?"

My amusement fades. "No, why would I be?"

Wyatt clears his throat. "It was a bit hard to, um, come out in a place like this."

"That's because this is bum-fuck nowhere, Indiana. Civilized society doesn't give a shit about that stuff." I roll my eyes. "I don't care who you fuck."

"I kind of care *what* you fuck though," Drake points out. "If you have a corpse on this property that you fuck regularly, please do it outside of our visiting hours."

I grimace as I try not to think too hard about that. Wyatt cracks a smile this time.

"I'll keep corpse-fucking to a minimum while you're here."

Drake shakes his head, but I don't miss his smile as he turns away. "Gee, thanks."

18

Daisy

"Ok, do you remember what I told you?"

My eyes won't stop scanning the property across the street. The boring, cement building nestled in the middle of an empty parking lot houses the small coroner's office. There's only one car there now, two down from the typical three.

Out of the corner of my eye, I catch Kingston's nod.

I swallow back my hesitation. It's time to put my faith in someone other than myself for the first time in a long time. If it was anyone else, I wouldn't be so confident as I slip out of the driver's seat and slam the door shut.

But this morning Kingston carved up two bodies and helped me bury the pieces without any problems. Not once did he turn green, throw up, or complain. He simply did as he was instructed, and whenever he finished his task, he asked for more. Then we bathed in the river and chowed down on some granola bars as if nothing had even happened.

We make a good team. I remind myself of that as I cross the

empty road and jog into the parking lot. Rather than head straight for the front doors, I go around the side of the building to the back. Once at the back door, I pull out a thick, heavy duty magnet I'd stolen ages ago and hold it to the keypad. It takes only a few seconds to disable the old mechanism. The lock disengages, and I'm able to open the door without issue.

I bend down, pick up a rock, and jam it between the door frame and door before slipping inside. For a second, I hold completely still. The sterile hallway is empty, the fluorescent lights bright and uncomfortable. The only noise comes from the other end of the hallway. By the sound of it, my victim is enjoying a podcast.

My feet start moving in that direction.

I'm not purposefully quiet, but my feet don't make a sound as I approach the room where the radio is playing. When I get there, I find the door cracked open. I pause just outside and listen again.

"—global warming. It's fucking ridiculous. Teachers and these big shot companies are feeding our kids this bullshit that they need to go green. Urgh, what does that even mean? Going green? Bo, your thoughts?"

"You're right, Sean. The Earth heats and cools naturally. Just because things are hotter now than they were a year or two ago doesn't mean our planet's dying."

There's a hum of approval by a non-radio speaking individual.

"Look, it snowed a foot in October up at my parent's house in Vermont. If that's not proof global warming isn't real, then I don't know what is."

"Right? Alright you guys, we'll be right back. Here's a word from our sponsors."

As a commercial starts to play, I can hear someone sigh. Reaching forward, I push open the door and step inside.

The man in the room looks up as I enter. Standing behind his desk, half bent over, I manage to get a good look at him. He's in his mid-forties. His blond hair is losing its luster, and there are lines beginning to show in his face. He's tall, probably just over six feet, and well-built.

Jeff Herring doesn't look all that different from the last time I'd seen him. The only change is he's not covered in someone else's blood.

"Who are you? You're not supposed to be here," he asks, frowning. "If you need something, you need to wait up front until Rita or Tonya come back from lunch."

I smile. It comes so naturally in situations like this. "Do you truly not remember my face, Jeff?"

The man straightens in surprise as I use his first name so flippantly. He steps around his desk with a frown, straightening his sleeves as he does.

"No, you don't look familiar at..." His brows furrow as he really studies my face.

I give him a minute. Despite how important I was to his plans all those years ago, I know time muddles memories. At least some of them. I wish time would erase some more than others for me.

"You do look familiar." He takes another step closer.

My smile splits into a grin. Excitement hums in my veins as my prey approaches.

"Let me jog your memory," I offer, keeping my voice sweet. "The first time I saw you, you stormed into the room I was being held captive in, you took one look at me naked and chained to a mattress, and *laughed*."

Jeff opens his mouth, his face twisted with confusion, but then I see it. "Oh... *Oh*!"

Understanding floods his features, shock trailing in its wake. Jeff's face slackens. His jaw drops, his eyes bulge, and a hand reaches backward to catch himself on the edge of the desk as he stumbles away from me.

"Do you remember me now, Jeff?"

The man has the audacity to scoff at me. After a second of being flustered, his mouth twists with a coy smile and a familiar gleam brightens his eyes.

"I do, Daisy Murray. What a surprise that you've come home at last."

Home. The word holds no meaning for me. Home is where you belong, where one finds solace. But I've not known peace for far too long. There is no place for me to run to escape the horrible nightmares that live deep inside of me.

"I have." My smile slips from my face. "Though I have a feeling I won't be welcomed with open arms this time around."

Jeff tsks. "Nonsense. Everyone will be thrilled to know you've come back from the dead to serve your purpose."

I laugh though it lacks any amusement. "You knew I was alive this whole time."

Jeff shakes his head, "Not after Tobias and I found Oliver's body in his house. It was poor timing on your part, leaving that day. I'd brought Tobias, knowing he didn't like my father either. I wanted him to see everything unfold. I was *so close* to getting everything I wanted."

"I'm sorry that handing me over to Francis for him to kill me didn't pan out." I roll my eyes. "What made you think I was dead if you knew I had escaped?"

"Tobias and I hired a tracker to see if you'd survived out in the woods all by your lonesome, but that was a dead end. Those woods go for miles, and the bears and coyotes that hide in them? Given the poor state you were in, I had no doubt you'd been eaten or died from exposure. I'm pleased to see I was wrong." He claps his hands together. "Well now, why don't you take a seat? I have a phone call to make."

"To Francis, or your father?"

"To Francis of course," Jeff rolls his eyes. "My father can go fuck himself. When I bring you to Francis's door, he'll *happily* kick my father to the curb to let me take his seat at the table. I thought this dream was lost, but I suppose Zarzuz has a plan for us all and this was his for me."

I saunter around the first surgical table, running my fingertips over it, leaving streaks but no prints. *That* was Jeff's doing. Oliver never once considered removing anything that could identify me.

"Did you or Tobias ever end up telling Francis you had me?" I ask curiously as I approach him. I look up from the table to find him pulling out his cell phone.

Jeff pauses to look up at me. "Of course not! Could you imagine what he would do to me if he found out I knew where you were all those years? Do you know the amount of money it took me to pay off Tobias to keep him from going to Francis? It was worth paying it though. Anything to avoid Francis's wrath."

Jeff walks back around his desk, phone in hand. He stops a few feet away to continue with whatever he's doing.

"You won't have to pay me to keep quiet about your fuck up," I assure Jeff as I start my slow stalk toward him. I won't be telling Francis anything. Not now, not later. The only thing Francis will hear coming from me, is the whistle of my blade as I plunge it into his heart.

He gives me a smug smile. "I know you won't."

Jeff must have some type of plan to subdue me. I'm almost tempted to let him go through with it to show him just how much I've changed since the last time he saw me. I'm not a weak, sniveling young girl anymore.

"Before you make that call, can I ask you something?"

"Sure."

"Do you remember Abigail Wellstone, Marie Chavares, or Jessica Blakely?"

Jeff's brows pinch together as he thinks it over. After a

moment, he shakes his head. "No, no I don't think I know any of them. Who are they?"

"Those were just some of the women you raped and tortured in Oliver's room of horrors. There are more of course. But I feel like since you didn't bother learning the names of the women you tormented, it would be a waste of my breath." I shove my hand into my jacket pocket, grabbing the thin object resting there.

"They weren't worth knowing." Jeff shrugs. "Now take a seat. I'd prefer to do this the easy way if you don't mind."

I laugh loudly, earning me a scowl. Jeff stomps over to me, closing the distance between us until he stands directly in front of me.

"What's so funny, *Chosen One*?"

"You were never a fan of the easy way before, why start now? You like a bit of struggle. I remember how much you enjoyed shoving your dick into screaming girls."

The screams still haunt me. Their trauma rolled into me, and I carry the heavy load wherever I go.

"Ab-so-fucking-lutely I did," Jeff laughs as he reaches out to grab my arm.

It's expected. I grab his incoming wrist, yank it forward to pull him off balance, and pull out the object in my pocket. The syringe slams into his neck. I empty the contents in the same motion. Jeff gasps, his eyes going wide. I let go of his wrist and let him stumble back. He reaches for the syringe sticking out of his neck.

His fingertips barely skim the plastic syringe before he's down on his knees.

"W-what, what's happening?" he gasps, his upper half swaying. "What have you done?"

"This, Jeff, is the beginning of the end for you." I straighten just as the door is unexpectedly pushed open. I freeze, my breath catching in my throat.

No one is supposed to be here.

I let out the breath I'm holding as my gaze lands on Kingston. Content that I'm safe, I turn back to Jeff just in time to see his eyes roll up into the back of his head. He falls face first onto the linoleum floor and doesn't move.

"You're not supposed to be inside, King." I start moving, pulling out the zip ties from my pockets and pulling Jeff's wrists together.

Kingston prods forward. He snatches the extra zip ties from my hand and gets to work pulling Jeff's feet out and binding them together. As I stand, King finishes and looks up at me from the floor.

"I can't stand to be away from you."

Though his expression is masked with a look of cool indifference, it's his eyes that shine in earnest. My stomach twists anxiously.

He loves me, the thought brings forth a wave of trepidation even as my heart flutters.

Is this what love is? To worry about another individual to the point you throw caution to the wind? An impatience to be back in each other's presence after only a short period of time apart? The willingness to cross dark lines without a second thought?

Or is this just madness?

Swallowing back a lump gathering in my throat, I sigh.

"Alright, well, since you're here, you can help me get him into the trunk." I pause. "Please tell me you thought to move the car like you were supposed to?"

Kingston nods. I start to bend down to grab Jeff's arms but stop again.

"How much of that did you hear?"

Kingston's gaze doesn't waver as he answers. "All of it."

Of course he did. I brace myself for the questions, the pity or concern. Kingston just stares at me, his eyes piercing. When he doesn't say anything else, I relax. I guess King won't push for answers. Good, because now is not the time. He'll get them soon enough.

Squaring my shoulders, I force myself to focus on the task at hand. "Alright, let's get this bastard out of here."

19

Wyatt

Drake and Owen are waiting for me outside the school as I stroll out the doors, having already locked up my classroom and released my students for the day. I bolt across the parking lot and hop into the back of Drake's truck. Owen slides open the window that blocks me from the cab as Drake pulls out of the emptying parking lot.

"Brought your stuff with us. It's in the duffle bag." He nudges his head toward the bag in the back with me before asking, "Did you take the next few days off?"

I flash him a grin. "I took two full weeks off. This is going to be the best vacation ever."

"You should've just quit. I did," Drake says over his shoulder. "Had a feeling I wasn't coming back."

"That would've looked super suspicious." Daisy may not have outright said what we're doing quite yet, but I have a feeling that by the time she's done here in Briar Glen, we won't be able to stay. The less attention I can place on myself now, the longer we should be safe here.

"That's probably a good call since we're already being watched," Owen points out. "Instead of heading straight to our meeting point and just waiting around for nightfall, we're going to head to Chasm and grab something to eat over there. Once it's dark, *then* we'll go meet Daisy."

Watched? I look around as Drake drives through town. At first, I don't see anything. But the more I look, the more I notice the stares from pedestrians walking down the streets we pass. Some raise their phones to click pictures, attempting to look casual. The car behind us is tailgating, the owner not bothering to back off when I make eye contact with him.

Well shit. What's this about?

"Did you guys have any problems today?" How could the town possibly be suspicious of us when we haven't even done anything yet?

"Not really." Owen shakes his head. "We went and pretended to help with the search party they had for Kingston. When that dissolved after lunch, we drove around to study the damage. No one really said anything to us. There were some whispers behind our backs, but everyone was relatively friendly."

"Then why do you think we're being watched so closely?"

Drake snorts. "We're technically outsiders now, Wy, and outsiders have never really been welcomed in Briar Glen."

That's true. When someone new blows into town, whether they're just passing through or stopping to bunker down for a bit, the entire town makes it a point to know their business, and if they don't like said business? Well, Briar Glen is good at icing people out.

Daisy invited us to be a part of her plan, whatever that may be, but did she consider how much attention we'd draw given that two out of the three of us would now be on the town's radar? My jaw clenches as my fists curl. It doesn't matter. They can stare all they want. We'll do whatever Daisy wants. After what this town put me through, what my own *parents* put me through, after her disappearance, the townspeople deserve everything that she has in store for them. I'll hold their gazes when I strike the match that will burn this place to the ground.

As we drive past my old neighborhood, unwanted memories surge forward.

"See? It's rubble. It's always been this way," my father said, forcing me to get out of the car to stare at the empty lot where Daisy's house once sat. For a week, I'd tried to get them to look into Daisy's death, but they weren't listening.

No, it was worse than that, they didn't believe *me. They didn't believe Daisy even existed. Which is unfathomable since she was over all the time. But where her house had been is no more. I stare in horror at the scene before me.*

"N-no, we used to hang out on the front porch and swing on the play-set out back..." My eyes scan the property but find no sign of the two-person swing set that once sat in her backyard. "T-this, this isn't right! Daisy would force us to watch Mary Poppins in her room all the time, and she used to hide notes for us in that tree!" I point to the oak standing tall in what should have been the front yard.

But where was the house? It looks like nothing has been here in ages. H-how could this happen? It was just *here a few days ago!* Daisy *had been here just a few days ago.*

"You're confused, son, there was never a Daisy. You saw that movie in school and the four of you became obsessed with it." The way my father's hands had pressed into my shoulders was painful.

"This madness has to end!" My mother wept from behind us. "Why can't you see it was all in your head, Wy? We thought this was a phase but... red-hooded figures? A ceremonial knife? None of that makes sense!"

I'd shaken my head, determined that I knew what I was talking about.

"Then explain my bruises!" I'd whirled around to face them, and they both scowled.

My dad huffed, rolling his eyes before pinning me with a steely look. "Kingston has always had a temper. He must be forcing you to tell us this to cover up for his own handy work."

"Kingston's an ass but he never would've beat us all up!" I'd fought.

Even after three years of my parents being dead and gone, I still hold on to the hatred I had for them. It took me until after their deaths to realize why they'd been so adamant about gaslighting me into believing Daisy wasn't real.

They'd been in on it. My parents were part of the cult that lurks in Briar Glen's shadows.

My stomach still hurts thinking about the truth of that revelation. How'd I not see that when I was younger? It wasn't like there was proof to find after their deaths, but it's so obvious that I feel foolish for not coming to that conclusion earlier.

With a sigh, I lean back against the cab and watch as Briar Glen passes by; thankfully my parents are no longer around to help the town gaslight me into believing I'd gone mad.

"I NEED TO SAY SOMETHING," I declare as we trudge through the thick brush.

The sun set a while ago. After grabbing a quick bite in Chasm at a deli, looking through a few shops, and filling the truck up with gas to kill time, we booked it to our designated meeting spot. The dirt road that Daisy had told us about had been difficult to find, even with her specific landmark details. We'd doubled back over a dozen times before finally finding it. After parking, we were quick to hide our vehicle with whatever brush we could find, just as Daisy instructed.

Now, we're on foot, nearly to our destination point. As we walk, however, a growing sense of importance gathers within me. Something has been irking me since we left Briar Glen, and I need to get it off my chest.

"Why are you announcing it? Just tell us," Owen huffs from behind me.

Right, of course. "I just want to say I'm sorry I didn't make more of an effort to reach out to you before Daisy first wrote to us."

Neither one of them says anything to this. I'm not sure if they're holding in their feelings, a grudge, or don't care enough to respond. With a sigh, I let it go.

Time ticks by as we walk. It's Owen that finally breaks the silence.

"My family and I left, Wy." He clears his throat. "Growing apart would've been natural in that instance anyway. But after what happened? I wanted nothing to do with Briar Glen or the people in it. If you had called or written, I would've ignored it."

Ouch. His confession stings.

"That doesn't mean *I* couldn't have put more of an effort in," I mutter. "And Drake, you still lived here. I could've done more to see you."

"You would've been wasting your time." Drake's response comes from farther ahead, where he's moving easily through the woods despite his larger size.

"Trying to keep what we had wouldn't have been a waste, Dre." I frown. "We were inseparable for years and yet, suddenly, we were just not friends anymore."

Drake says nothing to this. Behind me, Owen sighs. "We'll do better moving forward."

I don't think we walk a hundred more steps before Drake's pace quickens.

"Masks on!" he orders over his shoulder.

I'd let my mask hang from around my neck, dangling behind me, but now, I yank it into place. Quickening my pace to catch up with Drake, I practically trip when we get into the clearing.

A *familiar* clearing.

My stomach drops as my limbs freeze up. Not twenty yards away is the stone platform that Daisy had been tied down to. Around it sit dark tiki torches. Set up in front of the stone are a few rows of seats made from split tree trunks, and in the middle of them, a firepit that now houses a small flame.

Blood drains from my face as Daisy's phantom sobs of fear echo in my psyche.

"Shit," Owen whispers behind me as he enters the clearing next. He pauses beside me. "We looked so hard for this place, remember?"

I do. We were sure if we could just show our parents where it happened, they'd have to believe us. The trouble was, trying to find our way back to this place had been impossible. It had been dark when we stumbled upon it, and no one knew just how far or in what direction we took from Solmer's Rock.

"P-please, don't do this."

A weak whine breaks through my shock. I follow Drake forward, toward the slab. He steps out of the way as he moves around it, and there stand Daisy and Kingston, dressed in their black jackets and masks.

"Good evening, boys," Daisy greets warmly, not taking off her mask. "I'm glad you found the place."

My heart swells at the sound of her voice. She's still here, she didn't leave. I didn't realize I'd been worried until just now as tension eases from my chest.

"How'd *you* find it? We searched high and low for it after that night," I ask, moving quickly to her side.

I pause just before I get there as my eyes land on the man zip tied at her feet. His eyes are only half-open, his mouth hanging slack with drool running from a corner of it. It's obvious that he's been drugged.

"I've been stalking Briar Glen for a long time."

Daisy's answer drags my attention back to her. The man lying at her feet is instantly forgotten. We'll get to him in a second.

"*What*? And you didn't think to stop by?" I can't keep the hurt from my voice.

"I did. Many times." At my gasp of surprise, she giggles. "I stood in your backyard many times, just to watch you get ready for bed or work."

I don't think I heard her correctly.

"Y-you did?" All these years wondering where she was, and yet Daisy's been here, with me, this whole time? I'm not sure if I'm angry or touched.

"Then you must've seen Wyatt's boyfriend a time or two," Owen teases as he and Drake come join us. He glances down at the stranger at our feet but dismisses him quickly.

Daisy nods. "I saw him."

Heat rises in my cheeks as I try to think of all the times Brett and I had messed around in my bedroom. How often had Daisy been there, watching?

"He wasn't my boyfriend. Just a... ah, friend. If anything he's an *ex-boyfriend*," I correct, hastily. "You know it's rude to stalk people, Daze"

She laughs, unperturbed.

"You could've stalked me, Daisy, I wouldn't have minded," Owen assures her as he crouches down next to this guy. "Anyway, who—"

"I watched you *all* from afar for a while."

Everyone turns to stare at her. Owen rises to his feet slowly, his head shaking back and forth.

"What?" he asks.

Daisy giggles. "Yup. I watched you all." She looks over to Kingston who stands so close that he's practically an extension of her. "I would stand under the shadow of that oak tree while you and the other patients were allowed outdoor time." She glances at Owen. "You just recently opened up a small tech company in Greenwich, called Bitez, across the street from a bakery that makes the most mouthwatering chocolate croissants." Finally, she looks at Drake. "And *you*... you live in a small cabin on the outskirts of Anchorage. A small herd of moose likes to cross through your backyard. They're not very friendly. And there is a beautiful quilt with a daisy pattern that rests on the recliner."

None of us say a word. We all simply stare at her. The girl we loved, who we all thought was dead, had been alive this whole time and simply haunting us from afar.

Drake chokes. He attempts to clear his throat, but it takes a minute before he can form any words.

"Why didn't you...?" He fails to finish the question we all want to know.

"I couldn't, Dre." The amusement in Daisy's voice trails away. "I wasn't... I haven't been ready."

Kingston lifts his hand, and he grabs the back of her neck. The motion seems to steady her because she takes a deep breath and continues,

"When I escaped The Butcher, I wasn't in a good place. Those first letters I sent you could've been gibberish for all I know. I don't even know how I managed to track you down when I was so—" she shakes her head and shrugs "—lost. When things got better, up here—" she taps her head. "—and I needed a break from plotting, I'd come find one of you. I'd watch from afar, living vicariously through you. Or, in your case —" she turns to Kingston "—sending you as much hope as I could muster."

I move around the man on the ground, who's starting to squirm, to approach Daisy. When I stop before her, I grab her hand and stare down into her masked eyes. The rising tide of emotions, burning in my chest hotter than molten rock, makes it hard to find the words I want, but eventually they fall onto my tongue, and I give them life.

"I get it. I'm just glad you could find solace near us, if not with us. Maybe it was your presence that kept your memory and my love for you alive." I push up my mask and then pull hers up too so I can see her. "Because I've loved you this whole time and will continue to do so until my heart is nothing more than ash and my soul has withered away."

I lean down and kiss her. It's a swift kiss. I know if I lean into it, give in to the hunger, desperation, grief, and joy twisting in my chest, that I won't be able to stop until I've buried myself deep inside of her. Unfortunately, we don't have time for that right now. With a reluctant sigh, I pull away.

Daisy's eyelids flutter. Color gathers under her pretty brown skin. Fuck, she looks almost dazed. My grip tightens ever so slightly as I hold her hand and will myself to focus on the task at hand.

Looking down at the man at our feet, I ask, "So, what are we doing with this guy?"

Daisy follows my gaze. There's a short pause before she answers, "We're going to sacrifice him to Lilith."

20

Drake

"I'm sorry, I think I misheard you," Owen says, shaking his head. "Did you say *sacrifice*?"

Daisy nods. "You guys get him on the altar while I get everything else ready. I'll explain while I work."

I watch as Kingston and Wyatt let go of their possessive hold on Daisy, ready to do what she asks. A twinge of jealousy twists in my chest before I snuff it out. Wyatt and Kingston have never been ones to resist going after something they wanted. Of course they're going to stake their claim now that Daisy is back. I wasn't blind to how smitten they were with her back when we were younger. How could I blame them when I was, and still am, utterly obsessed with Daisy myself?

But she said she loved us all, and I'll be damned if I don't show Daisy she's mine just as much as she is theirs.

I stroll forward and grab under the man's armpits. While I take his upper half, Wyatt and Kingston take the lower end. The guy weighs a ton. How did Daisy and Kingston manage to get him all the way out here by themselves? My guess is by dragging him, but that would've taken all day.

I suppose they had the time.

Together, the three of us lay the man down on top of the stone altar. Daisy's victim seems to have come to enough to realize that he's in danger because once his back touches the cool stone, he starts to struggle. It's a messy twisting of his bound arms and legs and is pathetically sluggish.

"As I told you last night, the cult in Briar Glen worships what they believe to be a deity named Zarzuz." Daisy moves over to a backpack and begins pulling items out of it. "The story goes, Zarzuz was a rising god that fell with Lucifer from the heavens. Lucifer erased Zarzuz from history, knowing that if he had worshippers, Zarzuz may become strong enough to take over his throne in hell. He uses Lilith to watch over Zarzuz, giving her powers that help subdue the misunderstood demigod.

"Well, a century ago, a blood moon rose into the sky at the same time a man was seeking answers from a divine being. He reached out into the universe, offering up his soul in exchange for guidance and power. Somehow, the blood moon carried his plea into the underworld where Zarzuz heard and answered the call. That man just happened to be Lionel Winslow."

I swallow, looking away from her. Shame and regret are a hard plaster around my heart. I shouldn't know this story. If my parents had been *normal* this story would all be new to me.

But they weren't and this isn't.

"*No*," the man moans on the altar. "They do not deserve to hear about our Lord! You bitch. The Butcher should've just killed you."

My hands curl into fists at my side. "Shut up."

"Lionel was granted riches and longevity," Daisy continues, ignoring the brief interruption as she moves over to us with an armful of items in her hand. Carefully, she places a bowl, grinder, and herbs down onto the flat stone surface and gets to work throwing the dried leaves into the bowl. "In return for bestowing such gifts, Zarzuz told Lionel that he must spread the word of his existence. With the power of prayer granting him strength, Zarzuz promised he could do much for those who loved him. Lionel happily obliged, spreading the news of this new god around Briar Glen. Thus, the start of the Zarazuzians."

"No, no, no!" the man wailed.

Daisy pulls out matches from her back pocket and hands them over to Owen.

"Light the tiki torches please."

Owen takes them without a word and moves to do as he's told.

"As High Priest, or the voice of Zarzuz, Lionel delivered many messages from their beloved god. One message was that Zarzuz wanted more from his followers. Another was that prayers and donations were alright, but if they want to be truly blessed, they must give Zarzuz something much more valuable than their time or savings. For those that want eternal blessings, you were required to offer up blood. Thus, the start of human sacrifices in Briar Glen."

"Shut up! Bitch, bitch, bitch!" the man cries out. His movements are growing stronger. Whatever Daisy had drugged him with, it's definitely wearing off.

Daisy shimmies off her jeans.

"Daisy! What are you doing?" Owen gasps.

She shoots him a wink as she leaves them in a puddle at her booted feet. I eat up the sight of her bare legs and cotton thong like a starving man.

Daisy climbs onto the flat stone altar, then removes her shirt. My entire body locks up in horror at the thick scarring that mars her skin. It's the same symbol as the one on the tombstone last night. The sign of Zarzuz. As I stare, Daisy tosses her shirt behind her, where it flutters to the ground and is immediately forgotten. Standing tall in just her thong and thin bra, she stares down at the man before her.

"Are you ready, Jeff?"

The man, Jeff, tries to spit at her. His loogie flies up only to come back down and hit him in the face. With a laugh, Daisy sinks to her knees, straddling him. Jeff's struggles become harder. When he nearly bucks her off, I step forward and land a fist against his cheek.

"*Oh*," he whimpers, sagging.

Pushing through my shock at the rune on her skin, I reach up and help steady Daisy, who makes herself comfortable on his lap.

"Thanks." Daisy reaches for her bowl and turns to Owen. "Light a match and throw it in here please. Kingston, do you have the camera?"

I glance over to King and watch as he steps closer, lifting up a polaroid. Jesus, where do you even find those anymore? His mask has been pushed up where it rests on top of his head and his eyes are trained on Daisy. His gaze hasn't left her face once this evening, not even when we stepped out of the woods. And he hovers even closer than the rest of us.

The guy has it bad.

On Daisy's other side, Owen comes over and lights the herbs in her bowl. It doesn't take long for the smell of sage, lavender, and other herbs I can't place to fill our small space.

"The sacrificing of children continued all the way up until I was born," Daisy continues after a moment.

"Why'd they stop?" Wyatt asks softly, riveted by the story.

I don't want to hear her say it. The words don't belong in her mouth.

"Because a greater sacrifice had surfaced," I answer, taking everyone by surprise. "Zarzuz had foretold that his bride would arrive on the night of a blood moon, on the thirteenth day during the harvest month a hundred years after his initial contact with Lionel. And when Daisy was born—"

"—she was born on Friday the thirteenth in October," Wyatt finishes, putting the pieces together himself.

Nodding, I add, "Daisy was Zarzuz's Chosen One."

Daisy's eyes land on me, surprise lighting her face up.

"How the hell do you know that, Dre?" Wyatt asks sharply.

I can't pull my eyes off Daisy's face as the light starts to dim, and wariness creeps into her beautiful face. Not wanting her to latch onto that feeling, I answer quickly.

"My parents were involved in the cult. When I confronted my parents that night after you fell, my mother told me everything." I suppress a flinch as gasps of surprise pepper the clearing.

Daisy doesn't gasp. She holds my gaze, her expression shutting down completely. My heart leaps up to my throat.

No! She can't pull away from me. Not when I've just gotten her back. *Not ever.*

"I didn't know before then, I swear it." God, I hope she can hear my sincerity. I push up my mask and stare into her face. "My parents weren't there that night, but they knew what was going to happen. They got upset that I interrupted the ceremony. Together, my mother and father beat me for days, and those beatings got worse when I tried telling other adults about what went down. All four of us went to everyone we could but no one would listen to us—"

"That's because they all knew," Jeff croaks, interrupting me. "More than half the town are followers of the Mighty Zarzuz. No one was to speak of the Chosen One."

That explains a lot. Wyatt and Owen glare at Jeff but Kingston and Daisy keep their attention latched onto me.

"I tried fighting for justice, Daisy. I really did. And I never would've stopped but my parents decided to silence me. It wasn't as dramatic as what Francis did to King, but it was effective. They pulled me from school, shoved me into that stupid little closest under the stairs, and kept me there for a year." I swallow hard as I recall the fear and loneliness I'd felt in that tiny space. "When I say they didn't let me out, I mean it. They gave me a bucket to piss in, fed me gruel when they felt like it, and their beatings continued until I *finally* caved and promised to stay quiet about everything. They probably would've kept me there until I was eighteen but then my father died, and I think my mother was ready to focus on other things."

Wyatt and Owen gasp. Kingston says nothing and Daisy... She frowns.

"I should've kept fighting but you were gone and I... All I wanted to do was get out of that damn closet and then eventually, Briar Glen." Shame causes my words to be stilted. My chest prickles with tension as the emotions from my past try to simmer up.

Daisy nods slowly, her gaze finally peeling off my face. Though she isn't wearing her mask, I can't quite read what she's thinking. It leaves me feeling anxious and off-kilter.

"Alright, so I think I understand everything," Owen hedges after a tense silence. "So what are we doing here tonight? Sacrificing this guy in the name of Zarzuz in your stead or something?"

Daisy doesn't answer right away. Her eyes are trained on Jeff who groans and whimpers softly. Kingston reaches up and squeezes her leg. She flinches at the contact. Kingston doesn't let go and after a second, Daisy relaxes.

She licks her bottom lip before she answers. "Jeff here will be sacrificed to Zarzuz's enemy: Lilith."

Jeff gasps in horror. The sound causes Daisy to chuckle.

"The Zarzuzians believe she's his mortal enemy. That the only thing standing between Zarzuz and them is her. So, I figured why not play into their stupid little ideology?"

Wyatt let's out a single, surprised, ha. "Now I understand

why you burned her name into the middle of town. The Zarzuzians' enemy is within their midst."

"But that doesn't explain who this is?" I nudge my head toward the man beneath her who is struggling frantically again.

"The High Priest has four Blessed Priests beneath him who help him run the cult. Jeff Herring here, is the son of George Herring, one of the appointed leaders. Unbeknownst to anyone else, Jeff also happened to be a friend of The Butcher of Briar Glen. He would come to visit every so often and use The Butcher's house as his own playground for demented games." Lifting her mask so that he can see it, she asks, "Recognize any of the names of these women? You should, since you helped them *stay* missing."

"They were nobodies—"

"No, no," she cuts him off. "Don't waste your last words on dismissing these women." Shaking her head, she looks around at us and continues. "What I have planned for Briar Glen is both dangerous and beautiful. It will collapse in on itself by the time I'm done. To make sure Briar Glen can't rebuild, I'm going after each and every Blessed Priest until only their High Priest is left, and then I'll kill him too. Mayor Tobias was first, George is next. Using Jeff here is twofold: I get revenge for the women he wronged, *and* George Herring will have his only son ripped from him by Zarzuz's very own enemy."

Kingston shakes his head once. "You mean *we*."

"King's right. You have us now," I agree with a nod.

"My father will kill you," Jeff grunts out.

"I highly doubt that." Daisy shrugs. "He's next, so you won't be in hell by yourself for very long."

"Fuck you!"

"Cut off the head of the snake and stir up some trouble in Briar Glen? I think that's doable," Wyatt says, grabbing her attention. "It's only fair since they tried to tear us apart."

Owen lets out a shaky laugh. "Fair, and a little crazy. Whatever you need Daisy, all you have to do is ask."

Daisy nods before slipping her mask back into place. She turns her head in my direction and lifts her hand to reach out for me.

"Come help me then."

I'm moving before she finishes speaking. Taking her hand, she helps me up onto the altar.

"Sit behind me and help me send a message. Maybe, if we're lucky and she exists, Lilith will bless us with the strength to see my plan through," she says as I straddle Jeff's legs right behind her. I take a shaky breath when I realize how perfectly her hips sit against my pelvis. Using both hands, she lifts the hunting knife above her head. "Drake, your hands on top of mine, please. We're going to aim straight for the heart. We'll need a decent amount of force."

It's been a few years since I've killed someone. My heart slams against my ribcage as a sick excitement rushes through my veins. The absolute delight lighting up my insides isn't good for anyone. It's hard to turn this dangerous part of me off when it's just me. But having Daisy, the woman I've hungered for all these years, egging me on while in my arms? Oh, I could be a very deranged but happy man at this rate.

I reach up, which isn't very far considering how short she is, and allow my hands to cover hers and the hilt of the knife completely.

"You won't get away with this. They'll kill you! They'll fucking kill you," Jeff whimpers, tears sliding down his swollen face.

"Jeff, if you could look at the camera and say cheese, I'd appreciate it." Daisy's body trembles as she giggles. "For the rest of you, masks back on."

Quickly, I pull my mask back on as Kingston raises the camera. Just as my hands wrap around Daisy's once more, there's a flash from the polaroid. It must be Daisy's cue because she moves.

I feel the tug as her hands move to plunge the knife downward. Moving with her, together we sink the knife deep into Jeff's chest. His cry of pain dies off in a wheeze. He twitches a few times beneath us as he chokes up blood. I stare at Jeff's face in wonder over Daisy's shoulder. A sick smile tugging my lips upward. This man hurt others— how can I even consider feeling bad for him?

There're two more flashes of light as Kingston takes pictures.

Against me, Daisy's back trembles again as she laughs loudly. I smile at her viciousness. She's gone mad in her absence. But, I suppose if we're going to stop a whole town, a little crazy is exactly what we're going to need.

"You know something?" Owen asks, watching close by. "Lilith is supposed to be the Mother of Demons, meaning she rules them. They flock to her when she calls for them, and they do her bidding."

Wyatt doesn't drag his gaze away from the man beneath us. "What's your point?"

"Daisy is *our* Lilith. We're your demons, Daisy," Owen chuckles. "You summoned us to help you and here we are, ready to do whatever you need of us."

In my arms, Daisy's body relaxes.

"My demons?" Her head tilts to the side as she considers this. After a moment, her body trembles again as her amusement spills past her lips. "I kind of love that."

"We'll be the worst kind," I whisper into her ear. Still holding her hands, I twist the blade in Jeff's chest. The flash of the camera goes off once more. "Always make sure they're dead."

"Of course." I can't see her eyes, but I know they're rolling.

My smile comes easily. Relaxing my hold on the blade, I look at the others. My eyes stop on Wyatt who's inching a little closer to Jeff. He's staring at the body intensely and clearly sporting a semi. My smile shifts into a grimace, "Owen, keep Wyatt back."

Wyatt looks up at me and tilts his masked head, "What? Why?"

Owen grabs the back of his jacket and tugs him away, laughing. "Do you really have to ask?"

"What's wrong? Is Wy squeamish?" Daisy asks, turning to look over her shoulder at me.

I grin behind my mask. "We've recently discovered that Wyatt is *overly* fond of corpses."

"There's nothing wrong with an interest in death."

"Nope, nothing wrong with it at all." I nod, though she can't see it. "But if you don't want his DNA all over that body, keeping him away from dead things should be your top priority."

"What are you talking about, Dre?"

"That particular demon gets his rocks off to dead people."

There's a pause as Daisy processes this information. It's short lived. Her head rocks backward, hitting my chest, as she bursts into a wild bout of laughter.

"Wyatt, I'll get you a corpse to fuck. It just can't be this one!" she calls as Owen pulls him further away.

Wyatt sputters just as wildly as he had this morning when we'd uncovered his little fetish, which only draws a laugh from me.

"Alright, let's finish up here. Drake, Kingston, will you help me paint my body with Jeff's blood?"

There is nothing that could prepare me for my body's response to her words. My dick grows hard faster than I ever thought possible, while my breath leaves me in a sudden whoosh. I scoot back, hoping like hell Daisy didn't notice the way my dick tried to impale itself into her ass. Swallowing hard, I manage to growl out,

"You don't have to ask me twice."

21

Daisy

Hiding my car and slipping back into Briar Glen in the back of Drake's small pickup truck takes time. A lot of it.

On a high from a fresh kill, however, my exhaustion doesn't hit me until we arrive at Wyatt's house several hours later. After a short fight about who would clean up first, I'm pushed into the guest bathroom and King is taken, I suppose, to the one in Wyatt's room. I know I should be relieved at the sight of a shower. I'll be able to wash Jeff's blood off me along with all the sweat and grime from the day. Soap, hot water, and water pressure harder than a drain spout? I should be thrilled.

Yet I simply stare at it.

I guess I take too long to get moving because I'm still standing on the other side of the door when there's a knock. When I don't respond, it opens a crack.

"Daisy?"

"Yeah?" The single word wobbles. Wyatt must've heard because there's a moment of hesitation before the door opens the rest of the way and he slips inside the bathroom to join me.

The door clicks shut behind him. Wyatt takes one look at me before moving toward the shower stall. He reaches over, turns the water on, and then turns halfway around.

"I got you, Daisy. Come here."

My bottom lip trembles as the tension in my chest eases. It's such a stupid reaction, but the fact someone else has taken the first step makes the rest of the process more doable. Clenching my jaw to keep the emotions back, I move forward. Wyatt's hand wraps around my wrist, effectively halting my short trek to his shower, and he pulls me in close to his chest. When I look up, I find him frowning down at me.

"Are you ok?" His moss green eyes search my face as his eyebrows furrow.

Ok? Am I *ok*? Sure, I guess, physically. But mentally? Emotionally? No, no I'm not *ok*. Being surrounded by my guys again has somehow made breathing both easier and harder.

"I'm not alone anymore," I whisper, knowing he won't understand. "And I'm glad. But I'm not used to... to *this*." I nuzzle my face into his shirt. "It's a lot. It's overwhelming."

There's a pause before suddenly Wyatt is crushing me against his body. Any breathing, either hard or easy, is halted all together.

"God, I can't *imagine* how alone you've been all these years or what being surrounded by people for any amount of time must feel like, but god, Daisy. You'll need to get used to this, to us. We're not going anywhere," he says into my hair before pressing a kiss to the top of my head.

I wrap my arms around his body and hug Wyatt back, not caring that he's crushing me to death. My isolation was essential to not only my survival, but to others', after I escaped The Butcher. Even when things started getting better, I didn't linger around too many people. Isolation was both necessary and depressing.

Wyatt loosens his hold with a sigh and steps back so he can look at me again.

"How is it that someone can look even more beautiful with blood painted across their face?" he asks, his mouth pulling up into a half smile.

I snort, my face warming as I look away. "I'm wasting your hot water."

Wyatt snorts. "I'll live, and so will the others."

He steps to the side, moving toward the door. The minute he does, I can feel the trepidation rolling back in overwhelming waves.

"Wait!" I halfway reach out to grab him but stop and let my hand, and gaze, drop. My face burns with humiliation. Why is such a small task so difficult?

There's a pause before his feet come into view. "Daisy, do you want me to stay?"

Swallowing down how stupid I feel, I nod. "Yes, please."

"Alright, I'll be right here." The patience in his voice brings tears to my eyes. "I'll turn around so you can—"

I let out a tired laugh, looking up at him.

"Wy, you watched me practically get naked before I murdered someone tonight. I haven't gotten modest between then and now."

He smiles before leaning back against the counter. With a deep breath, I start to undress. I don't get far. As I pull my shirt off, I stumble as exhaustion makes me dizzy.

"Woah, there." Wyatt catches my elbow. "Here, let me."

He grabs the hem of my shirt and pulls it over my head with a gentle jerk. I'm grateful he doesn't mention the large scar on my body. He doesn't even glance at it. He must've gotten his eyeful earlier. I relax as he removes my bralette. Wyatt moves to kneel and grabs the button to my jeans. Seeing him on his knees does something to me. A shiver of awareness cuts through my fatigue. Rather than use his shoulders to steady myself, my hands move to his hair, where they sink in.

Wyatt's hands pause, my jeans coming to a rest at my knees. He looks up at me slowly. With his jaw clenched tight and his green eyes ablaze, he looks just as hungry as I feel. Oh hell, this isn't what we need to be doing. As much as I want to explore this possibility with Wyatt, I don't want to take advantage. He's just trying to help, not seduce me.

Licking my lips nervously, I pull my hands away. "Sorry."

His nostrils flare before he returns to the task at hand and shoves my pants the rest of the way down. I step out of them, and then my underwear.

"Come on," he orders, pulling me by my hand over to the steaming water. He helps me in and then lets go of my hand to slide the door shut.

The moment the hot water hits me, I groan. How have I lived without this for so long? Wyatt's water pressure is set up to where it feels like I'm under a waterfall. And the heat? It's scalding. Can it burn away the past? Sear away the nightmares woven into my psyche? I close my eyes and tilt my head up to the water.

A second later, the glass door opens, and a gust of cold air hits me. As I pull my head out from under the stream of water, Wyatt steps into the shower with me. I bite my bottom lip to keep from gasping. Wyatt has always been lean, but there's more muscle than I thought coating his body. His arms are toned, as are his legs. His chest is well defined and there is a thin trail of light brown hair that starts from his belly button and runs down to join the patch of hair around his erection, but other than that, his body is smooth and hairless.

And that erection... His dick is veiny, red, and straining toward me. I itch to reach out and wrap my hand around him. Instead, I look up, meeting his gaze.

"In case you haven't heard it recently, you look good, Wy."

Wyatt chuckles. "Turn around, Daisy, before you inflate my ego."

I do as I'm told with a giggle.

"I'm going to start with your hair, alright?" he says, and the sound of a bottle popping open follows. I nod.

His fingers dive into my hair, starting at my scalp. I groan as his short nails scratch gently at the base of my roots. Wyatt takes his time shampooing and conditioning my hair. Either I'm super dirty, or he's just enjoying the task. I can't tell. It doesn't matter. I love the magic he's creating, and I never want it to stop.

As he works the tangles from my hair, the muscles in my body start to unwind. I reach up, bracing my hands on the shower wall as knots I didn't even know I had all throughout my body start to loosen. When was the last time I felt safe enough to relax? I'm not necessarily safe here at Wyatt's house. I'm sure there are neighbors watching his every move, but here, in the confines of his shower, in the presence of one the men I adored, I feel secure.

What would it be like to be held in Wyatt's arms?

When Wyatt's done rinsing my hair, he twists it up into a bun and moves to grab the loofa next. With a deep breath, I risk finding out. I lean back against Wyatt's chest and catch his hand before it gets to the loofa.

"Daisy?"

Wyatt allows me to guide his hand down to rest on my lower abdomen. "Will you touch me?"

I lack experience in seduction. There hasn't been much cause for that particular skill. There's been no need. By the time I feel down to mess around, I'm shitfaced, as is my potential partner.

Now I wish I had learned a little. Especially when Wyatt's whole body stiffens, his hand freezing against me.

"*Daisy,*" Wyatt groans. He moves to pull away, but I hold him tighter.

"Please, Wyatt?" As I press into his chest, his erection sits firmly against my lower back.

There's a long pause. That doesn't feel like a good sign. I bite my bottom lip and hold his hand tight.

"You're making it hard to be a gentleman, Daisy." Wyatt huffs, his hand suddenly pressing into me on its own rather than me holding him there.

I'm not going to ask again. As desperate as I am to assuage the primal hunger coiling within me with one of the boys I've loved for so long, I don't want to ruin what we have. If friendship is all that he can offer, I'll take it gladly.

"I have a vicious appetite, Daisy," Wyatt mutters into my ear before nipping at the tip, startling me. "I want certain things and... I don't want to hurt you."

Certain things? I frown, thinking back to the conversation from earlier. "Oh, I see. Do you want me to play dead or something? Would that help?"

Wyatt sucks in a sharp breath. "No! It's not that. *That* particular interest is a one-off thing. I've never actually done anything with a, ah, well, you know." His soft laugh has an edge to it. "I just..." his hand slides down on its own accord and he cups my mound. "I've wanted you for so long and there's so much I want to do, but you're tired, Daisy. Do you even realize you're trembling?"

"It's not from being tired."

Wyatt's hand slides further between my legs, his fingers moving through my folds. We both gasp.

"Fuck, Daisy, you're so slick. So wet," His mouth slides up and down my neck slowly. I spread my legs wider for him. He chuckles, his chest trembling against my back. "Look at you, opening up for me like a flower. Are you sure you want this?

I've *dreamed* of this since we were young—you quivering against me."

Two of his fingers slip inside of my pussy as his palm presses against my clit. I groan. A heavy shiver rushes through me despite the hot water cascading over my body.

"Tell me, Daisy. I need to hear that you're absolutely sure," Wyatt presses, his hand freezing. "Because if we do this, there's no end in sight. I won't ever be through with you. Do you hear me?"

I squeeze my eyes shut, carefully snuffing out the wild blast of hope for a happy future bursting in my chest. There will be an ending, eventually. But until then? I can give Wyatt that.

"Yes, I hear you. Please, Wy, touch me."

He groans into my ear. "Please, huh?"

His fingers start pumping in and out of me, his palm pressing back up against my clit as he works. I let out a breathy sigh that I immediately suck back in when Wyatt's other hand comes up to roll and tweak my left nipple. At the same time, Wyatt plants delicate kisses along my neck. I lean more weight against him. He doesn't seem to mind. Reaching back with one arm, I wrap it around his neck and sigh as he finger-fucks me.

"Can you open your legs a little wider, pretty flower?" I do and he hums in approval. "Good girl."

As a reward, he inserts a third finger. Unable to stop myself, my hips thrust in time with his hand.

"I knew you'd be wet for me if I ever had this chance with you," he murmurs between kisses. "But I've barely touched you and your body is weeping around my hand. It's better than any fantasy I used to have of just the two of us."

Mustering up the ability to speak, I whisper, "You thought about me like this often?"

I can feel his hum as his lips vibrate softly against my skin along my shoulder.

"All the time. In my dreams, you were mine to do whatever I

wanted with, and you were a good little flower, taking it in stride." He pinches my nipple hard, causing me to gasp. "I wonder if you will be as amenable in real life? Would you let me tease your petals, let me pluck them until you scream? How far would you let me go, pretty flower?"

"As far as you wanted," I breathe as the tension coils between my legs.

"Truly? Or are you just telling me what I want to hear?"

"Yes, whatever you wanted, Wy."

His hum of approval vibrates down his arm. "Such a generous flower."

Wyatt's thumb brushes against my clit, circling it gently. The stimulation is all I need for my body to fall apart. I cry out softly as an electrical current courses through my veins. There's no stopping my hips as they jerk against Wyatt's hand. My arm around his neck shoots out to re-brace myself against the wall as I gasp through the aftermath.

"T-thank you," I stammer.

Wyatt pulls his hand free from between my legs, only so that he can rest both on my hips and turn me around to face him.

"Thank you? For what? Caring for my flower?" Before I can respond, Wyatt's lips crash down on mine. I moan into it as I grind my hips against his erection. He breaks the kiss and says, "Who says we're done?"

He sinks to his knees, his eyes never leaving my face.

"I need to taste you, Daisy." He pulls my hips closer to his face and presses his nose right against my clit. I gasp as he takes a deep breath in. "Good god…" His voice trails off as he tips his head forward and licks my arousal. I cry out as his tongue laps at my core then slides up to tease my oversensitive clit.

"Wyatt!"

One hand slides between my legs and his fingers slip deep into my pussy to pump vigorously in and out of me. I lean back against the wall and stare down at the boy turned man, and memorize this new face. This *handsome* face as he passionately devours me. I've watched him from afar for years, but seeing him up close? It's a whole different experience.

My body trembles and my nipples harden as the pleasure starts to mount once more.

I reach down to run my fingers through his hair, savoring the sensation of the slow moving tidal wave that's gathering in my lower abdomen. As focused as I am on his face, I don't realize where his other hand has gone until a finger probes my asshole.

My whole body stiffens with surprise. Wyatt pulls away from my clit but continues to pump his fingers in and out of me.

"Come on pretty flower, open up for me," he says, his voice breathless. "I know you can do it. Just breathe and relax." From his knees, he looks up to search my face. "I want all of you."

His finger continues to tease and probe until I relax enough to allow him to enter. When he does slide in, it's... strange. Not unpleasant but definitely different.

"There you go. What a good girl you are, Daisy, listening so beautifully," Wyatt praises with a sultry smile. "Now I need you to cum for me. Can you do that for me? God, I can't wait to feel you come apart again. When you cum, you radiate, do you know that? It's like looking at the sun, you shine so brightly. You were made to be used like this, you know that?"

Am I? I'm not so sure, but I allow his words to wrap around me in a cocoon of delight and fantasy as his mouth returns to suck and tease my clit. With his fingers pumping in and out of both my pussy and asshole, his mouth latched onto me as he suckles, it doesn't take me long to find my second release.

My hips grind against Wyatt's face as I groan loudly through my orgasm. As I cum, I look down to find Wyatt staring up at me, his green eyes watching me unravel.

Oh hell... A full body shiver ripples through me and saps what energy I have left. As my legs give out, Wyatt pulls away, catches me as he stands, and lifts me up. Instinctually, I wrap my legs around his waist. With a contented sigh, I sag against him.

"No, no, no, none of that, little flower. I need you to cum again for me," Wyatt says before kissing me thoroughly.

Another? I couldn't possibly. My eyelids are already dropping, and my body feels well used. Wyatt pulls away.

"You can give me one more, I know you can. Tell me you'll cum again, Daisy," he pushes as he kisses my chest, nipping at my nipple.

"Wy, I don't know. I don't think—"

"Yes you can, Daisy. Let me find your limits for you. Let me feast on your body until you're so overwhelmed that you don't know your name, that you can only call out mine," he begs. "Let me enjoy those pretty sounds you make. I haven't quite etched them into my memories yet."

His mouth goes back to my nipple. He teases it with his tongue and sucks hard. My breath catches. Without even being consciously aware of it, my hips settle over his erection and roll, teasing the head of him at my entrance. Wyatt groans.

"Is that a yes?" he presses, pulling his mouth away from my breast to look up at me in earnest. "Tell me you trust me."

My answer comes without hesitation. "Yes, and I trust you, Wy."

"There's a good girl."

With one swift jerk of his hips, Wyatt's erection slides straight into me. And keeps going. I stiffen in surprise as he slides deep into my body. My pussy clenches around him hungrily, pleased with this friction and fullness he's brought on.

"*Wy.*"

"Fuck, Daisy. You're so fucking perfect. I can feel your body holding me here, like I belong," he hisses through clenched teeth. "This was always meant to be."

Maybe. Or maybe not. I'm not a romantic by any means, but his words warm me from the inside out and it drives my body into action. Wyatt presses me against the shower wall, his hips thrusting upward, driving me wild with his hungry, animalistic fucking. My breathing becomes erratic, and my heart is flying by the seat of its pants as Wy takes me to new heights. I can feel the tension coiling between my legs.

I squeeze my eyes shut, blocking out the wave of happiness that threatens to overwhelm me in the moment. This can't, and won't, last but while I'm with my boys, I'm going to savor each moment, touch, and word we share.

"Come on, pretty flower," Wyatt mutters, his mouth skimming up my neck until he's kissing my jawline. I lean down and meet his lips hungrily.

When we kiss, my body unravels again. I bare down on Wyatt's dick as I cry out into his mouth. He eats up the sound before pulling his mouth away.

"I knew you had another one in you, Daze. You've done so well tonight," he praises through clenched teeth. He pulls out of me just before he finds his release. His cum splatters against my stomach. "You're mine now, Daisy." As he finishes, he leans his head forward until our foreheads touch. "I never stopped loving you. I never will."

Tears gather in my eyes. This is too much. Tired, well used, and emotionally spent, all I can muster is to bury my face in Wyatt's neck, hoping that he understands that what I feel for him goes beyond words. It goes for all of them. King, Owen, and Drake too.

"Come on, pretty flower," Wyatt says after a moment, holding me tight since I've used up all my energy and now just hang limply between him and the shower wall. "Let's get you cleaned up."

Wyatt's version of cleaned up, it turns out, involves two more orgasms, a soaped up loofa that scrubs me until I'm practically shining, and a wonderfully gentle towel-dry session. I'm barely awake as he squeezes the water out of my hair and when he carries me to a guest room. I think he helps me into a shirt but I'm so tired, I don't really notice. When Wy places me down onto the softest mattress ever, I'm ready to fall into oblivion.

"There you go, Daisy." His lips brush against my temple. "I'll bring your backpack and stuff in here so you have everything you need. Sleep tight."

I hum but don't respond.

Just as I'm about to succumb to the darkness behind my eyelids and drift off, the bed abruptly dips.

Opening my eyelids halfway, I find Kingston sliding into the bed with me. He comes up behind me and lays on his side before pulling me into his chest. I snuggle closer to him, feeling safer than I have in a long time.

22

Owen

I don't sleep at all that night.

Not that there was much night left by the time my head hits the pillow. I should try at least to close my eyes. Who knows what Daisy will have us do next? Yet sleep eludes me. Watching a man being killed, cutting him open, then painting my girl's body with his blood certainly doesn't make falling asleep easy. It was the first time I'd been up close to such an event. While he deserved it, I can feel the guilt trying to tease the edges of my conscience.

But that's not the only reason I can't fall asleep.

Daisy's here. Under *this* roof, not twenty feet away from me. It's too hard to believe. So hard, in fact, that I can't shake the need to keep an eye on her. Sleeping soundly in the other room, all I really need to do is peek in to see her. But why do that when I have a camera set up in there? Pulling up that feed and just having it readily available to stare at is so much easier and more discreet.

It's that logic that wins out over getting rest. So I stay up, watching Kingston hold Daisy in his arms while the two of them sleep.

It's probably wrong. No, wait, scratch that. I *know* it's wrong. The same way I knew it was wrong to watch those other women for all those years. It's an invasion of privacy. I should've told Daisy about the cameras before she passed out. Or at the very least I should've mentioned them to Kingston while he laid there for a while, simply watching our girl before he drifted off to sleep.

Neither of them would probably care about the cameras.

I mean, Wyatt clearly doesn't mind. He knows about them, yet he still decided to fuck Daisy in the shower. He knew I would be watching these feeds at some point. Did he do it for my benefit? Probably not but… What if he did? I pull *that* video up for the hundredth time and replay it. My dick is nearly raw with how many times I've gotten myself off to the two of them. It doesn't stop me now though as I palm my erection.

With the volume turned off, I can't hear what he says to her, but I can see the way he touches her and how her face lights up each time he helps her find her release. By her third orgasm, my balls are tensing and I'm cumming with Daisy and Wyatt.

With a sigh, I clean up my mess with my shirt and toss it to the floor.

That was the last time. It's a promise I need to keep. If I want Daisy, I can't hide behind books or a computer any longer.

Despite how fucking hot it is.

I push my laptop to the other side of the bed and force myself to close my eyes.

"You fucking sicko."

My eyes fly open at the sound of Drake's voice. As I sit up, I find the big guy glaring at me, his arms crossed over his chest. How long have I been asleep? It can't have been longer than a few minutes.

"W-what?" I blink the sleep away and yawn.

"You jerked off to King and Daisy all night? Jesus man, what's wrong with you?" he demands. I turn to see my laptop still open, the feed with the King and Daisy still up, and, to my horror, my dick still hanging out of my pants.

"No! I didn't—"

"Whatever," Drake interrupts. "Wy and I need your help with something."

"Yeah, sure, ok," I nod and slide out of bed.

As Drake stomps toward the door, he grumbles, "I'm waking Kingston."

The minute he leaves, I shove my soft dick back into my pants and grab a clean shirt from my bag. Drake's coming out of the other guest room with Kingston in tow when I slip out into the hallway. I stifle my embarrassment at being caught and shoot Kingston a smile. Hopefully Drake keeps what he saw to himself.

Given how the only time he opens his mouth is to hackle Wyatt, I don't have high hopes for that.

Kingston doesn't return the smile, though he does give me a sort of half nod before following Drake. I shiver as I trail behind him. This new Kingston is so different from the guy I knew. I have a feeling that the one in front of me is capable of anything. Good or evil.

A perfect match for Daisy given how feral she seems to have become.

Me? I'll do whatever Daisy wants of me. Even if that means climbing up onto an altar and stabbing a guy. But if I could *avoid* that, I will. Drake on the other hand—he hadn't hesitated last night. I look past King to stare at the back of Drake's head. He's different too. Quiet and watchful. His behavior reminds me of a predator just waiting to strike.

We move through the house and into the garage where Wyatt is waiting for us. He looks away from his whiteboard, his brows pinched together in thought.

"Good, you're all awake. I wanted to take care of this while Daisy was still sleeping," he says and looks back at his board. I come up beside him and stare at both the old and new information he has added.

Francis Winslow's name is at the top, written in all red letters. His name was there before, but now, beneath his name are four lines, connecting him to other members of the Zarzuzian cult. Tobias Bower's and George Herring's names have been added, along with two question marks that represent the unknown Blessed Priests. At the very bottom of the board, away from everything else, is Oliver Grayman's name.

"We know these three are part of Zarzuz's fan club," Wyatt says, pointing. "I left Jeff's name off because he was only an extension of the main group. I'd like to see if Daisy will give us the names of the other two, but for now, let's just work with them."

"Work with them how?" I frown.

Wyatt runs his fingers through his tousled hair. "Daisy wants to slaughter the town, and I'm fine with that—"

Drake snorts. "Of course you are."

I laugh but then Drake shoots me a dark look. "Don't get too much of a kick from his perversion. You got your own sick shit going on."

Wyatt's brow raises in curiosity, but I jump back into the initial conversation before we go down that route.

"What do you have in mind, Wy?"

Drake smirks as Wyatt turns his attention back to the board. "I want to see if we could use your skills, Owen, to crack into their personal affairs, find hard evidence of their involvement and start collecting it. When we're done here in Briar Glen, we'll send it to the proper authorities."

I nod even as I frown. "I can do that, but you know it won't clear her, or us, if we get caught, right?"

"That's not what this is about," Wyatt scowls. "This is about making sure the world *knows* what this place has been up to."

King nods in approval before adding, "And we're not going to get caught."

Wyatt blinks, confused. Frustrated, I shake my head,

"He said no one's getting arrested." I glare at Wyatt. "Did you completely forget everything Daisy taught us?"

Wyatt's face turns bright red. "I remember a little, but I stayed up last night for a bit and watched a few videos to brush off the dust." He clears his throat. "How do *you* remember it?"

"I took it as an elective in college." So I could keep those solitary moments of Daisy teaching me sign language alive. "And made sure to practice after I graduated. You need to re-learn this shit and fast," I snap. "That's not fair to Kingston."

Drake doesn't say anything, but he does give a sharp nod.

"I said I'm already on it, Owen," Wyatt rolls his eyes but then turns to Kingston. "If you don't mind just going a little slower until I get better, I'd appreciate it."

Kingston rolls his eyes but nods. With that settled, Wyatt returns his attention back to the whiteboard.

"Alright, so don't get caught and dig up secrets, I can do that." I tilt my head as I race through the different ways I can scavenge for data. "The latter will depend on if they keep their secrets digital. I can tell you right now, Francis Winslow doesn't have anything on him. I've tried looking into him over the past few years. The guy presents as squeaky clean."

Kingston's expression shifts to a sneer, directed at a man who's not present. "My dad is old school. Everything of any value, he keeps in a safe in his office. I doubt that's changed since he forced me out all those years ago."

I start to translate for Wyatt but he cuts me off with a glare. "I got most of that. His dad has a safe of information, thanks."

"Think we could break into his house and get to the safe?" Drake asks me.

I scoff. "Get what? The stuff inside the safe? I doubt it. I'm a tech guy, not a trained spy that can crack safe codes. Any chance you know the combination to it, King?"

Kingston shakes his head.

"Ok, scratch Francis off our list. For now, Owen, can you look into George Herring and Tobias Bower?" Wyatt asks, redirecting the conversation. "With one dead and the other about to be, we should collect what we can before the police wipe evidence of their wrongdoing away—if they haven't already with Tobias. We'll start compiling what we can during our downtime."

I nod. "No problem."

"Why is Oliver Grayman's name up there?" Drake asks, drawing my attention back to Wyatt's theory board. The Butcher of Briar Glen's name is low on the board with a question mark beside it.

"Because I don't know how he fits into all of this." Wyatt folds his arms over his chest. "The only connection to the cult is between him and George Herring's son, Jeff. What's his importance in all of this?"

"He has no other association to the Zarzuzians other than the fact that he created the monster that would destroy the cult he wanted so desperately to be a part of."

I jump at the sound of Daisy's voice. Turning around, I find her walking toward us, looking just as tired as she did last night.

"You should be sleeping, it's early yet," I tell her, concerned at the dark circles under her eyes and trying hard as hell not to stare at her bare legs since all she's wearing is my shirt I'd happily given to her the night before.

She shoots me a small smile as she comes to stand beside me. "I don't tend to sleep for long periods of time."

That much is clear. "Why not?"

"Because," she shrugs. "If I allow myself to really sleep, I get nightmares. In any case, I feel pretty rested."

Kingston reaches down and takes her hand. The causal ease of the motion causes jealousy to tighten in my chest. *I* want to take Daisy's hand and hold her. My hand twitches as if to take her free one.

"Nightmares are no excuse. You need to sleep to have a clear head," Drake snaps as he scowls at her.

"Ignore him, he's grumpy this morning," I mutter in a stage-whisper. Drake opens his mouth but whatever he wants to say is cut off as Wyatt asks,

"So, Oliver had nothing to do with the cult?"

Daisy presses her lips together as she stares at him. Her shoulders stiffen slowly, even while she releases a heavy sigh.

"Oliver knew about the Zarzuzians and desperately wanted in. Unfortunately for him, because he wasn't from Briar Glen, he wasn't allowed to join. When he found me washed up on the shore, Oliver knew who I was since he tracked the cult's activity closely, and he was thrilled," Daisy continues. "I was his lucky break. Oliver thought if he returned me to the Zarzuzians, they would welcome him into their group with open arms. Rather than tell the cult right away though, Oliver tended to my recovery and gloated that he would one day lead the Zarzuzian's to glory."

Washed up on shore... I cringe. From that fall, the types of injuries she would have received would've been extreme. There was probably no chance for her to run or fight back when she found out that the man who saved her was really a monster.

My stomach churns.

"How long did it take to recover?" Wyatt asks, his brows pinched together as he sinks deep into thought. "Certainly not five years, right?"

Daisy shakes her head. "No. At some point along the way, Oliver realized how much power he held. He loved knowing he had one up on the cult." Her gaze shifts away from us as it becomes unfocused. "He also loved having an audience to his madness and a toy to constantly play with."

Her whole body flinches as she sucks in a sharp breath.

Fuck it, how can I not touch her right now? I wrap my arm around her shoulders. Daisy rests her head against me, silent as she gathers her thoughts.

Or struggles to escape them.

"Hey, if this is too hard for you to talk about, we don't have to know," I assure her. "All I care about is the future."

Daisy blinks rapidly, her gaze refocusing on us. "It's the past that drives what happens moving forward."

I want to tell her it doesn't have to be this way. That we could stop and start anew somewhere else. But there must be a bloodthirsty part of me deep down inside somewhere because those words never leave my mouth.

"It was around the fourth year that he went out one night and got drunk at a bar. There, he proudly proclaimed he had the Chosen One under his roof. Jeff Herring just happened to be there that same night, got curious, and somehow managed to talk Oliver into bringing him back to the cabin. When Jeff saw me, he saw his own meal ticket. He wanted his father's position so he figured if he and Oliver presented me to Francis a few days before my twentieth birthday, exactly five years after the botched sacrifice, that Francis would bless the both of them on Zarzuz's behalf, giving them everything they ever wanted."

"Fucking disgusting..." I mutter.

"Did Oliver agree to hand you over with Jeff?" Kingston asks.

Daisy nods. "Yes. Over the course of that final year, the two of them became good friends. Oliver would allow Jeff to come over all the time to play in that room with his own victims, or to have Jeff watch him as he showcased his own skillset."

All while she'd been in that same room.

My stomach twists at the thought of Daisy in that situation. How did she manage to keep sane herself? The helplessness and fear she must've felt would've been crushing. Add to that, she probably knew we all thought she was dead. No one was looking for her. She knew no one was going to save her. The last bit is a sucker punch to my gut. Pulling her closer into my side, I hold her to me, hoping that I can protect her from experiencing anything like that again.

"Anyway, in the end, I escaped before that could happen."

Around us, the others wear grim expressions as they consider what she's told us.

"Do you think Jeff told his father about you?" Drake asks after a long stretch of silent contemplation.

Daisy shrugs. "Given that he wanted George's position, I doubt he would've told his father his plans."

Drake scowls as he nods. "If no one knows you're alive, then we might have the element of surprise for a while longer."

"Not for long. Not with the pictures Kingston took last night. They may not show Daisy's face, but nearly naked, it wouldn't be that hard to guess who it is," Wyatt points out. "I have a feeling we'll be using those for George, right?"

Daisy's head bobs up and down. "We are initially, though we'll be leaving them behind for the others to see. And I'm not necessarily trying to hide that it's me doing all of this." A half smile pulls at her mouth. "If they figure it out, my revenge will be even sweeter. As long as they don't catch me, I'm golden."

With our faces and most of our bodies covered, they probably won't be able to deduce who all is in the clearing. Still, the idea of leaving behind evidence of a heinous crime doesn't sit well in me. Then again, nothing that's happened in Briar Glen has. What's one more stone in my gut at this point?

"If they do capture you, Daisy, you realize they may try to sacrifice you again, right? We're only two weeks out from your birthday. This would be the prime time to nab you." I shake my head as terror tries to claw its way into me. "We need to make sure we get your revenge and then we get the hell out of—"

Daisy's body flinches so violently that it causes her to levitate a few inches off the floor. It's so unexpected that she manages to dislodge herself from under my arm and yank her hand free from Kingston before her feet hit the floor.

Wyatt and Drake take a step closer to her in surprise.

"Daisy," I look down to find her staring past Drake, her eyes wide with horror. I follow her gaze and find exactly what's startled her. "No, no, no! Don't worry about the cloak, Daisy."

Wyatt's eyes widen and his face visibly pales.

"It's not real, Daisy, I swear!" he says, taking a step toward her with a hand outstretched. "I got it made when—"

Daisy's not having it. Both Kingston and I reach out to grab her as she backs up, but she moves too quickly. Her head swings wildly back and forth as her body trembles. With a choking sound, she turns and rushes back into the house.

I don't think any of us hesitate to follow. Kingston makes it back into the house before me, but I'm close on his heels as we rush through the living room. We round the corner into the hallway just in time to see the door to the guest room slam shut. We stop in front of it, and I immediately start pounding on the door.

"Daisy? Daisy, c'mon and open the door!" I call out.

There's no answer. Kingston punches the door, his mouth twisted in a muted snarl as he glares at the barrier.

"Is she in there? Daisy?" Wyatt asks, joining us. He shoulders me and Kingston out of the way and tries the doorknob. It's locked. "Daisy, I'm sorry. I'll get rid of it. It's a replica, it's not real! I just wanted to have everything in order while I tried to piece together what happened that night. I'll burn it right now! You just gotta come out. Please! I'm sorry!"

We all wait, but Daisy doesn't answer. Wyatt swears and steps back. He turns to us and mutters, "She self-harms. I saw the marks on her legs last night. We shouldn't leave her alone while she's upset."

Marks on her legs? I choke back a groan. God, Daisy… *Why*?

Kingston shoots him a dark glare. "She won't do anything."

I open my mouth to translate but Wyatt seems to get it. "Still, we need to keep an eye on her. We don't know the shit she's been through and what could potentially push her too far."

"The camera," I remind him, keeping my voice as low as possible. "We can just check in on her through the cameras."

Drake glares down at me but says nothing. Probably because now there's a reason to creep on our girl.

"Right, well, let me go take care of the cloak." Wyatt huffs as he stomps away.

23

Daisy

There's screaming. Angry screams, fearful ones, and then there are the ones of agony. That's all I can hear. Even with my hands over my ears, I can still hear them.

I want to scream right along with the wailing in my head. It's been a while since I've heard them, but now that they're back they're so loud that they no longer feel like memories. The owners of the screams might as well be right there in front of me.

Though I'm not sure I'd notice them.

I'm not sure how long they go on for, but one minute I'm reliving nightmares, in the next— real, large, warm hands are wrapping around my wrists. The touch is so unexpected, I immediately start fighting. I lash out, my nails turning into claws and my teeth becoming weapons. Stuck in my head, I don't know who it is I'm fighting but I'll be damned if I go down without resisting.

As hard as I try though, I don't get very far. Arms wrap around me from behind, pinning my own to my side, and I'm pulled back into something warm and hard. I fight harder, knowing that if I don't, I could end up chained down onto a mattress for another five years.

I can't do it. Not again.

The floor beneath me vanishes as I'm plucked up and carried off somewhere. I fight harder as panic drowns me. I can't breathe. He's going to take me back to *that* room, with *their* screams that have stained the air.

"The devil can't get you here in my arms, darling," a deep voice murmurs in my ear from behind "You're safe."

Safe? No, I can't be safe. I'm never safe. I'll never *be* safe. But even as I think it and panic tries to well up, feeling someone's calm heartbeat against my back shakes me from my waking nightmares. My fighting ceases and I suck in a heavy breath.

"There you go. Come on back to me."

I squeeze my eyes shut, trying to focus on the breathing behind me. When I open my eyes, the room comes into focus. When did I get back in here? Wyatt's guest room is simple. There's a bed, a nightstand, a long dresser, and a relatively empty closet. Wyatt brought mine and Kingston's backpacks in last night and placed them by the door, but other than that, it's bare in here.

With another deep breath, I look down to find myself on someone's lap as they sit on the bed. Strong arms tighten around me. Judging by the blond hair on said arms, it can only be one person.

"Drake?"

"Yeah, darling, I'm here." He loosens his hold on me but doesn't drop his arms away. His mouth brushes against the shell of my ear as he asks, "You feeling better?"

Am I? I don't know. I don't even know how I got here. I flip through my memories until I remember what I'd seen in the corner of the garage. The red cloak. My chest expands as I pull in a sharp breath. I'd been triggered. The thought is dishearteninging. I was sure I was getting better. Before Kingston tackled me the other day in the hunter's perch, I hadn't melted down in over a year. Now that's twice in twenty-four hours.

I can't keep this up. Reactions like this will get me killed.

"Yeah, I'm fine now," I mutter, though I feel far from *fine*. In fact, I'm exhausted. I lean back against Drake's firm chest with a heavy sigh. "I didn't hurt you, did I?"

"No."

I don't believe him, so I turn and look up at him. Staring at Drake is like staring into the face of a complete stranger but with that nagging feeling in the back of my head that tells me I know him. There's nothing left of my soft, emotional boy. At least not outwardly.

Curiously, I reach up and touch his beard. "I never in a million years pictured you with a beard." I smile. "When I got to your house up in Anchorage, I thought I'd gotten the wrong address."

Drake snorts, his lips twitching in amusement. "After I got out of the Marines, I wanted to distance myself as far as possible from them."

Ah, so the long hair and beard make sense now.

Drake shifts me off his lap to place me on the mattress. As he reaches for something on the nightstand, I noticed the thin, slightly bloody nails marks around my wrists. I check my nails to confirm what I already know—I fell into old habits. In my state of panic, I tried to rip open my own skin to get to my veins.

I won't be taken alive. The thought is saturated with determination and desolation.

Pushing away the thought and dropping my hands out of sight, I watch as Drake grabs a tray of food that I hadn't noticed until now. I frown, confused. Drake places it between us on the bed. There are pancakes, fruit, fried potatoes, sausage links, and crispy bacon all plated up and ready to be eaten.

My stomach growls eagerly but the rest of me balks.

"Is everyone coming in to eat some?" I shoot a look toward the door. "Why is the door off its hinges?" *And how didn't I notice?*

"You weren't opening the door." He grabs a fork and stabs a diced potato. As he brings it to my mouth he adds, "The others are eating now. They'll probably barge in any minute once they realize I took the liberty of removing the barrier you put between us."

I locked them out?

"Sorry." My eyes fall to the fork, and I let Drake feed me.

When the utensil reaches my lips, our eyes meet. I watch as the hardness there softens just a touch. As I pull away to chew, he stabs a sausage link and brings it up next.

"Don't apologize. Whatever you've been through, I'm sure there are mental wounds that aren't healed yet."

I bite the sausage link in half.

If only Drake knew what wounds I had and how deep they ran. I wonder if he and the others would accept me back so easily if they knew what I was capable of.

They've already seen you murder someone. Kingston and Drake even helped without hesitation. They've got wounds that match yours.

For some reason, that settles some of my concerns.

"There is something you will not do, however," Drake says as I finish the link after a short pause. My eyes lift to his face. He glares at me. "You won't run from me, Daisy. From any of us, really, but *especially* not me."

As his voice hardens, a darkness gathers in his eyes. It speaks to my charred soul.

"I didn't mean to," I admit, but swallow when that darkness turns pitch back.

"Don't. Run. From. Me." Drake all but growls the words through his teeth.

"What if I can't help it?"

"Then I won't be able to help but give chase." His voice deepens. "And if I catch you, there will be consequences neither of us are ready for."

The way he's staring tells me I should be scared. His words are laced with a deadly promise, but all I see and hear is a delicious challenge. Danger is a drug I seek out gleefully now. My nipples harden and graze against the soft fabric of a shirt that's not mine. The breath I suck in catches in my throat as I think about this mountain of a man chasing me.

"Don't look at me like that, Daisy. This isn't a game."

Drake's brows slam together. But if he's supposed to be intimidating me with this look, he's failing miserably. Cloaks, *those* I'll quake at the sight of. A dangerous man with a large heart that possesses a soul as dark as mine? Well, clearly, my body will tremble for a whole other reason under that type of condition.

"What will happen if I run again, Drake?" I challenge softly, enjoying this side of him.

Drake huffs, breaking eye contact to shake his head. "We all have our own demons, Daisy. When it comes to you, my demons..."

His voice trails off as his nostrils flare. Drake attempts to stab at a grape but it just rolls left and right before shooting off the plate altogether.

"What happens to your demons when it comes to me, Drake?"

"You inspire them, and because of that, I might end up taking what I want like an animal if I let them get the best of me." His voice is steely as he cuts through the pancakes. "You trigger them when you run."

Good god, who is this man and what happened to my sweet Drake? And why does the thought of me being pinned down beneath this giant turn me on so much that I know there is a wet spot on the comforter right now? As discreetly as I can, I press my thighs together to ease the tension coiling between them.

"What if I don't want that?" I watch his face as he brings a bite of pancake to my lips.

"Then don't fucking run."

I suck in a sharp breath, stunned at his words. But while the warning is there, I still can't find it in myself to be worried. I allow Drake to feed me a few more bites of breakfast before I pull away.

"I can't eat anymore."

Drake scoffs. "You're going to eat every bite on this plate."

"I'll burst before I get halfway through what's on there!" I stare at the plate between us, noting how we haven't even made a dent in what's there.

"You will eat, Daisy. You're nothing but skin and bones."

I shake my head. "I'm going to *pop*, Dre!"

The thunderous look on his face nearly has me back tracking. But I bite my bottom lip and hold onto my resolve.

"You will eat, and you will sleep while I'm around... while *we're* around," he corrects, though it sounds a bit begrudged. "You haven't been taking care of yourself."

I scoff. "I'm doing just fine."

"Your protruding bones say otherwise." He shoves a piece of bacon in my face. "Now eat."

Glaring at him, I take the bacon with my hand and then toss it to the floor.

"I've been taking care of myself for years, Drake. I don't need you to baby me."

Drake glares at me before turning it toward the piece of bacon on the ground. His shoulders stiffen. After a moment, he looks back at me, all the stiffness slipping out of him with a heavy sigh.

"I *want* to take care of you, Daisy. It settles something inside of me," he admits with a frown. "You don't look well. If you want to survive these next few weeks, you need to be at your best. Do you think you could outrun *anyone* right now? You couldn't fight me off a few minutes ago. Hell, I'm pretty sure I can pick you up with my pinky, Daisy. How are you supposed to do any of the things you want, even with us by your side, if you're too tired and weak to finish a task? Food will help. Sleep will help. *I* will help you with anything you want and then some. I'll be your soldier, Daisy, but I need you to be a strong leader, ok?"

This is the second time in less than twelve hours that I've heard Drake string more than a few words together. Each time he opens his mouth, I swear it's only to say something important.

"Hey, Drake?"

He raises a brow expectantly.

"You know I adore you, right? Always have, always will." As surprise flickers across my giant's face, I lean forward and claim his lips.

Drake remains rigid for all of one second before he crushes his lips against mine. His hand goes to my hair and grasps it in a biting grip. He bites my bottom lip, and when I gasp his tongue dives in and greets mine with a sweeping warm welcome.

I groan. My heart slams against my chest wildly and my blood starts to boil. Before I can sink too deep into the kiss, Drake breaks it. My eyes flutter open to find him smirking.

"I love you too." His voice is gruff, and I swear I catch sight of a light blush on his cheeks. "Now let me feed you."

My heart swells. If he wants to take care of me, I'll let him. It's the least I can do as I drag him down this dark path I've taken. Besides, he's not asking for much. Without replying, I open my mouth and wait for the next bite.

A small smile pulls at Drake's mouth as he forks a piece of cantaloupe and brings it up. His smile is bashful and reminds me of the old Drake. I'm not sure which one I love more, or if I even need to choose.

As I swallow the fruit, we're interrupted.

"Hey! Why didn't you say you got the door open?" Wyatt demands, appearing in the doorway, scowling at Drake.

"Didn't think I needed to tell you every little thing I did," Drake responds with a half shrug as he feeds me another bite of pancake.

Wyatt shoots Drake a glare before softening his gaze as he looks at me.

"Are you ok? I'm sorry about the—"

"Don't worry about it, I was just taken by surprise." I don't want to talk about it. Looking at Drake I add, "And touching... if I don't *expect* it, I react the same way. Thus, the fighting."

Drake shrugs. "Just expect me to touch you from here on out and it won't be a problem."

A shiver works its way down my body at the thought of Drake's touch and where he would put his hands.

"I'll get rid of it," Wyatt continues. "In the meantime, do you have a plan to go after George Herring?"

Do I have a plan? Internally, I scoff and roll my eyes. I always have a plan.

"It's Saturday night, George will be home drinking and watching the evening news until nine-thirty or ten, then he goes to bed, so it should be relatively easy. That box I unearthed? It's filled with the ashes of his son's victims. I want their ashes freed so I'll create a bomb that we'll set off. We'll use it as a calling card for when we're through with the evening so the police can find his body." I lean forward, excited for this evening's events. "I can go over everything in detail if you'd like before we leave? We can divide up tasks to make sure this runs smoothly."

Drake nods immediately. "We'll tweak your plan to accommodate some of our strengths and weaknesses, then we'll go over it repeatedly until we can all recite the plan forward and back. If anyone has even a moment of hesitation, a well laid out plan can go awry."

I smile at him, pleased he's taking this seriously. When deciding to get everyone back together, I knew there was a chance not everyone would be game for a murdering spree. But my men haven't balked yet.

"Alright, I'll let the others know what's up and to get ready for this evening." Wyatt starts to turn but pauses and looks back at Daisy. "Care to fill us in who the others are by any chance?"

Now that I know they're totally onboard, I don't mind at all. "The last two Blessed Priests, after George, are Vincent Callaway and Ronney Maxwell. Then, of course, there's the High Priest himself, Francis Winslow."

Wyatt blinks in surprise. "Wait, Ronney Maxwell? As in the *Sheriff* of Briar Glen?"

At my nod, Drake snorts. "Who else would be there to clean up Francis's mess but the damn sheriff? Your friend is probably involved too."

I frown as I watch Wyatt open and close his mouth. His brows crash together as he shakes his head.

"No way is Brett involved." He looks at me as if expecting I'll agree with him but if that's what he's expecting, he's going to be disappointed.

"I don't know who the smaller fish in the cult are. Just the biggest."

Drake grunts. "As long as you keep Daisy and King's name out of your mouth, Wy, we'll all be safe."

Wyatt's face falls. "I would never breathe a word about them to him, no matter what."

I reach out to Wyatt, hating the crestfallen expression clinging to his face. He immediately moves further into the room to take it. Our fingers intertwine and I give his hand a squeeze.

"He might not be involved, Wy."

"If he is, then I have a real shitty radar when it comes to trusting people." He squeezes my hand. "Anyway, let me tell the others what's happening."

He drops a kiss on the top of my head before leaving me and Drake alone. My face flames hot at such a sweet and unexpected gesture.

"I don't know why you look so surprised," Drake mutters, pulling my attention back to him. He stabs a piece of watermelon and lifts it to my mouth. I take it, watching the hint of amusement dance in his eyes. "You should know we're all obsessed with you. Always have been. Always will be."

My cheeks grow hotter. I'm not sure how true that is, but they're here with me and that's all I could possibly ask for. Anything else is just being greedy.

"Then you should know I love you all," I confess. It comes out easy because not only is it true, but over the years I've learned how quickly you can lose the chance to tell someone that.

Now that we're all back together, I'll start to let them know how I feel more often. We won't always have each other. But when I'm gone, I want them to know that up until the end, they always had my heart.

Kingston

"—Ask the people of Briar Glen not to be alarmed. We will find both men, but it will take time," Sheriff Maxwell says on the screen.

Standing behind a podium in front of Town Hall, he and my father stare into the camera as local reporters bombard them with questions. The sheriff wears a look of determination; my father's expression is one of polite concern. Together, the two most powerful men in Briar Glen create a near perfect image of a solidarity. Their ability to make people believe they give a fuck about anyone other than themselves is a talent that could make even the devil jealous.

No wonder I didn't know how monstrous he could be until it was too late.

"Ed Fisherman and Harry Kramer are good hunters. They know what to do in case of an emergency. I have no doubt in my mind that they will be found shortly by our search teams," Sheriff Maxwell adds. "We do not believe that their disappearance and the fires that have happened around town are related."

"Are there any details about Kingston Winslow?" a reporter asks.

My father has the audacity to look disheartened as he clasps his hands in front of him and drops his head.

I throw the remote at the screen as Sheriff Maxwell clears his throat. "We have reason to believe he has left Briar Glen and is headed for freedom. Given the efficiency of our police department, he most likely would want to put distance between us. We have alerted the police departments in the surrounding areas about his escape and that, if seen, approach with caution."

Approach with caution? I snicker. They better approach with the intent to kill because I'm *not* going back.

"Ok, Daisy is all set up and is making a, um, *bomb* in my garage," Wyatt announces as he enters the kitchen from the side door. He shuts then leans against it. "I'm not sure whether to be scared or turned on that she knows how to do that."

Amusement flutters around in my chest. Daisy's new skill is impressive. After explaining how she was going to do it, Drake and Owen scavenged up whatever material Daisy didn't have in her backpack, and we've given her space to work. The fact that you can make a bomb with stuff laying around the house is astonishing.

"I'll have to have her teach me how to build one sometime. I want that skill on my resume," I tell him.

Wyatt's brows furrow with concentration. Oh, that's right. The fucker doesn't remember sign language. Just as I'm about to turn away, his face twists in horror and he groans.

"First, I don't know what type of job besides the military requires the knowledge of how to build a bomb, and second," he pushes off the door and comes to join me in the living room, "I don't know if I want her teaching you how to do that under this roof. I know the house isn't much, but it's something for now."

Huh, maybe he really does need just a simple refresher when it comes to signing. My mouth curls upward in amusement. It's strange to smile after so long not doing it.

"While I got a second with you, I just want to tell you that I'm sorry." Wyatt flops down onto the recliner. "When I sent letters to Riverbend, they were always returned unopened and you weren't allowed visitors, but I should've tried harder to get in touch. I can't imagine what nine years in Riverbend must've been like, thinking we didn't care enough to try to reach out. I just want to let you know that I didn't stop thinking about you. We're all relieved that Daisy is alive, but for me at least, it's like you've been resurrected too."

My eyes slide away from his face. I don't need an apology. There's nothing he could've done to change my situation. My father made sure of that. The power Francis Winslow has in this town is impossible to fight against.

Or it *was*.

Daisy's here now, dismantling his throne from right underneath him. I can't wait to see his fucking face when this is all over. Hopefully, when I stare into his eyes, they're lifeless.

With a sigh, I turn back to Wyatt to find him still watching me. I roll my eyes. "Don't get all sentimental with me. It wasn't like you all actually *liked* me."

Again, it takes a minute for Wyatt to process what I've said but when he does, Wyatt snorts. "I mean, you *were* an asshole. I don't think I missed the bullying so much, but I still liked you. You were one of my best friends."

"Who was an asshole?" Owen asks, walking into the room from the hallway.

"King, when we were kids."

Owen laughs. "That's putting it kindly. You were a dick,

man." He flips me the bird as he makes his way to the refrigerator.

"Remember when he stole Drake's shirt, that day at the river?" Wyatt asks him. "Drake *hated* not wearing a shirt when we went swimming, and King tore it off him and got rid of it. Oh, Drake was so upset."

It takes a minute for that memory to resurface, but when it does, I smile a bit. Drake had been really pissed and cried like a goddamn baby.

"Daisy forced you to take off your shirt and give it to Drake," Owen says as he plops down on the couch with a soda in his hand.

Wyatt laughs. "I forgot about that! That was, like, your favorite shirt, right? She demanded you give it to Drake, knowing it wouldn't fit but to put you in your place."

Heat rises in my cheeks. Yeah, I do remember that. While I don't remember what she said exactly, I do remember how her chastising had hit a little too hard.

"I learned my lesson, that's for sure," I admit after a minute. "That day at the river sucked."

"Not for all of us," Wyatt declares, his smile turning smug. "Drake had his first kiss."

First kiss? *That* day? I don't believe it. "With fucking who? *You*?"

The blond brute walks into the room at the sound of his name. He stops in front of all of us and when he realizes we're all staring at him, he scowls.

"What are you guys going on about?"

Wyatt's smile grows even more pronounced. "Oh, that day at the river Daisy pulled you aside and kissed you."

We all watch as the hard lines on Drake's face slacken with surprise. He tries to cover it up quickly—a scowl deeper than I ever thought possible nearly pins his brows together.

"How do you know about that?"

Wyatt shrugs. "I may or may not have pretended to wander off to pee and followed the two of you."

"Wait, was that Daisy's first kiss too?" Owen asks, sitting up straighter. "You guys were still in middle school when that happened."

I glance at Wyatt who shrugs.

"No, she'd been kissed before," Drake growls. "That guy Chad cornered her in the music room at school and kissed her."

He did? I stiffen as jealousy bulldozes through common sense. It was years ago so it shouldn't matter. Yet *that* guy got a taste of my girl before I did? Fuck!

"Daisy liked Chad?" Wyatt shakes his head. "I don't remember that."

Thinking back, I don't recall Daisy ever talking about her crushes. Even when it came to celebrities. Was it because she didn't like anyone? Or was it because, even back then, she loved us all and didn't want to make it awkward between us?

"I said he *cornered* her—not that she liked him."

Understanding ripples through the rest of us. My heart sinks.

"Did you step in?" I ask him. Where the fuck is Chad now? I wonder how much it would take for us to convince Daisy to add him to her hit list.

"I didn't have to," Drake smiles then. It's short lived but warm nevertheless. "She pushed him and punched him in the nose. Had two black eyes for a week and a half."

Owen and Wyatt laugh as I gape.

"Wait, I remember those black eyes." I grin, amused. "He said he got hit in the face by a fly ball during baseball practice."

Drake shakes his head. "Nope, those were from Daisy."

"Good for her," Owen says through his laughter. "Whatever happened to that bully? He was an even bigger dick than Kingston here."

I shoot him a glare, but Owen just flashes me a smile.

"He died about two years ago. Motorcycle accident." Wyatt grins. "Karma caught up with that guy."

"Thank god you didn't turn into *that* guy, King," Owen says with a sigh. "Anyway, I want to hear about this kiss with Daisy. Why didn't you tell us, Drake?"

Drake's face turns red as we all look back at him.

For the next hour, the four of us tease and reminisce. As I sit there interacting, I find the tension in my shoulders and back ebbing away. For nine years, I'd been ripped away from these guys. Before being locked away, I'd thought I was better than them. Held myself an arm's length away, and clearly, it shows as we recount our childhood.

The fact that we're here now, together, and they've welcomed me back with open arms despite how terribly I would treat them at times, tells me that I wasn't better than anyone. If anything, they were better people than me.

It feels good to be back with my rightful family.

25

Kingston

"King, you're holding me too tight!" Daisy trembles with stifled laughter that I can feel through my body which is pressed against hers.

Rather than release her, I press my chest harder into her back, which pushes her flatter against the tree as headlights from the car that's just pulled out of George Herring's house flashes in our direction.

"I promise they can't see us from here," she whispers.

She also promised that George would be alone tonight, but we just watched a woman slip out of his front door after they shared a passionate kiss. I'm not willing to risk Daisy being exposed. Even stationed where we are, across the street in a neighbor's yard, hidden between a few thicker trees, dressed in dark clothes, our faces hidden behind our masks and our hoods up, I'll be more than a little protective to keep her away from prying eyes.

"Ok, the car's gone. Time to give Owen the signal," Wyatt mutters from behind me.

I bring my fingers up to my mouth and let out a short, sharp whistle. The three of us wait, watching George's house with bated breath. Time ticks by. I'm not sure if we wait there for only a few seconds or a few minutes, but suddenly the lights in the house go out.

A burst of surprise pops in my chest. Huh, when Owen mentioned that he could cut the power supply and mess with any wifi settings from afar, I had my doubts. Those doubts, however, have been effectively squashed. I guess the guy knows what he's doing.

Against me, Daisy tenses. I keep her pressed against the tree. We don't move without his signal. It comes maybe a full minute later. A flashlight flickers on and off three times from across the street in a neighbor's yard from high in a tree, letting us know that even the motion-sensor lights attached to George's house have been disabled.

I step back and allow Daisy to straighten.

"Ready?" she asks, looking over her shoulder at me, then Wyatt. With her mask on, I can't read her expression, but gauging by her tone, she's excited.

I pick up her backpack off the ground. As I hand it to her, I nod.

"As I'll ever be," Wyatt answers, his muffled voice sounding a little strained.

I hope it's not nerves causing his anxiousness. There can't be a moment of doubt in any of this, or we'll be putting Daisy in jeopardy.

"Then let's move." Daisy's already slipping out of the protection of the dark shadows as she speaks, shrugging on her backpack as she moves.

Wyatt and I flank her sides as we hurry along with her. As we cross the street, using the bushes and trees that line the sidewalk as coverage, and approach the house, I search for Drake. Being as big as he is, hiding should be difficult, but as we creep up the driveway toward the garage and side of the house, I don't see him.

We reach the side of the house and then press our back against it as we continue onwards. We slip around to the back of the house, dart across an open space, and then pause under the small weeping willow. The back of George's house is made up of all glass, including the massive sunroom. Because of that, we can see George's pale figure moving blindly through the house as he walks by.

None of us make a sound as we watch the dead man walking.

My hand slides into my pocket where the hunting knife Daisy gifted me hides. Daisy wants to kill George and, if all goes to plan, she will. But after that initial kill in the woods, I want to do it again. I want to hear the death wheeze and feel their blood turn cold as it slowly stops flowing over my hands. Last night, I dreamed of carving up that hunter, and when I woke this morning with Daisy in my arms, I was smiling.

There's no better gift than the gift of a violent death, I'm sure of it.

When there's no more movement in the house, Daisy waves us forward. This time we make a mad dash toward the only part of the house that isn't glass. The spot is maybe five feet wide in length, right where the A/C unit sits. Behind it is a lattice wrapped in greenery that stretches upward against the house, nearly making it to the second floor.

We huddle behind the unit as best we can and wait again. When Daisy's ready, she sucks in a deep breath and looks at me.

"Ready to climb?"

I'm ready to kill. Any friend of my father's is an enemy to me. George Herring's time is coming soon.

I nod before I turn and reach up high. Gripping the lattice, I move to pull myself up. The lattice groans under my weight and shudders. I pause, waiting to see if it will hold me. When I'm sure it will, I make my ascent. It's a slow progression as I make sure it doesn't knock too hard against the house as I move. When I get to the top, there's about two feet between me and the lip of the roof. This is why I had to go first. I was the tallest of the three of us. Drake wanted to be here, but given what we had to do, the three of us weighed less.

Reaching up, I grab the edge and pull myself the rest of the way. When I get to the top, I immediately turn and lean over to help the others. Wyatt is next, climbing the lattice a little faster than me, but still cautious with his movement. I reach down and offer him my hand. Wyatt takes it and with a soft grunt, I pull him up. Daisy moves next, faster than either of us, and more nimbly climbs up the lattice.

She's halfway up when a whistle, short and soft, pierces the night. We all freeze. A second later, headlights from a car pulling into the driveway brighten up the backyard.

"C'mon!" Wyatt hisses down to Daisy.

I want to push him off the roof for breaking the silence back here. Instead, I glare at him then reach down for Daisy. She starts climbing again but only makes it a foot higher when a voice and the light of a flashlight drift toward us.

"—said I was here, didn't I? I'll do a quick sweep around back, and then I'll come in. I'm telling you, you're just being paranoid," a man's voice says. "Yeah, well, your son's an idiot. He's probably balls deep inside a whore over in Chasm. You know he can't resist a flappy pussy or blow."

The voice grows closer, coming near us as whoever it is searches the property. I wave Daisy on as my heart starts to hammer in my chest. Daisy nods, climbing the lattice faster than ever to get to the top. When the lattice ends, she reaches for us.

Shit. I knew she was short, but her arms don't stretch nearly as far as Wyatt's did. Wyatt mutters a soft swear beside me as he gets to his stomach. We both lean our bodies halfway off the edge of the roof, reaching for our girl. She takes my hand first. I grab her by the wrist and jerk her up. Wyatt catches her other hand, and in tandem, we pull her up.

I'm not all that surprised she's so easy to pull up. She's practically a feather. But I do make a mental note that I'll be on team Drake when it comes to pumping her full of food for each meal.

Just as we pull her onto the roof, a man rounds the corner of the house where we had just been standing. With a phone pressed to his ear, he lazily sweeps his flashlight around. The three of us watch him, unmoving.

"Yeah, yeah, I hear you. I'll be in to flip the breaker in a second." The man shakes his head and ends the call, shoving his phone into his pocket. "Old fucker… I don't get paid enough for this shit."

He moves to the middle of the yard, does a complete three sixty, and then sighs.

"I told the bastard it was nothing," he grumbles as he keeps moving to the other side of the house. When he's out of sight, we all let out a collective breath.

"Come on," Daisy whispers.

"Wait, we didn't plan for a second person to be here," Wyatt hisses, grabbing her arm. "What do we do now?"

"What we came here to do." Daisy's response is clipped and cold as she pulls her arm free.

I grin again as my cock stirs. Her bloodthirsty nature is utterly delicious. And infectious.

"I'll take care of the newcomer, you and Wyatt stick to the plan," I offer happily, pleased that I'll be able to get my hands dirty once more.

Daisy nods, but I catch Wyatt hesitating. Both Daisy and I sigh in unison.

"King is going to handle the problem. You and I are going to get rid of George."

Wyatt nods quickly. "Oh, right, ok."

The three of us get to our feet and creep along the rooftop over to the small window that, according to Daisy, leads to a guest bathroom. Crouching beside it, Daisy reaches over and pulls it up. Just as she'd promised, it's unlocked.

I stare at her a moment, marveling at how detailed she is. How long did she stand outside this house at different positions, plotting her attempt to get inside? When did she learn that *this* particular window always remains unlocked? It must've taken her ages.

She's absolutely incredible.

Daisy slips into the house first. Wyatt motions for me to go next, and I don't hesitate. I finagle my way through the small window and then find myself in an unimpressive bathroom. Daisy is standing by the door with it cracked, her head tilted to better hear what's going on in the rest of the house. Wyatt slips in next, then shuts the window behind him. Daisy holds up a finger and I hold my breath.

"—did she want?" the man who was outside asks as he moves about the house. It sounds like he's still on the first floor.

"What makes you think she wasn't just here for me?" That must be George.

"Because Terra Miller doesn't fuck anyone without an agenda. Everyone knows that."

I stiffen, as does Daisy and Wyatt. Terra Miller? Drake's mom? Was that who left earlier?

"She's none of your concern."

There's a scoff of disbelief and a creek of a floorboard. "She's trying to climb the ladder—tell me you know that?"

"Of course I do! Now quit your bitching and go check upstairs. No one pays you for your advice, just your gun, Cam," George hisses.

Daisy scoots away from the door. The sound of footsteps stomping up the stairs tells me whoever Cam is, isn't worried about anyone actually being in the house. Otherwise, he'd try to make it a little less obvious that he was coming. I pull Daisy behind me and push her toward Wyatt, who drags her under his arm protectively.

I shift my weight to the balls of my feet.

My heart rate increases as excitement and nerves simmer under my skin. My fingers flex at my sides. The hired gunman opens a door nearby. His heavy footsteps tell me he's making quick and sloppy work of searching the room beside us. He's muttering something under his breath as he moves. I open the door wide enough for the others to slip out and nudge my head.

Daisy nods and quickly slips out from under Wyatt's arm and out of the bathroom. Wyatt follows close behind, his hand landing on my shoulder briefly. I watch as the two of them slip into another room, then I swing the bathroom door so it's nearly shut again.

George's security moves out into the hallway. I track his footsteps as he grows nearer. As he approaches the bathroom door, my hand slides back into my pocket. Without pulling my eyes away from the door, I pull my knife out from its sheath. As the door is pushed open, I grab the handle and yank it open the rest of the way. The move startles Cam and jerks him off balance.

The man with wispy hair combed over a shiny bald head only has time to gasp. My muscles bunch before I spring into action. Jumping forward, one of my hands slaps over his mouth as I run him into the doorframe. Pinned between me and frame, Cam can't react fast enough as my other hand slams the blade of my knife into his neck.

I hold Cam's gaze. Fear and pain cause them to widen and water. I step forward, pushing the blade deeper. Amusement bubbles up in my chest. This man thinks he's in pain? He doesn't know the meaning of the word.

Out of the corner of my eye, I catch movement. I risk a glance and catch Daisy and Wyatt tiptoeing down the stairs.

Cam grunts and pushes at me, catching me off my game. I stumble backward, my knife coming with me. With his mouth free, he opens it to shout a warning. Only blood pours out. One of his hands wildly searches for the gun at his side while his other presses against the wound on his neck. A wild thrill rushes through me. When I suck in a deep breath, I feel more alive than ever.

Leaping forward, I laugh.

My knife slams in his chest, and while he flinches, I knock his hand away from his holster. He pushes at me, grunting in agony. Blood pours from the wound in his neck, creating a mess. I love it all.

Grinning behind my mask, I adjust the knife in my hand and then lunge for him again.

26

Wyatt

The pained grunts coming from upstairs fade as Daisy and I move through the dark house. My heart flutters with apprehension as we move. I let Daisy take the lead. I'm impressed with how she confidently prods through the house as if she owns the place, even with the lights off.

We move through the large dining room, then a family room that's nearly the size of my house, and down a hallway before the sounds of someone moving around reach my ears. Without breaking her stride, Daisy swoops down as her foot comes up and she pulls her massive hunting knife from her boot.

I copy her, pulling my knife from my back pocket. My hand tightens around the hilt while blood roars in my ears. The silence of the house mixed with the task at hand has my heart racing. Sweat gathers on my brow. As much as I wish to wipe it away, my mask prevents the action.

The two of us stop just outside of what must be his office. I can hear the sound of papers moving and George muttering to himself. Daisy takes a deep breath. I can hear her soft intake of air. As she exhales, she kicks open the door and moves.

I'm right behind her.

George jumps in his seat at the loud bang of the door against the wall. He's not quite as startled as I thought he would be. He glares at us as he pulls a gun from under his desk. Without hesitation, he points it at Daisy as she charges forward.

I reach out, grabbing the back of her jacket, and pull her out of the way. The first bullet flies by harmlessly. Letting her go, we both twist and duck. As I jump to the side and Daisy moves in the opposite direction, the second bullet hits the floor by my foot. I catch sight of Daisy throwing her knife. It misses his head by less than an inch. George gets to his feet, swings the gun around at Daisy, and snarls.

Time slows as panic kicks my instincts into overdrive. My feet move on their own accord as I cross the short distance between me and George. The gun goes off at the same time I slam my knife into his gut.

George roars in agony, his body freezing up as he tries to breathe through the pain. The gun in his hand clatters down onto his desk. The croaking that bubbles up and spills past his lips reminds me of a frog. His body flinches before he collapses down into his chair.

Something unravels inside of me. It's a lazy glee twisted with hunger. It spreads, causing my limbs to tingle with a renewed energy. My mouth stretches wide in a grin that I know would frighten me if I could see it.

I stabbed someone. I *stabbed* a living human being. I know I should be scared, or maybe even in shock, but I feel none of that as I slowly straighten. A calm voice whispers in my head, "*Finish him.*"

When I take in a deep breath, eager anticipation fills my lungs. I reach forward, ready to grab the handle.

"Why?" George gasps, looking up at me.

I pause as I stare down into the face of the older man sitting before me. Hatred floods my nervous system, nearly ruining the high that's making me giddy for more pain.

"Because you took my girl away from me," I hiss.

Confusion briefly flickers across his face. "W-who?"

"Me, George." Daisy steps forward and pulls up her mask. "But the fact that you need specifics to narrow down who he could be talking about tells me you've destroyed more than a few relationships."

George looks over to my girl and gaps. "No... Francis said it was you, but I didn't... I d-didn't believe him. You're back?"

Daisy plops her backpack down and unzips it. "Well, Francis was right."

"You're supposed to be—" George gasps for air before continuing. "Dead. Briar G-glen is crumbling because you didn't... die. Zarzuz needs you in order to send us... his strength."

I scoff. "Your god doesn't exist."

"He does. Z-Zarzuz awaits his bride."

His words piss me off. The way he stares so intensely at Daisy as she pulls out a baggy full of polaroid pictures disgusts me. It's like he's willing her to drop dead before him. I reach the rest of the way forward and grab the handle of the knife. Before I can pull it out and stab him again, Daisy stops me.

"Hold on, my eager demon." Somehow, Daisy has the ability to laugh. As she does, she opens the baggy and tosses the pictures down in front of George. His gaze drops from her to them.

"J-jeff? You k-killed my son?" George's words break on a sob. He tries to reach up to grab a picture, but his arm only makes it halfway before it drops, and he leans back in his seat. "*No*! I already gave Zarzuz my first son. Jeff d-deserved to live!"

His first son? George was one of the people who'd sacrificed someone? I don't know why this surprises me. Given his ranking within the cult, of course he would go all out for his beloved god.

Daisy giggles. "Don't worry, George, his death wasn't for nothing. I gave his life to Lilith, asking her to lend me strength in destroying you and the others."

She sits on the edge of the desk as George wails in horror. I watch him, wondering why I don't feel remorse or disgust. Is it because I know the type of person he is? Or because I'm a psychopath?

"Tell me something, George," Daisy continues. "How does it feel to be watched as your death closes in on you?"

George shakes his head, tears streaming down his face.

I step closer to him. "Answer her."

He sobs, "I-I feel helpless."

Daisy nods. "That tracks. I remember when I was tied down to a rock with a knife hovering above my chest. I felt the same way. Do you want to plead your case? Ask me to spare you? Or can we skip that part knowing *you* had no intention of sparing me as I cried beneath Francis's blade?"

"Zarzuz..." George wheezes. "H-he waits for you. To give you..." he winces. "A good afterlife by his side. You were never meant to l-live..."

I shiver. Maybe in *his* world Daisy wasn't supposed to be alive, but in the future I imagined as a kid, she was there with me. "He's not real."

"He is! H-he waits with open arms... for all h-his followers."

Daisy snickers as I scoff. "Only cold nothingness awaits you on the other side, George."

The man sobs harder, shaking his head in denial.

"I want you to know George—" Daisy moves a little closer to him "—that a little birdie has unearthed all your patient records; including the ones where you covered up a pregnancy that would result in a sacrifice. You were a physician, George.

Your job was to help people, and what did you do in your life? You stole countless lives."

By little birdie she means Owen, who dug up every single record George kept. The number of names on that list was horrifying. Being the only physician in town, George Herring carried out horrific crimes in the name of Zarzuz and had no one to stop him.

Daisy smiles sweetly at the dying man. "I've saved these records. I'll be combining them with everything else I've uncovered in regard to the Zarzuzians, and will be sending it to newspapers, government officials, and everyone else I can think of. *You'll* be remembered as a monster."

"Y-you're the monster," he wheezes out.

"Luckily for me, I've already been erased and forgotten. Monster or not, no one will ever know about my involvement in the chaos that will ensue here in Briar Glen."

As her smile falters, my heart cracks.

She's right. Even after all this, Daisy will remain a ghost to the world. Unease twists in my chest. We'll figure something out. Once she's had her revenge, she'll start a new life with me — with *us*. We're all going to have to sit down and discuss the future at some point.

I watch as Daisy scoots around the desk to stand beside George. He looks up at her, tears streaming down his face, his mouth opening and closing like a goldfish.

"He knows you're here. Knows this is you wreaking havoc. Zarzuz told him. F-Francis will find you and finish what he started."

"Francis can try." Daisy reaches forward and wraps her fingers around the handle of the blade sticking out from George's chest. "Tell your son, 'I told you so' when you see him."

Before he can respond, Daisy pulls out the blade and drives it back into his body. George screams in agony. His body twitches violently as he coughs up blood. The gurgling of liquid pooling in his lungs... I swallow hard as I realize how magical the sound is. As is the way the life drains from George's face. She repeats this motion of stabbing him over and over. Blood splatters everywhere. George's weak cries fade until all that is left is the 'thwomp' of the blade slamming through skin, muscle, and cartilage, and the sucking noise as it's being pulled back out.

I watch on in awe. Warmth gathers in my cheeks and my heart races for a whole new reason. My pants tent as my dick stiffens at the sight of a fresh body on display right before my eyes. Licking my lips, I step closer and just... stare.

It's not that George is attractive. No, that's not why I'm suddenly harder than rock. It's the lack of life, the shell of a human. It's just so heady knowing that I'm alive and he's, well, far from it. I try to breathe through the inappropriate reaction, but it does nothing to quell the sick desire beating at me.

I need to get out of here before I embarrass myself.

Blinking to pull myself out of the moment, I look up at Daisy. Her expression is absolutely blank as her arm comes up and she continues to stab. Her face and hands are covered in blood, but she doesn't seem to notice.

"Daisy."

She doesn't react. I try again.

"*Daisy*!"

Again, she doesn't respond. She simply keeps stabbing. Swearing mentally, I move toward her until I'm directly behind her.

"Hey, Daisy!" I catch her arm as it comes up again. Her body flinches and she lets out a soft gasp. "Hey, you're ok. He's dead now. You can relax."

Her body goes slack, the knife in her hand dropping to the floor. She doesn't move or speak. Daisy simply stands there, staring at George. I glance at him again and bite back a groan as my dick hardens further.

What is wrong with me?

"I'll never be ok."

Daisy's words pull my thoughts away from my throbbing cock and the dead man in front of me. I wrap my arms around her and pull her into my chest.

"Don't say that. You're perfect as you are."

"I'm broken, Wy." Her admittance is spoken softly but I hear the hint of hurt she's either trying to hide or doesn't realize is there. "He broke me. The *town* broke me. I can't trust, I can't live without hating, and..." She swallows so hard I can feel it through her body. "I want this—" she flicks her hand toward George "—to make me whole, but I-I feel absolutely nothing."

I squeeze my eyes shut, hating myself for not being able to reach into the past and undo everything. If there was anyone who could experience life to its fullest, it was Daisy. I know the old Daisy is here, I just know it. She's just a bit tarnished. After all of this, I'll make sure that one day, she shines again. With a sigh, I lift my mask up.

Turning her around in my arms, I capture her chin and force her face to tilt upward. Her eyes are unfocused, her brows are pinched together with uncertainty.

"For now, I'll feel everything you can't, ok?" I promise. "When you're in my arms, you're allowed to relax and find solace."

Daisy blinks. I can see her struggling to come back into the moment. My thumb, perched on her chin, smears blood as it slides over her skin. She's stunning covered in someone else's blood. And the vulnerability on her face? My heart swells, ready to break free of my chest just to wrap around her. Unable to stop myself, I lean down and capture her lips with mine.

When I pull away to stare down at her face, I can see life returning swiftly now. She gives me a soft, shy smile before she rolls onto the balls of her feet to reach up and kiss me again. I meet her halfway. Her hands come up to hold my face and she opens her mouth to sweep her tongue against my bottom lip. I open my mouth, eagerly accepting her invitation.

Daisy lets out a soft moan, and my already hard dick grows harder yet. Her hips lean forward and press into mine. Her soft chuckle as she pulls away brings heat to my cheeks.

"Hm, seems like this type of setting suits you," she teases. Glancing at George, she laughs louder. "Maybe it's not me, maybe it's something else entirely."

"It's definitely you," I assure her. "But I will admit... this is, ah, a new experience for me and I don't hate the spectator with us." I answer hastily. "Also, as it turns out, I might have been born a killer. I'm not as freaked out as I should be."

Her hand comes down and cups my dick. I flinch in surprise but then press forward, into her warm palm.

"Death is natural. Nothing to be afraid of or freaked out about," she assures me. "Clearly, it excites you."

It's not so natural when you get brutally murdered in your own home, like how George went out, but I don't point this out. Not with her hand squeezing me gently.

"We should go check on Kingston." She sighs and steps away from me.

The loss of her hand on my dick has me reaching out and grabbing her again, this time by the waist. She gasps as I lift her up and place her on the edge of George's desk.

"In a second," I mutter against her lips just before I kiss her again. My heart hammers gleefully in my chest with Daisy in my arms and blood covering the two of us.

She reaches up and cups my face, smearing it with George's blood. I groan, stepping closer into her body. My hips grind against her pelvis. God, I could blow just doing this. Daisy pulls away after a moment. When our eyes meet, I see her eyes twinkling in what little light there is spilling into the room.

"I have an idea."

I grin. "Whatever it is, I'm sure it's creative."

Winking, she hops off the desk, grabs my hand, and pulls me closer to George, who's slouched forward in his chair. She grabs a handful of his hair and yanks him back so that he's leaning backward. Keeping a hold of him, she uses her other hand to pat the desk directly in front of him.

"Climb up and sit facing George."

I frown. "Daisy, I—"

"Trust me."

My hesitation is brief before I do as requested. When I'm sitting, facing George, I look at Daisy, confused. Her smile turns devious.

"Unzip your pants."

I fumble getting the fly open, my hands shaking from excitement. Usually, *I'm* the one giving orders, but Daisy dictating what we're doing is hot, and in the moment, I'm sure I would do anything she asked of me.

When my dick is free, she reaches over and strokes me once, twice, and then gives me a tight squeeze. I groan. Leaning my hands back, I brace myself on the desk and watch Daisy as she shoots me another sly smile.

"Tell me if this is too much, ok?" she asks.

I snort. "Don't worry, I haven't found my limits yet— OH MY GOD, *DAISY*!"

Suddenly, my girl is yanking George forward. His hanging mouth comes down around my dick, and suddenly, it's hitting the back of his throat. George's saliva and blood pool over my cock, still surprisingly warm. His tongue flops against my dick and I suck in a sharp breath as I'm both horrified and absolutely fucking blown away by how turned on I am.

"You ok?" Daisy's question is practically purred, as if she knows *exactly* how I feel and is just taunting me.

I know my mouth is hanging open, but I can't seem to find

the strength to shut it. Looking from George to Daisy, I know in that moment, I would die for this woman. I'd carve up bodies, pluck out eyeballs, go to jail, hell, I'd do *anything* for her. I'm so fucking in love with Daisy Murray that my heart can't seem to stop ballooning as I stare at her.

"I-I... yeah, yes. I'm good," I manage to croak out.

Her smile turns into a full blown grin as she lifts George's head almost all the way off me before sinking him back down. My eyes cross as I groan at the strange and sick sight of a dead man on my cock. Without any sucking, it's mostly just the feeling of fluids dripping over me, but the sight of my girl pleasuring me with a dead body? It's further than I've gone even in my fantasies. When I was with Brett, we'd fuck *near* a body—but on or *in* one? Never. That was Brett's hard limit.

It should be mine. Hell, it should be *everyone's.*

But it's not. I'm a fucked up person with a perversion no one but someone equally as fucked up as I am would get.

Daisy is my soulmate. I know it.

I can't stop another heavy groan from slipping past my lips or my hips from jerking upward into the dead bastard's mouth. Daisy pauses a moment to scramble up on the desk beside me. She brings down George's head again, but this time she tilts her head up toward me. I oblige immediately, coming down to kiss the woman from my dreams.

Her soft moan in my mouth nearly sends me over the edge.

Up and down, George's tongue and fluids move on my dick while Daisy's tongue lazily explores my mouth. Could this night get any better?

When something lands on my shoulder, coming from a different angle than what Daisy could reach, I jerk away from Daisy's mouth, my heart leaping up into my throat. My breath catches in my throat as I find Kingston standing there, with his mask up, watching us. Oh shit... He has to be wondering what the hell he just walked into. Especially since Daisy doesn't stop jerking me off with a dead man's head. To my surprise, he smirks at me.

"King," Daisy calls to him.

His eyes flicker to her for one moment before he looks back at me. Slowly, he lifts something into view. I gape as he waves a severed hand at me. He reaches forward, letting the fingertips skim across my cheek. Fuck, why does this fucking cause my heart to flutter? Kingston snickers as he drops the hand beside me onto the desk.

"Need a hand in here?" Kingston asks.

Or it was something along those lines. I let out a shaky laugh. How is *he* not freaking out about what Daisy and I are doing? We all must be just fucking nuts.

Kingston walks around George's body to stand in front of Daisy. George's head pauses, his lips sitting around the base of my cock while the tip of my dick sits just beyond his tonsils.

"It was sweet of you to think of Wyatt. I think I have things covered in this particular department, but I could use some attention. Join us?"

He flashes her a grin. There's blood on his lips and teeth—Did he bite someone? She leans forward and he meets her halfway, kissing her hungrily. His bloody hands dive into her hair, and he leans into her.

My cock jerks in George's mouth.

Though he never admitted it, even after her disappearance, I'd always thought Kingston had a crush on Daisy. Despite how much he teased her and poked fun at some of the things she did, he always had this covetous gleam in his eyes whenever he stared at her and she wasn't looking. Now, there's no doubt about where his heart lies.

Without breaking her kiss with Kingston, Daisy starts to move George's head again. I groan, my eyelids fluttering halfway shut. Fuck, this has to be a fever dream of epic proportions. We should be rushing to get out of here, getting to Owen and Drake, who are probably freaking out as they wonder what's taking us so long.

But I can't find it in me to stop this madness.

I let it consume me, basking in the strange sensation casing my dick and watching two of the most attractive people I've ever encountered make out while covered in an alarming amount of blood.

It doesn't take me long. My back hunches forward as my hand comes down on the back of Daisy's where she holds George's head. My balls raise up just as the tension in my body snaps. When I cum, I can't stop the shout of ecstasy that fills the room. Daisy pulls away from Kingston, who simply leans forward to kiss down her neck, and she smiles up at me.

"You're going to be the death of me, woman," I rasp as I try to catch my breath.

Her only response is to laugh.

Besides Kingston slinking through the darkness a few minutes ago, there's no movement in George Herring's house. Gritting my teeth, I search every nook and cranny that I can see for any signs of life.

But there are none.

I'd almost stabbed the man who'd shown up twenty minutes ago while he lurked around the backyard. The only reason I hesitated was because I didn't want a neighbor to see me drag off a body. Dressed in my hoodie with my mask on, I probably wouldn't be recognized. Still, the least amount of disruption I can make while Daisy and the guys are inside, the better.

I take a small comfort in knowing that if the newcomer had seen Wyatt, Daisy, and Kingston, there would've been some type of commotion. Enough to warn me they needed help. So for now, I hold my position with bated breath.

Where is that man now? And is George still alive?

My entire body is locked up, ready to move if need be. I'll

give them just a few more minutes. If they don't show then, I'll—

There! Three shadows move through the house. My gaze swings toward the movement. I heave a sigh of relief. I watch as they approach the back door. Just as the shortest one, Daisy, reaches for the handle, headlights flash in the driveway. They must've seen the light too because all three stop moving.

Swearing, I slip through the darkness, back toward the driveway. The sound of a car door slamming shut is loud in the night. The sound of heels clicking against pavement follows. My footsteps falter. Shit.

She's back.

Did the others recognize my mother as she left the first time? Or had I been the only one lucky enough to see the traitorous bitch move through enemy territory as if she owned the place? Moving in the shadows until the front of the house comes into view, I catch Terra Miller as she stomps toward the door.

I reach for the knife that Daisy gifted me, which sits in its sheath on my belt.

She looks older. The blond hair I inherited from her is now faded and graying. It looks thinner too. Her face has more wrinkles than I remember, especially between her brows and around her mouth. But despite the signs of aging, she's dolled up like she's in her twenties and her makeup is over the top.

Bitter resentment pools on my tongue. This woman kept me confined for months, giving me as little food as possible, forcing me to shit in a bucket in a place where I had to sleep, all while touting that she's doing this to make me see things in a better light. As if I would *ever* want to be a part of her crazy-ass cult. She was willing to torment me, allow Daisy's grizzly and unjust death, and for what?

My fingers wrap around the hilt of the knife. Terra bangs on the front door, clearly pissed off about something. She'd never see her own death coming if I snuck up and slit her throat right now. My hand tightens around the hilt.

What about Bethany and Caroline? Can I take their mother away from them?

My sisters clung to every word my mother used to tell them. I have no doubt in my mind that they've been initiated into Briar Glen's cult. They had said nothing to stop Terra and my father from punishing me, nor did they seem to care when I was packing up my shit when I was heading out for basic training. I have no connection with them whatsoever.

Yet my teeth clench as I think about hurting them this way.

Letting my hand fall away from the knife, I exhale. I watch as Terra shoves her hand into her pocket and pulls out a set of keys.

Damn it, she can't go in!

I look toward George's car. The box of ashes Daisy dug up the other night is sitting just beneath it, within sight. The bomb she concocted is rudimentary, but the fact that Daisy knew how to build it without looking up instructions on the internet *and* had nearly everything she could possibly need for it, and for others like it, surprised me. On top of her knowledge of bomb making, Daisy managed to set up a detonator with it in only a few minutes.

She's a woman with many talents it seems. Dangerous ones at that.

I'm supposed to wait to set it off when the coast is clear, and the others have left the building. But as my mother slips a key into the lock, I make the executive decision. My hand slips into my pocket, and my finger presses the small button. The explosion that follows is instantaneous. George's car flies up a few feet into the air and explodes into flames. The sound is deafening, and the force of the bomb causes me to stumble backward.

The sound of my mother's scream is heard over the roar of the flames.

I steady myself and then take off toward the backyard again, keeping low and in the shadows. Just as I round the back, I catch sight of Wyatt, Kingston, and Daisy making a mad dash for the other side of the house where Owen waits in a tree. I follow, letting out a low whistle to let them know it's me approaching.

Daisy slows, turning halfway around.

"Go, go, go!" I hiss as I come up to her. Rather than wait for her to turn back around, I scoop her up and throw her over my shoulder. Her weight is inconsequential. She might as well be a backpack.

Daisy's laughter is soft and uneven as she's jostled around. Ahead of us, Owen jumps down from his tree and joins us. As we make our way to Daisy's car that we picked up earlier, the sound of sirens begin to ring in the distance. We jump over hedges, cut through properties as lights flicker on, and cut down streets swiftly.

We get to the car only a few minutes later. It sits in an alley between an old ice cream shop that's been out of business since before we were born and a laundry mat that's closed for the evening. I barely slow down as I put Daisy on her feet.

She unlocks the car, and we all pile in.

"Well that was fun!" Daisy hums happily as she peels out of the alley.

Wyatt snorts and yanks off his mask beside me. "That was *insane.*"

"God, I was so nervous," Owen admits, crushed against the door opposite of me. "I wasn't sure if I should turn back on the lights when you guys didn't come out right away."

"You did good, Owen," She assures him. "Drake, I need to tell you what I heard about your mother—"

"She's still involved, I know." I swallow bile that is trying to climb up my throat. "She was the one leaving while we watched the house, and she returned looking upset. If I hadn't blown the car up, she would've walked in on you guys."

"Shit," Owen whispers. "This is complicated."

"It complicates nothing. She was seeing George but now that he's dead—" I glance at Wyatt who confirms with a nod "—she has no connection to the upper leaders. We leave her alone unless she proves that she's a threat."

There's a short silence.

Daisy's the first to break it. "Alright, Dre. Whatever you want."

I'm not sure what I want when it comes to Terra Miller. Right now, she's not important.

Daisy reaches up and pulls off her own mask. If I hadn't been right behind her and watching the movement, I wouldn't have noticed the tiny flinch that follows the motion.

"What was that?"

Daisy's eyes flicker to mine in the rearview mirror. "What was what?"

"You're hurt, aren't you?"

In the passenger seat, Kingston's head whips around to stare at Daisy and Wyatt leans between the two seats with a gasp.

"What? Where?" he demands.

Kingston reaches out and snatches her by the wrist.

"It's nothing! I'm fine!"

"It's her upper arm," I growl, shouldering Wyatt out of the way. He shoves his shoulder back into me.

"Fuck, he's right." Wyatt gasps. "You were shot."

The blood drains from my face. *Shot*?

"Daisy! Are you ok? Why didn't you say something?" Owen demands. "Should we go to the hospital in the town over?"

Daisy sighs. "It's nothing. The bullet grazed me. I'll just need a bandaid—"

"No hospital. We're going straight back to Wyatt's house where I can take a look," I snap, cutting off her placating. "I'll be the judge of what you need. If it's stitches, I can do that. For now, pull over and let one of us drive."

I should've been the one to go in with her. This never would have happened if I'd been inside. Rage like no other surges forward. Why did I think I could trust Wyatt and Kingston, two people with no fighting, or killing, experience with Daisy's life? My hands turn to fists as I glare at her through the rearview mirror.

"Um, no." Her curt response is paired with an eye roll that she makes sure I can see. "This is my car, I get to drive. Besides, I'm not bleeding out and it's not hindering my movement. I'm telling you, I'm ok."

"And *I'm* telling *you*, if you do not at least pull over to let me see it right now, I will make sure that you sit out while *we* take care of the others," I tell her.

Daisy says nothing to this and for a second the car engine revs in a challenge.

"C'mon, Daisy, let us see," Owen pleas softly. "Give us a little peace of mind."

Silence ticks by.

"Dre, I'll let you check at Wyatt's house, ok?" Daisy asks after a moment, her voice tense. "Right now we don't have time for this. We have to hide this car, go get yours, and sneak back to Wyatt's."

As the other's concede, I fume silently.

THE MINUTE DAISY cuts the engine, parking down the hidden dirt path where my truck sits on the outskirts of town, I throw open my door and stomp around to rip open hers.

"Drake!" Daisy glares up at me as I crowd her space.

Her incredulousness only pisses me off. Have I not made

myself clear on my stance when it comes to her well-being? Guess not.

Reaching down, I yank Daisy out of the car by her good arm and bring her to her feet. The gasp she lets out causes Kingston to glare at me over the hood of the car. I ignore him.

"Careful, Dre," Wyatt warns as he slides out of the car next.

Careful? *Careful?* Where was his *care* with our girl while they were in George's house? I don't spare him a glance, knowing I'll deal with him later.

Daisy shoves at my chest, growling as she attempts to push me away. "Drake, chill."

Without waiting, I unzip her jacket and peel it off her. As it falls to the ground, I grab her arm and lift it. There, just below the short sleeve of her shirt, is a bleeding bullet wound. The air in my lungs is knocked out. *She's been shot...* Seeing it makes it real. It reminds me that we're only human and we're risking more than a slap on the wrist from the authorities. There's a real chance one of us could die.

Taking a deep breath, I study the wound.

Daisy's right. She probably doesn't need more than a thorough cleaning and a bandaid, but still. Just the sight of her blood dripping down her arm is enough of a chokehold on me that I can't stop the horrid chill from running through me nor can I calm the rapid pounding of my heart.

Or the anger that stems from Daisy trying to keep her injury from all of us.

"You will tell me each and every time you hurt yourself," I tell her through clenched teeth as I glare down at her.

Daisy lets out a short, sharp laugh of disbelief. "Don't be ridiculous."

"I mean it." I yank her closer, causing her to gasp. "Whether it's stubbing your toe or getting a papercut, I want to know."

"You're acting like an old mother hen." She tries to yank her arm back. I don't release her.

"I won't repeat myself." She can't get hurt. If something happens to her again because I wasn't there or able to prevent it, I won't be able to live with myself. The blood rushes loudly in my ears.

Around us the others are moving, opening the trunk and transferring backpacks and weapons from Daisy's car to mine, preparing to leave. But I can feel their eyes and the tension growing between all of us.

With a heavy sigh, Daisy asks, "Is this about our conversation earlier? About you wanting to take care of me?"

My body, riddled with too many emotions and with no reasonable outlet, trembles slightly. Unable to speak, I simply nod.

There is a short pause. Daisy rolls her shoulders before letting them drop, then nods. "Alright, Drake."

I let out a relieved sigh which allows some of the emotions to dissipate.

"Thank you. Now let's get back to Wyatt's."

28

Kingston

It's late by the time we get back to Wyatt's house.

Just like the night before, after we switch cars and drive back to town in Drake's truck, Daisy and I are dropped off at the house behind Wyatt's so we can slip into his unseen while the others enter through the front.

"I didn't realize before, King, but you're filthy," Daisy says as we all start turning on the lights in the house.

I look down at myself. My jacket and shirt are completely covered in dried blood.

"You're not hurt, are you?" she asks just as Drake grabs her by the hand and drags her into the living room. I trail after them, shaking my head.

"None of it is mine." I flash her a grin and she returns it.

"King, you can take a shower first," Wyatt offers, pulling off his jacket and mask. "Owen, the guest bathroom—"

"You can go. You're covered in blood too." There's something off in Owen's voice. When I turn, I find him with his hand on his stomach like he might be sick. "What happened to your pants, Wy?"

I snicker at Wyatt, whose face turns a deep shade of red as he dips into his bedroom.

"Things got messy!" he calls.

Owen nods weakly, "Messy. Right. Whatever that means..." Shaking his head, he looks at me. "I'm going to just change out of my clothes. If you throw yours over by the laundry machine, King, I'll take care of them in a minute."

Without another word he dips into his room. I scoff as I stare after him. Clean the evidence of my picturesque murder from my attire? Blasphemy.

Simply killing the guy in George's house hadn't been enough. I chewed through flesh, yanked out organs, and cut off fingers. The thrill of the experience is still coursing through my veins, amplified by the sight of Daisy using a corpse to get Wyatt off.

I can see the two of them as clear as day even now. My dick hardens. Fucked up. That's what we are. And hot *damn* if being screwed up in the head isn't a thrill!

Desire pulsates through my veins as I join the others in the living room. I watch Drake pull Daisy down onto the coffee table and place the first aid kit beside her. He kneels before her and opens the box. Without a word, she pulls off her jacket and gives him her arm. As he begins patching her up, I watch Daisy. With her lips pursed, brows slightly furrowed, and her eyes dark, she looks wary of Drake. But the rest of her body appears relaxed, so that can't be right.

What's she thinking?

"There, all done," Drake mutters, after cleaning and bandaging the cut.

"Feel better?" she asks him, which seems odd given that *he* is helping *her*.

"Yes."

Her odd expression melts as she gives him a smile. She reaches up, cups his face sweetly, and hums happily.

"Good." She stands and turns to me. "I'm going to take a shower, if you're ok with waiting your turn?"

I shake my head. "Go."

She reaches out, takes my hand, and squeezes it before she disappears around the corner. The minute she's out of sight, Drake stands. He moves so quickly, I'm not ready for his attack. His hands shoot out and he shoves me backward. I stumble and almost fall on my ass. At the last minute, I catch myself. I glare at Drake as I straighten.

"You two were supposed to be there to *protect* Daisy! How the hell did she end up with a bullet wound?" he demands.

Why is Drake being so *dramatic?* I roll my eyes. "We were having a little bit of fun."

"Fun?" He grabs the collar of my shirt and yanks me toward him. "You think this is a *game*?"

"Isn't it?" I counter, smiling. "This is chess. Briar Glen made its move, now it's our turn."

"Are you out of your *fucking* mind?" Drake shakes me. "This is Daisy's *life* at stake! Are you willing to risk her getting hurt for some *fun*? What if it hadn't been her arm? She could've gotten a bullet right between her eyes, King!"

My amusement fades as his words strike a chord. He's right. I should've been downstairs with her and Wyatt, not mutilating a corpse.

Drake lets go of me, his scowl deepening. "If you can't watch her back, I will, and *you* can stay outside holding your breath wondering what the hell is happening."

Rage flares up in my chest. Absolutely fucking *not.*

Pushing at Drake's chest, I turn and head down the hallway. On my way to the guest room that I stayed in the night before, I pause by the bathroom door. I can hear Daisy moving around, humming softly with the water running. Steam plumes up from beneath the door. She could've been really injured tonight. My fists curl at my sides as I move away.

I won't let myself get carried away again.

Just as I make it to the guest room, Wyatt pops out of his room, clean and wearing only a pair of boxers.

"Showers open in there if you want."

The pride of wearing another man's blood on my shirt has dimmed significantly. With a nod, I move past him.

"Extra towels are behind the door!" Wyatt calls after me.

I rinse off quickly. By the time I get back to the guest room though, Daisy's beat me. She looks up from the edge of the bed as I enter, her fingers busy braiding her hair.

"I could've sworn you were going to wear all that blood to bed," she mutters with a half-smile as I shut the door behind me.

I don't miss how her eyes trail down my exposed upper half. My dick stirs to life at the heated look she gives me when our eyes meet again.

"Another time." I move across the room until I'm standing in front of her. "I should've been there, helping Wyatt watch over you. I'm sorry."

Daisy's expression shutters, closing off whatever she doesn't want me to see. "I've been alone a long time, King. While I appreciate everyone's help and concern, I know that if it comes down to it, I am more than capable of getting in and out of sticky situations on my own."

"But you're not alone and you should be able to trust me with as much faith as you put into yourself." I crouch down in front of her, between her legs. "I wouldn't be able to live with myself if something did happen to you because I got a little too carried away. Do you know how much I love you?"

Her face softens. "You told me."

"But do you know how deep my love for you runs?" I push. Dressed in only a long white tee shirt Owen gave her the night before, her legs are bare to me. Does she wear underwear beneath it? If so, I'll remedy that soon enough. "If I could, I would unravel the very fabric of time and space, and then weave the fibers of my being into yours so that when I breathe, you do too. So when my love for you chokes me up, it drowns you too. You'd feel how deeply your name is etched into my soul, and how being apart from you has scarred my heart."

Daisy gasps as my hands fall to her thighs. My palms slide upward, pushing her tee shirt off her legs up to her hips. There's nothing between me and her core. My dick twitches, urgently needing to feel her heartbeat around it.

My lips follow my hands, planting kisses up her thighs. With each kiss, I suck gently, leaving a pale pink mark on her light brown skin. Without me having to say a word, Daisy's legs part wider, allowing me to scoot closer. As my kisses travel upward, I notice the thin, short scars lined up like tally marks on the inside of her leg. How did I not notice them before?

"She self-harms. I saw the marks on her legs." Wyatt's words echo in my head from earlier today.

First the gun to her head, now this? What else has she been doing that I haven't noticed? My stomach tightens.

I'll take care of her, I vow as my lips get to the apex of her legs. There, I'm greeted by the glistening of her arousal.

Tugging my gaze away from heaven, I look up at her. "I need you tonight, Daisy. Tell me I can taste you, that I can coat your insides with everything I've saved for you."

When they first started coming to my room at night, the nurses in Riverbend would pride themselves on making me cum, believing it was because of them. But it was Daisy, *always* Daisy, that I pictured when I couldn't hold on to my release any longer. That was back before I'd gotten good at denying them that satisfaction. Everything I am, everything inside of me, belongs with the woman in front of me now.

"Take me however you want, King." Her words are deliberate. Giving me free rein of her body. I swallow as I lean forward, my hands gripping her upper thighs in a tight grasp as I sink my face between her legs.

The perfume of her arousal reaches my nose and I breathe in the heady scent. Groaning, I run my tongue through her wet folds from her core to her clit. Daisy gasps softly, leaning back on her hands and relaxing. I repeat the motion, this time circling her clit with my tongue until I hear her let out a long deep moan. Her hips push toward me, encouraging me to continue. Lifting one hand, I wet my finger with her arousal before sinking it into her pussy.

The pretty sound she lets out causes me to smile. I pump in and out of her lazily, my tongue spurring on her pleasure. After a moment, I add a second, then a third finger into her tight pussy. Daisy's thighs creep toward my ears until they become my earmuffs. Still, I don't stop. I alternate between my fingers and tongue into her tight hole, lapping up everything her body gives me.

Her hips begin to grind against my face. Though muffled, I can hear her breathing turn into sharp pants. It takes no time before her body clamps down around my fingers. When she cums, her whole body quakes. Her thighs grip my face as she rides her orgasm. My heart squeezes in my chest just as tightly.

When her legs set me free, I rise to my feet quickly, licking my fingers as I do so. Dropping my towel, I take a step toward Daisy, but she holds out her hand to stop me. Instantly, I freeze.

"Let me take a look at you," she mutters, her eyes traveling down me.

"Take your time." I smirk when she rolls her eyes at me. It fades though as I add, "I'm all yours, Daisy."

She leans forward until she's rising to her feet. Lifting her hands, Daisy places them on my chest before running them downward, over my stomach, my sides, back up to my shoulders, and then down my arms. When our eyes meet, I swear I can see the glow of the fires of hell in their depths.

"You're mine," she confirms darkly. "I won't let anyone else touch you."

My heart flutters. "Yours."

I reach down and pull up her shirt. As I toss it away, I give myself a second to drink her in fully. I ignore the thick scarring, not allowing the moment to be soured by rage targeted at a group we've set out to destroy.

Leaning down, *way* down, I take her face between my hands and capture her mouth with mine. Her hands brace against my chest as I step forward and slip my tongue between her lips. She tastes of toothpaste. She must've swiped whatever she could find in the guest bathroom. The minty freshness is at odds with the copper taste of blood from earlier. My hands slide down her face, neck, sides, and stall at her hip.

I pull her closer, allowing my cock to nestle between us, to be warmed by her body heat. When that isn't enough, I lift her by the hips and walk her the few steps back toward the bed. There, we fall together onto the mattress, not breaking our kiss. Daisy's hands go to my hair as her legs come up around my waist, urging my dick to dive into her.

The warmth of her core brushing against the tip of my dick sends a brief moment of shock and horror through me. *No, no, no...*

I must've reacted without realizing it because Daisy's legs come down and she breaks our kiss quickly. I capture her hands before she can pull those away too.

"Are you ok? Am I going too fast?" she asks, her eyes searching my face.

I go to shake my head, but I pause, wondering at my reaction. Why did I panic? I want Daisy so badly that my dick is throbbing to slide home. Even now, as I ponder the situation at hand, a drop of precum drips from my body. So why is my breath caught in my throat? And though my heart hammers away with excitement, there's a little fear there too.

"Hey, look at me, Kingston."

I blink, realizing I've gotten lost in my own thoughts.

"If this is too much, that's ok." Daisy smiles in reassurance.

I pull away enough so there's space for me to sign, "I want to. I want you so badly, I swear I might die if I can't be inside you right at this very moment."

It's the truth. Yet there's still a tingling of confusion and hesitation sitting on the fringes of my mind.

Her smile never falters. "Then how about this? You're completely in charge. You decide when you're ready, the pace, and intensity. I'm here for you, King. Use me however you want. Or, if you're not ready, we can lay here, and we'll fall asleep together. Having sex for the first time, *consensually*, is a heady thing, but it's also nerve-wracking. If you're not ready, that's perfectly fine."

I see the understanding in her eyes. It's mixed with what she's not saying. I groan, hating our pasts. Leaning down, I take her mouth again. This time the kiss is less hungry and more soul-searing. I can't get enough of Daisy.

Daisy opens her legs wider for me as I press my body down onto her again. Skin to skin contact seems to be ok. My hands find her hips and I pull her closer. The tip of my cock brushes against her clit. Daisy shivers and leans into me, kissing me back just as deeply. Her hands are more cautious as they run across my body, allowing me to breathe easier. I test the waters again, brushing my dick against her hot entrance. The arousal there coats me instantly. This time, there's less panic. Still, I pull away to simply enjoy the way my dick slides through her wet folds.

When that sensation begins to burn away the lingering doubt and reservations, I position myself at her entrance and push inward. As the head of my dick is sucked into Daisy's perfect body, I instantly know that this is different from every other experience I've had.

We both break our kiss to gasp.

Good god, the hold she has on me is nearly enough to push me over the edge this very instant. I hold my breath, stilling as I try not to ruin the moment by finding my release too early. Beneath me, Daisy breathes heavily. As promised, she doesn't move, allowing me to control this moment. But I can feel her body tremble as she waits. Her pussy bears down like a vice around me. Her arousal is dripping down my cock as her body tries to suck me.

She needs me just as badly as I need her. That knowledge is exhilarating.

When I'm certain I can continue without immediately cumming, I sink deeper into her body. I throw my head back and squeeze my eyes shut as her body wraps around me. She's slick with her own juices, hotter than I could have ever imagined. I breathe through the intensity. Testing the waters, I pump my hips back and forth.

Daisy groans as her body stretches around me while simultaneously trying to hold me inside.

I could stay like this with her for the rest of my life.

"Oh god, Kingston, I—" Daisy swallows, her eyelids fluttering half shut as her hands fall to the mattress and grip the sheets. "You feel amazing."

I shudder at her words. Leaning down, I grab one of her nipples between my lips and suck as I start to move my hips more dramatically. Her body gushes around me, making the motion easy. I grab her legs and bring them up to my sides, causing her body to lift and tilt. When I sink all the way in at this angle, Daisy cries out her elation.

"Yes, yes, yes..." Her words are soft whimpers of affirmation that go in time with the way I pull in and out of her.

I suck on her nipple harder, nipping at it. She yelps and I chuckle before lapping at the hard bud.

I love you, I whisper in my mind to her. *I have always loved you. I'm sorry for everything. For failing to protect you, for not seeing through my father's attack before it was too late. For letting him capture me and allowing him to keep me from you. Despite my failures, I am desperate for your love, Daisy.*

My throat convulses as my guilty conscience twists my heart and causes my hips to snap harder into her.

I pull away from her breast and look down into Daisy's face. Pulling Daisy's legs tighter against me, she immediately knows what I want and locks her legs in place. With my hands free, I tell her,

"Hit me."

Daisy's eyes widen. "*Hit* you?"

"Please, Daisy." I slow the movement of my hips. "I don't deserve you. I know I don't, but I need to hear it from you. Tell me I don't. Hit me, choke me. *Beat me*. I can't stand all the... the *suffering*. What you went through all these years was because of me. I should've been able to save you that night. I don't deserve to feel this good around you."

My throat convulses as my hands fail to convey how I thirst for some type of retribution from her. I want her to take her anger out on me. If I had just been faster, we could have saved her. If I had been more observant in my parents' lives, I may have been able to prevent *that* night from ever happening. If I—

A hand cracks against my cheek, startling me from my spiraling.

"Don't you dare blame yourself for what happened, Kingston Winslow," Daisy hisses beneath me. Her hand makes contact with my cheek again, moving so fast I don't see it coming. The sharp burst of pain comes and goes swiftly. "You think I didn't know something was going on that night? That my parents weren't acting weird? Don't you dare try to shoulder all the blame."

She reaches up and grabs me around the throat with a surprisingly strong grip.

"You say you love me but are you sure? Or do you love the girl I used to be? Are you trying to hold out hope that she's still here? If so, I'm sorry to say she did die that night," she assures me through gritted teeth. I grunt as she cuts off my airway. "Fuck me, Kingston. Show me that you want *this* version of me, jagged pieces and all."

My hips snap forward hard, causing her to gasp. I repeat the motion. There's nothing sweet or gentle about how I pummel into her. Daisy's body bears down on me. I grunt as I struggle to breathe. Daisy lets go of my neck only to slap me again. The pain and shock mix with the pleasure that's building inside of me.

Her hands come up and she drags her nails down my chest. The bite of pain chases away the guilt that threatens to consume me.

Yes!

The pain is exquisite. My balls rise as my orgasm nears. Daisy's hand wraps around my throat again, cutting off my airway. Her hips start to move, meeting my hard thrusts with her own, but then she freezes halfway through the motion as she catches herself.

Keep going, I want to urge her. There's no need for her to be cautious anymore. All my vacillation has burned away. I've been in control, now she can have it. *Next time*, I promise her mentally. I lean down and capture her mouth as my body trembles in warning. My right hand comes down between us to tease her clit, hoping that she's as close as I am.

Her pussy locks down around me. I choke on my pleasure

as Daisy's orgasm washes over her. Her pussy milks me, flooding me with warmth and begging for my release.

"*Kingston*." My name, spoken as a soft prayer on her lips, sends me over the edge. Just as I cum, she lets go of my neck.

The rush of air back into my lungs intensifies the mind-numbing, soul-freeing orgasm that billows through me. My body hunches forward, my hips jerking in time with my cock as I paint her insides with my release. I catch myself with my forearm on the mattress before I can crush Daisy with my body weight.

When I feel like I've been turned inside out and am completely spent, I suck in a deep breath and use both hands to balance myself on either side of her face. Daisy smiles up at me. Her face has softened so much that I swear I *do* see glimpses of the old Daisy there.

"I didn't hurt you, did I?" she mutters, her eyes sliding down to my chest. I follow her gaze to see the red marks that she left behind. When her hand comes to my cheek, this time it's to rest it there gently. "The others are going to think there was a fight."

I move, taking Daisy with me. Falling to my side, Daisy turns into me. I lift her leg to rest over the top of my thigh. My dick is beginning to soften but I refuse to pull out of her warm embrace. The gentle fluttering of her pussy from her after-shocks feels amazing.

"I want these marks tattooed onto me."

"I'm sure Drake knows a tattoo artist we could go to."

The bed shakes from my silent laughter. As it dies down, Daisy brushes her lips against mine in a featherlight kiss. When she pulls away, she asks, "How do you feel?"

The question is absurd. I feel like I'm floating above my body, basking in a sea of bliss. My heart feels like it's beating correctly now.

"Free," I confess, feeling something wild and frantic settling down in my chest. "Those women... they don't own any part of me. Not anymore."

Daisy leans forward and kisses my nose.

"Good." Her eyes flutter shut. "I'm glad."

I pull her closer into my chest. When I'm comfortable, I bury my face in her damp hair and allow sleep to suck me away too.

29

Owen

"Owen, what are you doing up so early?"

I jump at the sound of Daisy's voice. Blinking rapidly as I peel my eyes away from the computer screen, I find Daisy standing in the threshold between the hallway and living room. Shit, I've been so focused on what I was doing, I hadn't noticed her moving around in the small window in the corner of my screen. As discreetly as possible, I type a few buttons and the little window of her bedroom disappears.

Dressed in a simple tee shirt, ripped jeans, and a flannel wrapped around her waist, she looks ready to start her day.

"Just getting some work done."

She moves toward me. "What are you working on?"

Not sure how long I was going to be up, I'd let Drake take the second guest room last night while I worked on the couch. Now, I regret it. My back is sore from sitting in the same position for hours. I roll my head to release the tension in my neck as she sits down beside me.

"Wyatt asked if I could look into the people you want to, ah, take out, so I have."

"Oh, like what you did for George Herring?"

I nod even as my stomach flips. Before hunting him down to kill the man, I'd gone ahead and searched through George Herring's digital footprint and uncovered how devious the man was. I thought hiding babies from the government after their birth, helping kill them in cold blood for a god that doesn't exist, and then performing surgeries on their bodies would be the most disgusting thing I would unearth.

Turns out that our next hit, Vincent Callaway, is just as cold-blooded and disgusting as George was.

"You should've gotten some sleep," she murmurs, resting her head on my shoulder. My heart does a somersault. "We did a lot yesterday."

"I just wanted to get a jump start on the work ahead of us."

Daisy hums, noncommittally.

I wrap my arm around her shoulders and pull her closer. "What are you doing up at—" I glance at the time on my laptop screen "—six-thirty in the morning?"

"Bad dreams."

I hold her tighter. "About last night?"

"No."

I wait for a moment, but Daisy doesn't elaborate.

"You know," I hedge carefully. "Talking about things can help sometimes. I know it can be painful to do, but if you ever need an ear…"

Daisy sits up and meets my gaze with a hard glare. "I don't need an ear, I need revenge."

"We're working on it." I drop my arm from around her shoulders to take one of her hands. "Would you like to see what I've uncovered on Vincent Callaway? It's pretty huge."

Daisy's smile brightens her face. "Show me."

I turn the screen toward her and point to the excel sheets I have up. "Last night I managed to slip past all of Vincent's security measures he has in place for his financial files. He has a ton of them, but I managed to sort through the Eveningstar accounts, you know the bank he runs here in Briar Glen, and his own personal accounts."

"Find anything of interest there?"

I shake my head. "There was nothing incredibly noteworthy about them, except he makes a lot of money. But then I found *the* account. Do you see all these numbers?" She nods. "These numbers just didn't make sense. I've been trying to track where they've been coming from, or rather *who* they've been coming from, and found an account labeled Z."

I grin as Daisy sucks in a sharp breath. She leans forward as I click a few keys and a massive excel spreadsheet pulls up.

"These are all the donations made by members of the cult over the past five decades. It looks like Vincent's been slowly going back and adding numbers, probably from handwritten accounting books. They're monthly donations, Daisy, and some of the amounts given are mind-blowing. I wouldn't have suspected most of the people in this town had this type of money to throw away."

I shake my head as Daisy's gaze rolls over the information.

"And I'm not sure they do." I click the keyboard again and certain numbers turn red, and others turn green. "The green is the positive flow of money into the donation account and the red is what's flowing out of it. If you look at the dates, ever since you disappeared, the donations have dropped significantly."

Daisy scowls. "I wonder why."

"Well, it wouldn't be such a leap to consider that since your sacrifice didn't go well, some of the members realized that this may be a big scam. An important ceremony botched? That could show weak leadership, cause people to question the entire process, and, hey, maybe some people had a come-to-Jesus moment and realized that maybe they shouldn't have tried to kill a young girl. Even though everyone was fucking compliant in covering up your disappearance, some of them may have been through with their involvement afterwards." I shrug.

"Hm, could be." Her skepticism is written all over her face.

I'm not sure I believe it either, but it's plausible.

"But what's more interesting is this." I run my fingers over the keys when another screen pulls up. "This is the main account that holds all the donations."

Daisy leans forward, frowning. "Seventy-eight million dollars... Why did I think it would be more?"

"Because it *should* be." I'm changing and splitting screens so she can see everything that I've uncovered over the past few hours. "It should come as no surprise that the donations were all going into the uppers' pockets. I found trails of money that lead to Francis, George, Ronney, Tobias, and Vincent's offshore accounts. They've been quietly dividing up their earnings, while also keeping some in the pot to use toward blessings."

"Blessings?"

I nod. "Yeah, occasionally it looks like they've put money toward granting members of the cult what they've labeled as 'blessings'. They've come in the form of a new roof for someone here, paying off a college debt for a member's child there, and random shit in between."

"They're acting on behalf of their god..." Daisy shakes her head as a grimace flickers across her pretty face. "Lovely."

Her sarcasm has me smiling. "Yeah, well the money was also helping keep Briar Glen afloat. The uppers have an account that they moved some money into to help keep businesses running, maintaining roads, and the like. And while that might sound like a good deed, can you see why it wouldn't be?"

Daisy considers my question deeply. Her brows furrow as she takes her bottom lip between her teeth.

"Well, without Briar Glen, none of these men have any real power. If it goes under, then they lose everything, right?"

"Exactly. But with fewer donations, there is less money to put toward that account. The uppers would rather continue to fill their own pockets than allot a little more to help the people they're stealing from. With fewer donations coming in and less money going back into the community, Briar Glen is doomed.

"It's amazing to see what these guys are spending their money on too. Tobias was having an affair with a woman in Michigan and funding her lavish lifestyle. Ronney's retirement fund is outrageous. George Herring was in the process of opening up two practices on the West Coast. Vincent has a mansion in Mexico, and Francis? He literally bought an entire town in Ireland, no doubt that's his escape plan."

Daisy takes a deep breath in as her body stiffens dramatically. A dark cloud seems to cross over her face, and for a second, I swear I see a flash of rage and madness, like lightning, in her eyes before her expression abruptly clears.

"I won't let any of them enjoy the money they reaped," she vows softly. "Can you copy all of these files and add them to what we already have?"

"It's already in motion." I pause, gauging her expression before I ask, "What do you want me to do with the money left over in this account?"

She looks away from the screen up to me. Her brows fly upward in surprise.

"*Can* you move this money?"

I grin. "Absolutely."

Shaking her head, Daisy chuckles. "God, to be as smart and talented as you... I'd be an evil genius, Owen."

"Who says I'm not?"

"There is nothing evil about you." Daisy's smile shifts as her pupils narrow onto my face. "The only issue you have is finding the wrong friends to hang out with. If you're not careful, I'll corrupt you."

I suppress a hard shiver. Last night, before I got to work, I watched her and Kingston have sex in the other room. She's so different with Kingston than she is with Wyatt but she's always been observant, knowing we have different needs. What would the two of us be like together? If what she considers corruption is love, I welcome it gladly.

"I'm your demon, Daisy, remember? You can't corrupt demons more than they already are." I hold her gaze. "Briar Glen has a fictitious god to worship, but I have something better, someone real to give my soul to. Or should I say that I *gave* my soul to. You have possessed me since the moment I saw you on the playground, and I've held you in my heart since you left us. There is nothing wrong with you. You're exactly what I need."

Daisy's smile slips as uncertainty ripples across her face. "It's not healthy to be in love with a dead woman, Owen."

"You're not dead, and you never were." I reach forward, taking her chin in my hand and leaning close. "Though at the time I didn't know that. In a sick and twisted way, I forced you to live on and created a world where you didn't die. Five worlds to be exact."

"What do you mean?"

Heat gathers in my cheeks as I pull away from her and turn my attention to my laptop.

"When I was in school, they taught us how to hunt down clues and crack codes, how to build firewalls and protect digital data. Using that knowledge, I flipped that skill and taught myself how to destroy and infiltrate. One day, while I was in my senior year of school, I was just messing around, trying to break into a home security system to test how much I already knew, and in the middle of class, I did it. I found a weak link, slipped in, and managed to see into different rooms of a house owned by a young woman. I was going to slip out and pretend I hadn't, my intention wasn't to stalk, but then I saw her making coffee and..." I pull up Sophia's home security network and turn the laptop back to Daisy who looks from me to the woman moving around on the screen.

Sophia Veros hums as she opens and shuts her refrigerator and moves around. Daisy watches her, a frown dragging her lips downward.

"Wait, is this live?"

I swallow nervously. "Yeah."

"I-I don't understand." Daisy looks back at me, confused.

"You don't? Well, I guess, to me, she looks like you... in a way. Minus the shaved head and piercings. But this was my Daisy for a long time. My first non-Daisy, Daisy." I hold her gaze. "After finding someone who kinda looked like you, I started searching for more women that could potentially be you."

Daisy blinks. "There are more?"

"I found four others— women that I could love from afar, pretending it was you. On my screen, you lived on past that night and grew up, got married, and had a family. Or you became a lawyer and you'd come home from a long day and spread out your caseload on the counter. In a different life, you run marathons, date a firefighter, but have an affair with the neighbor. I watched it all. This woman you see now, that's Sophia. She's expecting twins. To me, that's *Daisy* expecting twins. It's an alternate universe where you were never hurt."

Daisy's mouth pops open. She searches my face as embarrassment and contrition cause my cheeks to grow warm. What is she thinking? Is she repulsed? Horrified? Given that I did just admit I've been stalking women, those are probably the only *correct* reactions. Yet, as time ticks by, Daisy's expression melts from surprise to wonder and then absolute delight. The grin that stretches across her face causes my heart to swell, even though I have no idea why she's smiling at me.

But with the smile come tears that gather in her eyes. My stomach drops in horror.

"Shit, I shouldn't have said anything!" I move my laptop to the side and reach for Daisy, pulling her up onto my lap. I wrap my arms around her slight frame and hold her close while she buries her face in my neck. "I'm sorry. That was weird, wasn't it?"

Daisy shakes her head, laughing softly. "I'm not crying because I'm upset. I'm crying because I love you so much." She pulls her face away from my neck to look into my eyes. "Look at how much you loved me! This is the sweetest and strangest thing I've ever seen or heard."

I suck in a sharp breath at her words. She loves me? The doubt must be written on my face because she lets out a strained laugh before taking my face between her hands and kissing me thoroughly on the lips.

My heart comes to a complete standstill. The air in my lungs stalls and my body begins to burn from the inside out. Daisy, *my* Daisy, is kissing me. Her hands on my face hold me in place, as if I could even dream of moving away.

Kiss her back! The shouting in my head spurs me into action. I lean into Daisy's kiss, my arms wrapping her and pulling her close once more. She leans into me, and I feel like I'm teetering on the top of the world. Is this how Superman feels when he lands on top of skyscrapers and looks down at everyone on the ground?

But something about her words finally registers beyond the fact that she loves me. I pull a few inches away from her face.

"Not loved, *love*— it's present tense," I correct. "Didn't you hear me? I never stopped."

Daisy grins. "I have the world's best demons by my side."

I laugh. "Yeah, well, just so you know, I'm deleting access to their cameras. I have the real thing and don't need them anymore."

"You're right, you don't." Daisy leans forward to kiss my neck. She sucks the sensitive skin there, sending a hard shiver through me. I draw in a swift breath. I turn my head, ready to capture her mouth again but she pulls back a few inches, a strange smile splaying across her face. "Did you watch while their husbands took your Daisy?"

My gasp is followed by a heavy heat gathering in my cheeks. "Ah, maybe a few times..."

"Did you touch yourself as the Daisys on those screens got off?"

I close my eyes as my dick hardens and humiliation mixes with my desire. When I open my eyes, I confess everything, "I did. Every fucking time. I pictured myself in their place. I pictured you thrashing around under me. I even..." I swallow hard but hold her gaze as I add, "Sometimes, I'd hire women that looked like you and fuck them too. I couldn't really find a *perfect* look alike, but it was when they slept that they looked most like you."

"How...?"

"They'd let me drug them so they could sleep while I got off. I'd watch their face, your face, completely at ease while I buried myself inside of you. It helped chase away the look of fear I have permanently branded to my brain from that night."

Her eyebrows rise as her pupils grow wide. "While they slept? Owen, you're terribly kinky. I never would have known."

I let out a breath of relief that she didn't recoil at this information either. This new Daisy certainly is no wilting flower. "I don't know about kinky but... inventive? Sure."

"Did they cum in their sleep?"

My cock strains against my pants as I nod. "I can't unless they do, you know? It felt weird just taking all that pleasure for myself and not giving in return so... yeah, I'd make it good for them too."

Daisy licks her bottom lip as she reaches up and cups my face with one hand. "God that sounds thrilling."

"It does?"

She nods. "Think you'd want to give the real thing a go? I don't know if I could stay asleep without a little assistance but I'm sure we can work around that. Maybe if I allowed myself to get tired enough..."

My dick throbs so hard that I have to reach down and grab myself. She laughs and then kisses me thoroughly. I kiss her back, so hungry to dive into exploring her body that nothing else matters at the moment. I turn, reaching for her hips so that I can grab and throw her back onto the couch but our bubble pops as Wyatt rushes the room.

"There you are, Daisy!"

Daisy looks over her shoulder, her body stiffening. "What is it? Is something wrong?"

Wyatt shakes his head as he hurries over and flops down beside us. He grabs Daisy's waist and yanks her toward him. "No, nothing's wrong. Not anymore. I just... I woke up from a dream that you'd slipped out, and when you weren't in bed with King, I kind of freaked out."

He pulls her onto his lap and kisses her easily. Instantly, I'm flooded with envy. Wyatt makes everything easy. Talking, laughing, cracking jokes, he's never had a tough time bonding with anyone.

Daisy giggles as she pulls away to look at him. "You're ridiculous."

"Maybe a little," He flashes her a grin. "But you make me this way. God, how is it possible that you're back and we're all together again? I can hardly believe it."

She sighs.

"I won't say it's luck or a blessing, but it *is* a miracle." She shifts, climbing off Wyatt's lap to sit sandwiched between us. She takes both of our hands, and just like that, my envy disappears.

"Whatever it is that brought us together, I'm thankful for it," I tell her seriously.

"To be honest, for a while I tried hard not to envision this," she admits softly, looking at the two of us. "I planned for *years* how I was going to exact my revenge, but I knew the trouble I would bring to this town, and to myself, if I got caught. I couldn't ask that of you. I didn't *want* to ask it of you. But..." she shifts, her gaze falling to her lap. "I *missed* you. We never got a proper goodbye. I debated sending another letter. I almost didn't."

I suck in a sharp breath. "You weren't going to tell us you were coming back?"

"No." Her soft admission snaps my brows together. The color drains from Wyatt's face as he stares down at her.

"What changed your mind?" I demand. "The fact that you knew we'd eventually hear about what was happening here?"

Daisy opens her mouth but shuts it as her brows furrow in thought. Anger starts to coil in my gut. How does she not know the type of hope, heartache, and desperation she awakened with that first letter? After five fucking years of agony, she resurfaced and dredged up every awful thing that happened to us after her absence— then to never give us any type of closure? *Again*?

"No, though that was a brief thought," she admits after a moment. She opens her mouth to continue but Drake enters the room, followed by Kingston.

"I guess we're all early birds," I mutter.

"Oh, good, you came just in time. Daisy was just about to

tell us why she had planned *not* to tell us she was going to come back to destroy Briar Glen," Wyatt says sarcastically.

Drake shrugs, moving past us into the kitchen. "Who the fuck cares? She did so it doesn't matter, does it?"

It's a good point. The tension in my shoulders lessens a little as Kingston comes over, scoots by Wyatt and bends down to give Daisy a kiss. I start to pull my hand away as Kingston deepens the kiss, but Daisy's grip tightens before she breaks away from King.

"I don't give a fuck either," he tells her with a shrug and then moves to sit in the recliner.

"Well, it was already a given that you and I would see each other again," Daisy rolls her eyes. "It would've been pretty hard to break you out without being present for the entire thing. But I also gave you the option to leave, start fresh somewhere else. I wasn't going to make you stay." Daisy looks at me, then at Wyatt. "The same way I sent the letter and gave you your gifts. I wanted you to have the option to stay wherever you were and just know I was out there doing what I needed to do. But I also gave you the choice to come back, if you wanted that. We were kids when all that happened. For all I knew, you all forgot about me. But ultimately, I never wanted to force you into killing. Even when we met up in that clearing, I was sure you all had come just to say hi before backing out."

I laugh. It's bitter and causes everyone to look over at me. Well, everyone except Drake who begins to pull out food and pans from different cabinets in the kitchen.

"Daisy, I don't think you understand how much you meant to all of us back then. I would've tried to kill someone for you in those woods the night they tried sacrificing you if I could've." I shake my head before meeting her gaze. "Am I a natural born killer? No. But I won't hesitate to do what I have to for you."

Her brows pinch together in confusion. "But—"

"Turns out, I am, so no need to worry about not getting a

job done while you're in town," Drake says, cutting her off. "It's why I left the Marines. I was *too* good at it. I was worried I'd put myself in a situation where I'd hurt someone innocent." He pauses cracking eggs in a bowl to frown. "Actually, I think I was more worried that I *wasn't* worried about hurting people." He chuckles suddenly and shakes his head as if he's told a joke. "I'm a messed up motherfucker. I'm the perfect man to be on your team, Daze."

I squeeze her hand, even as I shoot Drake a worried look.

"Yeah, ok, well... that's not problematic or worrisome in the least," I mutter. Beside me, Daisy giggles. The sound unravels any lingering tension and I smile down at her.

"Turns out I don't have a problem with it either," Wyatt admits. "I stabbed George like he was a stick of butter. Who knew killing was so easy?"

Kingston grins. "I bit off a man's nose last night. The day before, we carved up two hunters. This has been exhilarating."

I gasp, which only causes Kingston's grin to grow wider. Daisy's laughter rings around the room.

"I guess we don't need you to be a killer, just the information guy, Owen," Wyatt looks over at me.

I don't hate the idea, but still... "I'll kill if it has to be done. Either way, we've been ride or die for you since the beginning, Daisy. Now, with Drake making us breakfast—"

"—I could use some help actually."

Wyatt immediately jumps up and moves to help in the kitchen.

I ignore Drake since I have no knowledge of cooking other than frozen waffles. "I want to show you something. Today's a down day, right?"

At her nod, I grin. Reluctantly, I let go of her hand to stand and walk over to grab the remote from beside Wyatt's TV. After a few minutes, I've pulled up a streaming service, plugged in my information, and pulled up a classic.

"Owen! Mary Poppins?" Daisy squeals from the couch.

There's a collective groan from everyone else that has Daisy and I both laughing. I look at her over my shoulder.

"It's been a while since I've watched it. Want to see if you still love it while we eat breakfast?"

"Absolutely."

30

Daisy

Drake and Wyatt move together seamlessly in the kitchen, as if they've been doing this forever. I don't need breakfast, but I know telling them that will be in vain. I'm getting food whether I want it or not. Apparently during our time apart, Drake has become somewhat of a mother bear, fussing over the well-being of her cubs. It's adorable, albeit a little annoying.

"Here, before this movie actually starts, I'm going to take care of some added security." Owen pats my legs and stands up.

"Added security?"

Drake grunts from the kitchen. "In addition to putting cameras outside *and* inside the house?"

Inside the house? I glance around the room. It takes me a moment to find it, but I do. There, low and behold, in the corner of the room is a small, discreet camera.

"Ah, yeah." Owen scoots by me and moves toward the hallways. "I'll be right back."

"The cameras are *everywhere* so if you don't want someone

to know your business, and by someone, I mean Owen, just be aware of that," Drake says once he's out of sight.

Now they tell me. I think back to what Owen could've seen and scowl. He must've seen me and Wyatt my first night here. While it doesn't necessarily bother me that Owen watched that, I do think it's an invasion of privacy if he had seen me and Kingston together. It was his first time— consensually speaking. I glance at Wyatt, whose ears are a little pink but otherwise seems unfazed. When I look over at Kingston, he simply rolls his eyes as he gets up from the recliner and joins me on the couch.

"We could have some fun with this information," he says before pulling me onto his lap.

If he's not put out by Owen having seen us together, then I won't be either. I kiss him swiftly.

When Owen comes into the room, looking more than a little ashamed, I wait until he sits back down beside me to comment.

"Did you get off watching me have fun with Wyatt and Kingston?"

"Daisy!" Wyatt's chokes from the kitchen. I ignore him.

Owen clears his throat. "I, um..."

"I caught him with his cock out the other morning," Drake announces, clearly amused by what he'd seen. Owen shoots him a dark look before turning his attention back to me, his expression apologetic.

"I wasn't purposely trying to catch you fooling around. I just happened to see things and then I—"

I shake my head. "No, no, I don't want excuses. Next time, if you want to watch, just walk in and take a seat. As long as that's ok with the others, I think it would be hot."

Owen's mouth drops open in surprise before sputtering with embarrassment. It's endearing. Wyatt chuckles, though it's a bit strained, and Drake just shakes his head. Kingston leans forward to nip my earlobe, his body trembling with laughter.

"Better yet," I lower my voice, smiling at the flustered look on Owen's face. "You could join in, if you want."

Owen's beautiful dark brown eyes search my face, the corners of his mouth pulling downward. Does he think I'm lying? Teasing? Hm, that won't do.

Just thinking about Owen's eyes on me while I mess around with one of the others, knowing how much he enjoys watching things happening from afar… It makes my blood boil. Leaning forward in Kingston's lap, I press my lips to Owen's full ones. I slip my tongue into his mouth as it pops open in surprise, and I deepen the kiss. Mentally, I smile victoriously when he lets out a moan and kisses me back fully.

Beneath me, I can feel Kingston's dick stir to life. Does he enjoy the thought of someone watching us too? With a sigh, I pull away.

"Now that we've settled that, what did you get for us?"

I look down to find a handful of devices in his hands and small rectangular plastic pieces sitting in his lap.

"I, ah, grabbed everyone's phone and brought these out." He lifts the plastic squares. "They're trackers. You can get them from any electronics place or online, but I've made modifications to them. This way, we can all wear one and know where each one of us are at all the time. We can put one on our backpacks, shoes, or wherever. I didn't think about using them last night, but after how things got a little chaotic, it might be a good idea."

"These are perfect." I grin at him. "Vincent, our next target, has a massive property. We'll have to spread out to case his place, so having something that will tell us all where we each are, will be helpful."

Owen beams at me.

"So why do you have my phone?" Wyatt asks.

"I'm going to add the program I created for these trackers to it. At the same time, I'm going to hack-proof them. Your lines will be completely secure." Owen leans back against the couch cushion, his brows furrowing as he gets to work opening someone's phone.

Wyatt looks up from what he's doing. "Do you need my password?"

I watch as Owen bypasses whatever password protection Wyatt has on his phone. Owen shakes his head,

"Nope, I'm already in."

Wyatt swears under his breath.

Drake chuckles again before muttering loud enough for us to hear, "I hope you don't have any nudes you don't want anyone to see."

Immediately, Owen denies that he'd search for such a thing and Drake calls him on his shit. Wyatt assures us that there's nothing on his phone and Kingston decides, given Wyatt's strange fetishes, that he doesn't believe him. Soon the room fills with laughter and banter.

And just like that, it feels like old times again.

Just like the day before, I'm given way too much food when breakfast is served.

But this time I don't mind. I take the plate Drake hands me as he wedges himself onto the couch. After a little protest from King and Owen, Drake pulls me onto his lap and takes the time to hand feed me as Owen pushes play on our movie.

Well, *my* movie. They hate it. Or so they claim. But as it starts up, all eyes are immediately glued to the screen, just like all those times when we watched in my parents' basement.

All eyes except for mine and Drake's.

Normally, I wouldn't find being fed hot, but watching

Drake's pupils grow wide as his eyes track the way my lips wrap around his fork does something to me. And with him growing hard beneath me? A thrill of power and excitement tumbles through my veins. He's *enjoying* this. And I'm enjoying the hardened version of my sweet, emotional boy, feeding into his desire.

When I absolutely cannot eat anymore, I take the plate and fork from him and place it on the coffee table in front of us.

"You're not going to eat that?" King asks.

"Nope, have at it."

Kingston hardly waits for me to finish talking before he grabs at the plate.

As he inhales the rest of my breakfast, I reach around Drake and grab the throw blanket. It barely has time to float down to cover me and Drake before my hand slips under it to stroke Drake through his jeans.

Drake jerks once, surprised I think, before stilling and leaning back into the couch. With a sigh, I lean back into him, readjusting my position on his lap so that I can quietly unzip his pants and pull his erection free. I'm eager and confident as I reach for him but when my hands wrap around the girthy appendage, surprise causes me to freeze. What the...

Small pieces of body-warmed metal line the bottom of his dick. In total, I count eight, but then, as my thumb slides over the tip of Drake's dick, I find a ninth one. This piercing is different. While the others are barbells, this one is circular. It protrudes from the slit of his dick before looping under half the head and disappearing.

Baffled and intrigued, my hand slides along each piece of jewelry. What are they for? Simply decoration? My face is directed toward the movie, but my mind wanders as I stroke and explore Drake's dick. What would these feel like inside of me, rolling against my inner walls? The thought has me squeezing my thighs together. It's hard given how they are stretched over Drake's long ones.

As I play, precum gathers at the tip of his dick collecting and spinning along with the piece of jewelry protruding from his slit. I try not to smile. Slowly, I collect what his body is offering so freely onto my fingers, and when I have enough, I pull my hand free, and tilt my head just enough so I can see his face as I suck it off my fingers.

Drake's nostrils flare and he sucks in a deep breath.

Lazily, he shifts me, his knee situating between my legs. He leans back further against the couch and his other hand, already wrapped around me, dips under the blanket. Drake makes easy work of slipping into my pants.

I bite my bottom lip as his fingers brush against my clit. He circles it a few times. I swallow hard, stifling the moan in my throat. I press my back harder into his chest as it starts to feel a little too good. To my dismay, he suddenly stops. Rather than continue to work me up that way, he slides his fingers into my wet folds. I choke on a noise as he runs his fingers back and forth through the mess.

Then he pulls his hand out of my pants altogether. Drake doesn't go far. He drags his wet fingers over his cock and strokes himself.

Oh... My pussy flutters, jealous his hands get to wrap around his dick and not it.

After a few seconds, Drake's fingers return between my legs to collect more of my arousal. He teases my clit again, causing pleasure and tension to mount. My nipples harden and it becomes hard to breathe. But Drake leaves me wanting as he continues to gather my arousal and coat himself with it.

I try to focus on the movie and breathing evenly, but my eyes can't help but drop downward to watch the blanket move ever so slightly as he gets off. I don't know why we're trying to hide this. Hadn't I just told Owen I wouldn't mind being watched or that he should join in?

Still, I try not to draw attention to the man pleasuring himself with my arousal beneath me.

After a few minutes, Drake's body stiffens ever so slightly. His breathing doesn't change but his muscles tense and I know what's happening. Heat gathers in my cheeks. Oh hell, he just got off to me and I barely even touched him. Rather than move to excuse himself, Drake simply relaxes and stares at the movie screen.

Grinning, I lean back and enjoy the rest of the movie.

"Go attach this to something that you wear or carry around with you all the time," Owen says, shoving the little plastic square into my hand after dinner. "Me, Wyatt, and Drake have the app that will keep tabs on it. We'll have to get you and Kingston a phone soon, but for now at least, if we split up, we'll do it where either of you are with someone who has a phone."

I take the object and slip away, stifling a sigh of relief.

It's not that I'm unhappy to be around everyone, but after a full day of touching, talking, food, and laughter, I'm over-stimulated.

When I get to the guest bedroom, I shut the door behind me and lean against it. I squeeze my eyes shut and try to slow my racing heart. This is too much. How do people interact with others all the time? All I want to do is peel my skin off and hide in a dark corner.

Guilt rolls in like a slow moving storm.

What is wrong with me?

I love my guys. All of them. So why do I want to put space between us? Am I so far fucked up that I simply can't *people* anymore? Sure I can put on a face and interact like a normal individual for short periods of time. But this? All day? It feels... Impossible.

Irrational tears gather in my eyes as I push off from the door. I'm not right. There's something *wrong* with me. I let one tear spill down my cheek before I take a deep breath and prod across the room. When I get to my boots and backpack, I crouch down, unzip my bag and rummage through it until I get to the bottom. The handle of the revolver has long since lost its effectiveness in shocking me back to reality. Still, I pull the old revolver free, the weight of it a small comfort. This morning, I'd gone without pressing the barrel to my temple. I can't let another go by.

I need to stick to my routine. My routine helps me stay in control. Without it, I'll start spiraling.

I can't spiral. Not yet. Not until this is done.

After a quick check that the barrel is still empty, that I hadn't unconsciously slipped a bullet into the chamber, I lift the gun and press the end of it to my temple.

What if I just ended this before I got someone hurt? Someone who didn't deserve to end up the in the crosshairs?

The thought helps me pull the trigger. The click and the sound of the chamber rotating are loud in the quiet room. Its familiarity helps a little. While I'm still here, the knowledge that I know I can change that if I wanted to, helps clear my head. If only for a moment or two.

But it doesn't absolve my guilt that I'm in here, and not out there with the others.

With a sigh, I shove the gun back into my backpack, its job done. Just as I finish tucking the tracker Owen gave me between the shoelaces and tongue of my boot, the door cracks open. Lost in my own thoughts, instincts take over before my mind can keep up. All my muscles lock up. As I turn around, I slip my hand under my boot and snatch the knife hiding there, then whirl around to meet whoever is trying to creep up on me.

Kingston closes the door behind him, leaning his back up against it as he watches me closely. His shuttered expression gives nothing away to what he's thinking.

"*Oh.*"

I try to let go of the tension in my shoulders and loosen my grip on the knife. My body doesn't respond right away. Kingston pushes off the door. He moves toward me with the confidence of a man that knows he won't get stabbed.

Or doesn't care if he does.

"Sorry, I didn't mean to, well, you know." What am I apologizing for? Clearly, it was a mistake. I straighten as Kingston stops in front of me. He reaches down and grabs my wrist attached to the hand that holds my knife. He brings it up and has me press the tip of the blade to his throat. I hold it there as he lets go.

"I won't ever fault you for your instincts to survive." He presses his neck harder into the blade. "I'll never find fault with you, *ever*, Daisy."

My heart swells so dramatically that it works its way up into my throat, choking me. I drop the knife away from his neck and take a step back. Not sure what to say, I simply turn around and slip my knife back into its hiding place. When I turn back around, I find Kingston has moved toward the window. He pulls the curtain back and peeks out. With a sigh, he drops the material and looks back at me.

"I think I might prefer the perch in the woods. I like the fresh air... and space."

I look away from him, understanding exactly what he means.

One minute he's by the window, the next he's beside me again. His arms wrap around me to pull me into his body. I lean into his chest, and loosely return the hug.

"We're probably safer out there too," I admit into his chest. "It won't be long before the town riots against the others, thinking they're behind all this. But for now, we have access to food, water, a roof, and cable."

The last bit causes Kingston to laugh. His body shakes and I can't help but smile.

He pulls away, reluctantly letting his arms drop. "And we get to be with the others."

"That too." Why do my words feel so stilted?

His icy blue eyes watch my face. When his pupils narrow and his mouth presses into a tight line, I cave.

With a sigh that carries my shame with it, I add, "It's just a lot, you know? I'm so used to having myself as company. Even then, I can turn everything off. Go into autopilot mode. But here? I can't. To be present, forced to feel things and acknowledge everything all the time..." I don't know what else to say so my words trail off.

Kingston grabs a handful of my shirt and tugs me over to the bed. I follow him without any hesitation. He sits down and holds his hands out for me. A smile tugs at my mouth as I go to him, sitting in his lap with ease.

"I know what it's like, to be bombarded with so much after going so long without. After a year of isolation, coming back to the general population was—" Kingston shakes his head.

His face remains utterly impassive, but his eyes grow colder. I watch them curiously as he works through whatever thoughts or feelings he's struggling with. A poisonous rage wraps around my heart like barbed wire. I can't wait to get my hands on Francis.

After a stretch of silence, Kingston continues, "It helps to just throw yourself in like this. It's a lot at first, but you acclimate quickly."

I nod, my eyes dropping to my lap. Kingston shifts. His lips brush against my cheeks, his hand cradling the back of my head. I turn into him, allowing him to seize my lips. King's kiss is soft but sure. I lean into him, using him as my anchor as I allow myself a moment to just push everything to the side and enjoy this time with him.

Who knows how many of these moments we'll get moving forward?

I open my mouth, hoping he'll deepen the kiss. Instead, he pulls away. My pout doesn't go unnoticed. King flashes me a grin.

"Don't think I didn't notice your little stunt with Drake earlier."

I gasp. "Why are you so nosy?"

"I'm only nosy about the things I care about, and the only thing I care about is you. Meaning you get all my attention," he assures me, without a trace of sarcasm or mockery. My cheeks heat with surprise and delight. "Maybe if, between the four of us, we can keep your mouth and body busy, we'll be able to make your transition easier."

I pretend to consider this before flashing him a grin. "I think that could work."

Kingston mirrors the expression on my face. "I thought it might."

31

Daisy

"You're the Chosen One for Zarzuz, but you're my *Chosen One too, Daisy. You're going to be my in. My salvation. You'll see..."*

The smell of cheap whiskey burns my nose. Oliver's whiskers brush against my face. With my eyes blindfolded, I can't see him, but I know his dick is out. It's always out when it's just the two of us. And when he's just killed? He's even more ready to play. Thankfully, these times are easier to handle than when he's sober. In those instances, his touching can last for hours, sometimes days as he edges himself over and over, showing how good he is by resisting my flesh.

Despite already being unable to see, I squeeze my eyes shut.

"Please no." The words are useless. Never have they stopped him before, but still, I will beg, plead, and fight each and every time he comes to me. I try to pull my limbs in toward my body, but with each one bound to a corner of the mattress, I'm not successful. Hands caress my thighs. The cool, thick liquid coating them smears over my skin and I choke on a sob. "Please, no!"

He's killed her. My newest friend. Chelsea had been trapped in this room with me for three weeks, longer than any of the others. It was hard not *to bond with her when all we had was each other. But now, her blood is on my skin, soaking into my pores. I can feel him smearing it all over me, re-creating the rune he's carved into my skin. My heart struggles to beat properly. It's been broken and re-broken so many times, I'm pretty sure it's only being held together by sheer will.*

A mouth latches onto my nipple and sucks. I shake my head, struggling against my restraints.

"No, no..."

"Such a pretty bride you'll be," Oliver coos.

"Don't touch me."

Oliver groans. The sound of skin lightly slapping together tells me he's enjoying himself. "Do you want to feel her lips against your skin? Have her worship you too?"

My stomach balks. "No!"

Oliver laughs harshly. "She had such pretty lips. I kept them so we could both enjoy them."

Flesh skims across my stomach, up my chest and neck. Then a strange, wet kiss is pressed against my cheek. Oliver moves, the bed dipping as he skims what I know to be a part of Chelsea across my face, toward my lips. His other hand finds the juncture between my legs. I try to turn my head away, to pull my lips inward.

"Ah, c'mon, Chosen One. Zarzuz won't want a boring bride." Oliver's bloody hand caresses my freshly shaved pussy, a job done by him only a few hours ago. "I'll make you feel good, like I always do. I always take care of you, don't I? You'll tell Zarzuz about me, won't you?"

Trapped in place, I can't stop him. As fingers covered with Chelsea's blood push into me, I scream behind my lips.

"Daisy! Daisy, c'mon darling, wake up!"

Hands touch me. My body trembles as rage and helpless surge forward until I can't feel anything else. Squeezing my eyes shut tighter, I pray for the end. I can't keep doing this. Kill me, kill me, kill *me!*

"DAISY!"

The scream, lodged behind tightly pressed lips, chokes off as my eyes flutter open. My rigid limbs abruptly start to fly as I realize I'm not bound. Someone swears at the same time something crashes and breaks. I suck in a sharp breath, but I can't seem to fill my lungs. My eyes, momentarily blinded by sunlight, burn with tears.

"Jesus Christ," someone mutters. "Someone go get her water."

"On it."

I can't breathe, I can't see. Where am I? Where's Oliver? Sweat trickles down my neck, feeling eerily like fingertips.

"You're ok, Daisy! Hey, it's us. It's your demons!"

"Daisy, look at me. Look at me Daisy!" Hands come down on my shoulders.

I can't stand the contact. My heart goes into overdrive. Unable to stop it, I scream. Again, someone swears. The timbre of their voice is familiar, and as my scream dies, the room comes into focus. Kingston, Drake, and Owen have surrounded me on the bed, all in various stages of reaching for me as I scramble away from them.

"Wait, watch out—" Owen's warning comes too late.

My hand reaches out behind me to shuffle further away but finds no purchase. The next thing I know, I'm falling off the edge of the bed. My back hits the floor and half the sheets come toppling down on top of me. There's no pain, but it does knock the breath out of me.

"Shit, Daisy, are you ok?" Owen's crouching down beside me before I can drag in a breath.

I look up into his face, but the room seems to spin around behind him. My stomach lurches. Scrambling to my hands and knees I croak, "Gonna puke."

"I got you," he says and without warning, scoops me up and hurries me out of the room.

We make it to the toilet with no time to spare. All the food I ate yesterday comes up and out as I lean my head into the porcelain bowl. As I puke, soft words are spoken just outside the open bathroom door. Owen kneels down behind me and rubs my back, which is a small but nice comfort.

When there is nothing left to upchuck, I brace my arms on the seat, place my forehead on top of them, and try to breathe deeply.

"Here."

I look up to find Wyatt crouching beside me, holding out a glass of water.

"Thanks." I take it with trembling hands, ready to throw it back.

"Easy there. Smalls sips or it'll come back up," he warns.

Nodding, I do as requested. When the glass is empty, I sigh and hand it back.

"Feel better?" Owen asks me. Looking up at him, I find concern etched all over his face. My heart twists as I find the same expression on Wyatt's face too. I nod.

"Y-yeah. Better."

"Drake and Kingston are working on scraping together breakfast, but it's going to take a bit. In the meantime, do you want a shower?" Wyatt looks at Owen. "Can you grab the clean towels out of the dryer?"

"Yup, be right back." Owen scurries out of the room, giving me a little more space to breathe.

"Hey, are you ok? Really?" Wyatt asks, moving from his knees to his butt and scooting closer. "That nightmare seemed... intense."

I shake my head. "I'm fine. It's over now."

I'm not just talking about the nightmare. The day I bashed

Oliver's head in with a mallet was the day all that torment ended. It had been the best decision of my life.

Wyatt reaches forward, tucking a strand of hair behind my ear. "Do you want to talk about it?"

"*No*." The answer comes out too sharp. I know it the minute it slips past my lips. Wincing, I try again. "Sorry, I just... I don't want to remember those times with Oliver, but there are nights my mind won't let me forget. I definitely don't want to rehash that particular night *again* after just reliving it."

"Alright, if you change your mind let me know." He pauses before tacking on, "It took us forever to wake you. Owen noticed King in the camera trying to wake you and started yelling. But when we all came in and tried to help, it was like nothing we did was getting through to you. Is there something we should do next time?"

I flinch at the prospect of the *next* time. My nightmares are inevitable. As lightly as I try to sleep, eventually exhaustion will creep up on me and take me under like it did last night. Looking down, I find my borrowed shirt drenched in sweat.

"No, not really." I run my hand down my face as I try to wipe away any lingering traces of Chelsea's lips against my skin. "I'll sleep on the couch or floor tonight, so I don't bother anyone."

"Don't be ridiculous," Wyatt snaps, surprising me. When I meet his green gaze, he glares at me. "Not one of us is going to go through hell alone anymore. Do you understand me, Daisy? You could be engulfed in flames, and I would step into your embrace so you wouldn't burn on your own." He reaches up and cups my cheeks, his expression softening. "I'm here for you."

My tired heart skips a beat. Giving him a half smile, I whisper, "You're crazy."

Wyatt's brows raise high, nearly disappearing behind his thick bangs. "Says the one who laughs as she stabs someone."

Somehow I find the ability to laugh still within reach. Though weak, it brings a smile to Wyatt's face. Owen comes back into the room just then, with a white fluffy towel in hand.

"Here you go, Daisy. Do you need anything else?"

"No, thanks guys. I appreciate this." And I mean that from the bottom of my heart. If only they knew how many times I've gone through this on my own. Snapping out of those nightmares is mentally and emotionally draining. "I'll take a quick shower and join you guys in a second."

"Don't rush," Owen assures me. "King's giving Drake a hard time about what we should feed you this morning, so breakfast won't be ready any time soon."

I roll my eyes the same time his phone vibrates. Owen shoves his hands into his pocket and pulls it out.

"Shit, Wy, your friend just pulled up in front of the house. Daisy, you may have to put your shower on hold and hide."

Wyatt and I are on our feet at once.

"Go to my bedroom, hide in the walk-in closet," Wyatt orders, moving out of the bathroom quickly.

Owen grabs my arm when he doesn't think I'm moving fast enough and drags me out after him. "Go, I'm going to stick with the others. It'll look suspicious if I'm not with Drake and Wyatt. Here." He shoves his phone into my hand. "I showed Kingston yesterday how to finagle through the different views. You'll be able to see and hear us in the living room."

"Got it." Just as I finish speaking, the doorbell rings.

"Go!" He shoves me down the hallway the same time Kingston jogs toward us.

Kingston snatches my hand and together we slip into Wyatt's bedroom, making a beeline for his closest. Inside, we scoot to the far back, pulling clothes in front of us and then crouch down. I pull up the screen for us to watch as Wyatt's ex walks into the house.

Wyatt

"What the hell is going on, Wyatt?"

Brett's greeting as I open the door is instantly irksome. As is the way he scowls over my shoulder at Owen who's headed toward the kitchen behind me. Tampering down my irritation at his over familiarity and possessiveness, I try to act normal.

As if I don't know about the hell that's been raised here in Briar Glen.

"I don't know what you're talking about, Brett." I step aside, feigning a look of concern. "C'mon in. We're just making breakfast."

"You hate breakfast," he points out, stomping into my house as if he owns it.

I shut the door slowly, taking every second to settle my already frazzled nerves. Daisy's freak out is still at the forefront of my mind. Whatever she'd been dreaming about, it must've been horrific. I've never seen anyone's body so tense. Her muscles and tendons were straining, tight against her skin. A thick vein in her head had been throbbing, tears forced their way through her closed eyelids, and her jaw was clenched so tight I was afraid she was going to break a tooth. Just before I'd left her to answer the door, there were still shadows in her eyes, as if she still isn't quite present.

"Yeah, well, my guests like it, and Drake has taken over cooking duties so..." I let the sentence hang as I shrug. "Drake, make sure you add a little extra for Brett."

From the kitchen, Drake grunts.

Brett moves to sit down in the recliner but seems to think better of it. He whirls around to face me as I stand by the door and glares at me.

"Do you know the shit I've been dealing with the past few days?" he demands. "It's been a fucking shitstorm in Briar Glen."

I roll my eyes. "A shitstorm, really? No need to be dramatic, Brett."

"I'm not!"

He was always a little theatrical. I don't point this out however.

"What, did all one hundred of Tina's cats escape from her house again?"

Brett shakes his head, his dark hair unmoving thanks to all the gel holding it in place. "This isn't a joke, Wyatt. People are dying. Then there was the bombing, those fires, the asylum—Briar Glen is in the eye of a storm, Wyatt!"

Yeah, and that storm is Daisy Murray.

I try not to smile at that thought. "I'm sure it's just a bunch of kids trying to go viral with the fires—Wait, what do you mean people are dying? Who?"

Mentally, I check my facial expression, hoping that I'm showing the right amount of shock. If there's even a lick of amusement showing, Brett will be able to detect it. He's terribly observant.

Brett crosses his arms over his chest. “George Herring and his son, though we’re still looking for Jeff’s body, and some guy who was in George’s house when we found him.”

As far as I know, Jeff is still lying on the altar where we left him, unless some of the wildlife decided to drag him off somewhere.

Shaking off that thought, I try to think about how I would normally react to this information. “Wait, I’m confused. There was a man in George’s house? Was he George’s killer? Could he have been Jeff’s? Hold on,” I scowl. “How do you know Jeff is dead without a body?”

Brett’s lips purse even as his shoulders sag. Before he responds, it’s Owen that speaks up from the kitchen.

“This town has really gone downhill since I was here last. Thank goodness I don’t live here anymore.”

“This town was shit even when we did live here,” Drake grumbles, the sound of eggs being whisked follows.

“Then why come back?” Brett demands, sharply, suddenly strolling past me toward the two of them. “Why are you two really here?”

I turn and track Brett, scowling at the edge in his voice. *That’s* not the tone of a cop— it’s one of a jealous ex-lover.

“I can’t have friends come and stay—”

“Your friends haven’t been back to Briar Glen in over a decade, and I never *once* heard you talk about them. Now here they both are, out of the blue, just as chaos erupts all over town,” Brett interrupts. “According to rumors back in the day, your friends were pretty vocal about their displeasure with Francis Winslow for one reason or another. Quite a coincidence that they come back, and his son is suddenly free.”

Drake scoffs while I frown.

“I was vocal about Kingston’s injustice too,” I point out, choking down my annoyance.

Before Brett can respond, Owen sputters before his brows

snap together. "Are you accusing us of aiding and abetting a criminal and of arson? Because that's fucking bullshit."

"I'm not accusing you all of anything. All I'm doing is pointing out some suspicious happenstances," Brett objects coldly. He turns to look back at me while he points a thumb at Drake, "This one's truck has been seen driving around at all hours of the night."

"I'm right here. No need to pretend I'm not," Drake drawls. "And am I not allowed to cruise around at night?"

"What have you been doing out so late?" Brett counters, turning his attention back to him.

Drake shrugs. "Hunting, drinking, getting some fresh air to clear my head. War really fucks you up here." He taps his temple. "Staying still too long gets me too much in my head."

The skepticism on Brett's face follows him as he glares at Owen. "And you? What are you doing at night?"

I can see the mischievous look in Owen's eyes, but I don't get a chance to stop him from opening his damn mouth before he says, "I spend my nights with my *good* friend, Wy. We've already made some great memories so far. I'm hoping all this craziness in town doesn't take away this special time we've had together."

My jaw drops as I throw up my hands. *Why would you poke the clearly irate bear?* I want to shout.

Brett's face turns an alarming shade of red. I take a step towards him, worried he might be having a heart attack.

"The city is getting ready to host another election in the next coming weeks but at this rate, we have *no one* interested in running. Sandra Mullens, the realtor down the street from you, has been receiving a record number of phone calls from people asking to put their house on the market." Brett takes a steadying breath, though it doesn't help his coloring. "The police department is overwhelmed with the work we have thrown at us, and we're understaffed and spread thin. I swear I think Ronney is starting to drink on the job again. The guy just sobered up a year ago."

I get his frustration, I do. But I don't have it in me to feel guilty or bad about making his life a little difficult. Briar Glen doesn't deserve any reprieve from the hell that's rolled in.

"Look, Brett, I know you're probably exhausted with all the work you're putting in. I don't know what to tell you except that maybe, instead of shouting at me and my friends, you get some sleep. If we can be of any help to you, let me know. Otherwise, I'm at a loss on what to do."

Brett sighs heavily, the tension leaving his body in small increments. He walks over to me and takes my hand.

"Can we talk, just the two of us?" he asks, softly, his eyes searching my face.

Could Brett be a part of Zarzuz's following? Or is he just stuck between the Blessed Priest running the police department and our revenge?

With a nod, I pull Brett toward the hallway. Once there, he moves to push open the guest bedroom door, the same room Daisy and King have been staying in. I jerk his hand back, pulling him to an abrupt halt. Who knows what Daisy and King have left out that could give their presence away?

"We can talk here, they won't bother us," I mutter, pulling Brett a little closer than I normally would since breaking up, hoping he won't notice how deliberately I've stopped him.

Brett frowns but nods. He opens his mouth to say something, but something catches his attention behind me.

"Since when do you have cameras inside the house?"

I look over my shoulder at the discreet little video recorder in the corner at the far end of the hall.

"Since all this shit started happening in town." I shrug and look back at him. "You can't be too careful."

Brett seems to accept this response because he lets it go. He closes the distance between us and presses his forehead against mine. Everything in me screams to back up. With a great deal of effort, I allow Brett this personal moment.

"Look, I know it may be hard to believe, but the town is starting to talk. They think it's those two in the other room starting this shit, and honestly? While I know you have good taste in guys—" he gives me a flirty smile that's short lived "—those two in the other room are trouble. I can feel it. Wyatt, this all started when they came into town. They probably helped their old friend, Kingston, escape, and they were probably the cause of the fire through downtown."

I pull away, unable to maintain the contact.

"C'mon Brett. That's a stretch. They planned a whole escape for Kingston while they were out of state just to make a scene the first night they got here? Without me noticing? Unless you're insinuating that I could be involved…?"

"No of course not!" Brett shakes his head in disgust. "You don't have a dangerous bone in your body… Well, except for one."

He laughs softly, the outrage fading. With a smile, he reaches up to cup my face. My whole body recoils in disgust. I'm tired of him touching me.

"Cut it out." I take another step back. "You come barreling into my house spewing shit about murder, throwing around baseless accusations about my friends, and now you won't stop flirting. Brett, you've gone too far."

"Wy, I'm just concerned. The people in this town don't take kindly to trouble, and if they think you're somehow involved with what's been going on…?"

I scowl. "Then do your job and figure out who it is before I get lynched. But to come here in a jealous rage is ridiculous."

Brett at least has the grace to look ashamed, even if it only lasts a few seconds before looking like a petulant child.

Just as I open my mouth, the sound of a window shattering cuts me off. Brett and I freeze for a fraction of a second before we break into action. At the same time, Owen starts shouting.

We burst back into the family room to see smoke and a small fire as the couch starts to burn. Owen is hurrying over with a glass of water to put it out but is forced to duck when something flaming flings through the broken window.

"What the fuck? Who's attacking us?" I demand, moving toward the door.

"No! Back up!" Brett grabs the back of my shirt and practically yanks me off my feet as he pulls me behind him. From his utility belt he yanks out his gun and charges toward the door.

"Wait!" My protest falls flat as he flings open the door and disappears outside.

I chase after him, Owen right behind me. Brett skids to a stop in the middle of my front yard, gun raised and pointed at a big, lifted truck as it peels around in the middle of the street. Five guys in the bed yell and throw another object on fire at us. Brett ducks but it sails by harmless and lands in my grass.

"Damn it! That's the Truman guys," Brett snarls. "I'm calling for backup. I'll get them, Wy!"

"Still think it's us?" Owen calls after him as Brett races to his squad car. "Asshole."

I turn to glare at him, but out of the corner of my eye, I notice the flames burning my carpet. Swearing, I rush back inside. Drake gets there before me, dumping whisked eggs onto the floor, putting out the flames.

"I'll get more water!" Owen rushes to the kitchen while I hurry over to the couch.

I yank the cushion off and throw it to the ground before stomping on it. As I work to tamper it down, I somehow catch the bottom of my pants on fire. I shake my leg, putting it out, just as Owen comes over and dumps a cup of water onto the cushion.

The fire goes out, sizzling in protest before it's just smoke.

"There." He steps back. "You'll never see the hole if we flip the cushion over—"

"Hey, you guys."

My head whips around to see Daisy standing in the threshold of the room. Blood covers her face, hands, and shirt. She flashes us a manic grin which is at odds with the words that fall from her mouth next.

"We have a problem."

33

Daisy

There's nothing like ripping out the intestines of a redneck to get your blood pumping or to chase away old nightmares.

Thankfully, Wyatt kept his knife out on the nightstand and Kingston had his on hand or this would have been a lot harder.

Unfortunately, now I have bodies to deal with. No, wait. That's not right. *We* have bodies to deal with. The five of us stare down at the four rednecks piled in the middle of Wyatt's master bedroom. Wyatt's too busy gaping, Drake is too busy laughing, and Kingston is merrily drawing a bloody heart on the forehead of a body to notice that Owen is swaying beside me.

As casually as I can, I hook an arm through his to steady him.

"They came in through the window while you were dealing with your visitor," I tell Wyatt.

"And you couldn't have just let them prowl into the rest of

the house while the *police officer* was here to detain them?" Wyatt asks, his voice strained.

I suppose I could've done that. But watching them attempt to be discreet as they moved through the backyard toward the house with guns in hand spurred me into a murderous rage. The need to defend my guys outweighed common sense. The minute the first one shimmed up the window into the room, they were dead men.

"It's no big deal." Drake shrugs. "They shouldn't have been here anyway."

Wyatt whips his head around to stare at him incredulously. "No big deal? There are four *bodies* in my house!"

Drake sighs. "Yeah, we see that. Don't go popping boners on us though, this isn't the time."

Kingston laughs silently. His head tilts backward as his shoulders shake with mirth. I try to stifle my own amusement, but Wyatt's outraged sputter is hilarious. Attempting to steer the conversation in a different direction, I offer, "If you're worried about the blood, we'll replace the carpet. I'll watch some videos and figure it out. No one will be the wiser."

"It's not hard— I've done it before in the cabin," Drake says absentmindedly as he kicks the leg of one of the dead guys.

"This isn't about the carpet!" Wyatt reaches up and runs his fingers through his hair with frustration. "Whatever. It doesn't matter. It's not like we're planning to stay here long anyway."

"We aren't?" Owen speaks up then for the first time since he walked into the room.

"Well, once we're done killing every fucker on Daisy's list, I doubt lingering in Briar Glen is a good idea." Wyatt pauses. "We'll burn the house, I'll collect the insurance, and then we disappear."

That plan came to him quickly. Or did it? I frown. Has Wyatt been thinking about this a lot in the past few days?

"Daisy, do *you* have a plan for the future?" Owen looks down at me curiously.

He's not the only one. Suddenly, everyone's looking at me. As casually as possible, I let my eyes drift down to the bodies on the floor.

"I haven't thought that far ahead." It's not necessarily a lie. However, the omission of the truth has my stomach knotting. The knowledge that no one will be alone after this eases my guilt. "This has been my primary focus for years."

This must seem like a plausible excuse because the guys turn their attention to the problem at hand. Drake crouches down to stare at the nearest dead man. "Tonight we have a bonfire and get rid of them in the woods."

Owen's soft but audible gulp causes my lips to twitch. Fighting down the urge to smile, I pull him closer and allow him to lean on me.

"Or we dump them in the river, then we go after Vincent. With Tobias's death and now George's, it'll be obvious who we are picking off." I smile at the thought. I hope these men are terrified. "Owen, you drained the cult's account, right?"

I look over at him to find his brown skin looking a little ashen.

His nod is jerky. "Ah, yeah. I did it yesterday after breakfast. I didn't leave a single cent. It's currently sitting in several different offshore accounts for when this is all over."

That's much better than Wyatt waiting around for an insurance check to come in the mail.

I grin. "Perfect. I'm sure Francis and his Blessed Priests are feeling the pressure now. Vincent especially, since he was in charge of the funds. The others are probably furious with him right now."

"A man backed into a corner will fight the hardest." Drake stands and looks back at me. "I have a feeling he won't go down as easily as George."

"George was a boring kill anyhow." I pause before adding, "But you're right. I'm sure Francis and the rest of his Blessed Priests are going to start preparing for trouble. We'll have to get a bit more creative."

Kingston rocks back on his heels. "My father won't like that someone is playing with his finances. Money was his world." Kingston looks at Owen. "You made sure the activity can't be traced back to us, right? Because he'll hire a team of people to look into this— if he hasn't already."

"He'll never know who moved the money." Owen's voice is growing weaker.

Looking up at him, I ask, "Why don't you go save the camera footage from the attack up front. Get it ready to give to the police. Then you should delete the footage of these guys creeping through the backyard. We'll move the bodies, rip up the carpet, and clean up."

He doesn't say anything, but he shoots me a grateful smile before practically sprinting out of the room.

"Guy looked a little green, didn't he?" Drake asks, coughing to poorly cover up his chuckle.

I shrug. "This isn't for everyone. Anyway, let's get moving. I'm sure the cop will be back to take everyone's statements."

Wyatt swears. "Yeah, he'll be back with buddies now."

"No problem. Let's go get a tarp."

Cleaning up the bodies and moving them out into the bushes propped up against the house takes a lot of work. Mostly because I can't go out to help and risk being seen, and because, well, carrying bodies isn't a forte of mine. Getting Tobias's body out of the window so he ended up hanging by the neck after I'd killed him had taken time and a lot of finagling.

Just as the last body was taken out back, Wyatt's ex comes

back. This time, he has five other cops with him. While they're here, Kingston and I are limited to what we can do—meaning cleaning up the crime scene has to come to a temporary standstill. But once they're gone, we all work to cut the bloody carpet out of the bedroom and bag it up.

Finally, at long last, I manage to hop into Wyatt's shower and rinse away the evidence of my nightmare and my kills.

When I'm clean and scrubbed nearly raw, I step out of the master bathroom with a towel wrapped around me only to find Drake sitting on Wyatt's bed waiting for me. In his lap is a plate of breakfast.

"You and food." I roll my eyes but approach him. I'd completely forgotten about eating.

"You and ignoring your own health," he counters as I stop at the foot of the bed.

I smile as his brows pinch together in a deep scowl. He's quite a striking man. Nearly Viking-esque in size and stature, but this hard exterior definitely adds to his intensity. What would he be like if I could crack it? The thought warms my blood, and I can't stop myself from sizing him up. The thought of eating right now turns my stomach. Fighting Drake on this might be a losing battle though. Unless... I bet I could distract him enough that food will be the last thing on his mind.

Drake's pupils narrow on me. "What are you thinking, Daisy?"

Feigning indifference, I simply shrug. "Nothing."

"Liar."

I can't stop the curve of my mouth as he calls me out. "Ok, well, with you just sitting so innocently on the bed, my mind started to wander."

The suspicion on Drake's face doesn't waver. In fact, it grows more intense. My smile grows as I move closer. Without giving it any thought, I drop my towel. I give Drake some credit, his eyes remain on my face for all of three full seconds before they drop and drink me in. My stomach tries to twist into knots as he takes in the thick scar tissue that creates the rune on my body. When his eyes drop further, I breathe a little easier. Slowly, I lift one knee and place it on the edge of the bed, right beside him.

"Did it hurt, Dre, to get those piercings?" I make sure to keep my voice low so that he has to focus on what I'm saying.

With a deliberate slowness that causes my nipples to tighten, Drake drags his eyes back up my body before meeting my gaze. Where his pupils had been narrow only moments ago, they're now blown wide. His jaw works and nostrils flare. Finally, he answers me.

"Like a bitch."

I bet. Bringing my other knee up so that I'm kneeling beside Drake, I find myself almost eye level with him. "Are they for you? Or more so for your partners?"

"Both."

My hand lifts and perches on his shoulder. My other one reaches down and grabs the plate of food out of his lap and moves it out of the way.

"Yeah?" I lean down and kiss his cheek.

Drake surprises me when his arm shoots out, wraps around my waist, and yanks me into his chest.

"Oh!" I'm off balance and forced to hold onto his shoulders with both hands.

"I know what you're doing Daisy."

"I don't know what you're talking about." I lean forward and brush my lips against his.

Growling against my lips hard enough that I can feel the vibrations through his chest he says, "I'm going to make you eat every fucking bite of your meal. And if I have to fuck you until your limbs are too weak to fight me off, until your mouth opens as you pant for air, and your pussy is still choking on my cock, then I will."

Well… *damn*. I blink in surprise at his words and pull back. Drake grins up at me, a wickedness gleaming in his eyes.

"You want to play, Daisy? Fine, but it's best to know what you're getting into. I'm not a sweet lover. I'm not *nice*."

I shiver as excitement twists down my spine and my heart speeds up. "Let's see what you got, Dre."

With the gauntlet thrown down, Drake responds immediately. His mouth crashes against mine. Teeth clash as our tongues dart out, meeting one another and instantly start clamoring for dominance. My hands go to his hair, tugging his blond locks out of the loose bun perched at the back of his head. As my fingers weave through his hair, I make sure to drag my nails against his scalp.

Drake's hands grab my thighs and shift me so that I'm straddling him. The bulge in his pants is impossible to ignore. Circling my hips, I rub my clit against it, enjoying the friction the motion creates. It doesn't take much for me to grow wet. After watching the way he'd so effectively used my own arousal to get himself off yesterday, my body hummed with a neediness all day. While I knew King would have been happy to sate that need if I'd initiated something between us as we fell asleep last night, it felt wrong using him when I was thinking of Drake.

All that neediness comes rushing back, warming my body and causing my pussy to clench. Drake allows me to grind against him for a few more moments before he moves. I'm tossed to the side, further onto the bed. I land on my back, bouncing once before coming to a stop. Suddenly, he's between my legs. He grabs my legs and yanks them up, bringing my butt up with them. Without warning, his mouth is on my core.

I cry out in surprise as his tongue plunges into pussy. He brushes his nose against my clit, and I can't stop the heady groan that slips loose. Drake's thorough, using his beard and jaw to brush against my labia deliberately as he feasts on me. I arch into his mouth, loving all the stimulation.

My body begins to tremble. It doesn't take Drake much to work me up to an orgasm. Just as I'm about to snap, Drake pulls his mouth away.

"W-wait, I'm so close," I pant out, trying to lift my hips to reach his mouth.

"Take a bite of your breakfast."

The command doesn't register at first as my body clamors for release.

"What? No, Drake, later—"

I'm flipped over onto my stomach so quickly that it takes a moment for me to process what's happened. Before I can say another word, a hand slaps down on my bare ass, hard. Hissing, I bow my body away from him.

"Let's try this again," he says in an annoyingly disinterested tone. "Take a bite of your food."

I glare at the offending plate sitting a few inches in front of me. My hesitation has consequences. Drake brings his hand down again, the smack ringing loudly. I squeeze my eyes shut as I suck in a sharp breath. When the brief pain fades, I reach out with a shaky hand and grab for a grape. I plop it into my mouth without any more protest.

This time, I'm rewarded.

Drake grabs my hips to hoist me up onto my knees and two thick fingers are shoved into my pussy. Their presence brings satisfaction, an intense stretch, and relief.

"Oh!" My body sucks in Drake's fingers and he chuckles darkly.

"God you're so fucking wet, Daisy. So responsive." He pumps his fingers roughly in and out. I bite my bottom lip as my body trembles harder, so close to an orgasm I can practically taste it. Just as my toes curl, Drake stops again.

"Eat the toast."

"Fuck the damn toast!" I snap back. My hips move, trying to use Drake's fingers that are still inside of me to find my release.

Drake removes them. I open my mouth to protest but suddenly one finger is shoved into my asshole without any preamble.

My howl of surprise and pain has Drake laughing. I press my face into the mattress as my body adjusts to the intrusion. Other than Wyatt's finger, I've never had anything back there before and oh god... I don't know if I can do this. His finger is much thicker than Wyatt's. The way it stretches me is extreme.

"What did I tell you?" Drake asks after his laughter trails off.

Breathing heavily, I lift my face up and reach for the toast. I grab it and force it down. When it's halfway gone, Drake moves his finger. I hiss, but he just tsks.

"If you breathe and relax, you might actually enjoy it."

Yeah right. Still, I try. With a deep breath between bites I try to relax around his finger as he begins to pump it in and out of me. By the time I'm finished choking down the dry bread, I start to see the appeal of butt play.

"There you go," Drake murmurs.

To my surprise, pleasure starts to unfurl in my gut. My pussy spasms around nothing as Drake works me up in a whole new way. My moan is soft, but I push back into his hand, and he hums his approval.

"Think you could take my dick, pretty Daisy?"

I think about the girth and the piercings that adorn his dick. He's a thick guy, and as curious as I am about the jewelry, I'm not sure if I'll live to enjoy them. I might be split open if he tries to drive into me. Though the thought isn't unpleasant.

Drake doesn't seem to need a response. He just continues his thorough finger fucking of my ass. My legs shake as it gets to be too much.

"Look at you, dripping for me," Drake groans. "I've pictured taking you so many ways since I learned you were alive, Daisy, but reality is so much better than any of my fantasies. Taking care of my girl while listening to your moans and heavy breathing? I can't get enough of this."

Casually, Drake snakes his free hand beneath me and circles my clit.

Just like that, the mounting pleasure in my body that has me in its chokehold snaps. I cum with a weak cry. The wave of ecstasy is powerful, keeping me from taking a deep breath to settle myself. But Drake doesn't seem ready for me to come down.

"Now, let's see if we can get those slices of apples down." He withdraws his finger to grip my hips.

"No." I shake my head, still breathing hard. "I can't—"

Drake jerks my hips backward, and suddenly the head of his cock is there, pressing against my entrance. My pussy tries to swallow him in as his bulbous head presses against me.

"Sure you can. Don't you want to know what it's like to take a dick full of metal?" he taunts, pressing in just a little further, stretching my opening but not going far enough to actually be inside of me. "Weren't you just saying how curious you were?"

I try to press back into him, but Drake holds my hips so I can't go any further.

"Yes, but—"

I howl into the mattress as Drake thrusts forward in a slow but determined motion. Oh god, I may have bit off more than I could chew. There's pain as my body stretches to fit Drake inside of me but the way the metal barbells rub against my pussy walls creates a mind-blowing friction that chases the discomfort away. Still, he's a lot.

"*Drake*!" I'm choking, as if his dick is down my throat rather than up my pussy. My body grips him tight.

There's a sharp breath behind me and a stifled groan. "God-damn, you're so fucking warm and wet. You love being manhandled, don't you? No, no, you don't have to say a word. I can tell by the way your pussy drools for more that you do."

He bottoms out inside of me then stills. My body flutters

hungrily around him. He feels exquisite. Before I can open my mouth to beg for him to move, a voice from the doorway asks,

"Well, what do we have going on here?"

Turning my head on the mattress, I find Wyatt and Kingston standing in the doorway. My face flames hot at being caught with Drake's dick deep inside of me, but the hunger on their faces has my whole body quaking with need. Drake grunts as my body clenches around him.

"Tried to feed her but, fuck, she's hungry for dick this afternoon, not food. The sight of you two just about milked the cum from my balls," Drake growls. "Get in here and help me feed this wench."

I laugh breathlessly at Drake's words. "It's well past lunch time. I could've just waited until dinner."

My response earns me a hard slap on the ass. As I cry out, Wyatt and Kingston move into the room to join us. Their gazes never leaving my body.

"Well, look at you, looking like a flower in bloom," Wyatt mutters as he sits down beside my head.

With a huff, I get to my hands and tilt my head up. My body squeezes down around Drake as Wyatt swoops down and takes my mouth with his. I try desperately to move my hips, to enjoy the strangeness of the piercings Drake has, but Drake holds me still. Wyatt breaks our kiss, leaving me wanting as he turns his attention to Kingston, who's climbing onto the bed with us.

"King, hand me the plate," Wyatt orders. "We should feed our flower before she wilts away."

I snort. "It's going to take more than a missed meal to—"

Drake pulls his dick nearly all the way out of me and then slams back home. I shriek, my whole body tensing. Those barbells rotate around just enough to massage my insides, and fucking hell, they feel amazing.

"Shut up and eat the food, Daisy," he snaps. "You've become a brat in your old age."

My laughter is cut short as Wyatt shoves an apple slice into my mouth.

"There, eat up," Wyatt coos. As I chew, Kingston scoots closer. His hand comes down to stroke down my spine. I arch my back into his touch as Drake pulls out and slides home, this time slower and for pleasure, not punishment.

"You know we need you at your best," Wyatt says conversationally, feeding me another slice of apple as Drake fucks me. I chew it quickly, afraid I'll choke overwise. Kingston's hand travels over my butt then dips under me to play with my clit.

My breath catches in my throat as my eyes flutter shut.

"Keep that up, King." Drake grunts as he moves. "Fuck... She feels so good."

"Yeah she does." Wyatt confirmation rings with pride. "Did you think it would be any other way? I knew it was going to be like paradise. You're that special, you know that, Daisy? You're doing so well, eating these apples without a fuss. Such a good girl."

Weirdly enough, I flush under his praise, but words are lost to me as all my nerve endings start to quiver a warning. My body bears down around Drake's.

"Come on, finish one more slice before you cum," Wyatt urges. "I know you can hold out a little longer for me."

Kingston shakes his head, drawing my attention to him. "Not if I can help it."

He reaches down and pinches my clit hard. The flash of pain causes me to arch my back and bear down harder on Drake's dick, which in turn causes those barbells to massage my inner walls. It's all I need to tip over the edge. My cry is met with a slap on the ass as Drake lets go of my hips so that I can ride him through this orgasm.

When the pleasure subsides, I collapse onto my stomach, exhausted.

"You didn't finish what's on your plate." Drake pulls out his dick. The moment he's free, I feel bereft and weak. "Maybe the three of us can teach you a lesson."

Wyatt brings a slice of apples to my lips and automatically I open my mouth. "Good girl." He looks up at something. I follow his gaze but don't notice anything. "Or we can teach two people a lesson at once."

"What if we show him what he's missing? What if we all take Daisy?" Kingston asks. "And make Owen suffer from afar?"

I gasp.

Kingston's grin is almost feral as his pupils blow wide and he reaches down to yank off his pants. Soon, he's completely naked, his dick standing tall and straining toward me. His pale skin is nearly flawless, except for the thick pink scar around his throat that stands out when he tilts his head to regard me. My mouth dries as I stare at him.

"Think you can handle that, pretty flower?" Wyatt asks as his hands come under my shoulders to help lift me up.

A nervous giggle slips past my lips. "I'd sure like to give it a go."

"She can do it." Drake's confidence in me is humbling and terrifying. "I call your virgin ass. The idea of filling you with my cum back there is making it hard to stay sane."

34

Daisy

"*What?* No!" My gasp is met with laughter from all three guys as they begin to reposition themselves while they rearrange my limbs.

"What did I say when we started this? If that plate isn't clear, then I haven't finished with you," Drake growls into my ear as he pulls my back up against his chest. His dick sits between my butt cheeks as a warning.

Wyatt rolls across the king bed and reaches for his nightstand. When he returns, he tosses something to Drake who catches it easily. His body trembles as he laughs.

"I shouldn't use this." He brings the little bottle down to my eye level so that I can see it's lube. "It shouldn't take all three of us to get you to eat."

I give him a one shoulder shrug that is more bravado than true indifference. "Fine, I don't care—"

"You can raw dog her ass when we don't have places we need to be later, or when she no longer is in a position where she may have to run for her life," Wyatt snaps, glaring at Drake while he undresses.

"Oh, she'll be fine."

As they bicker, I turn my attention to Kingston, who's leaning up against the headboard with his legs splayed out in front of him, cock in hand. He strokes it slowly as he holds my gaze. I lick my lips and shoot him a wink. With his thumb, he wipes away the thick drop of precum. My mouth curves into a smile as I pull away from Drake, get on all fours, and crawl toward King. I open my mouth for Kingston, ready to taste him. Rather than let me have what I want, Kingston smears the salty liquid around my lips.

I chase his thumb with my tongue and watch as he sucks in a shaky breath.

"You can be Drake's brat, or Wyatt's pretty flower," he signs. "But you'll always be my everything."

I shiver at the harsh intensity burning in his eyes. "Yes."

He leans in and kisses me thoroughly. My eyes flutter shut as I melt into the moment. His tongue dives into my mouth as his hands come up to cup my face. The sound of a top popping and brief conversation is ignored as I feast on Kingston's mouth. How did I get here and end up deserving any of this? I'll never know, but for now, I won't question it.

It's not like I'll ever get an answer anyway.

Reaching up, I grab Kingston by the neck. I can feel the way his pulse quickens. A heady groan slips past his mouth as I apply pressure. I grin against his lips. Before we can go any further, I'm grabbed by the hips and torn away as Drake moves the two of us toward the headboard.

Kingston chuckles as I pout. "I wasn't done."

"Here, put this in your mouth rather than Kingston's cum," Wyatt brings a bite of egg up to my mouth, using his fingers. Without hesitation, I take the offering. The eggs are cold now, but I don't care. I'll do whatever they want, as long as they keep touching me.

Sitting beside Kingston, Drake leans back so his neck is supported by the headboard, and he brings my hips back onto his erection. In this position, my back faces him while I stare at Wyatt. The stark desire on Wyatt's face causes my pussy to clench with excitement.

"You ready for this, pretty flower?" Wyatt asks.

Drake's cock nudges at my back door. The lube coating it is thick and warm.

"You're ready, little killer," Drake whispers in my ear.

As he pulls me down onto his cock, slower than how he inserted his finger, I think I feel myself actually splitting in half. I open my mouth to scream as the head of him breeches my body, but nothing comes out as the stretching blinks out all ability to do anything but *feel*. My eyes flutter shut, but the eyes of the others, Wyatt and Kingston, are pinned to my body, watching with intensity.

"Look at my flower as she's fed a beast of a cock," Wyatt murmurs, the bed dipping in front of me. "You're doing so well. You needed this. You need *us* don't you, pretty flower?"

"Yes." My confirmation is whimpered as I feel the first and second barbell enter me. Another slips out as I lean my back against Drake, which takes him further into me. My body trembles from the exertion, my breathing nothing more than sharp quick pants. What was I thinking? I can't do this. It hurts, god it hurts. Yes, there's pleasure, but it's too much.

My hands dig into Drake's thighs. He has to stop, *needs* to. Yet just the thought of disappointing everyone in the room, keeps me from tapping out.

Suddenly, something hot and wet twists around my clit. My eyes flutter open as pleasure overrides the stretching. Looking down, I find Wyatt between my legs, sucking and licking my clit. *Oh*... I groan as the pleasure he's working from my body this way clouds the pain going on behind me. Wyatt's tongue slides through my folds, lapping up my arousal like a starving man, before he returns to my clit. He seems unbothered by Drake's cock that's not even an inch away from his face.

Kingston comes up to my side. He reaches up to turn my face and takes my mouth again. I gasp into his mouth before moaning as his tongue sweeps into mine. His hands go to my breasts, tweaking my nipples and teasing them. He tugs and pulls, rolls and pinches. It's too much. All of this is too much. All the sensations combined cause the tension to build to new heights. One I'm scared to fall from.

But fall I do.

King eats up my scream as my body jerks and thrashes against Drake's chest and Wyatt's mouth. I can feel my arousal pool out of me in a rush, but I don't have it in me to be self-conscious about it. And, given how Wyatt's mouth latches onto my core to lap me up, he doesn't mind.

When my orgasm subsides, Drake shifts enough so that he's laying down completely, and takes me with him. Wyatt pulls my legs out on either side of his waist as he crawls forward to hover above me. His skin is warm and the hair on his lower abdomen tickles my stomach.

"Ready to take me, pretty flower?" Wy asks, smiling. "I know you can do it. You want to be filled with our cocks, don't you?"

I'm nodding but doubt is a gray cloud in my mind. Kingston scoots closer, his cock in his hand.

"Tilt your head back for Kingston, Daisy. Open your mouth," Drake orders, his hand coming up to hold me by the front of my neck. He applies a little pressure to keep me trapped against his chest.

Wyatt chuckles darkly as he looks over his shoulder at whatever caught his attention earlier. "Hey, Owen, you can watch us fill all her holes, or you can join us." He turns back to look at me, grinning devilishly. "Either way, smile for the camera, Daisy."

My weak laughter is cut off as Kingston slips his dick into my mouth. I suck on him immediately, using my tongue to caress the underside of him as he sinks further into my mouth.

"Good, just remember to breathe," Wyatt says, pressing his cock against my entrance.

Just as he nudges into me, Owen's voice rings out somewhere in the house, "Wait!"

He comes barreling into the room the next second, a tripod in hand and a phone in the other. Wyatt freezes, and Kingston pulls his dick from my mouth. Owen sets up his stuff, fumbling with it until he has it exactly how he wants it.

"Really, Owen?" Drake asks with exasperation.

"Guess who'll get to relive this moment over and over while you guys just get to use your head?" Owen says as he strips down to nothing and hurries over. His cock is thick and straining, nearly as girthy as Drake's.

"King, care if I take her mouth?" he asks, eagerly hopping onto the bed.

"If you want, we can both take her warm cunt, King. Just come up behind me, I'll scoot forward. We can make it happen," Wyatt offers just as he starts to sink into me. Together, we both groan as my body stretches beyond belief. I'm completely at their mercy and I love it, even as they tear me apart.

My eyelids slam shut as I simply try to breathe. It's a struggle. My pussy pulses around Wyatt's dick and my body bears down on Drake's dick that's already buried deep inside of me. Tears sting my eyes but suddenly hands are on my nipples and someone plays with my clit. Slowly, I'm worked up as someone moves around.

My legs are lifted upward as Wyatt moves his body, scooting up high and kneeling over me.

"Please..." I don't know what I'm asking for, but I beg for it anyway.

"Hold on, Daisy," Owen coos. One of his hands leaves my breast to cup my face. I open my eyes halfway to look at him. "God, you're fucking beautiful."

He swoops down to kiss me.

"She'll look even more beautiful as she leaks cum from every hole she has," Drake rasps behind me. His body is as stiff as a board. There's a slight trembling radiating from him that, at first, I thought was me. Clearly, I'm not the only one struggling.

Kingston comes behind Wyatt, taking my legs and holding them in the air as he leans his hips forward.

"She's so wet, King," Wyatt hisses, he buries his face in my neck before kissing me there, sucking gently on the skin while one of his hands continues to play with my clit. "You won't need the lube to enter her."

I feel it as Kingston's dick presses against my entrance, his cock pressing up against Wyatt's to fight to get in. My whole body tightens, and everyone hisses. I turn and open my mouth, knowing that if I don't accept Owen now, I'll be lost to all that's going on.

"You sure you got this, Daisy?" Owen asks, worry briefly crossing his face.

"Let me taste you," I beg weakly.

He grins. His dick moves forward, and I take his dick into my mouth. I lick the underside of his dick before giving him a hard suck. Owen lets out a loud moan before moving his hips back and forth.

It takes work on everyone's part to make sure they all fit. The stretch of my pussy is beyond imaginable. But somehow, the guys manage. Wyatt is talking to me, his hands all over my body. I think Drake and Owen are saying something too. But there's a ringing in my ears that muffles their words. I'm burning from the inside out. All the horrible things I've ever been through don't stack up or compare to how *right* this feels. I'd do it all again if I could just stay in this moment with our bodies locked together. I can't fathom how Kingston and Wyatt are managing, but somehow they begin to move, finding a rhythm of short thrusts that move me up and down Drake's cock. I suck on Owen, taking him as far back as I can go.

If someone had told me I'd be able to find enough pleasure to find a release in this intense moment, I probably would have laughed. But the pleasure that is building is like nothing I've ever felt before. This one is like someone putting live wires in water, sending intense shocks to my nervous system. It crackles up my spine and into my head before shooting back down all the way to my toes.

Just before it hits, Drake cums. His dick twitches and I can feel the hot splash of his release reaching deep inside of me. My orgasm follows, causing my body to grip him and the other two so tight that everyone is forced to still as I fall apart. The room goes black. Sound becomes muted, and all that's left of me in that moment are molecules humming with life and ecstasy.

Somewhere in the back of my mind, I can feel the others reach their own release. I can feel it spilling inside of me. But I simply bask in the endless sea of bliss I'm floating in. Is this nirvana?

I'm aware enough to notice when Owen pulls out of my mouth. As I blink the room back into existence, he cums. His hot release lands around my neck. I look up to see him staring down at me reverently.

"There, a necklace just for you," he teases.

Smiling, I close my eyes again and grasp for the fading afterglow of my orgasm. The world outside these walls may be dangerous, but here? Right now? I've never felt so safe.

Or loved.

35

Daisy

"Ready? On my count. One, two, three!"

I watch as Kingston and Drake fling the first redneck into the water. Here, at this section of the river, the water is deep, and the current is strong. It captures the corpse and steals it away without issue.

It'll wash up later but by then, any DNA left by us will have been corrupted.

"These fuckers are heavy," Owen grunts as he and Wyatt lift the second guy. He drops the body's feet and takes a few steps back. Judging by the look on his face, he could be sick at any minute.

Through clenched teeth, Wyatt huffs, "It's like carrying around a bunch of dead weight."

"Jokes? Now?" Drake asks, exasperated.

"Why not now?"

Owen swallows before bending back down to pick up the feet again. "Just throw the body in, Wy!"

I watch them from a few feet away. Their banter keeps me

from spiraling too deep into my memories of my time in that cold current. But it's not enough to ease the quiet terror completely. I capture the inside of my cheek between my teeth nervously. My stomach twists as Drake and King move to pick up the third body.

Anxiously, I take a step back to put myself a little further from the water. I'm at a safe distance now, but you can never be too sure, right? One step turns to two, and then three. I don't realize how much distance I put until my foot hits a tree.

I jump, startled, then I chuckle at my own stupidity. Leaning against the tree trunk, I close my eyes and try to settle my nerves. It's just water.

I survived that river before and if I fell in now, I know I could survive again. We're not standing on a cliff with a hundred or so feet between solid ground and water. If anything, I should be afraid of heights. It was the fall that made my time in the water unbearable. A broken collarbone, ankle, and fractured hip probably wouldn't be a pleasant experience in general. But the water had bounced me around, jerking me left and right, amplifying the pain tenfold.

The memory of the pain makes me lightheaded. I suck in a sharp breath.

"Daisy?" My eyes pop open to find Owen jogging toward me. "Are you alright?"

"Yeah." I straighten as the others approach.

Owen's frown tells me he doesn't believe me. "Do you want to go back to Wyatt's house? We don't have to go after Vincent tonight."

Yes, actually we do. Without money, I've immobilized the leaders of the Zarzuzians. But a cornered dog isn't a dead one. If I don't move, Vincent, Ronney, and Francis might find a way to strike first. It's best we take out another leader before they can strategize.

"No, I was just..." I sigh as the others join us. "Being around the river makes me a little anxious."

Drake grabs my hand and pulls me away from the tree. Kingston grabs my other one and tugs me away from Drake to tuck me under his shoulder. I giggle as Wyatt tries to steal me away, but Kingston guides me out of his reach, sticking out his tongue as he does.

"You can't hog her," Drake grumbles as we all head into the woods in the direction we'd come from.

King shoots him a smug smile over my head. Before he can respond though, Owen clears his throat.

"Speaking of staking a claim, Daisy," Owen looks over at me nervously. "We, ah, well none of us used protection earlier. Should we stop at a drugstore tomorrow to grab some condoms for future activities or are you using some type of birth control?"

The other guys freeze in surprise. I open my mouth to reply but Wyatt lets out a choked noise, cutting me off.

"Shit!" He shoots me a panicked look that makes me laugh. "Daisy, that was so selfish of me. I didn't even think—"

"Wy, it's fine. There's nothing to worry—"

"I'm not worried," Drake cuts me off as he shoots the others a smug smile. "I'm clean and if I end up knocking our girl up, I call dibs on naming the little demon."

I gasp in surprise at his declaration. Wait, *what*?

Kingston shakes his head. "If I have to eat your cum out of her pussy just to make sure *I'm* the father of a demon spawn then I'll do it."

My head whips around so I can gape at King properly.

He ignores me as Drake taunts, "You sure you can handle that task? I got full loads—"

"You guys!" I interrupt with a squeak of surprise twisted with a little horror. Kids? *Kids*? I pull away from King and Wyatt to look around at all four men. "You don't need condoms. I won't get pregnant."

All four men look down at me clearly confused.

"What? How do you know that?" Owen asks. "It's a real risk, Daisy. To be on the safe side—"

"I *can't* have kids," I interrupt quietly but firmly. My shock and amusement wither away. "Oliver... he made sure of that."

Wyatt frowns. "I don't understand."

The painful ache of what was taken from me all those years ago has lessened significantly over time. Having a family was the old Daisy's dream. I haven't been her for a while.

"Five years is a long time to go through what I endured without ending up pregnant." I bite the inside of my cheek as I cast my eyes downwards. "It happened once. Oliver was thrilled and I was... not." To say the least.

The thought of bringing life into a world as dark and sinister as the one Oliver created, tortured me more than anything else up until that point.

And knowing that *thing* was an extension of *Oliver*? Bile creeps up my throat. Even if I had escaped the next day, I never would've kept that monstrosity.

"It didn't last long. A week or so after I found out, I had a miscarriage. Oliver went in with this... this *thing* saying he had to scrape the tissue out of me or I could get sick and die..." Flashes of blood on my thighs and on the mattress come and go before I can suppress them. Then there was Oliver, digging around inside of me. "It was extremely hard on my body and it messed things up inside of me. After that, it never happened again. I went to a clinic not that long ago where the doctor told me there's too much scarring. That I would never be able to get pregnant again."

While the news would have devastated a lot of women, the relief I felt had left me reeling for days afterwards. I survived Oliver Grayman in order to take lives, not create them.

"Daze..." Owen stares at me, his eyes bulging. The others wear various expressions of shock and horror.

"It's fine." What Oliver did to me was definitely *not* fine. But that was the past. I'm here now and what I went through has only made me stronger. Forcing a smile, I continue in the direction of the car. After a few steps the others follow. Kingston's arm comes back to rest along my shoulders and Wyatt recaptures my hand. "Anyway, no, we don't need to worry about protection. Now, let's put some distance between us and that river. I wasn't exactly having a great time the last time I was in it."

There's a short pause. Without looking, I know the guys are all exchanging looks over my head. I ignore them.

"How long were you in the river for?" Owen says from behind me after a moment of silence. "You know, after you fell?"

An eternity. "Just a few miles. But I'd broken a few bones, and I kept hitting rocks..."

Against me, I feel Kingston stiffen. I wrap my arm around his waist at the same time Wyatt squeezes my hand in reassurance.

"When I washed up on shore and Oliver found me, I was so relieved." I think back to that night. I'd been semi-conscious when the water pushed me up onto the pebbled shore. I can't remember how long I'd laid there, drifting in and out of consciousness. When a man bent over me, his eyes full of surprise, I'd been so sure I'd been saved.

"What were the chances you ended up in The Butcher of Briar Glen's possession?" Wyatt grumbles. "As if what you'd gone through hadn't been enough."

I frown. "As terrible as this sounds, if Oliver hadn't found me, I probably never would've been able to do what I'm doing now. I *want* revenge. Everyone I knew and trusted, besides you four, knew what was going to happen to me and were fine letting it happen. Including my parents. Thanks to Oliver, I have the nerve—" and the right amount of insanity "—to pull this off."

I could let the conversion drop. Up until this point, I've been purposely vague about what happened that night and the years that followed. But my men are willing to kill for me. They've moved bodies for me. I feel like I owe them more than just the scraps I've been feeding them. And after admitting to the miscarriage, the rest should be a walk in the park to talk about.

"The Butcher of Briar Glen did horrible things. He let me befriend his victims and enjoyed my suffering when he forced me to watch as he tore them to pieces sometimes for days at a time. I watched him try all sorts of different methods on those women, those *girls*. At some point, something inside me snapped." I struggle to breathe through the words that need to be said. "Toward the end, what he was doing no longer disgusted me. It enraged me, made me feel helpless, but he destroyed the part of me that saw blood and death as something to recoil from. When he forgot to tie me back down to the bed the night of my escape, I could have just run. But I didn't. I wanted to feel his blood coating my hands. I wanted to experience that high he got when he killed those women. He was my first kill, and probably the most satisfying thus far."

The guys are silent as they listen on. They've given me the stage and await my darkest confession. I brace myself for what I have to say next. Here in the woods, under the light of the stars, surrounded by the people I love, I'll give them everything.

"After I killed Oliver, I was lost for a year—trapped in my head. Touch triggered me more often than not, as did the color red. I-I did a lot of horrible things." I shake my head to dispel the cloudy memories.

While everything during that time might be hazy at best, I do know that I was feral. Death came swiftly to the unfortunate individuals who tried to get close to me. The things I put in my body to survive and the places I slept... Disgusting and dangerous, I'm sure of it. Rabid animals probably looked timid next to me. I wish I could say that part of me is long gone. But it's not. It's a vile and malicious entity inside me. It's what's wrong with me. Keeping me from being the old Daisy. It's merged with my soul for me to carry around as long as I live.

"What about the first letter you sent us?" Drake asks after some time has passed. "If you were so far gone, how did you find us?"

I frown as I ponder the answer. "Honestly, I don't know. Maybe even as lost as I was in my own head then, I missed you all and thought to reach out. Is that possible?"

"Daze, anything is possible," Owen assures me. "The mind is an incredible thing."

"I think the only thing that kept me going were the memories I had of you four. Maybe that carried over once I was free? I loved you all so much and clung to the good times when Oliver would—"

I choke on the emotions bubbling up.

Kingston leans down and brushes his lips against the side of my temple. I lean into him while absorbing the strength Wyatt sends me as he gives my hand a gentle squeeze.

"Anyhow, eventually I started becoming more like myself. When I realized how damaged I was, I tried to fix those parts of me. I threw myself into activities where touch was common," at least I got paid for those activities, "and I painted my makeshift homes in red." Cardboard boxes or underpass walls were the common places I found shelter back then. "And eventually, I got my first real job. It wasn't much, but waiting tables at the little dive in that small town in Idaho gave me a chance to learn how to interact with people again. The structure helped me settle down. I started reading and doing research."

"And plotting your revenge I'm guessing," Wyatt murmurs thoughtfully.

I nod. "Yes. I had a lot of time to think about this."

The trees begin to thin as we approach the road. Soon, we'll be headed to Vincent Callaway's house. Around me, my men huddle close. None of them appear fazed by the fact that I'm not whole anymore. That the girl they knew is now, in part, a wild, unstoppable force of nature created by a devil.

I don't bother to stifle the small smile that I can feel curling the corners of my lips upward. They love me. Darkness and all. My confession will stay here, in the woods, but their love will follow me all the way to the end of this wild ride.

My footsteps feel a little lighter.

As the car appears, Wyatt tugs on my hand, forcing me to stop. He steps in front of me and places his hands on my shoulders.

"Thanks for sharing that with us, Daze." His eyes search my face as he gives me a soft smile. "There wasn't a day in my life that I didn't think about you too."

"Don't be corny, Wy." Owen walks around us.

Wyatt doesn't look back at Owen as he flips him the bird.

I grin. "Come on, let's go have family-murder time."

Kingston's body shakes as he laughs, and behind me, Drake chuckles.

36

Drake

"Do you have the map that Daisy drew?"

I look over my shoulder, back at Owen, to find him looking around anxiously.

"We don't need it."

Owen huffs and mutters something under his breath.

"What was that?" I can't help but smile. Owen was never one for doing things outdoors when we were younger, and he doesn't seem to have outgrown that now.

Thank god *I* did. Nature is now my place of solace. In the woods is where I belong. I don't feel much like a man as I move through the trees, but what's so great about feeling like one anyway? The emotional turmoil and heavy set of a conscience is hindering. Here, I can shed all that baggage to live in the moment.

"Are you sure we're going in the right direction? I feel like we should've made it to Vincent's house by now."

I look up, checking the placement of the stars before answering. "We're going the right way."

Daisy's rudimentary map that she had drawn of Vincent's property is etched perfectly in my head. With landmarks, directional markers, and even the number of steps between certain points, she was thorough with her explanation and drawing.

She's been watching Vincent for a long time.

The thought is unsettling. How often did she stalk through these woods on her own and with deadly intent? The fact that she knows the layout of the land so perfectly she could describe it so that there was no question where we each needed to go, tells me it was a lot.

She should've called us sooner. Especially me. I could've helped her plan, even execute her revenge earlier, if only she'd asked for help.

"Daisy said that from where we split up, his house should be in sight within an hour."

"What time is it?"

"A quarter past midnight."

I do the math real quick. "We have five more minutes."

Owen lets out a soft groan but falls silent. I'm surprised he's talked at all. Since disposing of the bodies earlier this evening, he's been pretty quiet.

And green. Even with his mask on now, I know his face probably hasn't recovered its color.

A serial killer's lifestyle isn't for Owen. I'm pretty sure Daisy's noticed that too and paired Owen with me for that reason. At least *one* of us will be able to kill without hesitation.

Or maybe he's quiet because he's mulling over what Daisy shared with us. I had to stop thinking about it. My heart can only break so much before I go mad from the pain.

Our journey comes to an end exactly five minutes later when the lights of a house come into view. Given our arrival is at the exact time she told us it would be, that means she, Wyatt, and Kingston have made it to their spot on the other side of the house about now too.

"Damn, she's good," Owen whispers.

I open my mouth to voice my agreement, but the snapping of a twig has me closing my mouth and moving quickly. Twirling around, I grab Owen and yank him down into a crouch with me. Owen's eyes widen in alarm, but I put my finger to my lips as I reach for the knife attached to my belt. Another snapping of a twig follows a moment later, followed by the crunching of leaves.

A man comes into view just behind us, strolling loudly through the woods. His camouflage gear is old and worn, but the rifle hanging off his back looks much newer. Is this security? Daisy didn't say anything about people combing the woods. It must be new. I'm sure she would have mentioned it otherwise.

If this is security, his lazy demeanor won't save Vincent. The man doesn't even take a full look around before stomping off loudly. Discretion clearly wasn't in the job description. As if to confirm that, the man loudly hacks a loogie, spits, snorts, and then takes a heavy drag of his cigarette.

Definitely not a professional by any means.

When he's out of sight, I scoot closer to Owen and whisper, "Text the others there's protection detail out and about."

Owen nods and pulls out his cell phone. As he sends them a text, I shove my knife away and stare at the three-story mansion. Vincent Callaway, the owner of the singular bank in town, is clearly loaded. I wonder if he even needed the donations of the parishioners of the cult to own this type of place. The cedar-shingled house has large windows, a grand front porch, and a steep roof line. Without any houses nearby or trees to obstruct the view, the house sits proudly for all visitors to admire.

In the circular driveway are four nice vehicles. They shine in the dim light of the stars. Who do they belong to? Are they all Vincent's, or do some of them belong to his hired help?

When Owen's done, he shoves his phone back into his jacket pocket and looks up at me.

"What do we do now?"

On the ground, we're bound to be seen. We need a better place for cover. The shadows won't do it for us this time.

"We need to get higher." I look around us and spot a good vantage point. "Over there. Can you climb that tree and get a few feet into the thicker foliage?"

Owen follows the direction of my finger. "I haven't climbed a tree in a while, but I think I can manage."

"I'll give you a boost if you need it."

Though I can't see it, I know Owen is glaring at me through his mask as I mock him. "I think I'm good, Dre. Where are you going to be?"

He better be good. "Close by."

After making sure the coast is clear, we break. I watch as he gets to his tree and pulls himself up. He's rusty at it, but he manages to get off the ground and out of sight quickly. Once I'm sure he's ok on his own, I find my own spot a few yards away, in view of his tree and the house.

Climbing up is easy. Once I find a sturdy branch, I make myself comfortable and turn my attention toward the house.

I'm not surprised to find all the lights on in the house at this hour. After the gruesome death of a second one of his buddies and his buddy's son, I'm sure Vincent will be sleeping with the light on for quite a while.

But he's not alone.

Movement captures my attention on the second floor. A red cloak walks by the window before it's suddenly drawn, blocking my sight. Shit, is there a cult meeting tonight? Or is this a special gathering?

Time creeps by. Over the course of the next hour and a half, three different hired hands pass under my tree. Three more circle closer to the house. There's no more movement coming from inside. No shadows pass by windows, no sounds drift across the vast space from there to here. It's utterly still.

Another half hour ticks by.

At the tail end of it, the front door opens. Five armed men, dressed in camouflage, come out with guns drawn. Behind them, four people emerge. From this distance, there's no chance at identifying them.

Each person climbs into their car, the guards helping them in and looking around as they protect their clients. One by one, each car turns on and pulls away, down the long driveway and out of sight. With their clients gone, the hired guards linger around the front door, talking among themselves.

Some of the noise from their banter and laughter make it to where I am, but it's not loud enough to hint at what they're talking about. After a few minutes they turn, ready to go back inside.

Then a gunshot rings out.

My whole body locks down, freezing in surprise. That sounded like it came from the other side of the house, where Daisy and the others are. Even my heart pauses, making sure it's beating doesn't hinder my hearing as I listen for any other sounds.

The men by the door all freeze too, but only for a minute, and soon I understand why.

The crackle of a walkie talkie a few feet away from my tree comes to life and a voice says over the system,

"Man down. Stab wound to the neck. I'm on the northeast side of the house. I'll—"

The voice cuts off abruptly.

"Dale? Dale, are you there? Can you hear me?" the security detail beneath me calls into his walkie talkie. When Dale doesn't answer, he swears.

In my pocket, my phone vibrates. As slowly as I can, I reach in and pull it out.

Wyatt: Cover's blown. Take the guards all out.

Wyatt: We're going in when the coast is clear.

Grinning, I brace myself for some fun.

Owen

The guards by the doors spring into action, sprinting down the front steps and rushing around the house toward where the gunshot was fired. My stomach knots as I twist around to see if there's any danger beneath me before I start to climb down.

A heavy grunt from somewhere close behind me causes me to pause. I twist around the trunk of the tree to find Drake already on the ground. His knife, dripping with blood, hangs from his hand, and the body of a dead man rests by his feet.

Shaking my head, I climb down my tree and join him, sticking a few feet back. The smell of blood in the air doesn't seem to sit right with me. Or maybe it's the lifeless eyes. Either way, best to keep my distance if I want to keep dinner down.

"The others are going to need our help. Those guards out front just went around the house after them," I tell him.

Drake nods, but instead of us rushing off, he crouches down and grabs the walkie talkie attached to the dead man's pocket. He brings it to his masked mouth.

"Two masked men on the southwest side of the property have machine guns and bombs. Need back up, quick!"

I gape at him as he chuckles and drops the walkie talkie as he stands up.

"You're going to get us killed!" I hiss at him as he strolls past me and breaks into a jog.

"Naw, we'll be good. Let's go."

Turns out, we're not as good as Drake has promised. We barely make it a hundred yards before bullets ricochet around us.

"There! I see them!"

We both throw ourselves to the ground as bullets spray just where we'd been standing. When the bullets stop, someone asks,

"Think we got 'em?"

"Let's go find out. We're getting paid too good to do a shit job," a second voice whispers.

They're closer than I thought they were. How'd we not see them? I try not to draw too much attention as I crawl under a bush for more coverage. The sound of footsteps draws near. Holding my breath, I reach down and grab for my knife.

I hate the way my hand shakes as it unsnaps the sheath and wraps around the handle.

Legs stroll past my hiding place. Then a second pair. I turn and watch them, not sure if I'm this lucky or if they're planning on doing some type of sneak attack. To my horror, I watch as the two men share a look as they come to a sudden stop. Smug smiles spread across their faces before one of them brings a gun up and points it in the direction of where Drake would be hiding.

My stomach drops at the same time a steely resolve shoots through me. I'm on my feet half a breath later. The grip on the handle of my knife is tight, and when it swings through the air, my aim is true. I watch as the blade sinks into the side of the man's neck like he's made from warm butter rather than flesh and bones. Blood spurts out from the wound, flying in all directions. The choking noise he makes draws his friend's attention.

As the second guard turns to look over his shoulder, I yank my blade free and push the body of the first man forward, into him. He swears, instinctually turning to catch his friend. His curse is cut off as Drake shoots up off the ground, yanks him around by the shoulders, then stabs him in the gut over and over. The blade moves so quickly that I hardly see it. On the last strike, Drake drags the blade down the man's abdomen before stepping back and letting him fall.

My eyes travel down with the body.

"I'm proud of you, Owen. I could've sworn you didn't have it in you to kill a fly, let alone a person," Drake says, coming up beside me, giving me a pat on the shoulder. "We should go."

He strolls past me, heading toward the others. I hesitate, still staring at the man I'd killed. Holy shit. I really did it. There's a dead man on the ground and it's because of *me.* Unable to believe it, I use my toe to nudge him. Nothing. Not that I really expected anything to happen. His blood pools out of his neck and seeps into the ground.

I wait for the guilt to flood me. Killing shouldn't have been that easy. This is definitely going to weigh on my conscience. A few seconds tick by, but nothing happens. I don't feel ashamed. I'm not appalled. If anything, I'm a little tired, but that could have a lot more to do with what time it is than the dead body on the ground.

Really, the only thing bothering me right now is the smell of blood that reaches me through my mask. My stomach twists and I can feel sweat gathering on my forehead. Why does blood have to smell so bad? I take a step back, sheathing my blade so that I can wipe my hands on the jacket Daisy gifted me.

I can shower when we're done here, I tell myself as I turn and chase after Drake who's already a good distance ahead.

We meet up with Daisy, Wyatt, and Kingston, a short time later. Surrounded by bodies and covered in blood, they look like they've been bathing in death. Kingston lifts his mask and flashes a grin in our direction.

"You guys ok?" Daisy asks, stepping forward.

I reach forward and drag her into my arms to hold her tight. "We're fine. You?"

"All good here," she assures me, returning the hug.

Oh god, the copper tang in the air… I drop my arms the moment Daisy attempts to move away, glad to get some fresh air. Even the thickness of our masks can't hide the perfume of death.

"What happened?" Drake demands.

"We were spotted," Wyatt sighs. "Well, *I* was spotted when I tried to get closer to the house. There's a gazebo that I wanted to see if I could get to but failed in the process."

Kingston shoots Wyatt a glare. "I told you not to go."

"We couldn't see anything from our vantage point!"

I'm glad to see Wyatt's managed to brush off the cobwebs of his sign language. Though I don't think the middle finger Kings gives Wyatt really ever needed translating.

"We should get moving. I'm sure Vincent heard all the noise out here and is preparing for trouble," Daisy says sharply.

Shit, right…

"What's the game plan?" I ask.

"We charge in there and kill him. He's alone," Daisy says as if she's talking about the weather. "Back door is unlocked. Two hired goons came from there, and I noticed it didn't latch when it swung shut."

I nod, pulling my knife out. "Then let's go."

The five of us cluster together and break for the house without any more preamble. It's Drake that reaches for the back door first. It opens without issue. The mudroom area is dark but nearly every single light is on in the rest of the house. Without having to discuss it, we all remain quiet and split up into our original groups to search the house.

It takes us all of fifteen minutes to determine that the first floor is empty.

We move up to the next floor. Each room I peek my head into, I'm sure it's about to be blown clean off. It doesn't ease my nerves when it doesn't happen. In fact, I'm a trembling ball of energy by the time we creep up to the third floor.

There are only two doors up here, one on either end of the hallway. Both are closed, but beneath each door comes the glow of a red light.

That's certainly not ominous.

Swallowing hard, we split up again. Drake and I move to the right, the others go to the left. Even with our weapons drawn, I don't feel good about this. Why wouldn't Vincent keep some security in the house with him? When we get to the door, we both pause. This time, it's me that reaches for the doorknob instead of Drake. With a deep breath, I twist and push.

Only to find it locked.

At the same time, the others open theirs. The loud bang of a gun going off stops time. A bullet slams into the door Drake and I stand in front of, mere inches from my face. There's a scream of rage and there's another gunshot. Sucking in a deep breath, I twirl around just in time to see Kingston, Wyatt, and Daisy spill into the other room.

Drake and I move as one, rushing back down to the hall. We get to the open doorway just as the gun goes off.

In front of us Daisy, Wyatt, and Kingston scatter to avoid being shot. Another bullet whizzes by my head, way too close for comfort. I don't stop moving, afraid that if I do, I'll become an easy target.

"Don't you get any closer. I'll fucking blast your faces off!"

I know the warning should drag my attention to the man standing in the middle of the relatively sparse room, but as I skid to a halt, my eyes land on the massive creature that looms over us.

The statue, made of plaster, is some sort of bull-like being, similar to a minotaur, with red gems as eyes. Above it is a red light, turning the white plaster pink. Around the statue, candles burn. The light catches in the depth of the gems, causing them to glitter. On the walls around the beast, and us, are weapons of all kinds. Some I recognize, like axes, maces, spears, and swords, but others are foreign to me.

When the gun in Vincent's hand swings in my direction, I refocus on the true danger in the room. The older man, who must be in his early seventies, appears in shape, tall, and is clearly pissed off. His pale face is pink with rage and strands of his poorly dyed jet-black hair falls in front of his eyes as he breathes heavily. His button up shirt is soaked with sweat. The large spot in the middle of his crotch looks less like sweat and more like piss.

I try to see things from his perspective. A singular man against five people wearing masks with missing women on them, horns, and blood spatter. I'm sure we're terrifying.

Yet I can't find it in me to feel anything other than disgust and rage. This is the man who was willing to sacrifice Daisy to some bullshit god. He also oversaw other sacrifices over the years, took money from parishioners, and pretended to bless those that pleased him and Francis. He's been stealing money and profiting off death and naivetè. Vincent Callaway is a disgusting piece of shit and deserves everything coming to him.

"Put it down, *Vinny*," Daisy taunts behind her mask.

"The cops are already on their way," Vincent hisses. "You're going to stay where you are until they get here."

Daisy steps toward him, triggering Vincent to swing the gun in her direction. "Actually, what's going to happen is you're going to meet your maker, and we're going to slip out of here without a scratch."

"You think? Maybe I'll make an example out of you," Vincent sneers.

No! Panic causes my foot to take a step toward him, as if the knife in my hand is any help against the gun in his. My movement is picked up, and again I'm facing down the barrel of a gun.

"If you shoot him, I'll have you wishing for death," Daisy promises. She reaches up to push back her hood and pull up her mask. "How about you point that in my direction since I'm the one you want to see dead."

Vincent keeps the gun trained on me but looks back at Daisy. He gasps.

"*Daisy Murray?*"

The barrel of the gun drops a few inches, so it's no longer pointed at my face. I'm not sure if I don't prefer that over it being pointed at my junk.

"Alive and in the flesh." Daisy's voice is strange. I glance toward her to find a twisted smile clinging to her lips. Her eyes are pinned to Vincent and they somehow both radiate chaotic madness and are utterly empty at the same time.

"Francis foresaw things turning around. Zarzuz told him..." Vincent's voice trails off as he suddenly turns the gun back to her.

Drake, who's on my right, takes the opportunity to subtly shuffle further behind Vincent. On the opposite side of the room, Kingston mirrors Drake's movement.

"Do you know how much fucking trouble you've given us? Briar Glen is going under because of you!" Vincent roars. "You were supposed to *die*, and we were going to be rich!"

Daisy shrugs. "Your financial situation is no concern of mine."

"What financial situation? There is no more money left! It's gone!" He takes an aggressive step toward her. "Was that you? Did you steal my money?"

Spit goes flying as he speaks, his face going from red to purple with rage. My heart hammers in my chest as my mouth dries.

Please don't let anything happen to her...

Daisy shrugs. "Maybe. Maybe not."

Vincent shrieks. The sound echoes around the room. "Do you know the *shitstorm* you brought upon us? We have nothing now because of you! *Nothing*! I was so close to retiring, so close to a life made for a *king*! You have been a blight to this community. Your parents were supposed to give you to us, and in return, we'd be blessed for eternity. We were so close! Then all hell broke loose."

Daisy rolls her eyes. "How *unfortunate* life didn't pan out for you the way you wanted it to."

Vincent's finger tightens on the trigger. Wyatt and I take a step closer in unison. Vincent snarls, waving his gun at us before turning back to Daisy. "Your parents were beside themselves, you know. They wanted to see your blood run red just as much as we did. We took their lives in retaliation. I helped kill them myself. Their fucking pathetic whimpers and pleas weren't nearly as satisfying as their silence was."

If he's trying to get a reaction out of Daisy, it's not working. Her face doesn't give away any of her thoughts. Did she know they were dead? Or did she believe they just took off? Surely she's seen the empty lot where her house used to sit. Did she wonder about that?

"No? Nothing for your poor mother and father who raised you to be a *good* bride? A smart girl with good morals for our Zarzuz? Well, no matter. You can hash it out with them in hell." Vincent steps closer to her.

My heart leaps to my throat.

"If you kill her, I won't even consider moving the money

back," I call out, distracting him. "I suggest pointing the gun elsewhere."

Vincent turns. When our eyes meet, Kingston moves. He jumps Vincent from behind, Drake following his lead. The older man screams, and the gun goes off again. The bullet hits the ceiling. To my surprise, Vincent doesn't go down easily. Despite his age, he fights off Drake and Kingston as they try to subdue him. In a panic, Vincent's hand continuously squeezes the trigger of his gun. Bullets create holes in the wall around us.

Shit, someone is going to get hurt.

I lunge forward and grab his wrist, keeping clear of the end of the gun. Just as I manage to wrestle it away from him, a fist appears, landing in the middle of Vincent's chest, knocking the breath out of him. He sags forward. As he wheezes, Kingston and Drake grab either arm. Wyatt kicks Vincent's legs out from under him, sending the man to his knees.

"You'll be arrested, the lot of you!" Vincent gasps. "Thrown in jail where you'll rot. But you, Daisy, you'll be given to our god. Ronney will make sure of it. The Almighty—"

Wyatt's fist strikes the side of Vincent's face and his head snaps to the side.

"Yes, I've heard this many times before," Daisy says from somewhere behind me.

Behind me? What the hell is she up to?

I turn to find her by the wall, attempting to reach for a massive battle axe hanging as decoration among the other weapons. The thing is nearly as big as she is. The sight is so absurd, I find myself laughing in disbelief. Hurrying over to her side, I reach up and take it off the wall. When I hand it to her, however, she nearly drops it.

"Here, let me—"

Daisy huffs and manages to throw the weapon over her shoulder. She turns and trudges back toward the others. As she moves toward her latest victim, she starts to sing.

"*Just a spoonful of sugar makes the medicine go down...*"

The tune sounds ominous as she moves toward the man, weapon in hand.

"I know who you are. All of you," Vincent pants, looking up at us with a swelling right eye.

"*Medicine go down.*"

"Wyatt Challahan, Drake Miller, Owen Woodlock, and let me guess, one of you must be Kingston."

"*Medicine go down...*"

"Ronney already knows you're trouble. He's just waiting, buying his time. He'll get all of you. You're all dead."

Daisy stops in front of Vincent, staring down at him. He glares up at her, struggling to get away from the others.

Drake and Kingston yank his arms out to his sides. Wyatt grabs a handful of Vincent's hair to hold his head still. I stay beside Daisy, ready to help wherever I can. Daisy pops her hip to one side, the axe hanging off her shoulder. Her grip tightens on the handle as a grin stretches across her face. But it doesn't reach her eyes which now seem dead.

"The boys you knew are dead. Have been for quite a while, Vinny." Her giggle almost sounds childlike. "The creatures before you are my demons, gifted to me by the lovely Lilith."

"Lilith?" Vincent spits. "That fucking she-devil—"

"Is my mentor, my mother, and my guardian angel," Daisy interrupts. "She's using me to send a message. One Briar Glen will never forget. Are you ready to hear it?"

"The cops will be here any minute. Ronney knows I record everything. If you do anything to me..." Vincent's voice trails off as she hoists the weapon up, over her head. "No, please!"

Vincent's eyes widen as the axe comes down.

My breath catches in my throat as I watch the blade glint in the strange red light as it flies downward. Vincent squirms but the others hold him still. The axe slices through his left arm, cutting it clean off. His scream pierces the room as Drake drops the limb and steps back. I wince. Wyatt let's go of Vincent's hair to lift the severed limb. He laughs as he waves it around.

My stomach lurches.

"That was Lilith saying, Zarzuz will never escape," Daisy says. She lifts the axe again. This time when it falls, his right arm is removed. The contents of my stomach roll around, no longer content to stay put as blood pores heavily from either stump. Vincent's screaming doesn't help. I take a half step back, to put distance between me and the red liquid. Kingston grabs a hold of the right arm.

"Hey, King?" Wyatt lifts his hand.

King looks over at him and catches on immediately. With shoulders shaking in a silent laugh, he raises his arm, and together they high-five one another. The blood drains from my face. Can this please end soon? Dinner is not going to stay down for much longer.

Daisy ignores the guys, her focus solely on the dying man in front of her. "That was her saying 'fuck you'. Did you get that in the translation?" Vincent groans. Drool dangles from his lips, his eyes rolling. Daisy lifts the axe again. "Can you do me a favor, Vinny?"

Drake reaches forward, grabs a handful of Vincent's hair and yanks the Blessed Priest's head backward. He's clearly on some sort of wavelength to Daisy's thoughts.

"Tell Tobias and George that I say hi."

This time, instead of bringing the axe straight down, Daisy swings it. The horrific thwack is followed by the blade getting stuck in the side of Vincent's neck. I stare down at him through my mask and watch his eyes go wide as his jaw drops open.

"Hm. That's no good. Here, lemme try it again." Daisy yanks on the axe until it pops free.

It takes five solid chops to get Vincent's head off. I'm relieved when the cutting is over. The metallic smell drifting through the air and the sound of a body being chopped up is enough to make the room sway.

Vincent's head topples off his body and rolls toward Kingston, who immediately drops the arm in his hand and starts to kick Vincent's head around like a soccer ball.

"Three down, two more people to go," Drake declares. I'm pretty sure that's pride in his voice.

"Owen, the recordings?" Wyatt says cheerfully, pointing the arm in his hand at me. "Think you can take care of those?"

I nod. "I just need to figure out where he keeps the device."

Drake points his thumb at the statue. "There's a door just behind this stupid thing. Given that I didn't notice any recording equipment in our search for Vincent earlier, it has to be in here."

Good bet. I follow him around the statue as Wyatt speaks to Daisy. Drake opens the door and inside is a small room, hardly bigger than a closet. As we step in, I find security cameras and video feeds of five different angles of the house. Glad to give my mind something to do other than focusing on the smell of blood, I move toward the screens and desktop setup.

"I'll erase everything here," I mutter, pushing my mask up off my face before my fingers begin to move over the keyboard. "Our presence won't even be a blip on their radar."

Drake hums but it doesn't sound like it's in agreement. It's confirmed when he says, "I'm sure we're very much on everyone's radar."

I grimace. "Well, yeah, maybe."

Behind me, there's a soft gasp. Drake and I turn to find Daisy standing in the doorway. She's not looking at us though. Her eyes are pinned to something just to the right of the door. I follow her gaze and groan.

There, situated on a mannequin, is a red cloak. It looks well-worn but the deep red is still as ominous as ever. A chill slides down my spine, leaving a sharp pain of frostbite and terror in its wake. Wyatt's replica cloak was close, but I swear this one radiates evil. How did I not notice it before?

Peeling my eyes off it, I look back at Daisy to find her rooted to the spot.

"Daze…?" I call.

I watch as her body flinches as if she's been electrocuted before she takes a single step out of the room.

"Breathe through your panic," Drake growls, taking a step toward her. "You're safe with us."

Daisy's head whips back and forth, taking another step back as her breathing turns to gasps.

"Don't. Run. Daisy."

With a groan of despair, Daisy turns and darts out of the room. Drake takes a deep breath before taking a step in her direction.

"Wait, Drake!" I hiss. "Vincent said he called the police. If he was telling the truth, we need to get out of here before they show up."

Drake swears. "I'll get Daisy. Erase what you can and then we'll meet you at the car in an hour."

"On it!"

He's out of the room before my fingers make it to the keyboard. I've barely gotten started when Wyatt calls into the room,

"Where the hell did those two take off to?"

"Don't know. Daisy panicked and took off. Drake went to make sure she was ok. The police are coming, so get ready to run. I'm just—"

"Owen, look!"

I huff but turn around. Just inside the doorway, Wyatt is standing with his mask pushed up. He's carefully juggling with a pair of… My stomach lurches so hard, I bend at the waist and gag.

"Aw, come on, you know this is cool," Wyatt says. "I'd be the star of a freakshow if those things were still around."

I try to straighten but at the sight of the dismembered bloody foot and hand going around and around, I gag again. Where the hell did they get that foot? Have they been chopping Vincent up into smaller pieces? Wyatt snickers.

"Hey, King, come here! Show Owen what you got."

"Please... you guys, we don't have time for—" My back spasms as I bend over again and gag hard.

Wyatt laughs loudly. The fucker is loving this. As sweat drips down my forehead, Kingston strolls into the room with a grin so wide it practically splits his face in two. I groan at the objects in his hand. Both eyes and a tongue? But *why*?

"What is wrong with you two?" I gasp.

"Real quick, let's show Owen what we can do," Wyatt insists, turning to Kingston and ignoring the very real possibility that a ton of my DNA might come barreling out of me at any moment.

The two of them face one another, grinning like idiots, and begin tossing body parts at one another. Together, they create a two person juggling act. As they juggle, blood flies everywhere, covering the floor, ceiling, them...

This time when I gag, I go down to one knee. I retch and retch, but thankfully nothing comes up. As I suffer, the others laugh.

"What's wrong, Owen? Don't worry, we won't leave you out. If you wanted to learn how to juggle, you could just say something. Here, let me teach you—"

"I swear to god, if you bring any of that over here, I'm going to dismember *you,*" I vow weakly. "Get rid of those and give me a second of peace to wipe these security cameras. The longer we're here, the more likely we'll get caught."

Wyatt's laughter overpowers Kingston's wispy one.

"Damn, you held down dinner. I bet Kingston here we'd get you to puke."

I'm not sure that's not off the table quite yet. Ignoring him, I turn back to the cameras and get to work.

38

Daisy

They're coming for me.

The people in the red cloaks. The men and women that I grew up around and trusted, they're coming to kill me. I won't let them take me. Not this time. I'll die. I'd rather throw myself off another cliff, tumble into cold raging waters with broken bones and a shattered heart, all so they don't get the satisfaction of winning.

I can hear them call my name some distance behind me.

My legs pump harder. I don't know where I am, but the darkness helps hide me. My breathing comes in gasps as I run as hard as I can. Trees. There are trees around me. I'm back in the woods. How did I get here?

Panic causes my lungs to seize and my strides to falter. I'm not moving fast enough. They're going to catch me.

The shouting gets closer. Footsteps thunder behind me. Crunching leaves and snapping twigs are my gauge on how close they are. My knife! I need my knife. I'm not helpless this time. With practiced steps, I lift my foot a little higher in this rotation, my body twisting down and my hand reaching. My fingers snag the hilt and pull the knife from my boot.

The heavy weight of the weapon does nothing to quell my terror. In fact, it makes it worse. For all the killing I've done, for all the self-harm I've inflicted with it, the weapon suddenly feels foreign in my hand. My grip tightens around it. It doesn't ground me as it normally does.

The footsteps are growing closer.

No, no, no I can't be taken again!

What feels like a semi-truck, hits me from behind and I go crashing to the forest floor. There's no chance to gasp or catch my breath. Whatever hit me lands on top of me, making it impossible to breathe.

But air isn't my priority. Escaping is.

As my lungs burn, I twist the knife in my grip and swing it awkwardly behind me. It sinks into flesh. The person above me grunts. I yank the knife free and try again. This time, however, someone catches my wrist. Their grip is biting. I hiss in pain and drop the knife as the weight increases on my back.

I attempt to thrash around. Without air, I can't scream, but I'm not going to make this easy for them. I don't care that whoever is on top of me is about the size of a mountain. I'll fight until the end.

No amount of kicking, scratching, or thrashing seems effective. As my vision begins to blur and my movements become less frantic, whoever is on me grabs both my arms and yanks them behind my back. Their weight shifts. A knee presses into the middle of my back and someone's hot breath hits the shell of my ear.

"What did I tell you about running from me, Daisy?" The deep voice rumbles through my head, blasting through the haunting memories of my past. My struggling comes to a slow stop. "I'm pretty sure I warned you not to, or you may not like the consequences."

That voice. I know this voice. But it mixes with the chaos inside my head, becoming garbled. A hand comes down and grabs the back of my neck, applying enough pressure to keep my head from moving.

"Now look at what you've done." The voice returns, louder than the others in my head. The weight presses harder into my back, causing me to cry out. A nose appears by my ear, and it sucks in a deep breath. "You've turned me into a predator. And you? You've turned yourself into my prey."

I can't breathe with the weight bearing down on me. The world begins to fade as the voice registers in my head.

"Dre...?"

"No," the voice overhead snarls. "I'm not your Dre, Drake, or even your demon, Daisy. I'm the fucking devil you've lured out of hiding. You ran from me once, all those years ago, and escaped. This time? I've caught you and I have no intention of letting you free. You're *mine*."

The pressure of his knee relents. I suck in a deep breath, my vision coming back into focus. But Drake doesn't release me. His hand leaves my neck only so that he can grab both of my hands and raise them above my head. He transfers them into one hand and pins them to the ground.

"Drake, what are you doing?"

"What I told you I was going to do," he snarls. It sounds like, if I looked over my shoulder, there'd be foam dripping from his lips. The air practically vibrates with a dangerous energy. "I've caught you, now you're mine to do as I please."

A hand yanks down my jeans harshly, exposing my butt to the night air. I gasp as I realize what he's saying. Fear and disgust should wipe away my surprise but at the sound of Drake's zipper coming down, my body trembles with adrenaline and twisted excitement. I cling to those feelings as they burn away the fear of the people in the red cloaks.

"I should carve my name right here." A sharp stinging slap

hits my bare butt, causing me to yelp. "Let everyone know I've captured my prize and have laid claim to it."

Drake shifts his weight. His large body covers mine, pressing me into the ground. He feels enormous above me. The weight bearing down on me calms me more than my knife ever has.

"Daisy, I can't stop myself." He pauses, dragging in a deep breath. "I'm not *well.*"

My body shakes slightly as I try to come down from my panic and focus on his words. "W-what are you talking about?"

"I've been broken and reshaped, my pieces don't match. My thoughts are jumbles. I. Am. Not. *Well.* And the person you feel pressed against you now is a dangerous motherfucker," Drake groans, his hips pressing into my ass. I can feel his hard dick, lined with those fascinating piercings, against my butt cheeks. A thrill shoots up my spine. "The horrible things I want to do, *need* to do to you, Daisy... You broke me when you left. Now it's my turn to break *you.* Then I'll take all the pieces of you and swallow them so no one else can have what's mine."

The possessiveness in his hold, the wildness of his words... It's doing something to me. My nipples tighten.

Drake rubs his erection back and forth along my butt crack. "I-I'm trying to fight it, Daisy, the thing that I've become, but I told you not to run."

The strain in his voice twists my heart. His implications are clear, and the threat in his voice is menacing. Yet I can't find it in myself to feel scared. Instead, my body grows warm and heavy. I can feel a dampness gathering between my legs.

"I don't want to hurt you, but—" Drake lets out a deep pained groan that twists into a dark chuckle. "—finders keepers, am I right? And I can do whatever I want with what's *mine.*"

Suddenly his teeth are sinking into my shoulder. I cry out and try to wrestle out of his grip as the bite breaks skin and draws blood. When he relents, I pant heavily—placing my cheek down on the rough, dead leaves on the forest floor.

While I recover, he yanks my hips back with one hand, the other still pinning my hands to the ground. My breath catches in my throat as the tip of his dick comes to rest at my entrance.

"Drake—"

"*Mine*," he hisses.

He thrusts into me with one long, sharp jerk and bottoms out inside of me. My scream is choked off as my back tries to arch and accommodate the sheer size of the man behind me. The pain is explosive. My whimper is met with a harsh laugh.

"Shh... No, no, don't scream. We've only just begun, *Daisy*," Drake mocks as he pulls back out, his piercings rubbing against my inner walls that spasm around him, creating a strange sensation. It feels good but the pain as my body tries to adjusts to the intrusion overshadows the pleasure. "I would save your voice for later, when we get to the good part."

He pulls all the way out again only to slam back inside of me. My howl echoes around us. This time, Drake doesn't take it slow as he pulls out of me. He yanks his hips back and then pushes into me again, then again, and soon it's a constant, hard, punishing fuck.

It's too much.

Tears spring to my eyes and I let out a harsh sob. I try to pull my hands free, but Drake has more than a hundred and fifty pounds on me, at the very least, and all of it is pressing down on me, holding me locked to his hips and to the ground. I'm trapped beneath this mammoth of a man, who's swept up in a dark place inside his mind and can't escape his own demons.

Tears spill down my face. My body jerks under Drake's harsh thrusts.

Something shifts inside of me. A realization unravels and understanding soothes the ache. My once sweet boy, now turned demon, needs this. Hadn't he just said he needed to claim me? I never realized I wanted to be owned, but the thought doesn't scare me. Drake wants me. He *needs* me. In his insanity, he's taking what he needs to survive. A delirious exhilaration floods through me.

Drake's movements become sharper, his grip on my hip and wrists grows tighter.

"I can feel your pretty cunt growing wetter. Who knew you'd enjoy being punished? Then again, you're just as fucked up in the head as I am." He laughs harshly. "We were made to be insane together."

"Yes," I breathe, my body starting to enjoy the way his piercings roll and massage against my pussy and how full he fills me.

He growls. "*Fuck*, this was the best prize I could've won."

My pussy flutters around him at his words, and I try to arch my hips as the discomfort is joined by a desperate need to cum. My attempt is in vain. Drake's hold on my hips tightens, not allowing me to move. Before I can open my mouth to whine, Drake roars. His hips slam against my ass and he stills, his releasing spurting into me.

A smidgen of disappointment twists in my chest. I'm not sure what it's from or why it's there, but Drake doesn't give me time to analyze the feeling. He pulls out of me when he finishes and lets go of my wrists at the same time. I sigh, sagging down onto the ground as he gets up. My pussy quivers in the absence of his dick. A fire has been stoked, but I need more.

Drake doesn't give me a long reprieve. Before I can stop him, Drake has my wrists wrapped in an intricate binding with what looks like paracord.

"You know, these nifty survival bracelets can be used in case of an emergency," Drake states conversationally. "You just cut it at one end and unravel it. Then you have a ton of heavy duty rope at your disposal."

"Drake, what are you doing?"

To my surprise, he yanks me up to my feet with the extra

tail of rope. My gasp of surprise is met with a humph. He steps forward and glares down at me.

"Did you think I was done with your punishment?"

I blink in surprise. "You're not?"

His angry grunt is my only answer. But when he turns and throws the tail of the rope upward, I slowly begin to understand why. Why waste words when you're going to *show* me what's next? The rope makes it around a thicker branch and falls back around. Drake grabs the end, shoots me a dark look, and then yanks on the rope, hard.

I scream as my arms are yanked upward. My wrists and shoulder sockets protest along with me as I'm pulled upward.

"What did I say about saving your breath?" Drake asks as he yanks me higher until my feet dangle a foot or more off the ground.

Tears run freely down my cheeks, but I won't beg for him to stop. Begging has never gotten me anywhere. Ever. In fact, it only made my torment worse as the people who held me captive or tried to sacrifice me basked in my terror.

Besides, Drake warned me what would happen if I ran from him, but I did it anyway. He's going to punish me, and I need to simply take it. I also trust Drake. He's not going to kill me, he'll just push me to a limit I've never dreamed of reaching before.

I can do this.

I can let my demon, who has so many emotions bottled up inside, explode and let out all his pent-up feelings. I'll weather this storm.

Drake ties the end of the rope to the base of the tree, then steps back. My wrists are screaming in agony as I slowly rotate around in a circle. I don't know how long I'll be able to stand this, but I've been through worse.

Drake steps up until we're face to face and grabs my shirt to hold me from twirling in another circle. His expression is stoic and hard, but his eyes... Even in the moon's light, I can see that there's a dark roiling madness in them as they remain pinned to my face. If Drake was sane, he isn't anymore.

His free hand reaches up and strokes my face. "My beautiful Daisy, you won't wilt for me while I teach you this lesson, will you?"

Will I? I honestly don't know.

"I need you to hear me when I say I will do *anything* to get you to understand that you don't get to leave my side ever again. Your tears don't faze me. Your cries for mercy won't sway me. The only running you get to do is *to* me, not away. Never away." He grabs my chin in a rough grasp. Even dangling from a tree, he's taller than me, so he's forced to bend down to sneer into my face. "If I have to set us both on fire until our souls melt together so you can't leave me, I'll fucking do it."

Good grief. That seems like a bit much. So, why do I love the sound of it so much?

His words unleash my own degeneracy. The cold chill of depravity that slithers from my heart is met with the hot burn of desire and the utter adoration I have for Drake.

"Teach me a lesson, Drake." I hold his burning gaze. "Show me how much you need me by your side."

He laughs softly, letting go of me as he does. He reaches down and yanks off my pants, forcing them over my boots. The cool night air causes my nipples to pucker tighter. Drake tosses the pants aside and sighs as his eyes drag over me.

Suddenly, he lunges forward, grabbing one leg to throw over his shoulder and grabbing the other to keep me from swinging back. Then two of his fingers shove deep into my pussy. The harsh intrusion causes me to scream out. My hips jerk, as if to pull away, but Drake won't let me go. His fingers pump hard in and out of me. I breathe through the intensity, choking on a whimper.

It doesn't take me long to get to the edge. I gasp and my body clenches around Drake's fingers. Just as I'm about to cum, he withdraws his hand and steps back. I whine as my body spins around without his support. It turns into a shriek, however, when his hand makes contact with my ass. This strike is hard and sends me swinging back and forth. I wince at the pain in my wrists and arms as gravity pulls me downward.

Drake turns me back around. Again, he pulls my leg up over his shoulder and shoves his fingers back inside of me. He hums in approval at the wet noise my body makes as he enters me.

"You salacious flower," he growls between clenched teeth as he stares up at me. "Are you craving your petals stroked so much that you've allowed yourself to be debased so easily?"

"Drake." I choke on his name as his fingers curl and brush against that sweet spot inside of me. My pussy quivers around his fingers. Again, he brings me quickly to the edge of my release only to pull his fingers out and step back. As I swing around, I know what to expect this time.

Or I thought I did.

Drake grabs my hips, and a hand slaps my butt. Not once, not twice, but ten times in rapid succession. They're all brutally harsh and send fire shooting up my spine and cause my pussy to weep. When he's done, I'm gasping at the sensations running through me. Have I ever felt so wildly, painfully aroused? My pussy flutters hungrily as Drake spins me back again.

"Look at you, darling," Drake purrs, his eyes between my legs. "You're soaking wet."

"Can't help it," I gasp as I try to breathe through the intense emotions choking me. "Drake, I need you."

"What you need is a lesson in obedience." His hands are back, this time he shoves three fingers into me.

I suck in a sharp breath that is let out on an equally sharp moan as he works me up.

"Your body is soaking my hand. You filthy, dirty flower." Drake's lips skim across my inner thigh, his beard tickling me. I squirm. This time when he withdraws from my body, I sob hard.

"Drake!" I hiss as I twist around. "Please, please, please!"

He helps the swing of my body, turning me away from him. As he does, he hums thoughtfully. "I didn't know flowers made music, but the sounds you're making could put Beethoven's work to shame."

When he spanks me this time, I receive fifteen hard strikes in the exact same place he'd struck me before. My back arches, my hips try to jerk away from the hits. The rest of my body is screaming for this to be over because this *hurts*. Tears continuously stream down my face.

I can't even sob as I try to gasp for air.

Drake turns me around to face him. He peers down at me with those wildly fierce, dark eyes. "What? No more begging? Didn't I just say how much I enjoyed it?"

All I can do is pant and cry. I watch him through teary eyes as he steps closer.

"What won't you do again?" he asks me.

I open my mouth but all that comes out is a croak.

"Come on Daisy, tell me. Tell me what I want to hear, and I'll give you what you want." He raises a single blond brow expectantly. I swallow and try again.

"Won't run," I rasp out.

"You won't, *what*? Come on now, I need to hear it." He grins viciously. "If you don't, I'll keep this up. I'll use your body how I see fit all night. Watching your ass turn pink and those tears streaming down your face is keeping me nice and hard."

I don't realize that one of his hands is wrapped around his dick until he strokes himself, drawing my attention downward. At the top of his dick is a drop of precum. Drake sees me eyeing him and chuckles.

"Want me to bury myself back inside you, Daisy? Do you? You know your body is my sanctuary. You know how much I want to, but I won't give you my cock until you tell me what I want to hear." He laughs. "Now, let's try this again, loud and clear this time please."

He lets go of himself to grab my leg to place back over his shoulder. His fingertips brush my swollen pussy, causing me to shudder.

"I-I won't run, Drake."

Drake tsks. "That's not enough. You won't run where?"

"Away. Away from you!"

His thumb brushes against my clit and my hips jerk toward him as I let out a mewl. "It sounds like you've learned your lesson, Daisy. Do you want to cum now?"

I nod frantically. "Please, Drake, please!"

Without another word, Drake shoves his fingers into me again. As my body gobbles them up, Drake uses his thumb to circle my clit. As worked up as I am, getting back to the peak is easy. *Painfully* easy. My body tenses, clenching down so tight onto Drake's digits that he grumbles a swear. His thumb applies a little more pressure to my clit and it's over. My world erupts into white light. My orgasm is so intense my entire body jerks around. My cry is muffled by a ringing in my ears.

When my body finally stops trembling, my vision clears. Drake's smirk sends another shiver through me.

"It took some time, but I'm glad to see you're a student worth teaching."

A noise beside us causes him to tense. I'm a little late on the reaction, given how tired I am, but I turn my head to follow Drake's gaze to see Kingston step forward, out of the bushes, covered head to toe in blood.

My pussy spasms hungrily at the sight.

"Kingston," Drake greets. "You're supposed to be with the others."

King flashes him a quick, half-smile. "Yeah, well, I came to make sure my girl is good."

"She's fine now, right, Daisy?" Drake's sneer causes my nipples to tighten further and my pussy to spasm once more.

Rather than play into Drake's hand, I look at Kingston. "He's gone mad. Help me."

Kingston's grin turns feral as Drake chuckles.

"Gone mad, huh? From the sounds of things, going mad is a lot of fun. Maybe I'll go mad with him?"

I gasp at the implications. At the same time, I can feel arousal dripping down my leg at the thought of being used by both of them.

"Wyatt and Owen?" Drake asks.

"Got out and are headed back to the car to wait for us. We have a bit before they grow concerned." Kingston steps forward. "We could do a lot in a short amount of time."

"Sure could."

"What happened to your leg?" Kingston nudges his head downward. My eyes fall to the same place. There, on the side of Drake's thigh, is a hole in his pants with blood staining the edges. I gasp at the same time Drake chuckles.

"I didn't know that daisy's had thorns but turns out this one does."

Kingston laughs. The airy sound brings a smile to my lips, though it's short lived from exhaustion. King looks back at me, his face twisting in a shadowy delight.

"Did you enjoy yourself? Do you still love this hulking beast in all his fucked up glory?" he asks me.

The question takes me by surprise. Kingston watches my face closely, as does Drake, who suddenly goes still. A giggle that's part hysterical and part amused bursts past my lips. How could he possibly ask me such a thing?

"Of course I do!"

Kingston nods, pleased, and the tension rolls out of Drake's shoulders. King looks over to him. "Well, it looks like your revenge didn't stick. She should be terrified of a brute like you."

"It wasn't revenge that has her strung up like this," Drake corrects him. "Daisy has put herself in a teachable moment. I can't help it if it's enjoyable for me too."

"Care if I join in?" Kingston stalks right up beside me, grabbing me just above my knee to keep me from swinging. "I have something I'd like to teach her as well."

"Absolutely. She's prepped for a proper education."

My pussy spasms even as I brace myself for trouble.

39

Kingston

I watched from a distance for as long as I could.

First, to make sure Daisy was actually ok with Drake's punishment. It must be brutal to hang there like that. But once I knew she wanted this, started begging for more of it, I simply wanted to watch the strain on Drake's face as he kept himself from his own release. It was a struggle myself not to fuck my hand, watching on as Daisy writhed around in both pleasure and pain. I knew it had to be even harder for him, doling out her punishment. Even now, Drake is holding onto his cock beside me.

Daisy stares at me, her gaze slightly glazed over, her cheeks stained with tears, and a small smile clings to her lips.

"What do you want to teach me, King?" she asks, her voice hoarse. Her tongue flickers out to wet her dry lips. I track the motion. When she's done, I look back up at her.

"That I plan to take care of you from now and until the end of days." I turn her toward me, enjoying how easy it is to do whatever I want with her like this. "From killing your enemies, to making you cum until you're utterly spent. You don't have to worry about anything."

Daisy's eyelids flutter closed as she lets out a pleased hum. I grab the hilt of my knife, pulling it free from its sheath, and hand it to Drake. He takes it without hesitation.

"Cover the handle with your blood."

Drake's brow raises in surprise before he barks out a laugh and gets to work. Daisy's eyes flutter back open, oblivious to the request.

"What are you two up to?"

"You'll see," I tell her, stepping closer.

Grabbing both her legs, I bring them up and throw them over my shoulders, so that my face is right there at the apex of her body. Daisy groans in relief and I know it's because in this position, her weight is resting on me rather than it bearing down on her wrists. I stare at the mess between her legs. God she's so fucking perfect. Does she realize how incredible she is? To take a punishment like that from a brute like Drake and still be capable of loving him? Will she love me just as much when I'm done with her?

Tilting my head forward, I run my tongue from her asshole through the mess between her legs and up to her clit. Daisy cries out, tensing in surprise.

"Kingston, wait!" Her body squirms as I circle her clit with my tongue before sucking sharply on the swollen bud. Daisy squeals. Chuckling, I pull away and look up at her. "Drake... His, ah, cum is still inside of me."

I raise a brow. Does she think I can't taste him there? That I would give a fuck? Holding her gaze, I lean forward again while tilting her hips upward, and repeat the motion. Her whole body tenses again, her legs closing in around my face.

I'm thorough as I lap up the arousal and seed dripping out of her body, and I'm attentive to her clit. My dick strains against my pants, aching something fierce, wishing it could be buried where my face currently resides. I lap, suck, and tease until Daisy's a quivering ball of nerves, her orgasm rushing through her swiftly. Her arousal drips from her body, cleaning out the rest of her pussy to make room for my own cum to fill her. I pull my face away as she sighs heavily.

Turning, my gaze lands on Drake. His eyes are on her face but when he feels me watching, he looks over at me. I nudge my head and direct him over. Drake's half smile is all knowing. Can he read my mind? He must have that power because he saunters over behind Daisy with the knife in hand.

With my hands on her butt, it's easy for me to spread her cheeks for him.

"W-what? King? Drake?" Daisy's hoarse voice trembles.

Neither of us pay her any attention. I feel it the minute Drake teases her asshole with the hilt of his knife. She gasps and stiffens dramatically.

"N-no! I can't, I can't do this," she cries out.

"Yes you can, darling. You can do anything if you put your mind to it," Drake objects. "Now breathe easy, or this is going to hurt... Well, more than necessary."

I laugh into Daisy's pussy before burying my face there again. This time, I'm working double time as Drake works the hilt of the knife into Daisy's body. Her cries of pain turn to heady moans, then back to sharp gasps. Her arousal is flowing freely now, dripping over my lips and chin. I lap it up as quickly as I can, hating that it's going to waste.

Daisy cums just as Drake steps back to admire his handy work. Her hips grind against my face as her weak cry floats through the air. With my tongue deep inside her tight, wet cunt, I can feel her pussy pulse around me. When she's spent, I pull my face away and carefully lower her legs off my shoulders.

She hisses as weight is reapplied to her wrists. Slowly she lifts her head to look at me while I take a step back and pull my cock free.

"You know I love you, right?" I tell her as my dick comes out. I stroke it, using the precum there to make the motion smoother.

Daisy nods.

"Good. Because I'm about to fuck you like I don't." I step forward again, grab her thighs, and pull them open. At this height, she's in a perfect position for me to plunge directly into.

So I do. Hard.

Daisy's chokes on a sob as I sink deep inside of her. Her pussy wraps and flutters around me, greeting me with more arousal. She's even tighter with the hilt of the knife buried deep in her ass. Fuck. For a second, I can't breathe. She's strangling me, but I'm more than happy to suffocate in this way.

Taking a steadying breath, I tighten my grip on her thighs then I start to move. My hips thrust in sharp shallow movements. I need to stay deep in her cunt, where I can constantly feel her heart beating. Behind her, Drake steps closer and I can feel him move the blade in time with my thrusting.

"My demons, my demons..." Daisy sobs softly, nearly delirious. I look up into her face and enjoy the sight of the fat tears streaming down her face. They meet at her chin and then fall from her face. God, she's breathtaking. "I can't do this. Shit, you guys... Oh, *oh*!"

Her body bears down on me so tightly that, for a second, my ability to move is completely hindered. But I don't need to move anymore, her body milks my orgasm from me with an impossibly delicious pulsating motion. My cum pours into Daisy's body, filling her to the brim and then some as it spills out between us. I struggle to breathe properly as I throw my head back and push in deeper, causing Daisy to cry out again.

When my dick stops jerking in time to Daisy's throbbing pussy, I pull myself free. Her head drops forward, her chin hitting her chest. Drake moves next, pulling the knife from

Daisy's body. She twitches but other than that, she doesn't move or make a sound.

"Hm... You know, lovers occasionally carve their initials into trees," Drake muses.

I reach up to hold Daisy to keep her from twisting around but look over to find Drake staring down at her legs, the tip of the knife pressed thoughtfully to his lips.

"Maybe we should uphold tradition?" Drake muses before looking up at me.

My heart races. Mark Daisy? Claim her in a wholly new way? I grin. Drake chuckles at the sight of my amusement and says,

"Yeah, I like the idea too. One second..." He crouches down and brings the knife toward Daisy's skin.

Her wail of pain is weak, her body barely capable of wiggling, let alone escaping the blade as it cuts through her skin. Drake's done pretty quickly. He stands and hands me the blade while placing his hand on her other hip to keep her from moving while I come around to see his handiwork.

At first, I don't see anything. It's not until I crouch down that I see on the inside of Daisy's right thigh is a small, bloody, crude heart with the initials D.M. carved beneath it. It's not super deep, hell it may not even scar much, but I like it. A lot. Chuckling, I recreate the heart on the other thigh and add my own initials. When I'm done, I stand up and move around to stand in front of our girl.

Daisy looks down at us, but I have a feeling she's not really seeing *us*. Her mouth is hanging open and her body is starting to tremble visibly.

"You're done, darling. We'll get you down," Drake says from her other side. "King, grab her hips while I cut her down."

I do so immediately. When the rope goes slack, Daisy sags in my arms. Jeez, she's so light. A small twinge of unease sweeps through me as I shift her into my arms so I can carry her easily.

She's *too* small. I know Drake has her eating more, but there's got to be a way to help her put on some more weight.

Drake comes forward and cuts the rope off her wrists. I take in the angry red skin, the slight purple of her hands, and welts immediately rising to the surface now that they have room. With the rope gone, Drake helps get Daisy's pants back on. She hardly moves, and she doesn't make a sound.

"Come on, let's meet up with the others," Drake says, brushing a hand over her face. Daisy says nothing, just stares up at the trees, breathing heavily.

I bend down and give her a quick kiss.

We got you, Daisy.

40

Wyatt

Last night was wild.

As I walk through the grocery stores, throwing random things into my cart, I have to remember not to skip or whistle. That would look odd. Then again, I'm already being stared at. Whatever. Their assessment of my character isn't wrong. It's just, they don't *know* anything.

Trouble. Deceiver. Killer. That's what they are whispering behind their hands, as if I can't hear them. Each aisle I walk down, I receive hostile glares or end up with someone abruptly turning around to avoid me. I'm sure Drake is receiving the same treatment, wherever he is.

"Here."

Speak of the devil. Drake comes up beside me and drops several packages of chicken breasts into the cart.

He has managed to throw in every food group imaginable and then some. It was a good idea bringing him. I've never been much of a cook but clearly, Drake more than makes up for my incompetency. I'm going to have to watch him carefully if

I'm going to be any help taking care of Daisy in this department.

He reaches down and swipes up the cookie dough I've tried to hide under a box of cereal.

"What's this? This isn't healthy."

I snatch it out of his hands. "Who gives a fuck about being healthy?"

"Me." He tries to snatch it back, but I pull it out of his way.

"Some of us have a sweet tooth." I stumble back when he reaches for it again. "Back off or I'll grab the tub of it instead."

Drake grumbles under his breath but gives up. Grinning in victory, I follow after him with the cart.

"I also have chips for walking tacos, but you can just use the lettuce I got with your taco meat and toppings if you want."

We head toward the checkout line where an older woman waits behind the cash register. As we approach, I notice the way her eyes narrow at us through her thick bifocals. Her thin lips, caked with makeup, purse together in disapproval. I want to roll my eyes.

Drake and I make quick work of adding the items of our shopping cart to the conveyor belt.

"Drake, baby? Is that you?"

I'm so focused on getting out of this store that I didn't even hear anyone approach behind us. I jump in surprise and turn at the vaguely familiar voice. There, standing behind us, is Terra Miller. The similarity between her and her son was more pronounced when he was younger. Tall, with a plump figure, a perfectly round face that now houses crow's feet and lines around her mouth, Mrs. Miller was always an imposing figure. Her epic scolding sessions when we were kids would last hours. She'd shame us all until we went home in tears.

She was such a bitch.

But her intimidation has lessened now that I know what I'm capable of. I'm a killer, she's just a fucking lackey in a sinister cult. And after what she did to Drake when Daisy died? She should be next on our hit list.

Mrs. Miller is looking past me, her eyes wide with surprise. They fill with tears as she takes a step forward.

"It *is* you! People have been talking, and I just didn't believe them. There's no way you'd come back to Briar Glen and not say hello to your own mother." Her voice wobbles as she moves around her cart to approach us.

"Take another step toward me and you'll end up with a black eye." Drake's words are cold as ice and stop Mrs. Miller in her tracks.

She blinks, clearly unable to process the threat that has spewed from her son's lips. "I beg your pardon?"

"You heard me. Now get fucking lost."

I want to laugh at the flabbergasted look on this cruel woman's face. I bet Drake *never* spoke back to her as a kid. At least he never did in front of us. His tears or blotchy red face would duck and he'd take whatever unwarranted scolding his mother dished out. The guy's definitely all grown up. Pride causes my chest to swell.

The surprised-mother act melts away as indignation causes Mrs. Miller to puff out her chest and lift her chin. "You don't get to speak to your mother—"

"You have never been a mother to me, so you can cut the shit," Drake snaps.

She opens his mouth to speak but I step forward and cut her off. "You heard him. Now, if you don't mind, we're trying to check out."

"Do you know what the town's been saying about you two?" she hisses. "You should be looking for allies at a time like this."

I snort. "And *you're* that ally? If that's the case, I think we'll pass. Besides, the rumors are absolutely asinine. You know how tongues wag around here when people get a whiff of drama."

"Hush your mouth, Wy. If your parents were still alive,

they'd be ashamed of how you've turned out! Sleeping with men? Possibly starting fires around town? And now you're bringing my son into your shenanigans. You disgust me," she snaps before turning her attention to her son. "I am your flesh and blood, Drake Micah Miller! I haven't heard from you in years, and this is how you treat me? The nerve—"

"You locked me in a closet under the stairs. So do you want to talk about poor treatment, or do you want the world to know what type of a shitty mother you are?" Drake demands loudly.

If they weren't already, everyone in a forty-foot radius stops and stares at us.

Drake's not done. He steps up beside me, his fists clenched, and he glares at her. "You want to talk respect? Why don't you worry about maintaining some for yourself. You're the power-hungry bitch, looking to be taken seriously when all you're doing is whoring yourself out. I know about you fucking George Herring, but do the police? When was the last time *you* saw him? The night of the murder maybe?"

Someone nearby gasps.

Mrs. Miller turns a bright red as she glances around nervously. "You've always been an insolent boy. Your sisters turned out so much better than you."

Yes, well, we all know Bethany and Caroline were suck ups. As children, Drake's sisters were annoying goodie-goodies that had nothing better to do than to try to get Drake into trouble. Their spying and constant berating of Drake were mirrored behaviors of Mrs. Miller.

Drake's mother backs away, cart in hand, glaring at the both of us. I chuckle as she yanks her cart out of the checkline and ducks down an aisle of food. Turning, I find Drake already pulling out his wallet and paying for all the groceries.

Outside, we make a beeline for my car. Quickly, we throw the bags of the food in the trunk and climb in.

"Well that was a shit show." I look in my rearview mirror as

I pull out of the parking lot. "At least the town will eat that up for a bit, rather than talk about what else is happening."

Drake's response is only a melancholy sigh. I shoot him a curious glance.

"You ok?"

"I'm fine. It felt good to tell her off. I wish I hadn't waited this long."

I snort. "She looked like she was going to faint."

"At least then she'd be quiet."

We both chuckle at that.

I'm about to turn onto Main Street but something in the rearview mirror catches my attention. Red and blue lights flash behind me, followed by a siren that causes my heart to drop. Drake peers at the side mirror and swears.

My heart hammers in my chest. "They don't have anything on us."

"That we know of," Drake grumbles as he shoves his hand into his pocket. "You better pull over though and see what they want. I'll call the others to let them know we might have trouble."

41

Daisy

"Please no! My daughter needs me!" Patty cries. "Please, don't do this!"

"Shut up, or I'll gag you. I'm in no mood to hear your screams this evening."

Oliver stomps around the room as he collects his tools of torture, picking them meticulously off the walls. Strapped down to the procedure table, her legs in the stirrups, Patty sobs. I sob with her but the gag in my mouth muffles my sounds.

I've already lost speaking privileges and the night hasn't even begun yet.

Oliver places the pliers on the steel rolling table beside Patty and claps his hands together. "Well, we should get started while the night is young, don't you think?"

The sense of dread that follows is cut short. In its place, a hot wave rushes through my body. It's unexpected and for a second, I stop sobbing as I try to place where it came from. Before I can consider it for too long, the sensation returns. My hips arch off the bed as my nipples pebble.

What's going on?

I don't get time to think. As Oliver reaches for the cutting knife, another pleasant wave of heat courses through my body. Rather than sob, I moan. The vision of Oliver between Patty's legs begins to blur as my toes curl and my breathing becomes ragged. Trapped on a filthy mattress with my arms and legs pulled and tied to the corners, I can't move, but for once I stop fighting the bindings as much. Another pleasurable wave creeps up and steals my breath away before it recedes, leaving me achy and wanting. Savoring this wild phenomenon that's chasing away my horrors and causing tension to gather between my legs is all I desire at the moment.

Heat returns, this time warmer than ever. When it gets to be too much, the entire room disappears and pleasure shoots into my trapped limbs. I groan as an unexpected orgasm rolls through me on Oliver's mattress.

As my body comes down from its unexpected high, I drift in the darkness. I'm dreaming. I know that now, but it's never been like this before. Somehow, I've escaped the nightmares. I sink deeper into the dark abyss with a grateful sigh.

Something nudges me. I can feel pressure between my legs. For a second, I panic. Oliver? I search around the darkness for him, but I can't see anything. Has he blindfolded me again?

"Sh, I got you, Daze. Let your favorite demon chase the devil away."

A voice. I know that voice. It doesn't belong to Oliver. Relief is chased by an electrical current of delight as the pressure between my legs intensifies. Something thick, hard, and warm buries deep into my body slowly, occasionally retreating only to return sinking deeper into me. Already warmed up, my body stretches easily for the intrusion. There's a need to move, to feel and demand more, but somehow my limbs won't seem to work. Rather than panic again, I simply relinquish control, allowing whatever is happening to me to continue.

It feels so fucking good.

Faint colors spot my vision. The stretching is glorious, and the friction causes a gradual tension to gather once more, this time coiling tighter. But it's not enough. I want to scream in frustration as the unhurried thrusting that's driving me toward my peak doesn't increase in tempo. My body feels like it's growing warmer. Am I on fire? If I am, it feels magnificent to burn. Slowly, the colors grow brighter. I can't seem to take a deep breath.

The tension inside me snaps abruptly.

My eyes fly open as I groan deeply into the neck of the person above me, their body covering mine. Automatically, my hips move to meet their thrusts as my pussy clenches around the hard dick inside of me. My entire frame is trembling. As I come down from the intense orgasm rocking my world, I'm gasping for air.

The person on top of me pumps into me one last time before stilling as they find their release with an airy sigh of relief. With each jerk of their dick, my pussy spasms in delightful little aftershocks. After another moment or two, our bodies still. Before I can blink the sleep out of my eyes, lips are on mine.

I chuckle against them, knowing who it is as sleep fades further and further away. When Owen pulls away from the kiss, he grins down at me, his eyes twinkling with delight.

"Wow." It's all I can manage and even that is a soft whisper.

"Wow is right." He kisses me again, this time it's just a peck. Carefully, he pulls out of me. I instantly loathe the empty feeling without him between my legs. "Hold on, I'll be right back."

"No, come back." I grab for him, but he laughs and easily pulls out of my grasp.

"I'll be quick." With that, Owen rolls off the bed.

He grabs his boxers to slip them on and darts out of the room. I sink into the mattress, feeling strangely rested even after having a nightmare. Usually, they leave me feeling drained.

Owen's back a few minutes later with a washcloth in hand. He climbs back onto the bed and pulls my legs apart.

"Here, let me clean you up. Then we can get some food."

"I thought Wyatt said he needed to get more food today," I mutter, watching him with hooded eyes as he wipes up the mess between my legs with a warm wet cloth.

"He and Drake are out at the grocery store now. They had an early start."

When he's done, he disappears with the towel in tow and returns without it to come lay beside me. I curl into him, throwing my leg over his hip and nestling close to his chest.

"Are you ok?" he asks, worry brings his brows together.

I chuckle. "I'm more than *ok.*"

"You said I could, and I just thought... Well, Kingston is glued to the TV, and with the others gone—"

"Owen, that was amazing," I assure him. He opens his mouth, I'm sure to press the issue, but I simply lean forward and kiss him.

He responds instantly, kissing me back fervently. His arm comes around my lower back to press me closer to his body. I sink my hips into his and lose myself in the moment.

A sharp knock on the door startles me and immediately I tense, pulling away from Owen. In the next breath, I giggle at my reaction and relax, already knowing who it is.

"What's up, King?" Owen asks, propping his elbow on the mattress and resting his head in his hand to look over me. "Oh, thanks."

Kingston's arm comes into view as he hands Owen his phone. As Owen answers it, I reach out and grab Kingston's wrist before he can pull away.

"Join us." I look up at him to catch his smile before he sinks down onto the mattress behind me.

He lays out on my other side, effectively sandwiching me. Their warm bodies are a comfort I didn't know I'd ever crave, but now that I have it, I know that it would be nice to wake up like *this* every morning that we have together. Kingston's hand lands on my hip, but immediately it slides forward, between my legs. His fingers find my clit and I let out a soft groan as he plays with the swollen bundle of nerves. I push my ass against his hips to find him already semi-hard. Turning my head to look over my shoulder, Kingston leans forward and greets me with a kiss.

"Hey Dre, what's—" Owen stops talking to listen to the frantic words on the other end. I stiffen as I turn to catch Owen's face falling. "*What*? Shit. Yeah, alright. I'll let them know. If I don't hear from you in an hour, we'll come—oh, no, you're right. *I'll* come find you guys."

I sit up at once. Owen hangs up with a sigh and sits up with me.

"Wyatt and Drake just got pulled over. They don't know what for yet, but you better get dressed. If they have any evidence that either one was at the scene of any of the crimes—"

"They'll try to get a warrant and come here next," I finish for him, already piecing the issue together.

The warmth of Kingston's body behind mine vanishes as he slips off the bed.

I follow him, my heart slowing as my panic is pushed to the far recesses of my mind. Freaking out has never helped me in the past and my body slides into the familiar autopilot mode as I get ready for trouble.

"Besides the blood on our clothes that no amount of bleach will remove, is there any other evidence here that could get them into trouble if they arrive?" I ask both guys as we all start to move around. I'll gather the clothes up, bag them and then shove them into my backpack to take them with us.

"Wyatt's been keeping body parts in the freezer," Kingston says.

"*Excuse me*?" Owen's voice shoots up three octaves in horror. "Please tell me you're joking, King. Where we keep the food?"

"Go see for yourself." Kingston's shoulders fall up and down as he laughs silently.

Owen stares, wide-eye in disbelief at him.

Any other time, I'd find this amusing. Unfortunately, we could all be in some serious shit. I don't have the luxury of laughing. Without another word, I leave the room and head for the kitchen. I yank open the freezer door, move some items around and, low and behold, there is a black trash bag. When I pull it out and open it, I find several fingers from different individuals, a hand that has all its digits, one big toe and one little, and an ear.

Owen appears at my side and looks down into the bag. His soft groan follows him as he stumbles away.

"*No!* No, no, no! This isn't ok! C'mon on, where is common decency? Wyatt should know better than to bring home souvenirs! That's so stupid. And why would he put it next to our *food*? Why would you desecrate the freezer like this? What the fuck?!"

As Owen has a mini meltdown, I run through a hundred different scenarios in my head as to what to do with these in our limited amount of time and come to a swift decision. Turning, I move toward the sink. Pulling out the small body parts, I shove them down the drain.

"What are you doing?" Owen asks.

Without answering him, I turn on the water then flip the switch for the garbage disposal. It's not the best method of hiding evidence but it will do in a time crunch.

"Oh no," Owen's voice sounds weak. "Not the kitchen sink."

As the garbage disposal does its thing, I look over my shoulder at him. "Owen, get your laptop and pull up a map. I have three different locations we can move to if this place is compromised."

I should've gone over this with the others beforehand, but I had hoped we could stay here just a little bit longer.

Owen inches toward the threshold of the kitchen and living room. He sucks in a sharp breath and nods. "Ah, right, let me get on that."

When all the little body parts are gone, I head for the garage door. Stepping out into the humid space, I look along the far wall and find a toolbox. Perfect. It doesn't take me long to find a saw to cut the frozen hand into pieces before shoving the parts down the drain.

Just as I finish up, Kingston and Owen appear. Kingston is dressed, ready to go, boots on and all. He drops both of our backpacks onto the couch and then makes his way over to me.

"You need to get dressed," he orders. "And we need to get as far away from this house as possible."

"I will."

"This may be nothing, guys," Owen starts as he sits down beside our stuff, clicking away on his laptop. "According to their trackers, they're still sitting on the road outside of the grocery store."

It *could* be nothing. However... "It's best to be prepared for the worst-case scenario."

I wash my hands, trot back to the garage, and wipe down the handsaw as best I can with a dirty rag I find, then place it back exactly how I found it. I come back in, throw the rag into the laundry machine, pour half the bottle of bleach into the machine, and turn it on. I repeat the process with the bleach in the kitchen sink.

When I'm done, I join Kingston and Owen on the couch to stare at the satellite view of Briar Glen on the laptop.

"I'll show you where each hiding spot is. They won't be exact locations, but at least you two will know what to look for when you get to the general area. I'll go counterclockwise, so if we ever split up and need to meet up, we start at one hiding spot but go to the next if it's compromised. Also, I'll show you where the extra car is stashed. I had it ready for King to use, but now it's just sitting out of sight," I start. "I'll make sure Drake and Wyatt know this too when they return."

If both of them return. My stomach sinks at the thought. If they aren't taken this time, I'm sure it won't be long before Ronney sends his men after us. He's a clever man. There's no doubt in my mind he's already taking all the precautions necessary to avoid being my next victim. Including striking first.

Leaning forward, with my mind half on this and half on formulating a plan to foil any attempts the Sheriff of Briar Glen has, I point to a wooded spot on the screen.

"This isn't a hiding spot, but in case anything goes awry and something happens to me, you need to know about it."

"Why? What is it?" Owen asks suspiciously.

Kingston looks at me, his brows coming together. I ignore his wariness and stare at the screen.

"For now, all you need to know is that *this* is plan B."

42

Drake

"Well, like I thought, they put a tracker in your car when they searched it," Owen declares as he enters the house. "I destroyed the motherboard inside but left the shell to throw them off in case they try to look for it."

He's ignored as the rest of us tackle our current conundrum.

"The police don't know anything," Wyatt protests. "If we just abandon the house, we'll just end up drawing even more attention to ourselves."

Kingston shakes his head. "It'll look like you took off and people might actually relax and let their guard down, thinking the threat is gone."

"I say it's too suspicious," Wyatt snaps.

"You know what's *actually* suspicious and will draw attention to ourselves?" Owen scowls in his direction. "Keeping *frozen body parts* in the refrigerator. There was a perfectly good steak next to your bag of death that you *ruined*. You don't put that type of shit near food, Wyatt!"

Wyatt rolls his eyes. "Where else am I supposed to keep it?"

"NOT NEXT TO MY FOOD!"

I'm with Owen on this but we're getting off topic and this is serious. "We need to get the fuck out of sight. Things are getting too messy. We were lucky when we were pulled over that all they did was put a tracker on the car and not a recording device."

"It's not like we're really leaving, we're just camping close by," Kingston objects. "Where are we more secure? In the woods, or surrounded by neighbors who are watching your every move? People have already tried to creep up on us before. Who's to say it won't happen again?"

"Uh, yeah, about that," Owen points out. "There's a missing person's alert for those guys. It popped up on my phone while I was outside looking for the tracker."

Kingston points to him. "Now people are aware they're missing. The fact that they came here and *then* disappeared doesn't really bode well for us. We should leave."

Daisy and I watch their bickering from the kitchen counter. With my back to the counter and Daisy sitting on one of the barstools beside me, I lean back and absentmindedly rake my fingers through her thick hair. When I get back to her scalp, I grab a handful at the roots and gently tug. She tilts her head toward me with a soft sigh.

The sound causes the tension in my body to ease. Since we got home over an hour ago, Daisy's seemed... *off*. She smiles and engages in conversation, worries, and plans with us, but there's just something not right. It's as if she's only partially here.

Is this how she deals with stress? By sinking into herself? Or is there something I'm not seeing?

Wyatt shakes his head. "I bet you a million dollars that they have dogs and people still combing the woods surrounding Briar Glen thinking that you're around. We're no safer out there then we are here."

Owen sighs and crosses his arms over his chest. "I can't believe we're *still* talking about this. We have the cameras set up around the house. We'll be able to see if anyone is coming."

"That didn't prevent people from trying to attack us," Kingston points out. "Last I checked, it ended up with four dead bodies in Wyatt's room."

Owen throws up his hands. "At least we saw them coming! Maybe we could lay out booby traps for the next time?"

Wyatt and Kingston open their mouths to respond, but Daisy cuts them both off.

"We're leaving and that's the end of it. We need to go soon, though. It may not be safe for you three to remain so conspicuous." I let go of her hair as she straightens, only to wrap my hand around her neck. "But we don't head for the hideouts. We'll probably have to use them soon, but let's hold off as long as possible. They're not necessarily comfortable. We'll go to Chasm. We can get a room or two at a motel."

Both Kingston and Wyatt grimace, clearly not onboard with that plan. I, on the other hand, approve.

"When was the last time you roughed it outside longer than a day or two?" I ask either of them. "This isn't camping, this is surviving. At least we'll be able to lay low but still be able to move around, get food, and have a roof over our heads. There may be people in Chasm who know about us, but they won't be as bloodthirsty or as wary as the people of Briar Glen are."

The fight leaves the both of them with heavy sighs.

"It may be safer for you and Kingston to slip out sooner, rather than later," I consider out loud as I look down at my girl. "If they're going to start watching us like hawks, the sooner you guys are gone, the better."

Kingston frowns. "We can leave tonight. When it's dark."

Daisy nods but Owen shakes his head. "No, we shouldn't split up. It's a bad idea."

"It's the safest way. What if they had pulled us over while

King and Daisy were in the car? They might try something again."

Owen shakes his head, but he doesn't have a logical argument against my point, leaving it up to the others to decide.

"I don't know about this..." Wyatt mutters. He looks at Daisy. "I know you're used to being on your own, and you'll have this psycho nut here," he jerks his thumb toward Kingston, "but it feels wrong letting you go off without all of us."

Kingston rolls his eyes but flashes a cold smile. "Don't forget she's psycho too."

"I don't think any of us are forgetting that anytime soon," Owen assures him.

Daisy shrugs. "King and I will be fine."

While I know that, and I'm sure the others do too, I'm not wholly thrilled about splitting up despite it being my idea. "We won't be far behind you. If you leave tonight, we could join you tomorrow. We'll gather up extra supplies, Wyatt can do whatever he needs to do before locking up the place for good, and then we'll head to Chasm. We each have a tracker, we'll give you one of our phones so you can see where we are, and we'll be back together in no time."

Beside me, Daisy nods and slides off the stool, forcing me to let go of her.

"I think it's a good idea." She looks at Wyatt. "I can't imagine what it will be like leaving your home, Wyatt." She turns to look up at me with a frown and then to Owen. "You each have your own place, but I don't know if you'll be safe enough to return back to them for a while after all this is over."

It's not the first time she's implied that she wouldn't be joining us. Whether it's intentional or accidental, I'm not a fan. There is no going back to the way things were. Daisy is here in our lives to stay.

"I've noticed you have a hard time with the word we. *We'll* return when it's safe, and if it's never safe for us," I shrug, "then we build a new home somewhere that will be safe."

"Don't forget, we have all that money we took from the Zarzuzians." The worry on Owen's face melts away as he looks around us. "We could buy a nice home and start fresh somewhere cool."

Daisy's expression is shuttered but she nods. The lack of confirmation on her end about any type of future sets me on edge.

"We'll figure it out," I growl through clenched teeth.

Daisy shoots me a smile that doesn't reach her eyes. "I'm going to lay down for a bit. Kingston and I will have a long trek to my car since we're leaving here on foot."

I wish I could offer to drive them, but slinking around on foot through the night will be safer for them than driving around in any of our cars, what with them being watched and all.

Daisy disappears out of the living room, and for a moment, we're all silent. Lost in our own thoughts.

43

Wyatt

My knuckles rap against the door.

It's almost time for Daisy and Kingston to head out. We're all as prepared as we can be. I've packed up the house, knowing that I probably won't be back. Ever. The thought is a little unnerving. I don't particularly care about leaving the house behind, my future is much more appealing than anything here, but I have a false sense of security here.

Letting Daisy and Kingston slip out into the darkness knowing people are just waiting for the chance to grab them, makes my stomach sick. My house at least provides a barrier between the wicked people of Briar Glen and those that I love.

"You don't need to knock," Daisy's voice drifts through the door.

I grab the doorknob and push the door open. Inside, I find Daisy sitting up, slowly blinking the sleep from her eyes.

"Is it time?" She yawns.

Is she still tired? "We can push this back a day or two. If you're still tired—"

"I'm fine, Wy." She smiles but it's cold and detached. "Slipping away, hiding in the dark, surviving? It's what I do best."

"It won't be like this for much longer." I can promise that, can't I?

My strides are long and sure, much more confident than I feel, as I come to join her on the bed. I sink down onto the mattress, right beside Daisy, sitting so close that we touch. She turns her head to look up at me. Her messy hair rests over one shoulder, but she unconsciously tucks a strand behind her ear.

"We're going to have an adventure of a lifetime after this, Daisy," I tell her. "You won't have to lurk in the shadows or scrape by anymore. Owen made sure that we'll be set for life. We'll go wherever you want—the beach, the mountains or anywhere in between."

I reach up and run my fingers through her thick curls, attempting to comb through the bedhead.

Daisy lets me fix her hair in silence. She tilts her head and slowly I work through the mess until I'm able to braid it. When I'm done, I tug on the thick plait.

"I'm serious, Daisy. No more just surviving. You'll be able to live."

The ice defrosts from her features. This time when she smiles, it reaches her eyes. "The beach? Really? Can you imagine poor Kingston under the sun? He'll fry."

I snort. "He tans better than any of us once he gets a nice base."

"And Drake? He'll scare off all the other beachgoers with a single glare."

"Then we'll have the beach to ourselves."

My response drags a short bout of laughter out of my girl. Unable to stop myself, I lean down and kiss her. What's supposed to be a quick peck turns into a deep kiss as Daisy opens her mouth and slips her tongue into mine. My heart hammers in my chest as I reach up and hold her face.

Daisy's hand slides under my shirt, skimming up my stomach to rest over my heart. Can she feel how it flutters under her touch? Or the strength of the love that radiates from it? I groan. If she can't, I need her to know.

I shift on the bed, pushing her back without breaking our kiss. Straddling her waist, I reach down and grab the hem of her shirt. We break apart only so I can pull her shirt off. Then my lips are pressed against her once more. My hands find her waist then skim upward. I can tell in just the short time we've spent together, she's put on a little bit of weight.

How long did she go without eating that just a few meals have made a difference? I push the thought away. She won't go hungry again. Not with us around.

My hands come up and cup her breasts. When my thumbs tease her nipples, Daisy groans into my mouth. I break away from our kiss to whisper against her lips,

"No more shadows Daisy. I'm going to drag you into the light." I bend down and take a tight bud into my mouth while I pinch and roll the other nipple. Daisy's gasp is beautiful as she arches her chest toward me.

I tease and suck her nipples, going back and forth between the two. Beneath me, Daisy begins to writhe and whimper. It's not enough. The desire to hear her cry out over and over, until she's begging for me to stop, rides me hard. Daisy deserves an all-encompassing life of love and affection. I'll give her a taste of it now, so we both have something to look forward to when this is all over.

My teasing becomes deliberate. From hard sucking, to feather light caresses, I drag pleasure out from my girl in a whole new way. I can feel the change in Daisy's body. Her breathing hitches as her fingers dive into my hair.

"Wyatt… Wy. I-I think…I-I…"

I pull away and blow cool air over one nipple. It does the job.

Daisy's surprised gasp is followed by a full body tremble and a heavy moan. Capturing her nipple back into my mouth, I suck and tease until her body sags beneath me.

"What the hell was that?" she asks, breathless. "You hardly even touched me."

I lift my head up and grin. "A fun little trick I learned, my pretty flower. Now, let me help take these off."

Reaching down, I yank her panties off.

"I need more from you, my pretty Daisy," I murmur as I lean down and kiss each breast again before trailing kisses down to her stomach.

"Whatever you want, Wy," Daisy replies breathlessly.

"A future." I kiss her mound but look up at her. Her eyes flash and secrets scatter out of sight. "I want a future."

"You'll have that."

I grab her legs and throw them over my shoulders, then yank her hips closer to my face. "I want it so that *we'll* have that."

My tongue circles her clit before I run it through her folds. Her body is already dripping with her arousal, so I lap it up slowly before sliding my tongue down between her cheeks. When I tease her asshole, Daisy tenses. Her hips jerk away from me, but I hold her tight.

"Damn, Wy, you were supposed to be helping Daisy get up, not fucking her down."

I laugh as I pull away and look over my shoulder to watch Owen saunter into the room.

"I couldn't resist."

Daisy's body shakes as she giggles, "And I wasn't going to stop him."

Owen moves over to the dresser where he stops and pulls himself up to sit on top of it. "Mind if I watch?"

"Not at all." I shoot Daisy a look for confirmation but find her already giving him a sultry smile.

"You could join us."

Owen shakes his head, already peeling his erection out of the zipper of his pants, "Naw, Daze. I want to watch you come apart. I'll have my turn when we meet up tomorrow."

I don't let Daisy have time to respond. Turning my attention back to the task at hand, I tongue her back door once more. Daisy hisses as her body tenses in surprise. As I work, her arousal leaks down, lubing up her tight asshole and coating my tongue. God, I can't get enough of it. Unable to resist, I run my tongue back up to the entrance of her weeping pussy and devour all the sweetness her body gives freely. Tilting my head forward, I rub my nose against her clit.

Daisy groans and her legs close in on either side of my head. My fingers dig into her thighs as I pull them away, knowing that it will only intensify the oncoming orgasm. As her body begins to tense, the bed beside us sinks. I look up to find Kingston lying on his side beside Daisy and leaning in for a kiss.

King eats up her cry as her second orgasm works its way through her body. I can feel her pussy quiver beneath my lips. I work my tongue into her body, needing to feel it all. Daisy's hips grind against my face and she cums harder. Her body floods my mouth as she continues to fall apart.

When her body begins to relax. I pull away, allowing her legs to fall over the edge of the bed as I stand.

Kingston takes advantage and rolls on top of Daisy, pulling away from her mouth to kiss her everywhere. I step back and watch Kingston greedily grab her breasts, kneading them as his mouth skims along her collarbone. Daisy's legs come up and around his waist. I'm almost positive it's just natural instincts that drive Kingston to grind against her almost desperately.

Daisy's fingers dig into his arms then drag down, leaving red marks in their wake. Kingston lifts his head and when he comes down to kiss her lips again, she bites his bottom lip, causing him to hiss in pain.

And it's like the pain turns him on further because he grinds harder against Daisy.

Movement out of my peripheral captures my attention. I turn to find Owen watching the two of them with rampant interest, stroking his thick dick with measured control. I grin as I pull off my shirt and pants.

"Think you could cum for me a few more times, pretty Daisy?" I ask her, as I join the two of them on the bed.

Kingston rolls Daisy toward me. Happily she climbs on top of me as he shifts to remove his own clothes.

"I don't know," she answers honestly, her mouth skimming against my jawline. "You guys seem to know my body better than I do."

She tilts her hips and runs her folds over my dick. The heat radiating from her core is excruciating in the best way. The way her arousal soaks my cock from head to base tells me she needs this as much as I do. As much as we *all* do. I almost cave, wanting to bury myself all the way inside of her, to feel her body wrap tightly around me. But then Kingston comes up behind her, completely naked, and begins to kiss along her shoulders, his hands moving all over her body hungrily.

It solidifies what I want.

"King, you can have her pretty wet cunt this time. I want her ass." And I want to watch the two of them fuck one another. Together these two are a dangerous combination. Both twisted and molded from their own personal hells and equally as attractive, Kingston and Daisy are a force to be reckoned with.

Kingston wraps an arm around Daisy's waist and plucks her up off my lap and drops her onto the bed beside me. Immediately, I miss the warmth of her body. Biting back a groan, I follow the two of them. As Kingston drags Daisy on top of him, she leans down to grab him around his neck. Her gripping is biting. I open my mouth to correct her hold, knowing that if she's not careful she could hurt him, but then I see the flare of madness in Kingston's eyes. His grin is nearly a snarl and his face flushes with excitement.

They know what they're doing. This isn't about safety. This is about how far they can push one another. If that's their thing, who am I to stop them?

As I scoot closer against Daisy's body, the door slams against the wall behind us, causing me to jump.

"What the fuck, guys?" Drake sighs. "This is the opposite of getting ready to leave."

"Shut up and get over here," Owen orders, his voice strained.

Daisy's body shakes as she giggles. Her ass vibrates against my straining dick, and I swallow at the sensation. With a groan, I grab her hips. As she sits up, I press the head of my cock against her asshole. Her arousal may be *just* enough to make this more comfortable but...

"Drake's right, we don't have a lot of time. This might sting—"

Daisy cuts me off as she presses back against me and impales herself onto my dick. We both gasp as her body wraps tightly around me. Hers is a mixture of pain and pleasure. I breathe for the both of us as I press forward, inching my way into her ass. Daisy arches her back into me, and Kingston watches from beneath us. His pupils are blown so wide that there's only a sliver of blue left.

When I bottom out, we both hold still, breathing hard.

"You good, pretty flower?" I murmur into her ear as I lean forward and kiss along the arch of her neck. My hands slide from her waist up to her breasts, where I tweak and roll her nipples. Daisy doesn't answer right away, she just continues to breathe hard. She shifts a bit before letting out a soft whimper, which concerns me. "Daisy?"

"Better than good, Wy," she answers, her voice stilted. "King...?"

Kingston doesn't need any more prompting. He shifts his hips beneath hers, his hand grabbing her upper thighs, and then he allows himself to sink into her.

"Oh fuck..." I hiss as Kingston's dick enters her body, causing the death hold Daisy has on me to tighten astronomically. There's no stopping the urge to move. I'm practically seeing stars as Kingston bottoms out inside of our girl. My thrusts are shallow though as I give Daisy time to acclimate to the stretching.

In my arms she's trembling, and I know it can't all be from excitement. She's so *small* that I'm surprised she can have sex with any of us without tearing apart. The fact that she can relax enough for more than one of us at a time? Fuck, it makes me love her even more.

"Hold on," Drake orders as he joins us on the bed.

"Hold on? Dre, do you not see what I'm doing right now?" Daisy demands breathlessly. "If I don't start moving, I'm going to combust."

"I want to see that happen sometime," Owen whispers from across the room.

Daisy shoots him a smile as Kingston starts to move his hips, much more aggressively than I dare to move. Her body clenches around us before she reaches down to slap him across the face. I freeze in surprise, but Kingston only gives her a vicious grin.

Letting go of her wrists he says, "Let's play, Daisy. It's Drake's fault he came in here last. Now do it again."

Daisy laughs harshly and slaps Kingston on the other side of his face, before leaning down and biting at his chest. He grabs the back of her head and yanks her towards his mouth to kiss her passionately. I watch in awe as her fingers go into his hair and she yanks at his head, almost like she's fighting him off.

At the same time, she moves her hips. The movement drags a groan from both Kingston and I as she figures out that she has control here. She uses both of our dicks, tilting her hips rather than thrusting, to enjoy us at different angles.

Oh fuck… I help her some, but I can't stop watching as she bites and scratches, nips and sucks at Kingston. He loves it. As his skin turns red and he peppers her with kisses wherever he can, I grow harder inside of Daisy. Their wild, chaotic mess of nails and teeth is a wonder. I've never seen such animalistic madness like this before.

The mattress dips to my right but I don't spare Drake a glance as I watch the sparing beneath me in awe.

"Look at me, Daisy," Drake orders, drawing closer to me on his knees with his pierced cock out.

Daisy tears her mouth away from Kingston to do as she's told.

"I want you to hold me inside your mouth while these two get off," he tells her. "Let them fuck you good and hard, while you take me deep in the back of your throat. You hear me, darling?"

Fuck her good and hard? I pause my movements, knowing that if I don't stop, I'll find my release too early.

Daisy nods and falls forward, onto all fours. Drake moves closer to Kingston's face, angling some so I can still see Kingston below Daisy. Without hesitation, Daisy takes Drake between her lips and into her mouth. Drake's sharp breath in is echoed by Owen, sitting there on the side lines. God, to see Daisy being used by everyone would be hot.

Maybe next time, I'll sit out and watch.

The minute I think about it, I dismiss the idea. Fuck that shit.

"I said hold me, not suck, Daze. Pay attention, I know you're dick stunned right now, but I told you what I wanted," Drake snaps as he chokes back what I think is a groan. "I'm not cumming this time. I'll savor that treat tomorrow."

Daisy hums and Drake hisses.

I smirk, knowing she did that on purpose.

With Drake in place, I start moving again. Kingston never stopped, he had simply slowed down, but now the two of us work together. My lips slide over Daisy's skin that grows damp with perspiration, reaching every place I can.

Beneath me, Kingston stares up at Daisy as if she holds the sun. His hands are all over her, not nearly as rough with her as she is with him. Daisy's eyes try to hold Drake's but they roll up and she squeezes them shut as her body begins to tighten and bear down on me and Kingston. Drool drips from her lips and slides down the length of Drake that she can't take.

All of it's too much.

But Daisy has to cum first.

Determined to see that through, I reach around and play with her swollen clit. Just as I lose my battle and cum inside of her, Daisy's body tenses so dramatically that she manages to stall my orgasm to cum first.

Her scream around Drake is muffled, but there's no hiding the intensity of it as she squeezes around me and Kingston. Liquid splashes around my hand as I continue to play with her clit. I hardly notice as my own orgasm barrels forward, unable to hold back anymore despite her body's death grip on me.

I cum hard into her ass. Continuous ropes of it coat Daisy's insides, leaving me breathless and frozen in a state of bliss. As I finish, Kingston's release hits. I can feel his cock swell just a bit harder inside of her before his orgasm strikes. The thin wall that separates our cocks does nothing to muffle the feel of his dick jerking inside of her.

As we all come down from the intense moment, I pull out first.

"Your mouth is a furnace, darling," Drake mutters, pulling his dick out of her mouth.

Daisy gasps as she collapses onto Kingston's chest, her body still trembling.

"Hold up," Owen says quickly.

He's suddenly on the other side of me, his dick in his hand. Owen's free arm wraps around Daisy's waist, and he lifts her off King. He stops stroking himself long enough to lay her down onto her back and straddle her. As Owen leans down to kiss her lips, his other hand goes back to his dick.

It takes all of three strokes to have him cumming. His release splatters all over her messy pussy. She gasps into his mouth and his body trembles with laughter as he pulls away and looks down at her.

"There," he grunts as he sits up and scoots back to take a look at his addition. Daisy spreads her legs wider for him. "I love seeing you filled and covered with cum. It's so fucking hot."

He uses his hand to smear his cum over her skin. Then his fingers scoop some up and he uses it to push deep inside of her pussy.

"I've never seen a woman actually squirt before," he mutters as he leans down to kiss her breasts, still pumping his fingers in and out of her.

Ah, is that what that liquid was? I grin. "We'll try to make that a common occurrence."

"Don't make promises you can't keep, Wy," Daisy teases with a tired smile as she relaxes. "That was a first for sure."

My laughter shakes the bed. "This is a challenge I definitely want to live up to."

With a sigh, Drake leans down and kisses her swiftly. When he sits up, he says, "If we're going to do this tonight, you and Kingston need to get ready to go. I'll make you something quick to eat while you clean up here."

He moves off the bed with a frown. His worry pops the

blissful bubble we've made in the room. My chest tightens with anxiety once more.

"This wasn't goodbye sex. We'll see each other again tomorrow. Relax," I tell him, needing to say it more than I needed to reassure him.

We each take turns kissing Daisy before pulling away. When I leave the room, I don't feel any better than I did before I came in here.

Maybe it's because Daisy said nothing about us all having a future together.

44

Drake

"Are you sure that's not too heavy for you?"

I eye Daisy's backpack as she slugs it over her shoulder. It was meant for hikers, meaning it's deep and full of pockets. By the look of things, Daisy has implemented a use for each one and stuffed the main part of the bag completely full. It's nearly as big as she is, and it probably weighs more.

"This is nothing to what I used to carry around." She zips up her black jacket and grabs her mask off the nightstand before flashing me a smile which is meant to be reassuring.

I feel far from reassured.

My stomach knots as I notice the hardness in her eyes. She's shutting down and pulling away. It has to be an internal protection mechanism. There were a few guys in my unit in the Marines who'd get this way when we were braced to see trouble. While I understand it, I don't like seeing Daisy do it. Grabbing her wrist, I yank her toward me. The movement causes her to stumble into my chest with a soft gasp. Letting go of her wrist, I reach up and pinch her chin and tilt it upward.

"We'll see each other soon, alright?"

Daisy nods. "Tomorrow night."

"You have Wyatt's phone, right? It's fully charged?"

"Kingston has it, and yes, it's fully charged. Both of our trackers are charged and attached somewhere on us too. We're good, Dre." I expect maybe an eye roll or an exasperated sigh, but she holds my gaze with a hard one of her own. "Kingston and I will be ok. I'm more worried about you three."

I lean closer to her face and growl, "God himself isn't a great enough force to stop me from getting to you."

Bending down, I steal a kiss, needing to taste her before she leaves. To my surprise, Daisy bites my lip hard. Jerking back to glare at her, I find her grinning. Like mine, it's more feral than friendly.

"No goodbye kiss."

Wyatt steps into the guest room and looks between the two of us. "Owen went back and checked the security cameras, nothing looks out of the ordinary and no one has come or gone down the street for most of the day. I think the coast is clear."

Daisy takes a step back from me only to be swept up into Wyatt's embrace. He takes her face and kisses her swiftly. When he pulls away, he just narrowly misses Daisy's teeth.

"I know, I know. I heard you tell Drake, but I have to kiss you now, or I won't for a full twenty-four hours, and that's simply too long." He laughs but the merry sound doesn't last long or extinguish the worry in his eyes. "I tried kissing King but then he punched me in my gut."

Kingston pops his head in and nods solemnly. I can't help it, I laugh.

"Alright, let's get you guys going—"

"Uh, Drake?" Owen calls from somewhere. "Your mom just pulled up to the front of the house."

It takes me a moment to process his warning. When it does,

Daisy, Wyatt, Kingston, and I all exchange surprised glances before I move to head toward the door.

"This is your time to slip out back," Wyatt tells the other two.

I pause halfway down the hall to see Wyatt follow the two of them to the back door. Before they reach it, the doorbell rings frantically.

"Want me to get it, Dre?" Owen calls.

Clenching my teeth, I turn and move into the living room and make a beeline for the door.

"She looks super upset," Owen mutters, passing me to head after the other three.

Ignoring him, I fling open the door to see the woman I loathe waiting on the doorstep. Her cheeks are tearstained, her makeup running. Strange, I don't think I've ever seen the woman cry. Even though she's visibly upset, she somehow manages to glare at me.

"Drake! We need to talk," she half-sobs. "I hated how we left off this morning and I can't... I can't let you go knowing that I could have done more to let you know how much I love you. That everything I've done has been for you. Please? Can we talk privately?"

For a moment, I'm stumped. Her sudden appearance, the tears, the words coming out of her mouth? They all seem so... unlike her. My mother is a cruel woman. Made from all sharp edges and worried more about her social standing than the well-being of her own family, Terra Miller is a grade-A bitch.

"Drake, don't just glare at me, *say* something!" she huffs before sniffling dramatically. "Can't you give your own mother a moment of your time? Whatever you're doing can wait a few minutes."

It takes another moment before I can find my voice. When I do, I'm not afraid to use it. "Get the fuck out of here with this bullshit, Terra."

My mother stiffens as if I've struck her. Her tears come to an abrupt halt, and she pulls herself up to her full height, which, thanks to puberty, isn't anywhere near mine now.

"How *dare* you," she hisses. "Your mother comes crying, and you turn her away? Where's the boy I knew who would do anything to stop someone from crying?"

I shrug. "He's probably still under the stairs in that fucking closet."

Taking a step back, I move to slam the door on her face. She reaches into the purse by her side and pulls out a gun, then points it at me.

"You're going to hear me out, *boy*," she grinds out between clenched teeth, turning into the woman I remember from years ago.

Except, she never had a gun then. I stare down the barrel, more amused than worried.

"You're going to put a bullet in my head?"

Her mouth twists into a perfect sneer. "Not me, but he might."

Before I can ask who, the sound of a safety being removed from inside the house snags my attention. The barrel of a gun is pressed to the back of my head, and someone says,

"On your knees and hands behind your back, you're under arrest."

Goddamn it. This was a fucking trap. I glare at my mother, who shoots me a smug smile and waves her gun at the ground, emphasizing the order. A part of me wants to fight. I could probably disarm the guy behind me, but my mother is a wild card. I don't know what she'll do. Despite being the woman that birthed me, she lacks any real maternal instincts.

There's also the fact that this guy behind me came in through the house another way. Which means there is a very real possibility that he, or whoever he is with, could've nabbed the others before searching me out. The thought sends a heavy chill rushing through me. I'll let him take me wherever he wants, as long as I'm with the others.

Slowly, I raise my hands to place them behind my head, and start to sink to my knees.

"You think you're better than me, Drake baby? Well think again," my mother says, the gun unwavering in her hand. "I'm so close to getting everything I wanted."

"And what's that?" I demand.

"Money. Power." She laughs. "With George and Vincent out of the picture, Zarzuz will help Francis pick the next leadership roles, and guess who's sacrificed more than anyone else?"

I shrug. "I don't give enough of a fuck to care."

Just as I make it to my knees, two gunshots go off somewhere in the house. There's return fire, followed by screaming. My mother's attention springs to the person behind me, who swears and tries to slap cuffs around me. I'm too fast. Back on my feet in half a heartbeat, I kick back. My foot smashes into the person's stomach before I twist and snatch the gun from their surprised hands. There's a bullet between his eyes before the cop has time to gasp. In the same motion, I twist around to point the gun at my mother.

Her mouth drops open in horror. She stumbles back, missing the small step, and topples to the ground. I'm on top of her in two strides. Picking up her gun, I point both weapons at her head.

"You should've just shot me," I snarl, holding her wide, frightened gaze.

"Freeze!"

The word is repeated loudly by several people at once from the street. I look up in time to see a handful of police officers flooding the streets, seeping out from the shadows of the neighbor's houses. Their guns are drawn, pointed at me.

Somewhere behind or in the house, there is more gunfire before everything suddenly goes quiet.

"Drop the guns!" three officers yell in unison. "Drop them now or we'll shoot!"

In my head I do the math; how many could I take out before they get to me? Four? Possibly five? Before I can decide, more cops come from around back. My heart sinks at the sight of Wyatt and Owen in tow, cuffed. Both look like they've been through a war, with their shirts torn, bloody lips, and scratches all over their arms and faces. Two cops walk on either side of Wyatt, clearly holding him up as his feet stumble and drag. He's practically unconscious. One of the cops holding him is his ex, Brett.

I swear violently under my breath. What the hell happened? And where are Daisy and Kingston? I gauge my situation again. I could probably take out a handful of these bastards, but not enough to make a difference or to give the others a chance at escape. Snarling, I click the safeties back on each gun and slowly lower them to the ground as I move to my knees.

The moment I'm on the ground, I'm being swarmed.

My mother scrambles out of the way as five different cops pounce me. Once cuffed, feet, fists, and batons batter me. Pain flares up my sides, in my face, and throughout my back. I refuse to make a sound as they beat me. Even when they shove me down and kick me in the face. My beating lasts until a sharp whistle cuts through the madness. Almost all of them back away, except for two that grab me by my arms and yank me to my feet.

Biting back a groan, I look up to see a man with dark brown skin, a thick gray mustache, and a wide-brimmed hat approach. The shiny badges on his chest, the swagger in his walk, and neatly ironed uniform tell me who it is even before the man speaks.

"Well, Drake Miller, you and your friends here have given us good people of Briar Glen a run for our money. It sure feels good to scoop you off the streets before you can do any more harm." Sheriff Ronney Maxwell cocks a brow as he holds onto his utility belt. "I hope you liked Briar Glen enough to rot here, because you're about to get a personal view of what I look like from six feet under."

"What happened to innocent until proven guilty?" I ask through clenched teeth.

Ronney chuckles. "That doesn't apply to you or your friends, son. Not when you stole everything from me." His cold amusement melts away as he steps forward until he's directly in front of me. "Lucky for you, I had another little Easter Egg hidden away."

I hold his gaze. Ronney thinks his shit doesn't stink but the stench of corruption and deceit is worse than the smell of manure.

"Hey, Sheriff! We got eyes on the other two!"

Holding my gaze, Sheriff Maxwell hollers back, "Remember, don't kill them! Francis wants both of them alive."

The blood leeches from my face. Daisy! Kingston!

"Well, boys, put them all in the van. No need to take a bunch of cars to the graveyard. One will do." Sheriff winks at me. "Next time you see me, I'll have a shovel in my hand."

45

Kingston

Our feet barely touch the ground as we sprint across yards, jump over fences, and cross streets. I can hear the cops in hot pursuit. Their sirens wail in the night and their lights appear on every street we try to turn down.

"Come on, this way." Daisy takes us between two homes.

Back here there are thick trees and overgrown bushes that we dive into. Immediately, I cover her body with my own and pin her to the ground as two cops peer into the backyard. When they disappear, I don't move. We take the moment to catch our breath.

"King, you gotta go," Daisy huffs. "You're faster than me, you'll make it further."

I don't spend the energy acknowledging her stupidity. I'll blame it on the lack of oxygen— we've been running for a while.

She nudges me.

"Seriously, I'm too slow. We'll split up and meet at one of the hiding spots, ok?" she whispers, sitting up, her mouth pressing against my ear. Her fingers attempt to wrap around my bicep, only getting halfway. "I can't let them get you, Kingston. We'll regroup and figure out how to help the others."

Again, I ignore her. What are we going to do? Briar Glen hasn't changed too much since I was locked away, but it's been so long since I've freely moved through the town that everything only seems vaguely familiar. I'm not equipped to plan where to go or pick a direction. The best I can do is put myself between the people of Briar Glen and Daisy.

The thought of them getting her turns my blood to ice, which, in turn, sends a hard shiver down my spine. If they get their hands on her, there's no doubt in my mind she'll be given to my father, which is a fate worse than death.

I reach over and grab the back of Daisy's neck to hold her for a moment, glad that we're safe for the time being. The others, they've been taken. Watching Wyatt take a baton to the face left me feeling nauseous. And when he went to his knees? Our eyes had met briefly, and I could see the fear there.

It hadn't been for himself. That fear had been for me and Daisy.

"*Go*," he'd mouthed before collapsing.

What's going to happen to them? Where are they being taken? To the police station? I didn't want to leave them, but it was between staying to fight a losing battle or getting Daisy to safety. The decision was a no-brainer.

Still, guilt curdles in my gut.

"We'll get them out," Daisy promises, as if she can read my thoughts. "You know I won't leave any of you behind."

"We need to get you to safety first," I sign quickly. "Then we'll figure that part out."

"King, I can find a tight spot to hide in or cause a distraction so you can run. If they capture you, you could end up in another asylum."

I would kill myself before I let that happen. Rather than tell her that, I shake my head. "We're not splitting up."

"But—"

The sound of soft buzzing overhead cuts off whatever she has to say. We both look up as a light flashes down on us.

"A drone!" Daisy hisses. "It's going to see us!"

As if fate could hear her, a police officer's voice shouts, "Over there! Behind the shed in the bushes."

We both reach for our knives at the same time.

"Look, if you run toward downtown, duck behind the old hardware store, then move north to the water tower, there're plenty of shadows to hide in."

I glare at her.

Her sigh of exasperation is followed by a hard nod. "Alright, let's go. We move together."

We're on our feet and running just as five cops converge onto the backyard with their guns drawn.

"Freeze!"

The order is ignored as we rush the four-foot tall, chain-link fence in the back of the yard and jump it. Two cops are already waiting for us on this side. Daisy grabs my arm and yanks me to the left. The six foot wooden privacy fence that splits these two properties is going to be impossible to jump, and climbing will take time. They'll grab us before we make it halfway over. I slow my gait, ready to turn and attack the cops behind us to give Daisy a fighting chance to make it over. My muscles bunch and my grip tightens on my weapon.

"Come on!" she snaps, running at full speed toward the fence.

I see why a second later. She shoves two boards forward and they actually raise up.

How did she know...? I don't have time to gape or wonder as I follow her lead, but I do grin, impressed with her ingenuity. Rather than continue to cross the next yard, we turn and head toward the front of the house. We cross the street, double back several times, and hide behind several trash bins. When the coast is clear, we make a break for the other end of the street.

We get there, only to come to a grinding halt. Two squad cars skid to a stop, blocking us. Behind us is the stomping of feet and the jiggling of items bouncing on utility belts. I tense, gripping my knife tighter as Daisy crouches into a fighting stance.

A cop climbs out of one of the squad cars, staying behind the door, and lifts a megaphone to his lips.

"Kingston Winslow and Daisy Murray, you are surrounded. Drop your weapons and get on your knees."

Daisy's knife goes flying. As the man lowers his megaphone, her blade gets him right in the cheek. The police officer staggers backward before collapsing. Other officers start to shout in outrage as a few of them try to charge us. I turn, knowing the ones behind us are closer. My knife throw isn't as clean as Daisy's, but it does end up lodged in a policewoman's throat, taking her out.

"Kingston, remember that I love you, ok?" Daisy's words, a whisper right behind me, are more chilling than the fate in front of us. Before I can turn to grab my girl up and promise her that we'll be ok, there's a loud bang.

Something hot rips through the skin, muscle, and cartilage of my shoulder before exploding out of it. The pain causes me to stumble forward and there's a ringing in my ear. Daisy's scream as I fall to my knees causes me to tense and focus even as the world tilts on its axis.

I look down at my right shoulder, where waves of agony are radiating from, to find a bloody hole.

"King?" Daisy whimpers, falling to her knees beside me.

I look up at her, stunned that she's still here. "What are you doing? Go, Daisy!"

The pain makes my signing sloppy, and with only one good

hand, I'm sure it looks more like a child's attempt at cursive rather than real words.

"I'm not leaving you!" she snarls before turning to face the wave of cops descending upon us. "You'll have to pry my cold dead hands off his body!"

I want to tell her to shut up. To run hard and fast away from here. But my fingers feel cold and lifeless as they dangle at my sides. The blood is draining from my face quickly. My stomach churns as spots skew my vision.

Daisy catches me as I pitch forward, making sure my face doesn't hit the sidewalk. The last thing I see before darkness takes me, is five men jumping on my girl with fists raised.

~

A FIERY BLEND of blinding pain and rage pulls me out from the darkness.

"Ah, there we go. You're awake."

That voice. Oh god... My heart comes to a full stop as it tries to process the unholy surge of terror that explodes from its depths. Then it breaks out into a race for its life. I blink as my eyes adjust to the lighting, straining to be present, to see the devil when he strikes me down for the last time. Something jerks out of the bullet wound in my shoulder causing me to wince.

As the world comes into focus, I find myself tied to a chair. My hands are bound behind me, my torso strapped to the back, and my ankles are tied to the two front legs of it. Whoever tied me up made damn sure I couldn't escape.

With a soundless moan, I force my drooping head upward.

Standing before me is the man I loathe most in the world. His blue eyes twinkle with mirth, his mouth curved into a small but victorious smile as I glare up at him.

I don't know what I expected as I stare at my father. Maybe

horns? A sign that he was clearly more insane than I am? But all I see is the man that raised me. The man who killed my mother, pinned her death on me, and then made sure I'd stopped touting what I'd seen him do in the woods to the people of Briar Glen, looks about as average as any clean cut, run of the mill, quiet millionaire.

"You know, I thought I would be quite happy to never see you again," Francis muses, pulling his hand away from me. He pulls out a handkerchief from the back pocket of his nice khakis and wipes my blood from the finger he had shoved into my bullet wound. "But, low and behold, I was wrong. I'm *delighted* to have you home again, Kingston."

Fuck you. I scream it in my head, hoping he sees the hate I have for him in my eyes.

He does and it only pulls his mouth up into a wider smile.

"What's wrong? No back talk or some vulgar profanity to spew?" He chuckles, shoving the cloth back into his pocket. "No? Well, I suppose that's hard when you have no voice."

Francis sighs and reaches out beside him to grab the metal folding chair. He drags it closer until it's directly in front of me and takes a seat. Without hurry, he crosses one leg over the other and straightens his button up shirt. As he prolongs whatever self-righteous rambling bullshit that he has prepared for me, I glance around the room.

Clearly, we're in a basement. I could say it's unfinished, but I think the dark glossy concrete floors are intentional, as are the painted red walls, tiled ceiling, and strange lengths of dark gray fabric draped loosely from the ceiling that block off certain parts of the space. In the area that I'm currently sitting, it's only me and Francis. There's no other furniture, no windows, not even a door.

"Yes, it's a bit different, isn't it?"

I look back at my father, who's watching me with interest.

He must see the confusion on my face because his smile widens.

"The basement, it's different, no? Since I had the house all to myself, I renovated the place. The basement is solely for the worshipping of our Lord Zarzuz now."

This is the basement of the house? I blink and look around again, not believing him. Where are the couches? The large TV that me, the guys, and Daisy would play video games on for hours? The foosball table is gone too. As are the bookshelves, posters of football stars, and the family portrait is missing too. He has even torn out the plush carpet.

"You know, I blame myself, in part, for how things transpired between us," Francis says, pulling my attention back to him. "I should've told you about Zarzuz from the moment you were born. It was how my father raised me. But I wanted you to have a normal childhood, something I never got. The late-night worship sessions, the never ending responsibilities... I'd loathed my father for keeping me from experiencing so much of the world around us. Your mother wanted some normalcy too. So we allowed you to grow up independent and to make your own choices. We sent you to public school rather than homeschool you, had you play sports, and make friends, all with the intention of having you join our world when you were of age."

He sighs and leans back in his seat, a thoughtful frown appearing.

"We just never expected you to befriend the Chosen One. Your mother and I were quite uncertain as to what to do about that, knowing she wouldn't be around long." His frown is replaced with a smile. "But she was a good girl, even at a young age, and we enjoyed having her around. She grew into a lovely young woman too. Smart, beautiful, and charming. Quite frankly, if she hadn't been the Chosen One, we would have arranged for you two to be married."

I jerk in my seat, shocked. The movement causes pain to radiate up my arm, but it's almost immediately forgotten as Francis laughs.

"Oh don't be so surprised. As if we would've let you marry just anyone off the street." He waves his hand dismissively. "Your mother and I had an arranged marriage. A union of perfection is what Zarzuz had told my father when he was informed who I'd be betrothed to. Unfortunately, the word of our Lord was clearly misinterpreted."

He sighs as he uncrosses his leg. Leaning forward, he braces his elbows on his thighs, folds his hands together, and rests his chin on the top of his knuckles.

"But alas, Daisy was already betrothed, and to a god no less. She still is, in fact." He smiles again, but this time not in fondness. My stomach twists.

Where is Daisy? Did she manage to escape? I highly doubt my father would be wasting his breath with me if he had her. I hold on to that thought as it inspires a sliver of hope.

"I don't blame you for the madness that's been going on in Briar Glen. I know Daisy has been behind it all. Though if you knew what was good for you, you should've just brought her here. *Maybe* I would have welcomed you home with open arms. I could have tried to forgive you for your sins and plead your case to Lord Zarzuz."

I'm tired of this conversation. My father has always loved the sound of his own voice. If I'm unlucky, this could go on for hours. With a sigh, I allow my head to droop. Focusing on the pain in my shoulder, I allow it to consume my thoughts.

"She thinks she's being clever, returning to avenge the life she thinks we stole from her. But this was always in the cards. I didn't know that, not at first. It was only after her fall from that cliff that Zarzuz told me she would return stronger and more fitted to be his bride. If only I knew how *creative* she would be, maybe then I could have limited the damage she's wrought on us all. In any case, I have her once more, and soon, she'll be at peace at last, by our Lord's side."

My stomach practically drops out of my body as my heart stalls. I look up, searching for a lie in his expression. He doesn't have her. He *can't* have her!

France grins. "Don't worry, you'll see her again before her wedding. This time, I'll give you time to say goodbye and get some closure. Maybe that's all you needed last time? You can let her go with the knowledge she will be cherished."

"No!" I scream it though nothing but air comes out.

"It is inevitable. The Daughters of Zarzuz are preparing her now, while the rest of the Council is busy at work alerting the members of the congregation of the arrival of the Chosen One. By sunrise, everyone will know the balance will soon be restored. The curse ruining this town will be nothing more than a dream. Those that continued to believe in Zarzuz after her disappearance will be rewarded immensely by our merciful god. And those who didn't believe that? Well, Daisy's sacrifice will eliminate the doubt of Zarzuz's word, and donations will come streaming back in. The money Daisy stole? It'll come back tenfold."

I struggle against my restraints as I scream muted profanities at my father. The pain in my shoulder increases but I fight through it. This can't be happening. Not again. Francis simply watches me, a deviant smile plastered to his face.

After a few minutes, he grows bored watching me and stands.

"I'll get someone to patch you up. I would hate to see you bleed out before the wedding."

He moves toward the curtains. Pushing them aside, he leaves without a backward glance.

I stare after him, my heart clawing its way up my throat. Where's Daisy? Who are the Daughters of Zarzuz, and how are they preparing her?

I can't believe this is happening again. Failing Daisy a second time isn't possible. Struggling against the rope is futile, but I continue anyway, not caring how much blood is seeping from my wound or how much the pain makes me ill. I can't just do nothing. If there's a chance I can loosen the rope enough to slip out, I'm going to take it. There has to be a way out of here. If this is my house, I know the layout. If I can just get free, I could start knocking down doors looking for her.

In my head, I scream.

46

Owen

I'm pretty sure I have a broken rib or two. The telling sign is that it hurts to breathe. The swelling of my nose doesn't help much, but I don't think that's broken. Just a little busted up.

It's not the only thing busted.

As Drake, Wyatt, and I are jostled around in the back of a cop van, cuffed and attached to metal hooks that keep us in place, all sense of hope for a future is dashed. There's no one to break us out like Kingston had with Daisy. We're on our own, and we're about to die at the hands of a corrupted sheriff.

On top of that, we all heard over the radio that they grabbed the others. It was just a quick "we got them," but there's no doubt in my mind who 'them' is. The cult has Daisy again, and there's nothing we can do about it. She's going to die. And Kingston? What will be his fate? Death, like Francis originally wanted? Or will his father throw him back into a psych ward and let him rot away once more? Both endings seem like a terrible fate.

I should've told Daisy I loved her more. Just confessing it and letting that be it was stupid. Every morning, I should have kissed her awake, looked her in the eyes, and told her how much she meant to me. Killing for her? Hacking into security systems and financial accounts? Those were just a fraction of the things I would've done for her. Does she know that? I should've told her there was no limit to the things I'd do for her.

Tears blur my vision as I hang my head and stare at the floor of the van.

The only bright spot about any of this is that all the information I've gathered on this cult since our arrival is in a file on my computer set on a timer. If I don't get back onto my computer and enter in a code, it goes straight to the FBI. Even if the sheriff has his guys sweep the house and destroy the computer, it's all in a cloud, ready to go. We might die, but hopefully the cult won't be far behind us.

The air in the van is stale. Like someone threw up and there was a lazy attempt to clean it not all that long ago, but what lingered has been marinating in the lack of A/C. I'm not sure if the air conditioning is broken or if this is a form of torture. That, along with the incessant rattle coming from the thin metal grate that separates us from the police officers in the driver and passenger seat is making everything a thousand times worse. I've given up glaring at the corner missing its screw.

How long do we have until our deaths? Sheriff Ronney mentioned burying us alive as he shut and locked us in here, but is that what's really going to happen? Or are we being taken to some undisclosed location where we'll simply be shot? I hope it's the latter. Suffocating to death under a pile of dirt sounds really off-putting. If we are headed to the graveyard, we're probably still a half hour away.

That's a half hour to replay all the good times I had with the people I love. And to wallow in hopelessness.

Beside me, Drake growls. The sound is strangely menacing and full of wrath. It's followed by an eerie snap and a pained grunt. Curiosity outweighs my despondency. Looking up, I find Drake pulling his wrist free from his cuff.

I gape. How the hell did he—?

The answer is clear when I catch sight of his broken thumb. Not only that, but the cuff is no longer attached to the wall of the van. Where the hook would have been, are now two holes that lead to the outside. Holy shit, did he yank himself from the wall when I wasn't looking?

Note to self: in my next life, I need to start working out.

With his free hand, Drake reaches into his pocket and pulls out a dime. I blink, confused. What does he think he's going to do with a dime? Subtly, Drake scoots closer to the metal grate and reaches up to the corner still attached to the van. Using the edge of the dime, he begins to loosen the other screw. I stare in disbelief his plan works.

A small balloon of hope swells in my chest. Pulling my gaze away from Drake, I look across the space to the other bench where Wyatt sits, his body facing us. He hasn't made a sound or moved since he went down in his backyard.

Just thinking about how quickly the cops had appeared as we walked Daisy and Kingston out... They'd been waiting for us. Maybe they didn't know we'd be splitting up, but they knew we were all at the house. They'd just been waiting, out of sight of the cameras I'd installed. I have no doubt that it was Brett that told Ronney about the cameras. I'd overheard him mention them when he came by to visit the other day.

I'm sure Wyatt's pieced that together by now. No need to point that out.

Using the tip of my socked feet, I nudge Wyatt's leg.

Wyatt doesn't acknowledge me. Is he still knocked out?

Frowning, I try again, this time a little harder. When that doesn't work, I give up being gentle and kick him in the shin. He groans but lifts his head to look at us. I try not to wince. The swelling on his face looks bad. His cheek might be broken. One eye is already so swollen and purple, I'm afraid he might lose it.

I tilt my head toward Drake once I catch his eye.

Wyatt's attention shifts to the big guy next to me and watches as Drake finishes. The brute catches the screw before it clatters to the ground and pockets it. He looks at Wyatt, then at me. He's trying to send a message with his eyes, but given that I don't have the power of telepathy, whatever he's trying to say is lost.

But whatever he needs, I'll give it to him. I nod. Drake looks over to Wyatt who only stares. I wonder if he's even with us or if he's too far gone in his pain to get what's going on. Without waiting for his confirmation, Drake stands and grabs the top of the metal grate. He pulls it away from the frame of the vehicle and begins to bend it back toward us.

"Hey!" the driver shouts as the van swerves.

"What are you doing? Stop that! Sit down!" the cop in the passenger seat shouts, turning around in his seat.

As he fumbles getting his gun out, Drake bends the grate back further. The metal groans under the pressure. When there's enough room, Drake reaches forward, grabbing the head of the cop sitting in the passenger seat and snapping his neck like it's nothing.

"No, stop! Leave me alone!" the driver screams, jerking the wheel left and right as Drake reaches for him.

Wyatt and I are thrown around. The only thing keeping me in my seat are the cuffs attached to the van. As my body weight yanks on the metal, my wrists scream in protest.

Drake's meaty fist slams into the driver's skull, snapping it hard to the left, where it cracks against the window. The van swerves harder before going completely off the road. I shout a warning as the front of the vehicle plunges headfirst into a thicket of trees.

We hit one dead on.

My body is thrown upward. I hit the ceiling of the van hard, flip over myself in midair, causing an excruciating pain to billow out from my shoulder, and then I'm falling. I hit the hard bench first, then the floor.

I gasp for air, trying to breathe through the pain. I hurt *everywhere.* How is it possible to hurt this bad and still be alive? I can taste blood in my mouth. And did I think my ribs hurt before? Well that's nothing to how they feel now.

Somewhere in the van, someone groans.

Fuck, who's alive? Please let it be Wyatt or Drake and not one of the cops. Opening my eyes and slowly lifting my head, I find Wyatt getting to his feet. His hands are still cuffed together, but the cuffs are no longer attached to the van. I watch as he shuffles forward and reaches over the grate. A second later he's sitting back down with a gun in his lap and a set of keys in his mouth. He brings his wrists to his mouth but the keys dangling from his lips fall before he can free himself.

With a broken cheek I can't imagine holding something between your lips can feel all that great.

I heave myself up slowly, wincing through the pain, and shift so that I'm kneeling. There's no satisfaction as I realize I'm no longer attached to the van. I hurt too fucking much to care. At the same time, Wyatt snatches the keys off the ground and looks up at me.

"I'll free you first," he says through clenched teeth. He gets up and removes the cuffs from my wrists. I take the keys from him and do the same for him.

"Where's Drake?" I look toward the front of the van to find his body lying on the scrunched up hood of the car, unmoving. The windshield has been completely shattered. What's left of it are bloody sheets of shattered glass. I can guess whose blood that is. My throat closes up.

Wyatt gasps. "Drake!"

The two of us move at the same time. We climb over the hanging grate and the two dead bodies strapped to their seats and work on opening the doors. I shoulder the passenger door and eventually manage to get it open at the same time Wyatt opens the driver's door. My feet barely hit the ground before the sound of a gun being cocked causes me to freeze.

"Put the gun down, Wyatt!" someone shouts on the other side of the van. "I don't want to hurt you!"

I know this voice. It takes me a second to place it, but when it registers, I roll my eyes. *Of course* Wyatt's ex is going to be the one to stop us.

"You don't want me *hurt*? Look at me!" Wyatt shouts back. "You were letting them take me to my *death*!"

"I wouldn't have let anything happen to you! Once we got to the cemetery, I would have gotten you away from the others. You have to believe me, I love you. I always have!"

Frantically, I look around for a weapon. I find one clipped to the utility belt of the dead police officer in the passenger seat. Fuck yes! I carefully remove the gun from the holster and creep around the back of the van where Brett must be. From here, I can see his squad car on the road. The lights are flashing, and the driver's door is open. We're not too far from it, so he must be directly on the other side of where I am.

"Bullshit! You're part of a cult. The only thing you care about is your crazy-ass god!"

"Zarzuz's love expands to even non-believers! I can love you *and* him without things getting complicated. I've been doing it this whole time! I know about your past, and I knew you wouldn't be interested in joining, so I thought I could keep things separated," Brett yells back. "Wyatt, you have to put the gun down. You and me, we can get out of here. We'll run away. I can worship Zar—"

I've had about enough of this madness. Unclicking the safety, I step around the back of the van with my gun aimed directly at Brett's profile. He sees me out of his peripheral vision. Quickly, he swings the gun stretched out in front of him toward me.

I pull the trigger.

Brett's body jerks back before he topples to the ground. My heart slams against my ribcage as I stare down at the body. I just killed another man. This is the second time I've actively taken another person's life. I wait a second, wondering if *this* is when the guilt and horror will roll in.

It doesn't.

Ok, well, it's official. I'm a psychopath just like the others. At least this way of killing is a lot easier than with a knife. Given that I have no experience with guns and still managed to hit my target? This may become my weapon of choice.

Wyatt comes around and stops in front of his dead ex-lover. I can't read the expression on his face, but he doesn't say anything for a long moment.

"Hey, Wy?"

Wyatt looks up, his face impassive.

"I didn't like your ex much."

Wyatt blinks once, but then a small smile slides into place. "Yeah, well, me neither. Is it strange I find him better looking without life in his eyes?"

"Absolutely, yes." I grimace even has Wyatt's smile grows incrementally as he teases me. It vanishes, though, as he looks over his shoulder.

"C'mon, let's get Drake."

My fluttering heart doesn't slow down as we both move toward the front of the vehicle. To my relief, as we approach, Drake groans and sits up.

"How the hell did you survive being flung out of a car and smashing into a tree?" I demand.

Drake sways. Blood drips down into his eyes and his clothes are stained with it. But I don't see anything life threatening. He probably has a ton of internal bleeding. What can be done about that? We can't take him to the hospital...

"I'm not dying until I know Daisy's safe," he grumbles.

I shoot him a weak smile. "That's convenient, thanks. And thanks for all of this." My hand waves toward the wreckage.

"Don't mention it." Drake takes a deep breath and moves to jump down.

Wyatt and I hurry forward and help him down. He stumbles and it takes both of us to keep Drake upright. When he's found his footing, he straightens.

"What do we do now?" Wyatt asks. "How are we going to find Kingston and Daisy? It'll be like looking for two needles in a haystack. And since I'm sure it won't take the others in the cult long to realize we never made it to our destination, we're probably going to find ourselves in more trouble soon."

Drake sighs heavily. "I got us out of the vehicle. It's time for someone else to come up with a plan."

I lean against the van and consider our options. There aren't many. We could drive around and just hope we find where the cult is hiding the others and pray we don't get caught. We could also just get the hell out of dodge and call for reinforcements. I'm sure the FBI would help in a pinch like this, right? But that could take too long. Who knows how long Daisy and Kingston have before the cult is through with them.

We have to find them first. But how?

"If I had access to our phones or at least a computer, I could pull up the program I created and find them using the trackers. Even if the cult found them and got rid of them, I'll be able to trace where they've been until they were destroyed or tossed out."

Wyatt nods slowly. His one good eye slides toward the squad car. "There's a laptop in Brett's car."

"Brett?" Drake looks at him confused.

"Not an issue right now," I tell him, then shake my head at Wyatt. "No, trying to crack through the police firewall so that I can upload my own stuff would take too much time."

Drake sighs. "Let's go see what's in the squad car we can use for weapons. If we're going to be scrambling for a while, we need to be better armed."

Nodding in agreement, we walk toward the road. Quickly, Wyatt moves around to the driver's side and pops open the trunk. Drake and I approach the back as it springs open. When my eyes land on the large, clear bags that fill it up, I laugh. The reaction causes my ribs to scream, but hysteria has given me the ability to ignore it.

"No fucking away!" I manage after I've gotten myself under control.

Drake reaches forward and rips open a bag and pulls out someone's black zip-up jacket. As he tosses the bag to the ground, a sheathed knife falls back into the trunk. We both stare at it before I break out into laughter again. In a bag just beneath the one he picked up are three blood-stained masks.

They took our stuff as evidence, but now we have it back. What are the chances Brett would be the one to drive around with the things they've collected from our house? This has to be sheer dumb luck. God knows we need it about now.

"Please tell me our phones are in there?" I don't wait for Drake to go searching. My hands reach for the bags, tearing them apart one by one.

By the time I'm through, Wyatt has joined us.

"No phones and no sign of my computer, but we have weapons and our get ups, so we're not completely defenseless." I look at both of them. "Now, if we could just find a computer, we'll be solid."

Drake grunts, before letting out a sigh. "Just any old computer?"

"Yeah, a home computer, a kid's laptop, whatever."

"Alright," he nods. "I know where to go to get one."

Wyatt grabs what must be his jacket and slips it on. Before he can grab the mask that's his, I reach down carefully, pick it up, and hand it to him.

"Let's get the fuck out of here," Wyatt says grimly. "If I have to kill every fucking person in Briar Glen to find Daisy and King, so help me god, I will."

47

Daisy

My skin hurts. In fact, it feels like it's on fire.

After receiving an enema, I'd been scrubbed meticulously with straight bleach by a bunch of women who dressed as strange looking nuns, so I'm not surprised I'm aching. It's not as bad now that it's been rinsed off my body and the smell is nearly gone after they held me under water in a bathtub full of heavily scented rosemary soap. Still, my skin burns.

I focus on that rather than how naked and exposed I am standing in the corner of Francis Winslow's bedroom, my wrists and neck caught up in a pillory that hangs from the ceiling. The holes are padded but tight, making it hard to breathe. It's also set up for someone taller than me, forcing me to balance on the balls of my feet or end up strangling myself. With my feet cuffed together, the job is even harder.

I can only imagine why Francis would have this setup here in the first place.

His room hasn't changed much. I only know because one

time, Kingston brought me up here to show me his dad's fancy pocketknife collection back when we were in middle school. The heavy four-poster bed is the same, the furniture around the room hasn't moved, and the walls are covered with boring wallpaper of people working in some type of field. This pillory though, this is a new thing.

Despite the burning sensation, my body shivers from the cool air. Having been freshly shaved everywhere, including between my legs, I can feel even the slight breeze all over my body.

I'm burning. I'm burning. I repeat the mantra in my head to keep from panicking.

Panicking will only lead to more problems. Just because I'm naked and at the mercy of yet another madman, doesn't mean I should just succumb to the hysteria. I squeeze my eyes shut, but in the darkness behind my eyelids, I can see Oliver sauntering over to me, his dick in his hand.

My eyes pop open.

The room is relatively dark, but the morning light is trying to push through the wooden blinds. There's a stream of light, no more than an inch wide, that lands directly on the door. So when it opens, Sheriff Ronney Maxwell is cast in an almost angelic beam. He flicks on the light, leaving me momentarily blinded.

"Well, Miss Murray, this has been a long time coming, hasn't it?" he asks, shutting the door behind him. He takes off his hat and tosses it to the bed as he eyes me up. "You know, we're putting on a party for you. By now, all Zarzuzians are waking up with a formal invitation in their inbox to your wedding to Zarzuz, taking place in two days. I don't think there's a single person who will miss this event. You'll be the talk of the town."

Normally, when The Butcher of Briar Glen would come to gloat or scare me, I wouldn't give him the satisfaction of replying. It drove him crazy when he couldn't make me scream. But this is a different situation and information could be my key to getting out of here or coming up with a plan.

"A wedding seems kind of strange given how it will end."

"It's how it was always supposed to be. Your death will inspire the good people of Briar Glen to renew their faith in Zarzuz." He stops a few feet in front of me, holding my gaze. "Once you're gone, I'll retire. Hang up the old belt and hat and take it easy. I've put in a lot of years in this position."

"Huh, it must've been hard to be a corrupt cop." I roll my eyes.

Rather than get upset, Ronney chuckles. "You have no idea. Destroying evidence, hiding bodies of those willing to expose us, and keeping people within the congregation out of trouble was a lot of work. Including my normal duties on top of that—I was a busy man."

"Sure."

"You wouldn't know the difficulties of holding a job, now, would you? Kind of hard to be a person out in the world without any type of ID or proof of existence. I helped George with that, you know. No DNA in the system, no dental records, nothing." As he talks, Ronney's eyes leave mine to travel down the rest of my body. "What'd you do to make ends meet all these years? Did you sell this pretty little body of yours? Or were people too repulsed by this mutilation? Oliver really did a number on you, didn't he? Look at these scars."

Focus on the burning. You're burning. Your skin is on fire.... I'm burning. I'm burning...

"I was perfecting the art of killing men like you." My voice comes out even. Hell, even my heartbeat remains calm as he steps closer.

His hand reaches out and traces the rune with a single fingertip. When he's done, he tweaks my nipple. I don't flinch.

He's expecting it, hoping for a fight. I can see it in the way his eyes find mine and he smiles.

"I erased you once, Daisy. I'll do it again after your wedding." He cups my breast, kneading it as he talks. "It shouldn't be so hard since no one but us knows that you're still alive. You're no more a threat now than you were all those years ago. Hell, I've been preparing for your arrival since you killed Oliver five years ago. You wouldn't even have come close to sinking your knife into me."

I blink in surprise. "You knew Oliver was dead? Yet you left his body there to rot in his cabin? Why?"

Why didn't you tell the world about all those women he had pictures of on the wall? Anger surges through me. The only reason I burned the woods around Oliver's house was so that no one could ignore what was inside that house or dismiss the lives that were taken under that roof.

Ronney grins. "Jeff stumbled in and found the body of The Butcher of Briar Glen with Tobias. Panicked, they both called me—told me everything. I came out and decided that no one would miss the bastard and left him there. Nothing to hide if I never found the place, right? We went searching for you, of course, but your trail ran cold. So, I prepared for you just in case you pulled something crazy. I didn't think to share it with the others until shit started getting wild around here. Francis suspected it was you, Zarzuz had already whispered it into his ears. But Vincent? He was skeptical. Unfortunately, I didn't get to tell George, Jeff, or Tobias."

Ronney's hand leaves my breast so his fingertips can skim down my stomach and dive between my legs. My bottom lip trembles as my mind starts to shut down. I can't panic in autopilot mode or when I'm trapped in the recesses of my own mind. Neither can I feel or be present in any way.

"I'm not a man who tends to like a freshly shaved pussy

but," he shakes his head, staring down at where his hand is. "Yours looks mighty fine."

My clit is toyed with. He circles and pinches it gently, watching my face carefully. Bile climbs up my throat and my legs come together as best they can.

I'm burning. I'm burning. My skin is on fire, I'm burning.

"Watching you become a woman, Daisy, was a thrill," he tells me softly. "When I found out what Oliver had been doing to you for years, I'll admit, I got a little jealous."

"You're disgusting."

He groans and the sound of a zipper being undone follows. "I'm not, but I want to do disgusting things to you, Miss Murray."

No, no, no! Not this, please. I want to beg. The words sit on the tip of my tongue. But I hold back. He wants to hear me beg. I won't cave.

Ronney steps closer. His hand vanishes from between my legs only so that he can hold my hips and pull me closer. I can feel the head of his cock press against my clit. I can feel him trying to move his hips in some type of clockwise motion to simulate the feel of his fingers.

"You're supposed to be a virgin when Zarzuz receives you," he tells me, suddenly sinking to his knees. His breath hits my pussy as he continues to speak from this new position. "I doubt you still are, but I'm sure as hell not going to risk his wrath by sinking my cock into you now. I'm sure he'll destroy anyone who touched you, his virgin bride. But that doesn't mean I can't *taste* you."

His lips skim up my thighs. They pull away for only a second before his teeth sink into my skin. The pain is hardly noticeable as my mind continues to shut down. I can feel myself receding further and further back, away from reality. He repeats this over and over on each leg, yet I find myself too far gone to notice it much.

Just as his mouth latches around my clit, the door flings open. Hastily, Ronney stands and tucks in his dick as Francis enters the room. No relief comes in the absence of the sheriff's mouth. Not with Kingston's father, dressed in his red robe, standing there.

Not the robe. Bumps rise and rush down my arms as the blood drains from my face. I jerk around but I'm trapped by the pillory. *Not the robe*!

Flashes of that night, of men hovering over me, chanting, come rushing forward.

"Get. The. Fuck. Out." Francis orders, spitting out each word through clenched teeth.

I hardly hear him as my own internal screams repeat from the night of my botched sacrifice.

"Yes, sir." Ronney hurries over to the bed, grabs his hat, and darts out of the room.

It's not until the door is shut that Francis walks toward me. His eyes hold mine as he approaches.

"You look so much better without all those piercings." He comes to a stop in front of me, his pupils narrowing. "It appears you are a temptation to even the most devoted. I'll keep an extra close eye on you. No one but me will touch you until you meet your maker, I promise you that."

Fear makes speech impossible. I simply stare at the leader of the Zarzuzian cult as my mind freezes up.

Francis's eyes drop down to my body. "Oliver actually did a decent job with the rune, but I want it fresh. That'll come later, I think. For now, it is time for your blessing, and to cleanse you from your sins. You may have been pure the first time around, but I have a feeling you are no longer an innocent woman."

Well that certainly doesn't sound like I'm going to like this at all. Rather than plead for mercy, I take a deep breath and tell him, "You know I gave my soul to Lilith, right?"

Francis's impassive expression cracks. His jaw clenches, and a small vein bulges from his forehead. "Your soul does not belong to her."

"Yes it does. I've given Lilith everything she required, and she has accepted me with open arms." My heart races, knowing I'm only going to make whatever Francis has planned for me worse. If he's going to hurt me, I want to make sure he loses it. If I can pass out from pain... Well, at least I won't feel anything. "She has guided my hand since I escaped from Oliver's house, and she has lent me the strength to destroy Zarzuz's followers."

"Is that so?" His voice is hardly more than a whisper as his face turns red. "Well, let's see if she'll step in to help you now."

He moves over to a small wooden dresser and opens the top drawer. He brings out a book that looks suspiciously like the Bible. The next drawer he opens is deeper and he has to rummage through whatever items are inside before he pulls out the next object.

When he does, my stomach sinks further. The whip unravels from the neat twist it's in, the tail falling to the floor.

"This may hurt a bit but trust me when I say you will feel so much better when I'm done," he assures me. "And then afterward, I'll take you to Kingston."

48

Wyatt

Normally, I'm not one to condone hurting women, or kidnapping them, or tying them up (unless it's consensual), but when it comes to Terra Miller, I'm open for all three experiences. When Drake pulled up in front of his old home in Brett's cruiser as the sun was coming up, drew his gun, and kicked in the front door, I was completely onboard.

Taking Terra down was easy enough. Her screams were cut short with a punch to the gut and, Drake managed to subdue her with some cord from the garage.

When it came to doing the same thing to his little sisters though, I was a bit more reluctant. I mean, they're not *little.* Bethany's twenty-two and Caroline's twenty. But I've known them since they were small. Seeing Drake take one down, then the other, without so much as breaking a sweat, didn't sit right with me.

That was, until they started spewing out nonsense about going to some fucking wedding the town's putting on for Daisy and how they looked forward to seeing her white dress turn red. Suddenly Bethany and Caroline were just as appalling as Terra.

"Ok, I'm in," Owen says from the kitchen table as he uses Drake's younger sister, Caroline's, laptop.

I don't take my eyes away from the three women tied up and pressed against the far wall. They all sob through their gags and struggle to get free, but Drake made sure the Millers weren't going anywhere.

I pull the frozen peas from my face, grateful the swelling has started to go down. "Have you figured out where they're at?"

"The program is searching for them now. It'll take a few minutes." Owen leans back in his seat, wincing. One arm comes around his chest as he takes a shuddering breath. "I'll find them soon enough. In the meantime, I found an email in all three of their inboxes. They're going to sacrifice Daisy during some sort of wedding-like send off in two days."

My eyes flutter shut as my heart squeezes tight. What can happen to Daisy and Kingston in two days?

"Hey." I open my eyes to find Owen looking at me, his bruised face pinched with concern. "We're going to find them. There isn't going to be a wedding."

"There might be, but she's not marrying a fucking fake-ass god," Drake declares as he strolls back into the room, looking refreshed after his shower. His clean clothes are tight on him, they're probably his dad's given the outdated apparel.

He has bruises climbing up his arms, along with cuts and scrapes, and there's a slight limp in his right leg, but overall, he came out of that accident relatively untouched. I'm almost positive that most of his wounds are from when the cops grabbed us at my house. He's one lucky son of bitch.

"Are you saying you're going to pop the question?" I snort at the thought of this broody bastard getting on one knee.

Drake shrugs. "It's not out of the question after all of this."

"Not if I beat you to it," Owen mutters from his seat.

Drake eyes him up. "We'll see about that. Want to take a bet?"

"What are you thinking?"

"Hm." Drake crosses his arm over his chest and considers the question. "How about, whoever asks her first, the other has to be the best man?"

Owen gives him a half-smile. "Deal."

"That's *if* we get to her before the cult kills her," I point out. "Now, if we're done with this bullshit, can we get back to the situation at hand?"

Drake drops his arms from his chest and digs into his pants pocket. He pulls out a small orange pill bottle. "Found these in Terra's medicine cabinet. Some oxy to help the aches and pains."

He holds them out for me, but I shake my head. "I'm just roughed up. Once the swelling goes down, I think I'll be good."

"Give those to me." Owen lifts a hand and Drake tosses them to him. "Thanks."

"Broken ribs?" Drake asks him.

Owen winces as he pops a pill back. "Yeah, I think so."

"I'll wrap them once you're done. It'll be easier for you to breathe and get some sleep once I do." Drake opens the refrigerator and glances inside.

I look down at his family, sitting there in tears. "What do we do with them?"

"For now, nothing. They'll sit there until we're done in Briar Glen." Drake doesn't look at them as he speaks into the refrigerator. "If they move, or pull something stupid, I'll shoot them in the goddamn head without hesitation."

His sisters squeal with terror while Terra goes limp in a fake faint.

My stomach twists as my head throbs. "Owen, how much longer until we get a location?"

"It'll be a little bit longer. The internet connection is slow here."

I nod. "Ok, just call me when you get something. I'm going to take a shower."

With a heavy sigh, I leave the kitchen and head up the stairs. I find the guest bedroom shower and turn on the water. Stripping out of my dirty clothes, I don't hesitate to step under the hot shower. A loud hiss escapes before I can capture it. Hot water burns all my open wounds. After a moment, I relax.

Well, as best as I can.

My heart doesn't seem to want to unclench. Not with the thought of Daisy and Kingston in trouble.

How did my world fall apart so quickly? We were supposed to be safe by splitting up. Now that we're apart, we're in more danger than before. I reach out and brace my hands against the shower wall. The breath that catches in my throat sounds suspiciously like sob.

Fuck... We were so close. All we had left was Ronney and Francis to kill, then we could've been in the wind. So what if we didn't have a plan for our future? As long as the five of us were back together, that was all I wanted. We could've bought an RV and just traveled around the continent. As Daisy napped yesterday, Owen had suggested buying a house with the money we stole. Drake and Kingston had scoffed, but me?

I took it to heart.

It was a suggestion, yet it might as well have been a seed of hope planted in my chest. A life with the people I loved all under one roof? Who wouldn't want that? It would've been beautiful. I've already seen glimpses of that life under my own roof. The laughing, bickering, the cuddles...

The love.

Fuck. I lost it all.

I allow tears to run freely down my face. Mixing with the hot water, they fall and drain away. After a long moment, I push away from the wall and start to get clean. As I rub the bar of soap over me, I think back to when I washed Daisy that first night she stayed in my house. The lost, empty look in her eyes when I stepped into the bathroom just about broke me.

And when she begged me to touch her? All the cracks caused by her dejection sealed shut. A way to take away her pain, her fear, and to show her I loved her? God, I couldn't have stopped once I started even if I wanted to.

I should've done more. Rather than dragging my feet, I should've just agreed to us all leaving my house yesterday morning. And when the cops came swarming into my yard, I should've tried to fight harder. It may have been four against one, but that didn't matter. Maybe I could've put more energy behind each punch.

Ultimately, Daisy and Kingston were taken by the enemy because I failed them. I fucked up my second chance with Daisy and there's a good chance I won't get a third.

There's a thump on the bathroom door, startling me from my spiraling thoughts.

"We found them!" Drake calls. "Hurry up."

49

Kingston

The faint sound of heavy footsteps coming down the stairs some distance away brings my struggling to a stop. My skin, rubbed raw from rope burn, throbs as I strain to listen.

Nurses have come and gone, doing the best they could to stitch me up while I fought them off, biting whoever I could. Then I'd been left alone for hours. *Hours*. Morning has most definitely come and gone, afternoon too. It must be getting close to the evening at this point. I've heard nothing about Daisy, and my dad never returned. The faint steps of people on the first floor come and go. Sometimes the sound of laughter drifts through the boards down here, but most of the time, it's silent.

I've been left alone with my thoughts, and they race. I've done this before. My mind is my own worst enemy. The tricks it can play, the memories it'll dredge up and put on repeat— I learned during a year in isolation that I can torture myself better than anyone else.

Or so I thought.

A moment later, the curtains are pulled to the side and two men emerge. Neither are familiar, but judging by the look of their leathery skin and wrinkles, it's safe to say we didn't run in the same crowds back when I was growing up.

They don't spare me a glance as they approach and I don't give them any more than a quick once over before my eyes fall to Daisy, laying limp, naked, and covered in long red welts in the larger man's arms.

My heart stutters, pauses, then breaks out into a frantic sprint. *What the fucking happened to her? Who did this to her?* My breath catches in my throat. Whatever happens to me is nothing compared to seeing Daisy like this. *This* is real torture. I failed to keep her from getting captured, and now I can't seem to keep her safe from harm.

"Put the chair over here. Not too close," the one carrying Daisy orders.

I didn't even notice the chair, or the rope around the second guy's shoulder, until now. He does as he is told, and together they sit Daisy down, taking a strange amount of care not to jostle her too much, and tie her up in a similar fashion to how I am. Her head lolls forward and remains there as they take a step back to double check their work.

The larger guy, the one who carried my girl down, looks over at me. "You're blessed, you know? Getting to be in the presence of the Chosen One is an honor. Your father must've forgiven you for what you did to your mother to grant you this opportunity." He looks back down at Daisy, smiling at her fondly. "She's been cleansed of her sins. Now she's right as rain, and Zarzuz will accept her with open arms."

"Fuck you and your stupid, pathetic fake-ass god!" I scream at them.

They don't hear me because no words actually pass my lips. They ignore me, unfazed by my silent outburst. They nod in my direction and leave us, disappearing behind the curtain before heading back upstairs. The minute they're out of sight, Daisy gets my full attention.

Her hair, wet and clean, has been braided and twisted up to sit on top of her head. The rest of her body has a slightly pink hue. I can't tell if it's from the marks that were inflicted all over her body, or if it's from something else. The welts crisscrossing over Daisy's skin are angry and raised. In several places, skin has split open where she's been hit in the same spot more than once. In these particular places, someone took the time to stitch the skin back together.

My eyes fall to her legs. With her ankles tied to each chair leg like mine, she's exposed to whoever comes into the room. The thought blankets my mind with murderous fury, but what really tips me over the edge are the teeth marks upon her inner thighs.

My body jerks forward as best it can as my stomach heaves. Breathing through the initial reaction is a chore. Rage, as hot and sticky as boiling tar, wraps around my heart then spreads to my other major organs. It constricts around my lungs, weighing them down and bringing spots to my eyes.

I'll kill everyone in this fucking house before I die, I vow as I stare at the horrific evidence of Daisy's abuse.

Needing to be near her, I try to scoot closer. I jerk around, throwing my body this way and that. The screeches of the legs against the cement are loud but no one comes to investigate even after about five minutes. In that amount of time, I get about an inch. There's still over four feet of distance between us. Daisy doesn't move or speak even with all the commotion.

Instead, I try a different tactic.

Taking a slow, steadying breath, I purse my lips and whistle. It's just a soft call, nothing to alert anyone upstairs or nearby, if there is anyone, but loud enough she would be able to hear me.

Nothing.

I try again but I get the same results. Determined to reach

out to her, I whistle our call sign. It takes three verses of a "A Spoonful of Sugar," but *finally* Daisy's body twitches. Her soft, pained moan is like a knife to my chest. I keep whistling until Daisy's head lifts. It's not much, but a minuscule amount of tension loosens in my chest as she turns her head in my direction.

Her glossy, unfocused gaze comes to land on my face.

"King?" Her voice is strained and hoarse, no doubt from screaming.

I want to tell her how sorry I am, or what I'll do to the people in this house if we ever get free. Most importantly, I need to tell her how much I love her and that if this all goes south, my soul won't rest until it finds hers somewhere on the other side. That even death won't tear her away from me this time.

Unable to say any of those things, I simply hold her gaze, hoping she can read all the desperation and rage in just a look.

She stares back all of five seconds before her eyelids flutter shut and her head lolls back to her chest.

Fuck!

50

Drake

"There is no way in hell we'll be getting past all that security," Wyatt says, staring at the pictures I'd taken with Caroline's phone after stealing Terra's car and driving past Francis's street to case the Winslow residence.

There had been over twenty cops lingering up and down his street and also surrounding his house. It didn't help that the rest of the force was out patrolling the streets of Briar Glen looking for us.

"You're right." I hate to agree but armed with only three knives and a police-issued gun, we're sorely outnumbered. "Keep scrolling, you'll see pictures of some of the townspeople already decorating."

Owen and Wyatt stare at the screen, their expressions twisting in confusion and horror.

"They're going to host this thing right in the middle of town?" Wyatt shakes his head. "How are they going to explain a human sacrifice to non-members who will be in attendance? Are they stupid?"

I shrug. "Don't know, don't care. We're not going to let the damn wedding take place anyway, so it's a moot issue at this point."

Against the wall, Terra glares at me while my two sisters sleep. I can feel the look burning into my skin each time I enter and leave the room. It's been easier to ignore her than I expected. Duct tape over the mouth really makes her more enjoyable to be around. I give her a second of my attention, smiling coolly down at her.

"If we could just cause a distraction, we might have a chance to get into the Winslow house," Owen mutters slowly, pulling my attention back to him. He looks a little better. The pain medication and wrapping his ribs seems to be helping a bit.

"I'm sure at this point Ronney is expecting something wild," Wyatt shakes his head. "There's not a big enough distraction that we could do to pull away all that detail around Francis's house."

Again, I agree. Francis has his prize possession with him and he's not going to risk anything to change that. Which leaves us empty-handed on rescue ideas. We're running out of time and we're nowhere closer to saving Kingston and Daisy. My hands curl into fists as my frustration rises.

"You would think, with all this planning Daisy put into killing these motherfuckers, she'd have some sort of backup plan," I snarl before letting out my pent-up energy. The wall is the victim of my fist. The drywall crumbles under the intensity. I yank my fist from the hole and breathe heavily.

"OH MY GOD!" Owen shuts suddenly. "She *does*! Daisy told me about it! Well, kind of."

I whirl around to face him and find Wyatt staring at him incredulously too.

"What are you talking about?" Wyatt asks.

"When she was showing me and Kingston her hideouts, she

also showed me the location of her Plan B!" He moves stiffly toward the table. He pushes aside the last of the frozen pizza we devoured for dinner and opens his laptop. "She didn't tell me exactly what her Plan B is, but she gave me a location and said that if anything went south, or if something happened to her, that we should get here."

I swallow back a string of profanities to growl out, "Why are you just *now* telling us this?"

"Because with everything that's happened, I completely forgot. Here," Owen spins the laptop toward Wyatt and I. "This is where Daisy said to go. She must've forgotten to tell you guys about it after going over where we're to meet up if we got separated."

I stomp over to the screen and stare down at it. "That's about twenty minutes outside of town."

Wyatt plods toward the threshold of the kitchen, grabbing the keys off the counter as he moves. "Then what are we waiting for? Let's go see what Daisy's Plan B is."

IT'S pitch black by the time we get to our location. Or at least the general location of it.

"Ok, GPS says it should be right here," Wyatt mutters and then points to the side of the road coming up. I pull to the side and cut off the car.

"Now what?" I push open the car door and look around. There's nothing here but woods.

"She said five feet off the road there will be a red string at eye level, wrapped around the trunk of a cedar. There is something buried just a foot down."

My exasperated sigh is mimicked by Wyatt who then asks, "First, how are we supposed to see anything with how dark it is out here, and second, *our* eye level or hers? That's a huge difference!"

"Just keep your eyes peeled." I brush past him and head into the woods. Eyeballing around five feet, I come to a stop a few minutes later and look around.

Owen stops a few feet away. "I don't know what a cedar looks like compared to any other tree."

"Just look for a fucking red string and shut up. My patience is at its end with you," I snap.

"I said I was sorry, you guys." Owen huffs. "You can't still be mad at me."

Rather than telling Owen that I certainly can be, I approach a tree, searching for a string. The three of us split up, feeling up and leering at every damn tree in the vicinity. Where is this stupid—

"Found it!" Wyatt calls.

I run over to him and find Wyatt reaching down to caress the string.

"Turns out, she means *her* eye level," he mutters before falling to his knees. I follow his lead. Together, the two of us start digging with our bare hands.

Behind us, Owen shifts his weight from foot to foot. It takes a few minutes of tearing through the earth but *finally* my fingers hit something.

"Here." I show Wyatt and he helps me move the earth enough to uncover a shoebox. I yank it out of the ground and fling the top away as I stand.

I'm barely erect when my body locks up in surprise. There are only two items inside of the box. One is a remote control for an older television set. The second is a map. Separately, the objects aren't all that menacing. But it's the words written on the small map of Briar Glen that have my blood freezing.

Wyatt steps closer and grabs the map. I know the minute he sees the words written in Daisy's handwriting because he gasps.

"Well, what is it?" Owen asks, trying to shoulder his way between us.

Wyatt hands him the map while I look back down at the remote in the box. A grin spreads across my cheeks.

"It's our way of saving Kingston and Daisy. Tomorrow, we will all be back together."

"Or be dead," Wyatt points out grimly.

Chuckling darkly, I nod, "Or we die."

51

Daisy

Usually, returning to reality after escaping into the recesses of my own mind takes a while. This time, it's different. My body is pulled forward at the smell of something savory wafting in my face. But while my mouth waters and stomach growls, my hunger is superseded by the stinging of the lashes from Francis's *cleansing*. Thankfully, I faded in and out of consciousness during his process, so I don't remember very much. Unfortunately, the aftermath is hard to ignore. The pain is bone deep. My body tenses up like I've been electrocuted. I gasp as my eyes flutter open.

Immediately, I notice I'm no longer balancing on my toes. My hands, legs, and chest are bound and I'm still naked, but this is much better. That small relief is snuffed out when the person sitting directly in front of me comes into focus. The skin around the warm brown eyes staring back at me crinkles as the woman I once adored smiles at me.

"Ah, there you are. I knew all you needed was a little pick me up," Mrs. Joanna greets. The owner of Ma's Diner lifts the bowl in her hand and smiles. "You must be starving. With all the activity about getting you married, I suppose taking care of the bride was forgotten."

Dressed in a habit like the nuns who'd bathed me, she looks nothing like the waitress and owner of a diner. A necklace dangles off her neck as she leans forward. My eyes lock onto the gold symbol and realize it's Zarzuz's rune.

I glance down at the bowl in her hand. This is where the savory smell is wafting from. It looks like a hearty beef stew with thick cuts of carrots and celery. My stomach growls again.

"Here, let me feed you, and then I'll take care of Kingston. Rumor has it, he's going to be your Maid of Honor... Or I guess he'd be called Man of Honor." She tilts her head to consider the title and then shoots someone to the right of me a curious look. "You'll have to let one of us know how to introduce you I suppose. No one wants to be politically incorrect these days."

I follow her gaze and find Kingston tied to a chair a few feet away. He's glaring daggers at Mrs. Joanna but she either doesn't care or doesn't notice, because she smiles at him just as warmly as she used to at all of us back when we were kids. Bitter resentment gathers in my heart. When she looks back at me, I make sure she feels every ounce of loathing through my own glare.

"Here, it should be cool enough to eat." She raises a spoonful of stew up to my lips.

Even as my stomach rumbles again, I hold her gaze and lock my lips together.

"Oh, come on, darling. I know you're anxious about what's to come, but really, you should be excited. You need a full stomach." Mrs. Joanna runs the spoon across my lips, letting the stew coat my lips. "I brought you your favorite dessert. Don't think I've forgotten about it. There's a strawberry banana milkshake upstairs with your name on it, but you don't get it until you eat."

My body shivers under the pain radiating through it, but it's chased by another tremor, and this one? It's full of wrath. This woman was just one of many who watched me grow up, welcomed me with open arms, and doted on me knowing that I would never live to grow up, grow old, and have a life. She *knew* and still pretended to care about me.

I open my mouth, still holding her gaze.

"There you go!" Clearly pleased by my willingness, she dumps the contents of her spoon into my mouth, careful not to let any spill.

It *is* delicious. Warm, but not hot, the stew is one of the best I've ever had. The blend of spices to keep the stew from being bland are perfect together. My stomach gurgles with excitement.

As Mrs. Joanna pulls away, I spit it all back into her face.

"Oh!" She freezes as her eyes widen and her mouth pops open.

Slowly, Mrs. Joanna takes the sleeve of her shirt and wipes her face. When she's done, she takes a steadying breath and rises from the folding chair in front of me.

"I was just trying to be nice."

I don't bother to respond. My glare remains pinned to her face as she glances at Kingston.

"I don't suppose you'll be any more receptive to kindness?"

In my peripheral vision, I can see Kingston shaking his head. The owner of Ma's Diner nods before she turns and leaves. She pushes aside thick curtains and disappears. Before I can turn to Kingston to make sure he's ok, the thundering of heavy footsteps coming down a set of stairs catches my attention. A moment later, the curtain is flung back to the side and a red-faced Sheriff Ronney Maxwell appears. He storms over to me as he stabs a finger at my face.

"Where are they?" he snarls at me.

"You'll have to be more specific about who you're talking about."

My comment earns me a strike across the face with the back of his hand. He hits me so hard my head snaps to the side and I see spots. Gasping for air, I slowly look back up at him.

"Your friends. I know you told them where to go in case things go south," he snaps. "You've been planning everything down to the fucking T so don't give me any shit about not knowing where they could be."

I frown in confusion as my heart leaps up with hope. "My friends? You mean Wyatt, Drake, and Owen? Last I saw them, they were supposed to be in *your* custody. How am I supposed to—"

Ronney pulls his gun from the holster on his belt with a snarl. "Fine, you want to play this fucking game, we'll play."

He stomps over to Kingston and points the barrel of the gun just between his eyes. My heart stops. Inside my head, there's screaming. It's not a single scream. It's the sound of many voices screaming. They belong to all the women who had become Oliver's victims. Their screams of denial, agony, and horror? They're all mine now as Ronney points the gun at one of the men I love.

"*He's* not necessary in any of this." Ronney smiles coldly at me. "So, if you don't want the company of a corpse down here with you, I suggest you better start talking. They escaped shortly after we arrested them thirty-six hours ago. That gives them plenty of time to run and find shelter. Shelter *you* probably set up for either yourself or them. So tell me, where the fuck are they? I won't let them ruin this night."

The relief that comes from knowing they've escaped is overshadowed by the terror from my current situation. Ronney's hand doesn't waver. He presses the barrel against Kingston's forehead and waits.

"I'm going to kill you." The words are a promise as I hold Ronney's stare.

He grins. "Sure you are." He removes the safety. "Now, your friends. Where are they?"

Kingston looks at me, his jaw clenched and brows furrowed. Just once, he shakes his head. He's willing to die to keep the others safe. My fragile heart swells. His loyalty is unwavering, and I love him so much for that.

"I can't give you an address." I lick my dry lips as my gaze drags up to Ronney's face. "But I can give you coordinates."

"Fine." He pulls the gun away from Kingston's head and holsters it. A second later, he has a pad of paper in his hand and a small pencil. Quickly, I give him the coordinates, and when I'm done, he shoves the information into his back pocket. "If this doesn't lead me to them, I'll kill Kingston without hesitation."

I nod, my heart racing. With that, Ronney hurries out of sight. When the sound of his footsteps disappears up the stairs, I look over at Kingston, whose face is twisted with confusion and worry.

"That should buy us maybe twenty minutes. When he realizes those coordinates are to his wife's gravesite, he's going to be extra pissed."

Kingston blinks before his face cracks into a wide grin. I'm glad he can smile at a time like this. With only twenty minutes on our side, and no clear way of escaping our binds, he could very well be a dead man.

TWENTY MINUTES COMES.

Then goes.

Ronney doesn't return. Whatever happened to keep him from making good on his threat is a small miracle on our end. During this time, I do my best to wiggle free. The lashes covering my body scream in protest as I wiggle my arms up the backrest of the chair I'm tied too. It takes time, a ton of rope burn, and a few pulled stitches, but *finally* I manage to get my arms over the back and between me and the seat.

I give myself a moment of rest to figure out what to do next. There's always the option of toppling over the chair and hoping it'll break. Given how sturdy this chair is, I have a feeling that plan won't go the way I want it to.

As I try to think of another plan, a stampede of activity by the stairs that are somewhere out of sight, has me pausing.

A few seconds later, Kingston and I figure out what the commotion is about. Francis appears, along with five women and four men. The sight of all five women dressed in their habits is more unsettling than the sight of Kingston's father for me. Between them, they all hold white fabric bunched in their arms, making it a point to keep it off the floor. They line up beside me while two of the four men come up behind me. The other two stand by the curtain as Francis approaches me.

He grabs the folding chair Mrs. Joanna sat in, pulls it back a few feet, and sits down. He makes a show of straightening his shirt and brushing imaginary creases from his pressed pants. When he's done, Francis leans back in his seat and crosses a leg over his other knee.

"It is time for your fitting, Daisy," he informs me. "You will look beautiful for your wedding tonight."

I could waste my words, spewing profanities or threats in his direction. It would make me feel a little better I suppose, though it won't do any good. I'd done that with Oliver for the first year, and nothing I said ever stopped him from completing whatever heinous activity he came into the room to conduct. It wouldn't be a leap to believe it wouldn't faze Francis either. So, rather than say anything, I say nothing at all.

"The Daughters of Zarzuz have brought you your dress. They will take your measurements to make some adjustments, and you'll be a good girl for them, won't you?" He lifts a dark brow. "I think I've beaten the wickedness from you but if I did not do a good job, I'll be more than happy to repeat the process."

At this, I can't help but smile. Did he really think a few lashes would do anything to assure my cooperation? Oliver did so, *so* much worse.

My smile is a taunt that doesn't get under Francis's skin. He simply nods as if I've confirmed my obedience and continues,

"Ronney has informed me of his failure to capture your friends. I tell you this not to give you hope that you'll be rescued like last time, but to share that the entire police force is out looking for them. They'll be on every street corner, in every shadow, and they surround this house. If seen, Ronney has given them permission to shoot on sight."

He might as well have kicked me in the gut.

"So let's hope that they have realized the error of their ways and have taken to the wind." He claps his hands together and sighs. "Now, after this, we'll refresh the mark of Zarzuz upon your flesh, letting him know that you are his. Rather than cut into your flesh," the corner of Francis's upper lip curls in disgust, "We'll be burning his crest right in the middle of your chest for all to see."

I hold my smile even as everything in me stills. He mentioned this before, briefly, when I was in his room, but at the time, I gave it no thought. Now, however, fear claws up my throat, strangling me.

Beside me, Kingston thrashes in his seat. His father looks in his direction.

"Maybe I'll purify you with the mark of Zarzuz too." Francis claps his hands and the men behind me grab my arms and start to untie me as the nuns rushes forward, fabric in hand.

52

Owen

"—Almost to the top," I grunt, with the phone pressed between my shoulder and ear.

"Well hurry up, I want to get those two out of there," Wyatt hisses down the line.

Don't we all? Rather than point that out, I continue to climb the ladder to the old water tower until I get to the top. It's getting dark, and festivities are just starting to get underway. According to the digital invitation the Miller family received, the wedding is supposed to happen at midnight. We need to hurry. With the others in position, hidden out of sight not far from Francis's house, we're nearly ready to enact Daisy's fail-safe plan.

My heart is racing and sweat drips down my forehead. Part of me is still in disbelief that Daisy managed to pull this off. She really did think of everything. How she thought she'd pull *this* particular plan off by herself if things got too bad to continue on her original path of destruction is beyond me. It would've been a death sentence for her.

It still could be, given how she set everything up.

But maybe that's the point? Trepidation creeps through me. Everything Daisy has done has been to the extreme. How far had she planned to go to get her revenge? Would she die to make sure it was complete?

The thought makes me queasy, so I push it away.

When I get to the top of the tower and climb onto the catwalk, I sigh in relief. I spare the town of Briar Glen a quick glance. I can almost hear the music from here. A few balloons escape and drift high into starry sky. If I was closer, I'm sure I'd be able to smell the pulled pork and funnel cakes.

The festivities going on made it easy to move around. There are cops out in full force, but with so many people, it was easy driving around and slipping through crowds. Tonight, Daisy's going to be sacrificed, and while a majority of the town knows what's going to happen, there's a good amount that think this is just some spur of the moment celebration. A fun night in the middle of a dark time in Briar Glen.

"Ok, I'm up here." I shrug off my backpack and carefully place it at my feet.

In my ear, I hear Wyatt let Drake know I'm in position. I'm envious of their role in our plan. Given the state of my ribs, I'll be no help in rescuing Kingston or Daisy. At least I can do this, and once I'm done, I'll be able to meet up with everyone.

God I hope this works.

Daisy's taken her bomb making and amped up the danger. Taking her homemade devices and taping them to the inside of a lid of a drum full of gasoline, she's really gone the extra effort in making sure Briar Glen is wiped off the map. They're scattered around town—hidden almost in plain sight or buried on various pieces of property. She's made sure there isn't a place that won't be touched. How did no one notice her presence all these years?

"Alright, we're ready," Wyatt responds after a moment. "Any questions before we do this?"

Crouching down gingerly, hissing at the ache in my ribs, I unzip my backpack and pull out the shoebox. Opening it, I grab the television remote with care and pick up the map. As I stand, my eyes return to the town below.

People are going to get hurt. Some might die. There will be innocent people in the mix...

"Are we sure we want to do this?" My question is spoken softly, more to myself than to Wyatt or Drake. "I know what we've done so far with Daisy has been... questionable. But this? This is a whole new level of crazy."

There's a pause. I swear I can hear Drake's exasperated sigh on the other end though I can't be sure.

"It has to be done, Owen," Wyatt answers solemnly. "Most of these people *deserve* this. Besides, Daisy's not evil. She's given time between the first few explosions to give people the opportunity to run."

I nod. He can't see it, but the gesture was more for myself than for him anyway. I'll do anything to help Daisy, even if that means becoming a domestic terrorist.

Bracing one hand on the railing, I let my thumb on my other hand hover over the power button.

"Alright." I swallow. "On your count, Wyatt."

I can hear him take a deep breath to steady himself. As he takes the moment, I look down at the map. There are fifteen Xs marked strategically all over Briar Glen, a small number written on top of each. The first three in the sequence are set ten minutes apart from one another, from there, the time between them gets shorter and shorter. The last X is directly over top of the Winslow house, not far from where Wyatt and Drake are. We'd talked about this, planned for it as best we could, but putting it in action?

This is terrifying.

With a push of a button, Daisy and Kingston could end up cooked. With no other options or time, it's a risk we have to take. A *big* risk. And if something goes awry on Drake and Wyatt's end—they could die as well. I'm the only relatively safe one, and that doesn't give me any sense of relief.

"Three," Wyatt says suddenly, cutting through the silence on the other end. "Two."

"One," I say with him.

I push the button.

53

Daisy

"Don't strike her face! She already has a bruise we have to cover!" Francis snarls as I flail about.

My feet come off the ground as I kick the man with the branding iron away from me. The two men holding me by my arms are struggling not to break them as I fight their hold.

"Daisy Murray!" Francis bellows angrily. "Sit the fuck down!"

I do no such thing. If anything, I fight harder. My right hand slips free of the person holding me. I curl my hand and punch the other in the nose. He swears, letting go of my other arm to hold his face. I duck as someone lunges for me, and I twist as the other recovers and tries to grab my hair that's fallen out of the bun.

There's nowhere to go. With four men plus Francis blocking the way out of this sectioned off space, I'm as good as stuck. But I'm not going to just sit around waiting to be branded then sacrificed.

I have to find Kingston and get out of here.

They took him an hour ago, during my fitting. He'd gone kicking and biting, but the guys who grabbed him were even burlier than the four standing in front of me now. When Francis wouldn't tell me where they were taking King, I'd lost it.

Well, maybe I'd lost it well before then, but whatever sanity I did have has gone right out the door. I bit, I kicked, and I'd stabbed a Daughter with a needle that I managed to nab when my hand was free while they were measuring the sleeves. It took a great deal of effort on their end to get the numbers they needed, but finally the Daughters hurried away.

And when they left, these guys showed up.

The man with the blowtorch in one hand and the branding iron in the other watches me intently. I hold his gaze.

"What do you think is going to happen here, Daisy?" Francis asks, gathering up his composure and attempting to sound reasonable. "Sit down and it will be over quickly."

"You do it!" I insist, not sparing him a glance.

Francis laughs. "I already have. We all have. Marty, show her."

One of the guys, Marty, lifts his shirt and shows me a quarter size rune burned into his skin above his heart.

"Great sign of devotion." I roll my eyes as he lowers his shirt. "But I already have his rune carved into me, as you can see."

Wearing nothing but my own skin, there's no way they *can't* notice it.

"My patience is growing thin, Daisy." Francis takes a step forward.

"Where did you take Kingston?"

Francis rolls his eyes. "For his own fitting. He'll be right there by your side this evening, watching on."

A small, cruel smile curls his lips upward.

And they call *me* crazy...

"High Priest!" someone shouts from somewhere on the other side of the curtain. "We have a problem!"

Francis sighs, his smile slipping. He turns to Marty. "Go see what's happening." Marty nods and moves behind the curtain. Kingston's dad waves his hand toward me. "Get her. I don't care if you have to break her leg to subdue her. She'll walk down the aisle with a limp."

The two men lunge for me. It's not a fair fight, and with renewed energy they pin me to the ground in only a few minutes. I breathe heavily as I continue to fight a losing battle. The man with the blow torch turns it on and reheats the branding iron.

Angry tears gather in my eyes, but they don't slow me down as I thrash around. When the iron is red hot and glowing, the brander steps forward and smiles down at me. It's almost a friendly one.

"No, no, no!" I scream as he hovers it over me.

As it starts to come down, the house shakes. Dust falls from the ceiling and something on the other side of the curtain shatters. Everyone freezes.

"What the hell was—" Francis's words are cut off as the house shakes again, this time a little harder.

"High Priest! We have to get you and the Chosen One out of here!" someone shouts from somewhere out of sight, and the thundering of footsteps down the stairs tells me I'm about to have more company.

As at least half a dozen men appear, the house shakes again. Even harder than the first two times.

"The entire town is under attack! Bombs are going off left and right, and everything's on fire. It's chaos!" one of them shouts.

"Ronney's been forced to do crowd control and took half the guys outside with him, but coming up the street—"

"—EVERY HOUSE ON THIS BLOCK IS GOING UP IN

FLAMES!" someone else finishes as the house continues to shake.

Francis whirls around to face me, snarling as he marches toward me. "What have you done?!"

I stare at his approaching figure with my mouth hanging wide open in awe.

They did it. My guys found Plan B. The relief that swells in my chest, pushing aside all fear and anger, doesn't come from the thought that I might be saved. The fact that I can feel the tremors of the explosions nearby tell me it's too late for that.

No, this relief is simple, and it stems from the knowledge that all my suffering is about to be over. There's a general sense of loss mixed with it, but I always knew there was no future after Briar Glen. It hurts knowing that Kingston will be here when the end comes, but maybe his suffering will come to a grinding halt with me. He won't be alone in his death.

Maybe in the next life, we'll all be together.

Before Francis gets to me, I'm laughing. Hard. My stomach twists and tears spring to my eyes. In my chest, my heart hammers away at a pace that will cause it to give out if I don't get it under control. But I'm not in control of anything right now.

So all I can do is laugh.

The house groans as the sound of another explosion makes its way through the foundation down to where we are. The bombs going off are getting closer, and the duration between each one is getting shorter and shorter. The domino effect is in full effect.

It must be a beautiful sight from the outside.

"Grab her and let's go!" he roars.

I'm yanked up off the ground and my feet, still laughing. Tears spill down my cheeks now, and the only sounds I can make are desperate gasps for air. I'm laughing so hard, my stomach hurts. The roar of explosions draws near as the curtain is pushed out of our way. I'm not surprised to see the rest of the basement has painted walls with Zarzuz's runes, or the statue, similar to Vincent's, on the far end by the door.

"Out the back, there!" Francis shouts as he runs ahead of us.

Oh shit. He wants to leave from there? My stomach cramps as I laugh harder. Francis is going to regret this so much....

We're halfway to the door when the entire basement is engulfed in flames. The world goes up in heat, smoke, and debris. As I'm caught up in a wave of destruction, I close my eyes, smile, and wait for death's sweet embrace.

Finally.

Through my old bedroom window, I could see the mushroom plumes of fire and smoke as each explosion got closer. Every other property is spared as the destruction raced for us. The orange and yellow, red and blue flames were magnificent.

Truly a work of art.

The Sons of Zarzuz noticed them too and when panic ensued, they forgot all about me. I was able to make it to the first floor without any issues just as the house splintered apart.

Being lifted off my feet to be flung backward along with pieces of the house took seconds. Hardly any time for me to process what's happening at all. But as my body hits the ground along with the rest of the debris, a bewildering pain nullifies all thoughts and feelings. There's a ringing in my ears now. Smoke clogs my lungs and burns my eyes. My whole body feels like it's vibrating, and the pain in my right leg? Extraordinary. So much so that it steals what little breath I do manage to suck in.

There's screaming somewhere nearby. A woman in pain,

pleading for help. There are soft groans that pepper the area around me too, but they fade pretty quickly.

I lift my head slowly, trying to get my bearings. With so much smoke in the air, I can't see much. I try to move but get nowhere. Bracing myself on my forearms, I push myself halfway up to find my lower half covered in debris, some of which is on fire.

Swearing, I take in a shaky breath and try to roll over, but there's too much weight on top of me for any sort of movement.

I try again, but rather than roll, this time I try to drag myself out. I get a few inches before being forced to stop or risk losing my leg altogether. Panting hard, I look around for something to help me, but all I can see is just fire and rubble.

Wait, where is the door to the basement? Where's Daisy?

A cold sense of dread and panic crushes me like a beartrap. I scream Daisy's name. It only results in a coughing attack. Desperation renews my need to get out from under this burning wreckage. I yank and pull at my leg, ignoring the pain in order to free myself.

"DAISY!" My mouth moves but my scream is nothing more than wispy air as I call her name over and over. My heart works as frantically as the rest of me, trying to claw its way out of my chest and drag itself to her.

Through the roaring of flames, screams of agony, and the continuous explosions happening outside, comes a sound. It doesn't process at first. Too busy trying to escape, I don't notice it. It's not until I have to stop to catch my breath that I hear it. With my cheek to the hot hardwood floor, my favorite song in the whole damn world drifts through the air.

Just a spoonful of sugar makes the medicine go down... Medicine go down. Medicine go down.

My head jerks up as I look around. Two dark figures appear, moving through the dust like shadows. One whistles while they creep along. I'm so relieved I could cry. Putting my lips together, I attempt to whistle as I wave an arm in the air.

Nothing comes out. My mouth is too dry, and the smoke and dust are too thick. They don't notice me. Clearing my throat and licking my lips, I try again. This time a little sound comes out. It's not much, but it's something. But not enough to gain their attention. They slip into the other room as they kick debris out of their way as they search through the chaos. I clear my throat, determined to get their attention.

This time when I whistle, the sound is loud and clear.

Just before I fall into a coughing fit.

The sound of stomping feet grows close, and suddenly two masked men in black jackets crouch down beside me.

"Jesus, King, we'll get you out of here." That's Wyatt's voice.

Together, he and what looks to be Drake start removing the rubble off my lower half. The minute enough weight is off, I drag myself free and to my feet. I stagger, but Drake catches my elbow to steady me.

"Shit, your leg." Wyatt crouches down and lifts his mask.

I don't even bother to take a look. The pain there tells me it's probably bad, but it's inconsequential. I'll deal with it later. After a quick check, I find that I can at least put some weight on it.

Turning to Drake, I tell him, "We need to get to Daisy."

"Where is she?" he asks, his voice no more than a growl behind that demonic mask.

"She was in the basement—"

"*Fuck*!" Drake swears as Wyatt comes to his feet.

"What? Where is she?" he demands.

"King says she was in the basement."

Wyatt groans.

My heart sinks at the sound. "What? Tell me."

Wyatt shoots me a pained glance before pulling his mask

down. "The bomb went off right by the basement's exit. It destroyed the foundation of the house. It's mostly caved in."

Everything tilts sideways as my breath leaves my lungs in a whoosh.

"We're going to find her," Drake snaps, grabbing me by the arm and dragging me toward where the front door should be. "Dead or alive, I'm not leaving without her body in my arms."

Wyatt follows behind us. "We'll look for a way down there, King."

I nod while silently collecting the pieces of my heart as they try to tumble from my chest.

This time there won't be any question as to what happened to Daisy Murray. She either died getting her revenge, or she lived to tell the tale.

55

Daisy

I'm pretty sure that whoever the Almighty Creator is, hates me.

Why else would I still be alive? Burns ravage my skin, and smoke threatens to suffocate me, but at the moment, I'm still here.

Damn it.

With a groan, I drag myself out from under two pieces of heavy concrete that tent over me, just enough to keep either one from crushing me. All around, pipes hang haphazardly from what's left of the ceiling and walls. Electrical wires flail around, and small fires are starting to catch on things it didn't touch the first go around.

What's left of the house will be ash soon enough.

In my daydreams, the ones where I pictured *this* outcome, I thought I'd be laughing from hell. Francis's home would be burned to the ground, the town that I grew up in would be in shambles, and the idea of Zarzuz would be over. I would have won.

Too bad that's not how this has panned out.

I'm very much aware of how alive I am, and I'm certainly not laughing, and Kingston? What happened to him? The thought of him burned, buried, or somewhere in between is too painful to consider. Pushing the thought away, I look toward where I think the stairs would be.

If there were stairs in that direction, they're gone now. In their place is rubble.

I need to get out of here and find him. Maybe it's not the Almighty but Lilith giving me strength to get to him. I *did* host a sacrifice in her name. Is this her lending me some strength to help my friend? Maybe if I can get Kingston to the others, or at least out of this rubble, I'll be ok to finally sleep.

And never wake up.

Moving hurts. There isn't a spot on my body that doesn't cry out as I crawl over pieces of drywall and scuffle around some live wires. Pulling myself up and over rubble is the hardest. I lack any real strength. It's mostly determination fueling my every move. My lungs burn as they breathe in and push out smoke. Dust sticks to my tongue and burns my eyes.

Still, I push through it all.

Someone wheezes. As a small breeze pushes the smoke out of my face, one of the Sons of Zarzuz comes into view. A piece of metal rebar protrudes out of his pelvis. His eyes stare upward, unseeing. From where I stand, I can see his chest struggling to rise and fall. I creep over to him, purposeful of where to put my weight.

His groans of agony make my lips twitch upward. When I get to his side, I look down at him. He doesn't look at me, but he must sense someone nearby because he raises a shaky hand.

"Please... help—"

"Just fucking die already."

Instead of helping him, I reach down and work the shirt off his body. The button up is torn and a little singed in some places, but at least it's something. He cries out softly as I jostle him around without care. Ignoring his whimpers, I shrug on the shirt and button it up. I leave the man, heading toward the direction the slight breeze is coming from.

Crawling under and over things takes energy I don't have. My body trembles with fatigue and the aches and pains that riddle it— I can feel each and every one. I stop to catch my breath. All I want to do is lay down. Sleep. I could close my eyes for just a few seconds, right?

No. I have to keep going.

I start moving again, slower than even before. A stronger breeze hits me a few minutes later. It clears the smoke once more, and there! A few feet away is a small hole leading outside. My heart doesn't have the capability to get excited. Until I know all my men are safe, I won't feel well, but this is my chance to find them. I move faster, ignoring the way my feet get cut up and my palms become bloody as I drag them over rough surfaces.

Just as I get to the hole, the foundation trembles.

I pause, wary of the impending danger all around me. It's the right call. Just where I had been looking to stand, debris crumbles down, effectively sealing off my chance at escape. I pull the shirt up over my face as I cough through the extra dust now floating around. When the coughing subsides, I stare at the dark place the hole once was. There's no breeze at all now. No way of getting out. At least not this way. I bite the inside of my cheek, fighting the urge to cry. I can't give up yet. There's a little left I can give.

But I need a moment. I'm just so tired...

I lean my hips back against some rubble and hang my head. What am I going to do? I suppose I could crawl back the way I came, look for a way to climb up to the collapsed first floor. The idea of expending all that energy is daunting. My shoulders sag further as my head droops.

"Daisy!"

Every muscle in my body tenses. I instantly regret that as my aching body protests the abrupt movement. My head jerks upward.

"Daisy! Daisy *fucking* Murray! You better be alive!"

A sob chokes out of me as the tears I've been fighting spill down my cheeks. I know this voice, the other one too. Pushing off the rubble, I get to my feet.

"Daisy!"

A whistled tune cuts through the air, my favorite song luring me toward my favorite people who wait for me on the other side of this burning hellscape. A heavy sob causes my chest to cave in.

"Daisy! Please, darling, say something! Anything!"

Their voices are growing farther away. *No, no! Please don't leave me*!

"Here! I'm here!" I sob again but cut it short to call out again. "I'm here! Drake! Wyatt! I'm here!"

There's a short pause. Did they hear me? Or have they moved on—

"DAISY!" they call in unison. I can almost picture the way they must've looked at one another before calling my name.

The image causes me to laugh, which only throws me into a coughing mess. When I catch my breath, I call back, "I'm here. I'm trapped!"

"We're coming, hold on!" Wyatt calls.

I can hear the sound of debris shifting as they work to get to me. Tears leak down my cheeks as I sob again. I don't even know why I'm crying now. It feels like years have passed before a breeze wraps around me, clearing away the dust and smoke surrounding my face. It's followed by light streaming into the tight space I've found myself.

"Daisy? Can you reach us?" Drake calls down.

I shuffle toward the light and the sound of his voice on

tender feet. When I get there, I look up. About a foot out of reach are Wyatt, Drake, and Kingston, looking relieved and staring down at me. My breath catches in my throat.

Kingston's alive.

A new wave of tears spills over, and I sob again.

"Oh shit, Daisy..." Wyatt chokes out as his eyes widen on me. "Fuck, ok, hold on. We got you, pretty flower."

Both he and Drake lay flat on their stomachs on the piece of concrete they're on and each reaches down with one arm. I reach up. Our fingertips brush against each other but I'm too short.

"Hold on," Drake grunts, scooting forward so his upper half bends further down into the hole.

This time when I reach for him, I leap up as best I can. He manages to grab my wrist and lift me enough for Wyatt to grab the other. Together, they hoist me up. I wince as my body protests the jostling. Once I'm out, two pairs of arms wrap around me. A heavy sob rocks my body but it's absorbed into theirs as they hold me. I'm safe. Free...

My eyes find Kingston's, who stands just a little way away. His eyes are misted over, and his jaw is clenched tight. Those dark brows are furrowed together, and under all that soot he looks extra pale.

"My dad?" he asks, his hands trembling slightly.

My shoulders move up then fall back down before I nudge my head toward the hole I'd been pulled out of. Francis should be dead. He was closest to the explosion after all.

But I survived when I shouldn't have.

Could Francis have somehow made it out? The thought that this could possibly not be over, that this nightmare isn't finished *yet* even after all of this... It's a crushing weight on my shoulders. If Francis isn't dead, I'll kill him. There's also Ronney to contend with too. He's somewhere running around

Briar Glen, doing only gods know what. I'll deal with him and everything else, but for right now, I'm with most of my men.

I wiggle an arm free and reach for King. Without hesitation, Kingston steps forward with his hand raised and weaves his fingers in mine.

"I love you," he mouths, his expression tortured.

I nod, knowing that with all my heart.

"Are you ok? Where are you hurt?" Wyatt asks, stepping back while not quite letting go of me.

Drake huffs, finally stepping back too. "What kind of stupid questions are those? Look at her! She probably fucking hurts everywhere. Come on, let's get out of here."

Taking in the sight of their cuts and bruises, they don't look all that much better off. What happened? I open my mouth to ask, but another question takes precedent,

"Where's Owen?"

A gunshot pierces the air. Drake's body jerks away from me as he grunts. Another shot rings out as I turn toward the sound. This time Drake goes down, hard, onto his back. Shock chokes me up as I stumble over and straddle Drake's body protectively. Before my eyes can land on the shooter, both Kingston and Wyatt are moving toward the threat.

"Get back!" Ronney shouts as he fires off two rounds, one at each guy.

I try to scream in horror, but my throat is so raw it's more of a choked screech. Thankfully, both rounds miss. Kingston and Wyatt skid to a stop as the sheriff snarls at all of us, his gun pointed at Kingston.

"You have ruined everything, you stupid bitch!" he roars, his eyes landing on me.

Standing in the middle of the singed and burning front yard of the Winslow property, covered in ash and shaking with fury, Ronney looks murderous. His uniform is soaked with sweat and his chest heaves. He's alone. The bodies littering the yard, his minions, don't move.

In the street, there are a few people screaming and yelling. Cars attempt to weave through the debris in the road and the sirens of emergency vehicles wail uselessly in the distance. There's no controlling this. Briar Glen is done for. Anyone who stays after a mess like this is going to be left with nothing.

"Years, Daisy Murray. We have been doing this for *years*! I have been able to thwart every fucking attempt to shut us down. Every single one, and I'm defeated by a fucking spoiled little brat!" He shakes his head slowly. "Now the town is practically gone. Police from every fucking county are on their way here, and I bet the FBI have caught wind of this shit. It's over. It's all *over* because of you!"

Me? Because of *me*? My jaw drops, staring at him incredulously. But my stupor doesn't last. I laugh, the sound stark and cold. It's just a singular ha but it's enough to get the gun aimed at my face.

"You brought this upon yourself." I take a step toward him, ignoring the weapon in his hand. "And just so you know, if you *don't* kill me, you'll be stuck looking over your shoulder for the rest of your life."

I'll fucking kill him. With a gun pointed at my face, I can't risk looking down at Drake, but I hear his groan so I know he's alive. For now.

Ronney laughs as the sound of tires screech and an engine revs nearby.

"You're cocky given the circumstances," he taunts. "I won't have to worry about you after this. In fact, I'll make sure to be the one to bury you."

Before he can pull the trigger as he clearly wants to do, a car rushes down the Winslow driveway. My eyes move from the deranged sheriff to the vehicle moving way too fast toward us. Ronney hears it too and turns.

He's not halfway around when the car comes up onto the yard and hits him. I gape as Ronney's body flies ten feet away before crumpling to the ground in an unnatural heap. The car that hit him skids to a stop, leaving tire tracks in the yard. Unsure of what to expect, I brace myself over Drake who's starting to sit up.

The driver's door is thrown open and Owen climbs out. He flashes us a grin.

"Turns out shooting people and hitting them with my car are my preferred methods of killing. Not a single gag!"

Wyatt laughs, though the sound is a little strained. Kingston does too, his shoulder shaking as he holds his stomach and doubles over. My ability to find amusement in the moment is lacking. Rather than feel relieved, my heart panics as I turn around. Drake is sitting upright with a hand covering his arm. I crouch down over him until we're practically nose to nose.

"Drake—"

"I'm fine, Daisy." He meets my gaze and holds it. "Just a graze to my arm and one to my thigh. Nothing more than scratches."

"One to the arm, huh? You'll have a matching scar with Daisy," Wyatt teases as he hurries over to us. "I'm a little jealous."

I grimace. "I'd rather get a matching tattoo."

"That could be arranged," Drake promises, a small smile appearing. I have a feeling, if he didn't have a beard, there would be dimples.

"C'mon, we need to get the fuck out of Briar Glen," Owen calls from the car. "I don't want anyone pointing us out and getting the other authorities on our case."

I move so Kingston and Wyatt can help Drake up. Stepping back, I watch as they throw Drake's arms around their shoulders and help him hobble toward the car. Owen says something as they approach, and the four of them laugh. My heart swells.

We did it.

Turning around, I give the Winslow house a last look. The once grand house is half caved in. The other side is up in flames. Soon, it'll all be gone.

I start to turn back toward the others but pause when movement by the line of trees in the backyard catches my attention. My eyes track it. The smoke makes it hard to get a read on what exactly it is, but when the wind picks up just a little, my view is clear, and I see who's slinking away into the burning trees.

Disbelief floors me to the spot. My mind goes blank as I suck in a sharp gasp.

As if a divine power was waiting for the opportunity to possess me, it strikes while I stand there in astonishment. Strength gathers in my muscles and a fire burning hotter than any in Briar Glen ignites in my heart. I find myself moving. First to reach down and grab a piece of steel rebar, and then to run. I don't even realize the actions until I'm nearing the entrance to the woods. Since when did I have the energy to sprint? Just moments ago, I was exhausted.

I don't question it further than that, allowing a demonic glee to fester and tarnish what's left of my soul.

As I plunge into the woods, I can hear the others call my name. Their voices fade as flames and shadows embrace me.

My bloody feet land on sharp rocks and twigs. The few stitches I have all over my body burst free and blood soaks the shirt I stole. None of that matters. Not when *he's* just ahead of me.

Francis must hear my approach. His hobbling picks up a bit of steam. But while he quickens his pace, I slow down until I'm walking.

"I know you're there," he snarls without looking back.

The trees break ahead of us and a small clearing gives me a full view of my last victim. He stops in the middle, dropping his head and shoulders in defeat.

"This wasn't how it was supposed to be." Francis turns around to face me, but I continue to lurk in the trees, and he doesn't spot me. "You've destroy Briar Glen, Zarzuz's following... *me*." His voice wavers as his head whips around as he searches for me.

I step out of the line of trees.

Francis's gaze finds me. His upper lip curls as he snarls, "You are nothing."

"Nothing? I beg to differ. I've been *chosen*— isn't that what you've been touting?" I smile. The piece of metal in my hand feels heavy, my adrenaline slipping away incrementally. This needs to be fast. "Unfortunately for you, I wasn't chosen by *your* god."

Francis studies me for a moment before a twisted smile pulls at his mouth. "You don't have the strength to kill me. Can you even pick that up?"

The thought of picking up my weapon feels impossible. My body is trembling like a leaf in a hurricane, and god, I'm so tired. Even keeping my eyes open feels like it's taking a great deal of effort. But I won't let weakness stop me. I brace myself, ready to finish this once and for all.

"She doesn't need to kill you when she has *us* to destroy her nightmares," a voice says from behind me.

I catch Francis's eyes widen in dismay just before I look over my shoulder. Emerging from the darkness one by one to stand shoulder to shoulder come Wyatt, Drake, Owen, and Kingston. The first two are wearing their masks and hold their knives in their hands. Owen carries a gun. Is that Ronney's?

My heart swells so swiftly at the sight of them that it's painful.

Kingston's cold stare is pinned to his father, but he shoots me a quick wink and a playful smirk. In that moment, I know it's not supposed to be me that kills Francis Winslow. He may have been the leader of the cult, the driving force behind the deaths of many lives, but that all pales to his true crime. He went above and beyond to obliterate the one life he should've protected and cherished more than anything else.

I hand Kingston my makeshift weapon.

He takes it, his smirk melting away from his face. I nod at him, then turn to face Francis. He's backed up, away from us.

"Why even bother with me?" Francis asks.

The guys walk around me, approaching him as one.

"You're wasting your time and energy. Just run already! Go and never come back. I'll leave you alone as long as—"

Owen shoots him in the good leg. Francis crumbles at their feet with a scream of pain. The four of them create a semi-circle around him. Owen, Drake, and Wyatt grab Francis at different spots on his body and hold him still. Kingston steps up, blocking my view of his father. He doesn't give any flourishing goodbye speeches, nor does he hesitate. Kingston simply brings the rebar up and then slams it down.

When he steps back, I can see the piece of metal has come down straight through the hollow of Francis's neck and came out the other side, and it is lodged in the ground, keeping the man's body leaning back in a kneeling position

We're all silent as we stare down at him.

I wait for the hum of satisfaction, the warm embrace of freedom, or for my heart to piece itself back together after a decade of being broken. Time ticks by yet nothing changes. The fire eating at the trees around us still burns. The sirens in the distance still holler. And me? I still feel... wrong. That monster molded by Oliver, fueled by revenge, and hidden in plain sight is still very much a part of me.

My shoulders sag. A soul-aching fatigue blankets me and the cumbersome weight of resignation inches into my heart. I'll never be free of the evil I've become. The Butcher of Briar Glen and The Zarzuzians have marked me up so well that there's no putting this monster back in a box.

With a sigh, Owen lets go of Francis and gives Kingston a hug. He whispers something into King's ear then drops his arms and comes over to me. His embrace is warmer than how I feel inside. I bury my face into Owen's chest and breathe him in.

There's some soft conversation somewhere behind Owen, but I ignore it as I return his hug. Suddenly three more pairs of arms wrap around me. Tears of exhaustion race down my cheeks. The combined weight of all four bodies bears down on me. My legs tremble as I struggle to stand upright, and my body hurts something fierce. It doesn't matter. I absorb the love that is coming off them in waves—letting the sense of being off-balanced and wrong settle.

I might never be whole again, and the darkness of my soul may only get blacker with age, but I have my demons by my side, and it's their love that will guide me the rest of the way through this life.

And maybe one day, I'll find some peace.

56

Epilogue

Kingston

Four Years Later

Perched up on the roof of the house, I can see for miles in nearly every direction. To my right, there's snow as far as the eye can see. Somewhere beneath it is a frozen lake. Drake's little fishing hut is the only thing that obscures the flatness. To my left is a woodland full of wildlife that is silent now as night falls. The trees are covered with fresh snowfall and groan ever so slightly under the weight. The sound echoes out here. It's ominous and eerily beautiful. In front of me are mountains stretching high into the sky, pointing toward the Northern Lights.

Out of all the places we've traveled and stayed at, this is perhaps one of my favorites. Strangely enough, the solitude isn't oppressive here. In a major city, surrounded by people, I found I feel more alone and alien. Here, I'm one with everything. I can breathe without feeling suffocated, and it's not like we're completely isolated. Town is only a ten mile trek by ATV or truck, giving us stuff to do without feeling bored. Not that I feel the need to go often. It's nature that calls to me on some level. I've started to appreciate its beauty this past year.

But my attention isn't on my surroundings tonight.

It's latched onto the person bundled up and lying in the middle of their snow angel.

Daisy's withdrawn again.

It was just a matter of time before she closed down and pulled away. It happens every other year or so. It's been a while since the last time, so she was due for a depressive episode. When she gets like this, we have to watch her even more closely than normal. If Drake didn't force her to eat, she'd lose the weight she's gained. Sleeping is either nonexistent for her or full of nightmares that wake her and us up. Her tendency to self-harm increases too.

She's in her silent phase now. For the past month she's hardly said more than a handful of words. There's no life in her eyes at this point either.

In my hands, I de-shell a pistachio. The shell falls into the snow and I plop the rest into my mouth.

The others are worried. They've talked about getting her on some medication, at least until she's feeling better. It's a conversation we've had over and over, with or without Daisy being in the room. I get their fear. At this point, Daisy is more a danger to herself than to others. We all want to rescue our girl from herself. But that's not how this works.

I know because I struggle with the same thing myself.

Though less frequent and severe, I suffer from bouts of depression too. Getting out of bed, showering, eating, or even watching television can feel like a monumental chore. I understand her suffering better than the others, which is why I pretended to let her slip out of the house, thinking no one noticed her departure, and why I haven't interrupted her moment of solace out here in the dark.

But it's getting too cold to remain outside, even with layers and a winter jacket.

With a sigh, I get up and make my way down to the second-floor balcony. Rather than trudge through the house, disturbing everyone, I climb over the edge of the railing, hang there for a second, and then let go. Without the snow, I wouldn't have risked the fall. But with almost two feet of cushion, I'm good.

There's no way to quietly walk through a wintery wonderland. The crunching of snow beneath my boot carries, and I'm sure Daisy can hear me as I approach. When I get to her side, I stop and stare down at her. Daisy's eyes reflect the stars up above as she stares at them. The reflection brightens up her face a little. The dark circles beneath her eyes and the hollows of her cheeks have given her a gaunt appearance. It seems despite Drake's best efforts, she's still managing to lose weight.

Daisy doesn't immediately acknowledge my presence. I'm not surprised.

Rather than force her to get up, I turn around, open my arms, and fall backward into the snow. I blow away the snowflakes that fly up and try to land on my face. With that done, I move my legs and arms. With the depth of the snow, making an angel takes time, but finally, I finish mine. I look over at Daisy.

To my surprise, I find her looking at me rather than up at the sky.

"Hey." Her whisper carries over to me and then beyond, into the wild landscape.

Smiling, I scoot a little closer to her and reach for her hand. She meets me halfway way, her mittened hand wrapping around my gloved one. With a heavy sigh, she turns her head and looks back up at the sky. Giving into the quiet moment, I look up and stare at them too. The rivers of green and white that make up a spectacular light show move, like water rippling. I don't think this gets any less beautiful the longer we're here. While longer stretches of warmer weather would be nice, this part of Canada is comfortable.

"King? Daisy? You out here?" Owen's voice drifts over to us.

I lift my hand and give him a thumbs up.

"Need some help?"

Thumbs down.

There's a long pause before I hear the sound of the sliding glass door shutting. But silence doesn't follow. The crunching of snow does. A lot of it. Suddenly Drake, Wyatt, and Owen appear. Each has a mug of something steaming in their hands. Wyatt and Drake carry two mugs, in fact. I sit up as the others circle around and plop down to join us. Drake hands me a mug. I look down to find marshmallows floating on top of a steaming cup of hot chocolate. Wyatt gives his second cup to Daisy, who lets go of my hand and sits up too.

Talking? Awareness? These are good signs.

"Drake was talking about making a fire and having dinner outside tonight. What do you think?" Owen asks me.

I shrug. Whatever they want to do for dinner is fine by me. I take a sip of the hot chocolate and enjoy the way it warms me from the inside out.

"I bought some better seasonings in town today," Drake says. "So the venison might be more appealing."

Wyatt rolls his eyes. "Anything is more appealing than a seasonless piece of meat."

"Well maybe if you had cooked it better—"

"Oh, right, blame me for a shitty dinner *you* were supposed to cook, Dre. Nice, real nice."

Drake and Wyatt's bickering comes to a halt when Daisy giggles. The sound is quiet and a little rough from lack of use, but beautiful nonetheless. We all look at her in surprise and she smiles, just a little bit before ducking her head with a sigh.

"I liked the venison."

The four of us exchange looks and smiles. Our Daisy's coming back to us again. Will that mean a few more murders to cover up? Maybe being forced to move one more time? Sure. But it's worth it. All of this is to see her happy again.

"Then we'll have it the same way as before," Owen declares.

"Well… maybe half of it can be seasoned," Wyatt hedges.

Drake nods. "And maybe a little less dry."

Daisy looks up at us through her lashes, another smile returning. "Sounds like a plan."

Flip the page for an additional bonus scene

57

Bonus Scene

Drake

1 Year Later

"Daisy! Where are you?"

The humidity is fucking ridiculous in Manaus, Brazil. Sweat drips down my face, coats my bare arms, and drenches the tank top I've thrown on. It sticks to my back and makes it hard to breathe. Mosquitos are out in droves, especially as night falls. They get stuck to my skin as I slap them away.

I fucking *hate* mosquitos.

Why I let Owen talk us into *this* being our next location is beyond me. Next time, we're going somewhere colder. Given that next time is soon thanks to Daisy's latest killing, I'm eager to get going.

"Come on, darling. I know you're out here. Don't make me come find you."

The garden has been Daisy's favorite place to hang out. Since moving into this nice single-story house just outside the major city nine months ago, this is where she's spent the most time. I almost thought it was enough to settle her vigilante tendencies. She's been so calm… I guess she's just been plotting.

My eyes scan the rose bushes, where a bench seat with floral cushions rests. Next, I check the hammock that's hidden by the hydrangeas. Nope, she's not there either. I huff as I stomp around the fountain toward the pergola.

The slight tremble of bushes nearby slows my trek. It's the wrong move. A knife sails by my arm, nicking me as it comes and goes.

"Damn it, Daisy!" I look down at the cut.

There's a snicker. "You better run if you don't want it to happen again."

I whirl around, heading toward the sound of her voice. The redirection earns me a small pocketknife lodged in my upper thigh.

"Fucking hell…" I snarl, staring down at the offensive weapon. It's so small, it won't cause any damage but damn it, this hurts!

"Remember when you once called me your prey?" Daisy's voice drifts around me as I yank out the blade.

I think back to that night I took her on the ground of the woods in Briar Glen then hung her up in a tree to fuck. My dick twitches to life.

"My how the tables have turned," she continues in a sickeningly sweet voice. "If you don't start running, you'll continue to bleed."

Oh boy, she's high off her kill. She's going to be trouble over the next few days, I already feel it.

I love her like this.

Grinning, I step backward. Her giggle brings my cock to full mast swiftly. So she wants to play? I suppose I can indulge her a bit. The thought of being chased has me hard instantly.

"Do you know what I'll do to you when I catch you, Dre?"

I can only imagine.

But I don't wait around to hear her taunting. Turning, I head back toward the house, hoping to lure her to safety and out of sight of the neighbors. With how bloody Wyatt came home, she's probably not much better.

Kingston and Wyatt are always feeding into her madness rather than trying to keep these moments contained to a singular spot or person. Given that she had two rapists in her sights this evening, I'm sure the two of them went absolutely wild. This flipping a coin business to see who goes with her is getting old. We need a new strategy.

Daisy will need a shower, and we need to pack. Maybe in between the activities I can fuck her wet pussy with my mouth and then my cock. Or maybe—

String stretching across the brick pavers, low to the ground and nearly invisible in this light, catches me at the ankles and takes me down. I land on my hands and knees. Swearing, I move to get up, only to be hit from the side by all hundred pounds of Daisy.

"Looks like I've bagged myself a handsome man. Hm..." Daisy straddles me as I roll to my back, and she grins. Blood is splattered all over her face and hands. Her eyes catch the fairy lights above us. They cause her brown eyes to twinkle with mirth and madness. "You won't be needing these anymore, Dre."

She reaches back and pulls out her big knife. Her *killing* knife.

"Daisy, we should go inside."

She ignores me. Grabbing the hem of my pants taut, she

uses her knife to cut a rectangular piece of material away. As she tosses what used to be my zipper aside, my dick springs free.

I glare up at her. "I liked these pants."

"And I like this cock," she shrugs. Leaning down, Daisy takes my lips with hers. I kiss her back hungrily. Our tongues clash and her heady moan causes my dick to twitch against her. She pulls away with a husky laugh. "Stay."

She stands and quickly discards her bloody attire. My eyes drift down her body. Other than the thick rune carved into her flesh and the scar left by her bullet wound, her body has healed perfectly. Having gained weight thanks to a strict dietary regiment, no bones show as she moves. Muscles ripple and her breasts jiggle beautifully as she comes back down to straddle me.

Without any preamble, she takes my dick and sinks down onto me, in one swift motion. She's so wet that the motion is *almost* smooth. With my piercings, it's never easy on her body, but she takes my dick like she was made for me. Together we groan.

"Oh fuck," I hiss, my hands coming up to her hips.

"Louder, Drake. I want the neighbors to hear you howl and think that wolves have moved into the area," she demands as she starts to ride me. Her body clenches around me and I gasp.

Daisy moves quickly, clearly ready to cum hard and fast. I help her, moving her hips up and down my shaft. Her breathing quickens. Watching her face as her brows furrow and her lips part is like watching magic happen. My balls rise. Neither of us are going to last long. Not like this.

"Come on, Drake. Cum with me," she whimpers as she throws her head back.

My hips come up, and together we find a rhythm that's just perfect. Her body clamps down on mine with so much strength, I can't move more than a few inches. But it's enough that as she cries out as her body spasms around me, I cum with her. I don't hold back my sounds, not giving a single fuck that the neighbors can hear, or if the guys are watching us from the glass patio door. Owen probably watched the whole thing from his office. Hell, he's probably even jerking off as I spill everything I have inside of her.

When we both come down, Daisy collapses onto my chest, breathing heavily. She lifts her head with a sigh to plant a kiss just over my heart. Can she feel it flutter wildly? I swallow hard as her gaze flickers up to my face.

She smiles before whispering,"I love you."

A shudder rushes through my chest. When I move, it's fast. Daisy doesn't have time to react as I pin her down to the ground. With my arms framing her face I have her effectively trapped beneath me.

"I know. You know I love you too, right?"

Daisy giggles. "I figured you did since you don't seem too upset that I threw a knife at you... and then actually stabbed you."

"Hm..." I lower my face so my beard tickles her nose. "About that..."

'SUP READERS?

Hello Dear Reader-

Did you know the best way to support an indie author is to leave a review? Whether you loved or hated this story, I'd appreciate it if you would leave one on Amazon's website. Want to leave a review on Goodreads or Bookbub? Even better!

Another great way to support an indie author is to never pirate their work. If you find a platform where you can read my book that isn't the 'Zon or my website- that means you're reading a pirated copy of my stories. Please, please don't support the narrow minded, selfish people who have stolen my hard work.

Want to read more of my stories? Make sure to follow me on social media to hear about my latest works in progress and new releases. Also, if you follow me, you'll see that I'm a big fan of giveaways. Giveaways that include: e-giftcards, signed paperbacks, and the occasional adult toy. If that sounds like something you'd want to participate in you should definitely come find me! I'll leave a link for you below so that you'll be able to follow me everywhere I'm active.

Additionally, if you join my newsletter, you'll occasionally be sent short, spicy, and dark stories for those one-handed reads I know we all enjoy from time-to-time. The sign-up to my newsletter will also be in the link below!

Thanks for reading my story and I hope you'll read more of my work!

Best Wishes,
MT Addams

Follow Me: https://linktr.ee/mtaddams

P.S. In case there are any questions or concerns about the content within my work, you can click the link above and then choose the "**trigger warning list**" to see if my stories are right for you.

BOOKS BY MT ADDAMS

Hidden Claws

Summon Us

Not A Peep

Bad For Me

(Anthology)

Show Me Mercy

(novella exclusive to newsletter subscribers)

Made in the USA
Columbia, SC
16 January 2025

51988443R00286